F
OGR   O'Grady, Leslie

Lady Jade

DATE DUE   H169 12.95

Lady Jade

Lady Jade

Leslie O'Grady

ST. MARTIN'S PRESS/
NEW YORK

For information, write: St. Martin's Press,
175 Fifth Avenue, New York, N.Y. 10010
Manufactured in the United States of America

Library of Congress Cataloging in Publication Data

O'Grady, Leslie.
  Lady Jade.

  I. Title.
PS3565.G68L3   813'.54   80-29120
ISBN 0-312-46429-0

Design by Laura Hammond

10 9 8 7 6 5 4 3 2 1

First Edition

To Hank and Corie Kelly,
artists and adventurers

Lady Jade

CHAPTER ONE

As May Monckton scanned the teeming Shanghai waterfront for any sight of her mother, she was beginning to regret not having left the ship with the other passengers. She could have appeared to accompany the fervent American missionary couple burning to salvage souls, the garrulous German silk merchant gnawing the stem of his smelly meerschaum pipe, or even the Hong Kong rice dealer bemoaning the fact that his seven wives were becoming much too demanding and quarrelsome. There was safety in numbers in this notorious open city, as May knew only too well.

She stood on tiptoe and gripped the railing so hard her knuckles turned white. Where *was* her mother? The telegram said she would be waiting when the steamer docked, but there was still no sign of her among the tide of people coming and going. May pressed her fingers to her forehead, where a headache was just beginning to form. She had often heard whispers of what happened to women who disappeared in Shanghai, and she shivered in spite of the blazing heat that made her dress stick to her and tiny beads of sweat rise on the nape of her neck.

Even in 1890, Shanghai was still no place for a woman alone.

"Don't be silly," she chided herself. "Margaret Fitzgerald can take care of herself. She's just late, that's all." But even that excuse had an unconvincing ring to her own ears.

"Begging your pardon, ma'am," a voice said at her elbow.

She turned to face the ship's steward, an amiable young man who had singled her out for his special attention ever since the steamer *British Queen* had left Hong Kong.

"Will you be going 'shore, ma'am? The other passengers have all disembarked, and we will be weighing anchor soon."

"Yes, I suppose I should." Then an idea came to her, so she flashed him a smile and said, "Would you mind escorting me past the docks? Those sailors are a disreputable-looking lot, and I'd feel safer with an escort."

He smiled in return and offered her his arm, unaware that she had no intention of rewarding him. "My pleasure, ma'am."

As he marched her down the gangplank, he said, "Have you ever been to Shanghai before, Mrs. Monckton?"

She nodded. "I was born and raised in China."

He gave her a suspicious glance out of the corner of his eye. "Oh? Were your parents missionaries?"

"No, merchants."

"I see. So I can't tantalize you with some local history, then."

"I'm afraid not," she replied. "I know Shanghai's story well."

As they stepped onto the dock stacked shoulder high with crates and bales and boxes, she was thankful she had prevailed upon him to escort her. Several burly sailors, their forearms tatooed and striped shirts sweat-stained, eyed her boldly as she passed, and ribald laughter rippled across the docks like fire. She could just imagine what they were saying.

The steward halted to stare them all down, a foolhardy gesture, considering he was outnumbered seven to one. "Are you being paid to gawk or work?"

One sailor cursed and made a gesture that caused May's face to burn, but their jeers died away into grumbling, and they returned to lugging and hauling the cargo onto the ship.

"Thank you," she said, her hands trembling slightly. "I would have hated to run that gauntlet alone."

The steward, sensing the opportune moment, moved quickly. "Is someone coming to meet you? Because, if you have nowhere to go—" He lowered his voice so only she could hear. "—I have rooms you're welcome to."

And how would she be expected to repay his generosity, she wondered, as she considered the best way to defuse him. "You are too kind, sir, but I do have accommodations. You see, I shall be staying at the Wright villa on Bubbling Well Road. Perhaps you know Nelson Wright? He's the Benton and Black taipan. Our families have been great friends for years."

The steward swallowed hard and retreated, as she had suspected he would. "Mrs. Monckton, forgive me . . . I had no idea you were a friend of Nelson Wright's. You must let me call a rickshaw at once and have you taken to his hong."

"That won't be necessary. I'm sure my mother will be here shortly, and she would be frantic if she couldn't find me. I'll just wait on the esplanade, thank you."

He looked desperate as he added, "And . . . and I would be most grateful if you made no mention of my impudence to the taipan. It would . . . cost me my position."

May smiled kindly. "I will not mention it, merely that you kindly offered to escort me."

The steward, realizing that he had both lost and won at the same time, said, "If you really think you'll be safe here. . ."

"My mother should be along shortly, and besides, it's broad daylight." As if that made any difference in Shanghai.

He looked relieved that she was absolving him of any responsibility, then saluted her and hurried back to his ship.

May started walking, and when she reached the esplanade, which stretched out before her in a long, tree-lined avenue, she closed her eyes and breathed a sigh of relief. Her seven-year absence had turned her into a foreigner seeing Shanghai for the first time, and she looked around in wonder.

The brilliant white buildings of the Bund shimmered in

the hazy heat, while the scents of burning camphor wood, hot peanut oil, and fresh fish hung thickly on the air.

And the people: May watched Chinese being pulled in rickshaws and pushed two at a time in Shanghai barrows by human beasts of burden. She even saw a richly robed young woman with bound feet being carried on a coolie's back, riding him with as much aplomb as she would a horse. And there were Europeans as well, white-suited men sauntering from their clubs back to the consulates, while women in gossamer white dresses strolled along the esplanade, shading their complexions with parasols, while their Chinese maids walked slightly behind. From the docks, English and French sailors swaggered away from their ships into the city, and on May's right two grim Sikh policemen went running in pursuit of some unseen transgressor. The scene was so familiar, yet alien somehow.

"You don't belong here anymore," she muttered to herself, shaking her head. But what was the use? Since the tragic, senseless death of her husband and the scandal that stained her life, London had turned a cold, hostile shoulder to her. She had nowhere else to go, except back to China.

Suddenly she heard someone behind her shout, "Look out!" and, before May could snap to attention, she felt a sharp blow between her shoulder blades that knocked her off her feet and propelled her forward. She flung her hands out to break her fall, but her cry of pain was drowned out by the rumbling wheels of a Shanghai barrow that narrowly missed her head. The driver didn't even slow his vehicle, or come to May's assistance. He just screeched a string of imprecations at her and rattled on his way.

Choking and sputtering on the dust that stung her eyes and throat, May raised herself on her elbows.

"What happened?" she heard someone ask as a small crowd gathered around her.

"I don't know," another replied. "She just walked right out in front of that barrow."

May was conscious of a dark man in a white suit kneeling down beside her and asking, "Are you all right?"

She nodded, still somewhat in a daze. "I . . . I'm more embarrassed than hurt, actually."

"Here," he said, rising and extending his hand. "Let me help you."

When his fingers tightened on her raw, skinned palms, May winced, and he instantly shifted his grasp to her wrists to pull her to her feet and out of the road.

"Thank you," she said breathlessly as she shook the dust from her skirts.

"Did you hear me yell the first time?"

"I'm sorry. I must have been daydreaming."

"Shanghai is no placer for dreamers."

May looked up at the man, who towered over her by a head, and found herself staring into blue eyes that were clear and candid, but as chilly as the North China sky in winter. When he reached up to whisk off his wide-brimmed hat, she noticed his dark hair was shot with silver, though she guessed he was no more than thirty years old. There was an air of independence and wariness about him, too, like the wolf who always hunts alone.

He obviously was not concerned with his appearance, for the suit he wore was a size too large for his lean, athletic frame and looked as though it had known a previous owner. And yet his speech was refined and pegged him as a man of some education.

An adventurer, May thought at first. But there was compassion in his face that belied the cynical set of his mouth, and she found herself intrigued.

Suddenly he broke into a wide grin, obviously amused by her frank scrutiny, and proceeded to assess her just as frankly. "Red hair and green eyes," he murmured, "a real Chinese demon if ever there was one."

His words forced May to recall herself as a terrified seven-year-old, being chased through the dirty, narrow streets of Paoting by dozens of Chinese children, who threw sticks and screamed "Demon! Devil!" at her as she ran home.

"Thank you for saving me," May said coldly, "but that doesn't give you the right to insult me."

"Insult you?" His smile died, and he looked genuinely distressed. "Look here, there was no insult intended. It's just that Chinese demons have red hair and—"

"I have lived here for most of my life, and I am well-versed in Chinese mythology. I do not find the comparison flattering."

Anger hardened his eyes to ice. "I can see now that I should have let the barrow run you over."

"You're insufferable," she retorted with a shake of her head.

"And you, madam, are ill-bred and rude."

He glanced around and spied her bonnet lying on the ground where it had rolled after May's fall. "Is this yours?"

"Yes," she snapped, snatching for it.

But he was too quick for her and pulled it away. "White straw and organdy roses . . . much too frivolous for a shrew. It doesn't suit you at all." And, as May watched in mounting horror, he pitched it back across the esplanade, where it rolled beneath the wheels of a passing rickshaw.

Tears of frustration welled up in her eyes. "My bonnet!"

"I'll buy you another," the man replied with an insolent grin. "Something that better suits you."

May was about to retort when the frantic calling of her name caused her to whirl around. There was her mother descending on them like a miniature typhoon.

"Let me guess," the stranger murmured with a devilish glint in his eye. "It's your governess come to rescue her charge."

She dismissed him with an exasperated noise.

As she watched her mother running across the grass toward her, May felt her mouth go dry. Would things be different between them this time? She was twenty-five now, not a child any longer but a woman who knew her own mind, and she hoped her mother would treat her as such.

"May-Ling! I can't believe it!" Her mother was breathless as she hugged her, enveloping them both in a heady cloud of the patchouli scent she always wore. "How are you? Let me look at you," she demanded, stepping back. "Why, you're beautiful. But, by the sword of Lu Tung-pin, you look as though you just fought the Taipings. And where is your bonnet? You'll get heat prostration if you don't keep your head covered."

The stranger, who had been quietly observing their reunion with a bemused expression, spoke up. "I am afraid I am responsible for your daughter's lack of a bonnet, but have agreed to replace it."

While her mother stared at the man, May said, "After I left the boat, I was nearly struck down by a barrow, and—"

"Good Heavens, May!" Mrs. Fitzgerald's head snapped around. "Are you all right?"

"I only skinned my hands, that's all."

"Well, we'll tend to them at the Wright's." Then she turned to the man. "It was certainly good joss that you were here, sir," she said. "I haven't seen my only daughter in seven years, and, on the day I'm supposed to meet her, the pony would have to throw a shoe. I thought I'd never get here."

Then she turned to May and said with a depth of feeling that surprised her daughter, "Oh, May, I had so many things I planned to say, and now that you're finally here . . ." She shrugged helplessly. "Words fail me."

May found her eyes filling with tears, as she hugged her mother again, then stepped back to really look at her.

She was surprised to find Margaret Fitzgerald virtually unchanged by the passage of time. A tall, striking woman in her early forties, whose forceful personality could overpower both men and women, she still dyed her hair black to "look Chinese," and, while she tried to keep her features composed, sooner or later, a quick smile or a raised eyebrow put an end to that. And even though she had forsaken Chinese garb today for a European dress of white gauze, she couldn't resist wearing several jade rings and a priceless black-jade pendant swinging from a gold chain.

Her mother hugged her again. "I can't believe you're here."

May smiled, slipped her hand through her mother's arm, and started leading her away. "Shall we go?"

"May-Ling, don't go leading me about like a child."

"Please, Mother. I've had a long voyage, and I'm exhausted."

"Very well. I'll have the mafoo collect your bags—where are they, by the way?—and, as soon as he hitches up the ponies again, we'll be on our way to the villa. Thank you again, sir," she added over her shoulder, "and good day to you."

"You haven't seen the last of me," the man called after them. "You can count on it."

"I sincerely hope not," May replied. She thought she heard him mutter "Demon," but she couldn't be sure.

"Nelson's carriage is over here," Mrs. Fitzgerald said, indicating a splendid, two-horse vehicle at the far end of the lawn. In the same breath, she said, "You were most rude to that young man, May-Ling, and after he saved you from injury too. Why we don't even know his name."

"I'm sorry, Mother, but he said something that made me very angry, and he had the affrontery to toss my bonnet away. Besides, he's just an adventurer."

"You could have at least asked him his name."

Then Mrs. Fitzgerald's mouth set in the determined line May knew so well, and she steeled herself for the onslaught, for her mother was a woman who always spoke her mind, no matter what the consequences. "Why didn't you write to me while you were in England? I received exactly three letters from you—one when you arrived, another when you got married, and a third when your husband died."

"Please, Mother, can't this wait until we get back to the villa? People are staring." She congratulated herself for resisting the impulse to argue.

"Your behavior was reprehensible, and I'd like an explanation."

"And you'll get one—later," was May's firm reply.

They walked in stiff silence to the carriage, and, when they reached it, Mrs. Fitzgerald ordered the mafoo to rehitch the ponies and collect May's bags, still sitting forlornly on the dock. When he returned, he secured the bags, gathered the reins, and set the matching Szechwan ponies off at a trot.

May glanced back over her shoulder as the carriage sped down the esplanade and circled the park. The man was still watching her, lounging with his weight on one hip and his right hand stuffed into a pocket. There was a curious expression on his face May couldn't fathom. Then a line of trees came between them and blocked him from view.

As she turned back to her mother, May felt as though the years that separated them dissolved and disappeared. There was so much she wanted to talk to her mother about, yet so little she really needed to say, even after all this time.

Margaret Fitzgerald cleared her throat. "So what was England like? Is Clara well? She was always catching all sorts of minor ailments when I knew her and forever coughing into a handkerchief."

May smiled at the warm memory. "That's Aunt Clara."

"And I know the country hasn't changed, so I won't ask you about that."

May sighed. "What you will ask me about is my shambles of a life."

"That can wait," her mother said emphatically, not allowing May the luxury of self-pity. "Now I'll tell you about Black Dragon House."

"Not now, Mother. Please."

Raised brows destroyed her attempt at keeping her face serene. "Well, if you don't want to hear about your home, you're certainly curious about Weng Ta-Chung."

"Perhaps later. I . . . haven't quite gotten used to being in China yet, so please don't bombard me with so many details at once."

"As you wish." And Margaret Fitzgerald turned her head to stare at the river of people parted by their dauntless carriage. But before a minute had passed, she said tentatively, "There's a hospital near Paoting now, and a wonderful, dedicated American doctor—Chad Gates—who comes to call sometimes. And there's a mission, too, run by a young man and his wife. They have four children, lovely tykes, but, oh, so lonely."

Most European children are lonely in China, May thought, as the carriage slowed to turn left onto Bubbling Well Road.

"How are the Wrights?" she asked, when the silence showed no signs of abating.

"Benton and Black couldn't ask for a better taipan than Nelson," was her mother's reply. "He's like Midas—whatever he touches turns to gold."

"And Emily?"

"Emily is the typical taitai. All she does is go to tea parties, gossip, and eat. She knows everything about everyone." Mrs. Fitzgerald shook her head. "You know I never could abide a useless woman. I can't wait to get home, to tell you the truth." She twisted a jade ring. "But you should see my Willie. He just turned ten last month, and what a bright, clever child. And to think that Emily produced him . . ."

Willie. The thought of a child gave May pain, and she turned her head so her mother could not see the tears that suddenly sprung to her eyes. Then she felt a hand on hers.

"I'm happy you're here," her mother said.

"As you said in your telegram, 'You must come to China.' And I had nowhere else to go."

"How long do you plan to stay?"

"Oh, until I heal, I suppose."

"And then?"

She shrugged. "Go back to England. This entire sordid affair will have blown over by then."

"I'm beginning to wonder if I was correct to send you back to Aunt Clara. But when your father died, I realized that you had grown up knowing nothing of your own people. Now I wonder if it was for the best."

"It was," May declared vehemently. "It was wonderful to walk through the streets of London and see women dressed like women instead of men." Her hand went up to touch her copper hair, the tresses Robin had called molten fire. "You can't imagine what it was like not to have to hide my hair because its color frightens people."

"Oh, you're exaggerating," her mother scoffed. "The

Chinese are used to us now. They aren't frightened by red-headed foreign devils anymore." Then, as an afterthought, she said, "Why, May-Ling, I never realized you resented your life here so much."

"You've made a place for yourself in China, Mother. I think I've always been just a visitor."

Mrs. Fitzgerald made no comment, just leaned out the window and announced, "Here we are."

As discouraging wrought iron gates swung open and the ponies trotted through, May craned her neck for her first glimpse of the villa.

There was nothing warm or reassuring about the Wright home, for it was a lavish, sprawling place designed to reflect the position and considerable influence of its residents. And in this respect, it was magnificent. Nelson's home was cool and white, like the buildings of the Bund, with more Doric columns than a Greek temple. Every room, from the public chambers on the first level to the family's private apartments upstairs, led out onto a long, roofed verandah, so guests could saunter from their rooms, look out over the gardens or the city beyond, and still be shaded and cool.

The only bits of color in the play of white against shadow were clay pots of vivid red geraniums set all along the upstairs verandah.

Like spots of blood on white linen, May thought. She shivered and looked away.

When the carriage stopped at the front door, a Chinese servant in white jacket and trousers appeared and assisted the women to alight.

"Missie Wright here?" Mrs. Fitzgerald asked in Chinese. "Emily forbids me to speak Chinese to them," she added aside to May, "but I do anyway."

The man nodded and said Missie Wright was in the solarium, so Margaret thanked him and dismissed him.

"We can find Emily ourselves later," she said to May. "But first we're going to stop at the kitchen and see if the cook has some salve for your hands."

The kitchen was small, hot, and crowded, but the cook

took time to cleanse the dirt from May's burning hands and apply an ointment that immediately drew out the fire. After thanking him, the two women went to find Emily.

"And how is your Chinese, by the way?" Mrs. Fitzgerald asked as their heels tapped against the foyer's slate flooring. "I should think you can't remember a word of it."

"I probably still speak it better than you," was her daughter's quick retort.

Emily was in the solarium, reclining like Madame Récamier on a divan and nibbling sesame sweets. The breeze from a punkah fanning slowly overhead felt cool on May's cheeks in this steamy room.

"Look who I've brought to see you," Mrs. Fitzgerald announced.

Emily's half-closed eyes flew open. "May!" she exclaimed in her light trilling voice as she sat bolt upright. "Oh, it's too hot to even move." She groaned and fell listlessly back against the cushions.

"Oh, Emily, this is nothing," Margaret chided her in exasperation. "Wait until July, when it's *really* boiling."

"It's so good to see you again, Emily," May said, bending over to kiss her. "You look as lovely as I remember."

Emily was as plump and contented as a pampered house cat, but the dark eyes that had broken so many hearts still sparkled coquettishly with schemes, and her conversation still veered off into a hundred different directions.

Now she held May at arm's length. "And you, my dear May, are absolutely ravishing. I could positively hate you. If you weren't already married, you'd have every eligible bachelor eating out of your hand. Come to think of it, they'll be eating out of your hand anyway." She stopped the rush of words long enough to look over May's shoulder. "And where is your lucky husband? I'm dying to meet the man who won your heart."

"In England," May replied lightly. "There was just so much work to do at the bank that Nigel couldn't possibly accompany me. So he sent me alone."

"Such an understanding man," Emily said. "I do envy you." Before May could comment, her hostess was off again.

"We have so much to talk about, my dear, I fear it will take weeks. I must hear all about England and your dear husband and your voyage."

So, for the next half hour, May answered Emily's every question about London's fashionable set, carefully skirted those about her "dear husband," and dwelled at length on the long, uneventful sea voyage.

Suddenly, Mrs. Fitzgerald announced, "I'm going to fetch Willie."

"Oh, don't!" Emily wailed. "He's probably right in the middle of a lesson, and Miss St. John will be furious."

Margaret ignored her. "Oh, a few minutes of visiting won't hurt him," and she bustled out of the room.

Emily shook her head. "I love your mother dearly, May, but sometimes . . ."

"I know, Emily. She always does what she wants, no matter what anyone says."

Emily sighed. "She's entirely too independent. She needs a man to keep her on a very tight rein."

May smiled slightly, but did not agree or disagree.

"Between your mother and Nelson," Emily went on, "Willie is terribly spoiled."

"I doubt that, Emily."

Suddenly, Margaret reappeared with Willie in hand. May first noticed the child's huge dark eyes, which overwhelmed even his round, rosy face. He resembled a cherub with his headful of chestnut curls—not one of the adoring, fair-haired angels beloved of Italian painters, but a rebellious cherub with a mind of his own. Despite his mischievous air, there was a compelling quality about Willie that drew people to him immediately. May warmed to him without hesitation.

"Is this Mrs. Monckton?" he asked with a broad smile, eager to make a friend.

"Yes, Willie, I am Mrs. Monckton, but I prefer just May," she replied, resisting the impulse to add, "My, how you've grown!" or something equally foolish.

"Aunt May," Emily amended.

May rose and extended her hand to him, and the child bowed over it with a courtly flourish that was both comical

13

and touching. "I am very pleased—no, honored—to make your acquaintance, Aunt May."

"And I yours, Willie."

"Do join us," Mrs. Fitzgerald said, seating yourself.

"Thank you. Aunt Margaret." And Willie sat down next to May.

"How were your lessons today?" his mother inquired.

"Dreadfully dull," he replied, squirming in his seat. "At least, Latin is. I prefer history, myself, and science. Miss St. John says I must learn my numbers, or I shall never be a taipan, like my father."

"I'm sure that will come in time," May said gravely.

"Actually," Willie began in a rush, just like his mother, "what I really like best is to ride my pony with Abbott down Bubbling Well Road in the early morning, before the sun is even up. He lets me gallop."

"And what is your pony's name?" May asked.

"Tartar. He's a Mongolian pony, you know. Do you like to ride?"

"I love to."

"Splendid! Then you must come with Abbott and me, and—"

"Willie, you're running away with yourself again," his mother admonished him gently.

May leaned forward. "Wouldn't a tall creature such as myself look rather comical on a Mongolian pony? Why, my feet would drag on the ground!"

"Oh, no, Aunt May," he replied, his face melting in adoration. "You would look beautiful on anything, even a camel."

Everyone laughed at that picture, then May said, "Why, thank you, Willie, but I think I shall confine myself to a carriage."

"Then I shall be your mafoo."

Footsteps heralded the approach of a young woman who wore the severe, drab dress and pinched expression of a governess. She trooped into the room and informed everyone that Master William still had lessons to recite. May assumed this was Miss St. John, and when introduced the plain young woman gave her a blunt look of disapproval.

At the sight of his governess, Willie's face fell, and after bidding all good day, he reluctantly left with her.

"That child . . ." Emily muttered, as another servant walked up to her and whispered something in her ear. "Lady Hertford! Yes, by all means, send her in," Emily ordered, rising, the heat forgotten. "Gracious! This is the first time Lady Hertford has ever called on me."

"May and I will go upstairs and leave you to your guest," Mrs. Fitzgerald said.

"No, do stay and meet her ladyship. She's just delightful."

"I have," Margaret replied, "and I found her to be a dreadful bore."

May felt embarrassed for Emily, whose finely arched brows narrowed in irritation. Her mouth tightened, but all she said was, "Do as you please. Number Six boy—or is he Number Seven? Oh, I can't tell one from the other—will show you to your room."

"No need," Margaret replied. "I know the way."

May followed her mother back out into the foyer and up the sweeping curved staircase of soft pink marble that led to the upstairs chambers.

"That Emily," her mother said with a shake of her head when they were safely out of earshot. "She does like to chatter so. She's so different from Nelson's first wife."

"Perhaps Uncle Nelson needed a little frivolity in his life," May suggested, recalling the somber, stone-faced woman who had been the first Mrs. Wright, before a typhoid epidemic had dispatched her to the European cemetery.

The two women were silent as they walked down a long, narrow corridor lined with closed doors and bright paintings of French country scenes in ornate gold frames.

Finally, Margaret said, "He certainly got what he wanted in Emily." She stopped before one of the doors. "Here's your room. It's the one you always used to stay in when we came here, the one overlooking the gardens." She patted May on the shoulder. "I'll give you an hour, and then we can talk."

May nodded wearily, then she walked inside and closed the door behind her with a soft click.

The room was just as she remembered it from years ago. The stark white walls and mosquito netting swathing the bed were its only concessions to the heat of the Orient, while the rest of the room was as desperately English as Emily could make it, with massive, carved furniture and sentimental bric-a-brac everywhere.

May collapsed with a sigh of relief into one of the chintz chairs, and she suddenly felt drained, emotionally exhausted, at the thought of the upcoming inquisition. Then she closed her eyes and rested her head on the back of the chair, letting her thoughts drift like smoke.

But those were too disturbing, so she rose, went to one of her bags, which were standing near the door, and fumbled to open it. Her fingers burrowed gingerly beneath the layers of clothing until they touched something hard and unyielding. She took out the leather-bound volume and ran her fingers lovingly down its spine, read the words POEMS—ROBERT BROWNING stamped in gold leaf and held it to her heart for an instant. It was all she had left of Robin—no photographs, no lock of his hair to be discovered by her husband, only a slim volume of verse and the memories burned into her brain.

But, oh, what sweet memories, enough to last her a lifetime.

"God's in his heaven, all's right with the world," she murmured, and the pain shot through her afresh.

Just as she was about to turn away, she caught a glimpse of herself in the mirror. "The ravishing Mrs. Monckton," the papers had called her, but personally she doubted their blandishments. Having been raised in a society where the standard for female beauty was established by dark almond eyes, straight black hair, and diminutive stature, May had always thought of herself as plain and gangly—with her pale, fine-boned face, round emerald eyes, and softly curved mouth, which had remained gentle in spite of all she had suffered in England.

"You are the most beautiful woman in Britain, and you act like you're the plainest," her husband used to scold her often and with some annoyance.

Since she felt she was not physically attractive, she never had been quite able to accept all the attention she received there. Men were attracted to her beauty, while women liked her in spite of it, for they discovered she was also sincere and guileless, and a staunch friend.

But when she stared at the woman in the mirror, she saw a different person. "Cheat," she accused. "Liar."

The woman in the mirror turned away, hurt.

May sighed, walked over to the bed, parted the netting, and flopped down. She instantly fell into a light, haunted sleep.

An hour later words, like pebbles flung against glass, jarred her into sudden wakefulness.

"May-Ling, wake up."

She started and opened her eyes to find her mother sitting resolutely on the edge of the bed and shaking her gently.

"What time is it?" May yawned and propped herself up on one elbow.

"It's time to talk," Margaret announced impatiently. Again the question, "Why didn't you ever write to me?"

"Why didn't you come to my wedding?" May retorted, still fighting off the aftereffects of her nap.

"It's a long, time-consuming, and expensive voyage from China to England. I would have been gone from Paoting for over a year if I had gone to your wedding."

China. She could never leave her precious China, May thought, not even for me.

She rose and paced the room. "Please, Mother, let's not argue like we did before I left."

"It's pointless, I agree." Mrs. Fitzgerald sighed. "Let's concentrate on the present. You're here, and I'm thankful for that." She was silent for a moment, then said, "What did happen to your husband, May-Ling?"

As May stared at her mother, she felt herself gradually thaw inside, then the tears started and wouldn't stop.

"Stop crying. You know how I hate tears."

"I'm sorry," May sobbed, wiping her cheeks with the back of her hand. "I haven't cried in so long I feel dried up inside."

"Don't apologize. It's understandable, I suppose."

May smoothed her skirt as she fought to bring herself under control. "Where shall I begin?"

"Perhaps you should start with your marriage."

"All right. You know I met Nigel through some friends of Aunt Clara's."

"Yes, your aunt wrote to tell me that much. Clara also told me he was fifteen years your senior, but that his family had been in banking since the time of William the Conqueror, or some such nonsense. Your silly aunt was most impressed."

May nodded. "The money never meant anything to me. When I first knew Nigel, he was the kindest, most sensitive man I had ever met, and I truly loved him. I would have loved him even if he had been penniless." May clasped her hands together to keep them from shaking. "And his family . . . did Clara tell you anything about his family?"

"Only that it contained more brothers, sisters, aunts, and uncles than her poor head could count."

"He had four sisters and five brothers, all married with tribes of beautiful children. After Nigel and I were married, they'd all spend weekends at our house in Surrey. The children would come spilling out of the carriages and be as noisy as they wished. They played soldiers in the yard, and threw sticks for our old collie to fetch, while their mothers and I played croquet on the lawn. It was idyllic, and I yearned for a brood of my own."

"Well, why didn't you start one?" her mother asked with her customary bluntness.

May stiffened. "I did try. For five long years. Finally, my doctor said it was hopeless." Her voice grew soft and wistful. "There was no use even trying anymore."

Her mother's eyes softened. "Oh, May-Ling. Why didn't you write to tell me about this? Why didn't you share this with me, rather than keep it to yourself?"

She shrugged. "I felt . . . ashamed, as though I had failed miserably somehow. Nigel was devastated when he found out. He wanted a son so desperately, so he would inherit and carry on the Monckton name. Day after day, night after night, I could see us growing further apart, and there was nothing I could do about it. Nothing. Finally, he became so cold and bitter and would say the most horrible things to me. I found it difficult to remember that we had loved each other once."

Her mother dismissed Nigel with a snort. "Men."

May took another deep breath and continued. "And then I met Robin Ashwood. He was a London publisher, highly respected in literary circles." Her gaze slid away, and she said, "We became lovers, Mother."

The silence in the room was shattering.

"Adultery? You, May-Ling? I don't believe it."

"I didn't mean for it to happen," May replied with a lame shrug. "But Nigel closed his door to me—just shut me right out of his life—and Robin opened his wide. We had to be discreet, of course, and couldn't be seen in public, because neither of us wanted a scandal. But he was an attentive lover, Mother, and made me feel whole again."

"But, my dear, adultery. . . ."

May raised her chin a defiant notch. "I don't expect you to understand, but I could never regret loving Robin. Never."

"Oh, credit me with a little perception," her mother said. "We Fitzgeralds are a passionate lot and were born to lead unconventional lives. It runs in the blood, I think. Look at your father and I . . . more Chinese than the Chinese. The ordinary, the conventional, that's not for us."

"I don't know about that. I, for one, found the conventional a welcome change after China, and I was leading what you would consider a very conventional life before Robin and what followed."

Mrs. Fitzgerald's eyes narrowed suspiciously. "What followed?"

"Nigel found out."

"And what did he do?"

The words stung May's throat. "One morning, he shot my Robin, then himself."

19

Her mother turned as white as the walls and, for a moment, looked as though she would faint.

"And," May continued, swallowing hard, "I found their bodies that afternoon."

Her thoughts flew back to that raw, Saturday afternoon in January, as the hansom rattled down the snow-strewn street to Robin's townhouse tucked at the end of quiet Laughton Street, facing the park, where children went skating in the winter and played cricket in the summer. She shivered in anticipation of the entire afternoon stretching before her, and, when the cabbie let her out, she nearly slipped and fell as she dashed up the ice-covered steps. She called Robin's name several times as she unlocked the door and let herself in. Robin was seated in his favorite chair, his back toward her, and she recalled laughing, as she removed her fur wrap, and saying, "My dearest, this is no time to be lost in thought. I am free for the entire day."

Then, as she removed her scarf, she saw Nigel where he had no right to be, sprawled on the sofa, his shirtfront stained scarlet, his eyes glassy and sightless, staring at the ceiling. She knew in one blinding instant of clarity and horror that Robin was dead, too, and her world was about to come crashing down around her.

"May-Ling?" Her mother's voice brought her out of her reverie, and she went limp, exhausted by the effort of recalling that day. Mrs. Fitzgerald ran out of the room and returned with a bottle of orange-flower water, which she proceeded to dab on May's temples and wrists.

May's teeth were chattering so hard she couldn't stop shaking, but she forced herself to continue, "Of course, there was a scandal. In a family as well-to-do as Nigel's, it couldn't be avoided. Once the rival newspapers heard the story, I saw my picture there every week. 'Mrs. Nigel Monckton and her lover meet in Laughton Street,' one illustration was called, and 'The beautiful Mrs. Monckton discovers the bodies of her husband and lover,' another said. People I trusted, people I thought were friends no longer called, and one day someone even poisoned my dog."

Her mother rubbed May's cold fingers with her own. "I'm so, so sorry, May, I really am. But you were right to come to me, to come back home to China. No one here knows what you've just told me, and you can forget about the past here."

She smiled feebly. "Thank you, Mother. I wasn't certain you'd be so kindly disposed toward me, seeing as how I neglected you so while I was away."

"Nonsense. You're my daughter. If I never saw you for a hundred years, you'd still be welcome in my house when you did arrive."

May reached over to hug her in wordless thanks. "I have no money as well as no reputation. Nigel changed his will before . . . before he killed Robin. But I'm glad. I wanted nothing of his after what he did. Nothing!"

Margaret was aghast. "How did you pay the fare here, then?"

"I sold most of my jewelry. Nigel was very generous in the early years of our marriage, and I had several expensive pieces. Oh, I have some money left, but not much."

Her mother looked thoughtful, then said, "Why didn't you find employment while you were in London?"

May stared at her. "Employment? You mean as a maid, or in a factory?"

"No, silly. On the staff of Benton and Black's London office. You know more about jade and Chinese artifacts than any person I know, so I'm sure they'd all fight over you."

"I never thought of that," May admitted, wishing she had thought of it before leaving for China.

"In any case, don't worry about anything." Then her mother stared out into space for a moment and shook her head. "I am still astounded by what you've just told me. What type of man would do such a thing?"

"A very proud man," was May's reply.

"I m glad I never did meet your Nigel, May-Ling. I don't think I would have liked him."

"I hate him now," May said simply and without bitterness, "but probably not as much as I hate myself for causing

Robin's death. If I had been strong enough to resist him, we would have never begun meeting, and he would still be alive today."

"Well," Mrs. Fitzgerald said brusquely, rising, "it's time to look forward to the future, not back at the past. We shall make a great team, you and I, scouring China for treasures."

"Shall I tell Uncle Nelson what I've just told you?"

"No, I don't think so. Ignorance is bliss, as they say. Besides, Shanghai is such a small town, as far as the English are concerned, and I wouldn't dream of jeopardizing Emily's exalted social standing."

Suddenly there came a knock at the door, and Number Six boy entered. He told them Taipan Wright was home and wanted to see them immediately.

CHAPTER TWO

Nelson Wright was not really May's uncle, but he had known her since she was a baby and was never thought of as anything but a relative, so she still called him that out of habit.

She had often heard the story about how Nelson and May's father, Timothy Fitzgerald, had come to China together in the mid-1860s as griffins, or junior assistants, to one of the great shipping magnates based in Shanghai. After years of hard work and shrewd dealing, Nelson succeeded his superior as taipan, or "supreme ruler," of Benton and Black, one of the most prosperous trading companies in China. Timothy Fitzgerald, however, with his facility for foreign languages and streak of Irish romanticism, succumbed to the lure of the Flowery Kingdom and spent the majority of his years roaming from the cold, windswept steppes of Mongolia to the wet, shimmering forests of Yunnan, trading jades, bronzes, lacquers—anything the Chinese were willing to sell or barter—learning more about China than even missionaries.

In fact, the only time Fitzgerald ever left the Orient was to return to England once for his beloved Margaret, who fortunately fell in love with China the instant she saw Shanghai. When they settled further north in Paoting, he remembered his old friend Wright and often traded with him. Both men grew wealthy.

Now, as the two women entered Nelson's study, they saw him standing before the French doors, his hands clasped behind him, surveying his domain beyond the verandah. He turned immediately at the sound of footsteps. "May, my girl! How wonderful to see you again," he said, crossing the room to give her a quick hug.

If anyone looked less like a merchant prince, it was Nelson Wright. A vigorous man of nearly fifty, he was short and so stiff he appeared as starched as his shirt collar. Blonde, he had a stiff brush of a mustache and a pink face that was more heredity than sunburn. Nelson Wright was a precise, methodical man who insisted on order in his marriage, business, and country, and, if anything disrupted that order, he acted swiftly and ruthlessly. People tended to underestimate him, until it was too late, and then they learned to their dismay why he was taipan.

"Thank you, Uncle Nelson," May said. "It's wonderful to be back."

He stepped back and said, "Let me look at you." The sharp blue eyes assessed her with the same shrewdness as if she were a piece of porcelain. "You're to be congratulated on your beautiful daughter, Margaret."

"I always said, Nelson, I'm glad she took after Timothy's side of the family, not mine."

"Oh, Mother . . ." May muttered, rolling her eyes.

"Well, ladies," Nelson said, "shall we go out into the folly? We'll have tea, as it's almost four o'clock, and May can tell me all about England. Or would you prefer the solarium? It's cooler there."

"The folly," May replied. "It's so secluded, and the scents from the garden are lovely."

"You're so unlike my Emmy," he said with a chuckle. "She is such a hothouse orchid, but I love her dearly."

After Nelson ordered Number Six boy to bring tea to the folly, the three of them stepped out onto the verandah, then started across the sunburned lawn. Nelson grilled May about England, asking if paper cones of hot chestnuts were still sold in Leicester Square, and if Brighton was still crowded with bathers and sightseers. Was it true the Queen was still in mourning after all these years and seldom seen by her subjects? It was as though he had been locked in prison and was quizzing a visitor about life far outside the high gray walls.

"Ah," he said dreamily, when they reached the folly and found shelter from the blazing sun beneath its roof. "It sounds heavenly. Someday soon Emmy, Willie, and I will go back for good. I'll buy a modest estate in Kent or Surrey and a house in town, of course, where Emmy can entertain to her heart's content."

Mrs. Fitzgerald gave a disdainful sniff. "Nelson, you've been saying that ever since I've known you, and you haven't left yet."

"But I will, Margaret, just you wait."

May asked, "And is your firm as successful as I remember?"

"More so," he replied, "and growing by leaps and bounds. Our godown is always full, thanks to my comprador, Wu. And my griffin, Abbott, is a good man, too."

"What items are you dealing in these days?" May wanted to know.

"Oh, just about anything you could think of. We're not particular. Teas, silks, porcelains—they're always in demand and fetch a good price. But you'll have to come see for yourself." He leaned forward, his eyes shining. "As a matter of fact, we've just received a new piece of jade—a boulder carving—that I'd like you to look at for me."

"I'd like that," May said.

Number Six boy arrived, staggering under the weight of a gleaming silver tea service, set it down on a small folding table, bowed, and departed.

"Margaret, will you do the honors?" Nelson asked, and while she poured, he added, "I wish your husband had come, May. I was so looking forward to meeting him."

"He couldn't come," she explained lamely. "Perhaps when you return to England to stay, I can introduce you."

"Wonderful." Then he asked, "Well, what are your plans? Will you two grace our humble home for a month or more? Perhaps two?"

"We'll be going back to Paoting soon," Margaret said

flatly, before May could open her mouth. Then she handed each of them a cup of delicate *famille rose* china and requested May to pass the sugar and milk.

Nelson just shook his head. "I don't know how you do it, Margaret, living in the interior as you do. I know there's that doctor living in Paoting now, and that missionary family you told me about, but aren't there any other Europeans for company?"

"When Tim and I first settled there," she replied, sipping her tea, "there was no one else except ourselves, and he was often away for months at a time, as you know. So I consider the doctor and the missionaries ample company."

Nelson shook his head again, and this seemed to irritate Margaret.

"I know you find this difficult to understand," she continued, with a testy edge to her voice, "but I find the Chinese fascinating."

"Fascinating?" Nelson sputtered. "If you consider using torture on prisoners and being a heathen fascinating, I'd say you've been living there too long, Margaret. You need a trip to England to put your life into its proper perspective."

"You're so close-minded, Nelson," she retorted with a shake of her head. "Nothing has value to you unless it's English."

"That's right," he said with calm assurance. "I don't want to have anything to do with the Chinese. Let my comprador deal with his countrymen. That's his job, and I pay him well for it. I'll just see that Benton and Black profits."

May looked from one to the other. "Are you two still having this same argument? Why, I feel as though it's still 1883, and I'm just departing for England!"

They both looked sheepish, and Nelson said, "It adds spice to our lives, because we can't convince the other we're right."

"Well, I *know* I'm right," Margaret said emphatically. "Now, if I can just convince you, Nelson."

The trio laughed, and Nelson added, "By the way, did I tell you Emmy's planning a party in your honor at the end of the week?"

"No, you didn't," Margaret said.

"Ah, yes. It promises to be the hit of the Shanghai social season, if I know my Emmy. Well, shall we finish this and adjourn to the parlor? I'm sure Emmy is desperate to hear more about England, as am I."

They all rose and went back to the villa.

"You'd think she was planning a coronation ball," Margaret said to her daughter later that evening after dinner, as the two women sat in May's room, brushing their hair and discussing the day's events.

After subjecting them to hours of party plans, Emily had invited them to an evening card party at a diplomat's residence, but they declined, for Margaret found card parties tedious.

"That's Emily," May replied. "I suppose she has little enough to do here as it is, with an army of Chinese servants to do everything for her." She looked across at her mother, who was busy plaiting her hair before retiring. "Is Nelson really going back to England at last?"

Margaret said, "May, I've lived in China for most of my life. Every man who has ever come out here vows to go back to England as soon as he steps onto Chinese soil. He is going back only after he makes a fabulous fortune, but I'll tell you, the cemetery's filled with most of them. Nelson is never going back, no matter what he says. I don't know why I still bother arguing with him about it anymore. It's pointless."

"He just seems so vehement, that's all."

"He's got such a good life here, May-Ling, whether he chooses to admit it or not. The house . . . the servants . . . he'd never be able to duplicate this in England. Never. And he knows it. Here he's the great Taipan Wright, confidante of the aristocracy and advisor to diplomats. There he'd be just another lowly, underpaid clerk scraping to survive." Margaret became silent and reflective. "And how are you feeling, May-Ling?"

"Please, Mother, just May. I'm not Chinese, you know."

"It's the name you were christened with," was her mother's indignant retort. "May-Ling . . . 'Beauteous Years.' "

"Still, I prefer simply May."

"As you wish." Hurt silence, then a tentative, "Your father used to call you Ling-Ling, remember? He said it sounded like bells ringing whenever he said it."

May stopped brushing her hair and looked across at her mother. "You still miss him terribly, don't you?"

She nodded dismally. "Yes, I still do, even after all these years. I know I never should have let him make that trip without me, but you know your father. He just looked at me with that rogue's grin of his and said, 'Maggie, allanah, don't you be worrying yourself now. Timmy Fitz has more luck than all the Kings of Tara.' "

May said, "I remember you always used to say to me, 'Don't worry about your father, May-Ling. He can smile his way out of any situation.' "

"It was true. But then . . ." Mrs. Fitzgerald's voice trembled. ". . . his luck ran out." She was silent for a moment. "The pirates must have killed him, May, that's the only explanation for it. I hope he died fighting and died quickly, that's all. You know how cruel the Chinese can be."

May nodded silently, then rushed over to put her arms around her mother, and they cried together for a little while.

Finally, Margaret sniffed and said, "Enough of this luxury. I know you must be exhausted after your first day in Shanghai, so I'll leave you now."

May hugged her. "I'll see you in the morning then."

The next morning, after a hearty English breakfast of eggs, ham, and sausage, everyone went in separate directions, Emily flitting off in her palanquin to make morning calls, while a sad-faced Willie reluctantly marched off to the schoolroom with Miss St. John. May and her mother joined Nelson in the carriage, which would take them to the Benton and Black godown.

After a short ride through the city, they arrived at the godown, one of many noisy, cavernous warehouses that lined the waterfront. It was bustling with activity this morning, and May, Margaret, and Nelson found themselves dodging impatient men moving crates and boxes. Everyone was so industrious, no one seemed to notice their taipan was in their midst, and this pleased Nelson because everything was running with its customary order and efficiency.

"Ah," he said, "some junks were due in from Peking today. That's the reason for all the commotion. Let me find Abbott or Wu, then we can go look at that carving, May."

May and her mother stood out of the way while Nelson wandered off, only to return a few minutes later trailed by two men, a young European and an older Chinese who must have been the comprador Wu.

Tobias Abbott was a thin young man, very pale and not healthy looking, who seemed shy and unskilled in the art of conversation, for he let Nelson do most of the talking. But he couldn't keep his eyes off May and only looked away when she met his gaze.

Wu, who was about Nelson's height and dressed in the stately robes of his station, did not come forward when introduced. Instead, he clasped his hands together and bowed in greeting. He had a round, common face that refused to register an impression in May's mind, and as soon as he turned his head, she forgot what he looked like.

Without further ceremony, Nelson ushered them all into a small back office that was barely large enough to hold them all.

Tobias Abbott, May discovered, could be absolutely garrulous when it came to art objects. "This is the piece," he said, tenderly lifting a boulder carving out of a crate and handing it to her. "The man who wants to sell it to us said it's been in his family for hundreds of years. He claims his great-great-great grandfather was Imperial Carver for one of the emperors, but I wouldn't be surprised if he stole it, knowing how these Chinamen are."

Comprador Wu glanced at him for a split second, but said nothing.

May ignored the pain in her hands as she took the pale yellow chunk of stone and carefully examined the carving.

"This is a scene from Chinese mythology," she said, after minutes of deliberation. "I would say it's the Lady Wang dining on the celestial peach of immortality—see the round object she's holding in her hand?—accompanied by the eight

Taoist Immortals. Here," she added, pointing to one figure, "is Lu Tung-pin with his sword." Next she closed her eyes, as her teacher, Weng Ta-Chung, had taught her to do, and let her fingers "see" the stone. Although she held the carving for a few minutes, the stone remained cold to her touch and did not absorb the warmth of her hand, and when she ran her fingertips along its smooth surface, it felt slightly oily.

"It's genuine jade," she said with conviction.

"Now let's see you date it," Nelson said, his voice holding a hint of a challenge.

May squinted, inspecting the piece carefully from all angles. "The stone itself looks old, as does the design, but we all know that doesn't necessarily mean the piece *is* old." May turned the carving upsidedown, and read a poem that had been engraved on the bottom. She smiled. "Here is K'ien Lung's seal, so it's not as old as it first appears."

"There," Margaret said with satisfaction. "May has exposed a copy, albeit a very good one. I suspect she's just saved you hundreds of pounds."

"Wu was able to do the same," Nelson replied nonchalantly, "but I had to test May." Then he smiled. "You are your father's daughter. He taught you well, May."

"Well, now that that's done," Margaret said with a sigh. "What else do you have to show us, Nelson?"

"Quite a great deal. Come along with me."

After bidding good day to Abbott and comprador Wu, they followed Nelson past the bulky, pedestrian items, such as teas and bolts of silk, to the finer merchandise—"the cream," as Nelson called it. May felt herself overwhelmed by the beauty and artistry of carved cinnabar boxes, pale-green celadon bowls of the Sung period, and blue and white porcelain decorated with cranes or dragons or pastoral scenes.

"It's all so beautiful," May said with a wondrous shake of her head, when all the treasures were packed back into their crates.

"These are treasures worth dying for," Nelson said in all seriousness.

"Possessions are never worth dying for," Margaret Fitzgerald retorted. "People and ideals—but never possessions."

May, too, looked at Nelson with a sense of dismay, then shrugged the feeling off. When Nelson Wright looked at objects—and people, too, May suspected—he judged their worth in terms of pounds and sovereigns, but her father had judged them for their beauty and craftsmanship. And that was the difference between the two friends.

"Now it's time for you two to get back to the villa," Nelson announced, "while I must get back to the hong, before they think I've been run over by a Shanghai barrow or dropped into the Hwang Pu."

When May and her mother arrived back at the villa, they found Emily and lunch waiting.

"Did you enjoy yourselves?" their hostess asked, toying with the beads at her throat. Before anyone could answer, she wrinkled her nose in distaste and added, "Nelson took me there once, and once was enough. All those boxes . . . all those rough, sweaty men milling about . . . But come, you two, Cook has prepared a delicious tiffin for us. I've spent the most delightful morning with Dorothy Charney and . . ." Emily drifted off toward the dining room, and Margaret just rolled her eyes and followed.

"We had an interesting experience yesterday," Mrs. Fitzgerald said, once they were seated and she could fit a word in edgewise. "May was nearly run over by a barrow, and she was saved by this tall man, slightly disreputable-looking, with dark hair and wearing a white suit."

"Good heavens!" Emily exclaimed. "Why on earth didn't you say something sooner? Were you hurt?"

"I'm all right," May insisted. "Please don't fuss."

Emily looked thoughtful as tiffin was served. "That sounds like Alexander Wolders, or the Dutchman, as some call him." Then she broke into a dreamy smile. "He's so dashing, don't you think? Half of the hostesses in Shanghai would love to invite him to their soirees, but he's something of an outcast, you know. None of the Europeans will have anything to do with him."

LADY JADE

May thought of her ruined bonnet and scowled disagreeably. "I can see why. I found him to be rude and offensive, even though he did save me."

"Oh, he can be," Emily agreed. "I remember the time he and Jason Devereaux got into a fight at the French consulate and tore the place up frightfully. He does fit in about as well as a bull in a china shop, but he is such a bit of fresh air compared to all the bland merchants and diplomats who come to these affairs."

"In what way?" Margaret demanded.

Emily dug her elbows into the table and leaned forward, her eyes shining at the prospect of choice gossip. "He's shockingly disreputable, you know. Rumor has it—and this is just rumor, mind you—that he keeps a Javanese woman in Macao. Some also say he's been involved in—" she lowered her voice to a dramatic whisper, "—white slavery."

"Emily, I see nothing romantic about a man who sells women into bondage!" May sputtered in disgust.

"But it's so tantalizing," Emily replied with a laugh, "to speculate whether he does or not! I just wish I could persuade Nelson to let me invite him to one of my parties."

Suddenly a houseboy carrying a small box entered the room and bowed. "Missie, man come. Asm for missie with red hair."

"Thank you, Number Three," Emily said, as she took the box and dismissed him with a curt wave of her hand. "Why, May, this must be for you," and she handed her the box.

"What, my dear?" her mother said. "An admirer already?"

"I doubt it," May replied, lifting the lid and peering inside at a solitary white flower. "Why, it's a lotus."

"Just a common lotus?" Emily sniffed. "They grow like weeds around here. Who sent it? Is there a note?"

"Yes." On the envelope was scrawled, "To the Chinese Demon," and May felt her irritation rise as she unfolded the paper. All it said was, "To replace your bonnet. A.W."

"Well?" Emily prodded, craning her neck to see. "Don't keep us in suspense."

May handed the note to her mother.

"What *is* this all about?" Emily was becoming agitated, for she hated to be excluded from anything.

When May explained about the bonnet and showed her the note, Emily said, "Wait until I tell Dorothy. She has been after Alex for months, and she'll be green with envy."

May shot her mother a look of helplessness and desperation. "Emily, I would appreciate it if you said nothing to anyone about this."

The words went right over her head. "But why does he call you the Chinese demon? How utterly mysterious!"

"If you bothered to learn anything about the people you live with," Margaret began, "you'd know that, in the Chinese hell, demons have red hair and green eyes."

May added, "It's obviously his idea of a joke, and I don't appreciate it."

"I'd be flattered if a man sent me a lotus for my hair," Emily said with a sniff.

"Emily, please, you're making much too much of this."

"Too much of this—!"

"Emily!" Margaret shouted, bringing her hand down on the table so hard the china and silverware jumped and tinkled.

Affronted silence.

"Please," May begged. "I have no interest in Alexander Wolders or any other man, except my husband. I'm a respectable married woman, and my reputation would be ruined if people found out about this."

Here at last was something Emily could understand, and she demurred. "Oh, why certainly, May. I'd never let that happen."

May smiled, and her mother just stared at the ceiling.

After tiffin, May took her lotus outside and set it in the fish pond. But she kept the note.

The rest of May's first week in Shanghai was an uneventful round of teas and luncheons, but Emily's party that Sunday more than compensated.

It didn't begin as a disaster. As a matter of fact, it began beautifully, with not a cloud in the clear, blue sky. Preparations had all gone according to Emily's carefully planned schedule. The lawn amah, Number One boy's elderly aunt who could do nothing else, stooped and scoured the lawn for any twigs or stones, while an army of gardeners—more of Number One's relatives—spent the week walking back and forth, pruning, cutting, and trimming, until the garden looked spectacular. The cooks had slaved in the hot kitchen the day before, all night and morning, filling the house with delectable sweet and spicy smells. Much to the nervous hostess's delight, acceptances came pouring in, so the day's success should have been assured.

May and her mother, in their cool, frilly party dresses and white organdy hats, sat near the fish pond, watching the goldfish zigzag back and forth, and the carp arch and leap into the air. They had spent the entire morning with Emily, standing in the villa's cool foyer and being introduced to an endless procession of people whose names May made no attempt to remember. Most of them were of position and influence, for Nelson was a consummate politician, as well as a businessman. But the person May most longed to see—Willie—had been exiled to the schoolroom with Miss St. John.

Now May watched the women, all in white, like languid moths, flutter together, exchange gossip, and disperse, while the men stood rooted to one spot, their drinks clenched in their hands as they discussed the state of the world and the British Empire.

"Do you see that buxom blonde over there?" Margaret Fitzgerald whispered from behind her fan.

"Fraulein Hummel? The one by the azalea bush?"

Margaret nodded. "Well, I predict the men will soon divide into two camps. Those who prefer ripe, mindless abundance will flock to our fair schnitzel and those who prefer cool, intellectual beauty will be at your side."

"Mother, what a cruel thing to say!"

She shrugged. "There simply aren't enough women to go around, but then, there never were."

A young man May remembered being introduced to her as an up-and-coming aide in the French consulate came across the lawn toward them. *"Excusez-moi, mesdames.* Would either of you ladies like some lemonade?"

"Thank you," Mrs. Fitzgerald replied, shading her eyes with her hand, "but we are drinking champagne."

"Ah, my favorite drink also."

Soon the ladies received four offers of refreshment, and when each man discovered his idea had been stolen, he stayed anyway.

May suddenly felt herself nudged by her mother. "Look," Margaret said, "there's that shy Mr. Abbott trying to muster enough courage to join us. Why don't you bring him into our circle?"

May rose and started for Tobias Abbott, and when he saw she was walking toward him, his eyes darted nervously about, as if searching for a convenient escape route.

"Why, good day, Mr. Abbott," May said brightly. "Isn't it a lovely day for a party?"

"Yes, Mrs. Monckton, it is."

"My mother and I decided we couldn't bear to leave you alone, so won't you join us?" She took his arm before he could protest or draw away.

"Why . . . why, yes, thank you."

When they rejoined the party, Mrs. Fitzgerald made the introductions, and the pale young man seemed relieved.

"You ladies live in the interior, I understand," Monsieur LaSalle was saying in amazement. "Aren't you afraid?"

"Oh, it's not for the faint of heart," Mrs. Fitzgerald replied with relish, "but I've lived there most of my life, so I'm quite used to it."

Tobias Abbott finally spoke. "I find the Chinese to be a backward race myself."

"Backward!" Margaret exclaimed, and he cringed at her vehemence. "How can you make such a claim, sir? Why, the Chinese had a flourishing civilization even before Christ."

"I mean they do everything backwards. The men wear dresses, like women, and the women wear trousers, like men.

They write and read backwards and when they're in mourning, they wear white instead of black. As I said, they're a 'backward' people."

All of the men tittered at his attempt at humor, but the Fitzgerald women wore frozen smiles.

When the conversation lagged, May turned her attention to one of the men who had lingered with their party, a British naval officer who greatly reminded her of Robin. "Sir," she began, "what ship do you command?"

"HMS *Bounding Main,* madam," he replied, his voice so much like Robin's, May's heart quickened. "We just pulled into port a few days ago, and I consider myself fortunate to be invited to this party."

"It is lovely, isn't it?"

"As are you, madam," he whispered, for her ears alone.

May blushed and smiled up at him.

"I say," Tobias Abbott murmured, staring across the crowd, "look who's here, and I don't imagine the taipan invited him, either."

All heads turned to see Alexander Wolders saunter into the yard, and everyone stopped speaking almost simultaneously.

"I can't tolerate the bounder myself," Abbott muttered, frowning in dislike.

Apparently the entire European community shared his opinion, for a palpable chill descended on the party, and no one—not even Emily, red-faced and fanning herself furiously—even acknowledged his presence with a nod. Except one—a stunning woman rushed smiling to Wolders' side, and he lowered his head to hear what she was saying.

"And who is that gorgeous creature flinging herself at him?" Margaret demanded.

"Dorothy Charney," was Abbott's reply. "Her reputation won't be worth a shilling after today."

Margaret's eyes were on her daughter when she said, "I hear he's involved in opium smuggling."

"If it's illegal or unsavory, you can bet the Dutchman's involved in it," Monsieur LaSalle said.

"Well, if Mr. Wolders's presence is so objectionable, why doesn't someone ask him to leave?" May asked.

Abbott looked horrified. "And risk a row? No, better to ignore his rudeness. He'll soon leave, if no one encourages him."

As if he knew they were discussing him, Alexander Wolders lifted his head and looked right at their group. May could feel the intensity of his cold gaze all the way across the lawn as his eyes met hers. He looked up at her white organdy bonnet with its frivolous roses, and his mouth tightened. Then he turned and strolled over to join Fraulein Hummel's admirers, with Dorothy Charney still clinging to his arm.

"Interesting," Margaret said softly. "I'm surprised."

"I'm not," was May's cool reply.

Wolders would not touch any drink as he wandered around the gathering, causing the women to redden and the men to glower when he spoke to them or tried to join in their conversation. Most turned a cold shoulder to him, but he just kept moving on, drifting from one guest to another.

When the buffet was served, Wolders alone refused to eat, even when a conscience-stricken Emily offered him a plate and urged him to join the other guests. May, however, was too interested in the captain to pay much attention to the ostracizing of Alexander Wolders.

His name was Joseph Forsythe, and, as May watched him cross the lawn with two plates filled with food, she marveled at the close resemblance between him and Robin. The captain had Robin's classical good looks, perfectly proportioned and pleasingly arranged, with intense brown eyes framed by heavy lashes. The captain coupled this handsome face with a trim, erect physique in a blue uniform, to cut a dashing, romantic figure, and he seemed to know just the right thing to say to everyone.

"What a charming man," May thought to herself, suddenly feeling admired once again.

As the afternoon wore on, the guests slowly started to depart, some going home in their carriages or rickshaws, while others drifted off to the park, to listen to the band, or down to the river, to watch junks with sails like dragonfly wings go lumbering up and down the Hwang Pu.

Captain Forsythe and May were taking a stroll through the garden when he gasped and clutched at his throat. "I don't want to alarm you, but I think the heat is beginning to affect me. Is there somewhere we can go that's . . . cooler?"

She nodded. "Oh, you poor man. Of course. Nelson's study."

As they crossed the lawn to the verandah, May kept casting worried glances at the captain, fearing he would collapse at any moment with heat prostration, for he did look as pale as Tobias Abbott.

"It does take some time to get used to the heat of Shanghai," she told him, "especially if you've just come from England."

The minute they were inside the cool semidarkness of Nelson's study, the captain miraculously recovered. First he closed the French doors, then the door that connected the room with the rest of the house. "That's to be sure we're not interrupted," he said softly, and May felt herself go pale.

"Captain Forsythe, I don't believe you are sick at all."

"About the only thing I'm stricken with is desire for you."

May almost laughed aloud, but he was so intense, she thought better of it. "I'm flattered," she said, taking a step toward the door, "but I must return to the others."

Before she could take another step, he encircled her with his arms.

"Please let me go this instant."

"No." Then his mouth came down on hers before she could protest.

With superhuman effort, May managed to pull her arms from his hold, twist free, and push him away. "Captain Forsythe! Such behavior! I'm surprised at you." May's voice was trembling with rage as she stood there shaking.

"Oh, are you, Mrs. Monckton?" The captain's handsome face was red and ugly as he grabbed her wrists, jerking her viciously. "Don't put on a lady's airs and graces with me, you trollop."

May was so stunned at first that all she could do was stare up at him. He smiled. "You don't like being called that, do you? Well, I have other names, all as unpleasant, but highly descriptive of women like you. Don't look so indignant, my dear Mrs. Monckton, because I know all about you. I was stationed in Southampton before being shipped out to this hellhole. Why, you look so pale all of a sudden, and I suspect you don't want to be reminded of England."

"I don't know what you're talking about," May said, suddenly frightened.

He licked his lips. "Oh, yes, you do. Your name was bandied about on every London street corner from Chelsea to Tottenham. 'The ravishing Mrs. Monckton discovers the bodies of her husband and lover,' I believe one illustration was called. Oh, yes, my dear, your name was well-known after what you did—after what you forced your poor husband to do. So don't pretend you're too good for the likes of Joe Forsythe."

He pulled her to him and tried to kiss her again, but May struggled and succeeded in pushing him away.

The captain drew back his hand. "Why, you—"

"Touch her, and I'm going to break your back," a voice threatened from the doorway.

Both of them spun around, to come face to face with Alexander Wolders.

"What in the hell are you doing here?" Forsythe growled.

"Thwarting your plans, obviously." Wolders walked into the room and loosened his collar.

"This is a private matter."

"I think not."

Forsythe hesitated for a moment, and May could tell he was measuring himself against the other man. With a slight shrug, he dropped May's wrists and started to march out, but whirled around for one last parting shot.

"You've won this round, but by this time tomorrow,

Mrs. Monckton, all of Shanghai will know what you are." And he left.

As soon as the door slammed shut, May collapsed onto one corner of the divan, without so much as a glance at Wolders.

A terrifying panic was sapping her ability to think, and she could almost feel her brain slowing down, then coming to a halt. She saw the man sit down beside her, and his lips were moving, so he must be talking to her, but his words were an unintelligible buzz and made no sense. The expression on his face went from concern to puzzlement, and finally, to alarm. He reached out, grasped her shoulders and shook her, but her mind still refused to move.

"I am going mad," a little voice shrieked within her. "I am finally going mad."

Suddenly the man brought his hand up and struck her. May felt the sting on her cheek, her head rocked to the side, and her mind awoke with a snap.

"I'm sorry," he said gruffly, grasping her hands. "I had to hit you. It was the only way."

"I know," she whispered as the tears trickled down her face.

"Are you sure you're all right? Perhaps I should get a doctor."

"No, that won't be necessary. I'll be all right."

"You're certain?"

She nodded.

"Well, you look a sight. You're as pale as Death's Head Abbott out there, and your hair's going to come down any minute." He reached over and brushed a strand off her cheek. Then he pulled a handkerchief out of his pocket and handed it to her. "Here. Dry your eyes."

May wondered if she had imagined the solicitous Wolders of a few seconds ago as she wiped the tears from her cheeks.

"That's better." He leaned back in his seat, his eyes twinkling. "You know, at the rate I'm going, I could make a profession out of rescuing you."

She laughed in spite of her misery. "I am grateful."

"And how are your hands?" he asked. Before May could reply, he reached out, took both her hands, and turned them over, scowling as he inspected them. "Well, at least they seem better."

"Cook put some ointment on them," May explained. "They seem to be healing nicely."

As their conversation trailed off, Wolders regarded her with a curious expression. "I can't for the life of me see what attracted you to Captain What's-his-name."

"Joseph Forsythe."

"Captain Forsythe. He's much too pretty to have any substance. China will kill him in a month."

May just shrugged and said, "He reminded me of some-one, that's all."

"I see."

She had a feeling he saw more than he should.

"Why are you afraid of him?" Wolders asked.

"Because he knows something about me I'd prefer to keep secret."

"And he's threatened to tell the world, is that it?"

She nodded dismally as she fought back the tears.

"The bastard."

"I'll wager not many women refuse Captain Forsythe anything," she said. "So now he's going to get even for my wounding his vanity, which seems to be considerable." She flung back her head and stared at the ceiling. "I was a fool to believe he was sick with the heat and to let him lure me into the house." *You were a bigger fool for thinking he was any-thing like Robin,* she added silently.

"Everyone makes mistakes," Wolders said gruffly. "Don't be so hard on yourself."

She laughed softly. "I seem to make more than my share." She shut her eyes as she wondered what the Wrights were going to think of her when the rumors reached them. May groaned aloud.

"Would it help if I . . . repaid Captain Forsythe for you?"

May's eyes widened in alarm.

Wolders saw her startled look and just grinned. "Not that way. Our friend is so pretty I was thinking more along the lines of selling him to the Empress Dowager as a concubine."

May laughed until her sides ached. "You're outrageous."

"Thank you. I consider that a compliment. Still, perhaps I can persuade the captain to keep what he knows to himself."

May sighed glumly. "He's probably told half of China by now."

"Told them what?"

She drew away, suddenly reticent. "I . . . I'd rather not say. It's personal and very painful."

"As you wish," he replied, as though he had more important things on his mind. Instead, his gaze traveled to May's hair, and he frowned. "Where's the lotus I sent you?"

"I put it in the fish pond, so it wouldn't die."

"Fish pond! It was meant for your hair."

A wry smile touched her mouth. "Such a beautiful flower for a demon such as I?"

He smiled and nodded slowly.

"Why did you come to this party?" May wanted to know. "I thought you'd have too much pride to go where you're not wanted."

"I usually do, but I wanted to see you again."

May felt a warm blush suffuse her cheeks, as she was caught off balance and could think of no quick reply.

He saw her discomfort and smiled gently. "Don't worry. You won't have to fight me off as well."

She returned his smile. "Twice in one day would be too much." Then she added, "Is it really true what people say about you, Dutchman?"

He laughed, a low, lazy sound. "You have your secrets, Mrs. Monckton, and I have mine."

"So, you know my name."

He nodded. "And everything—almost everything—about you."

"And yet all I know is your name. That's not fair."

"Perhaps one day you will know more." Then he rose and stood over her. "I wouldn't worry about Captain Forsythe, if I were you."

"Oh, but I do."

"Why should you? There's the great Taipan Wright to protect you."

She ignored the mockery in his voice. "I doubt if even Nelson could save me."

Annoyance flared in his eyes. "Where's your spirit? Are you just going to give up without a fight? Come now, Mrs. Monckton, I would expect more courage from you."

She looked across at him and sighed. "I've been fighting for a long time, and I'm tired."

Wolders took a step forward and looked as though he was about to say something. Instead, all he said was, "Good day, Mrs. Monckton."

"Good day, Mr. Wolders, and thank you, once again."

After he disappeared through the French doors, she irrationally wished him back. She should have been thinking about how to prepare herself for the inevitable consequences of Captain Forsythe, but she couldn't get Alexander Wolders out of her mind. He was so brash and brazen, with little respect for the conventions and traditions that held British Shanghai together like so much paste, but she couldn't help recalling the gentleness deep in his eyes.

A chill wracked her body, as she thought of the disapproving looks again, the whispers behind fans, the silences and stares that would greet her when she walked into a room. The women would become cold and distant, while their husbands became warm and very friendly.

"Not again!" she groaned aloud. "Please, Lord, don't let it happen all over again."

Finally, she stretched with a sigh and rose, wondering how long it would take British Shanghai to learn the truth about May Monckton.

Three days later, two topics dominated every conversation in the International settlement—a shocking rumor about the Wright's lovely houseguest and the disappearance of Fraulein Hummel.

CHAPTER THREE

Something was dreadfully wrong.

May realized this the minute she saw Emily's palanquin come rocking back down the drive a scant half-hour after it had left to carry her on her morning calls. May watched from behind one of the columns on the verandah as the coolies stopped and gently lowered the conveyance. But even before it touched the ground, Emily had flung open the door and was sweeping out, throwing the men off balance, causing their sinewy backs and arms to strain as they fought to keep the palanquin from teetering.

As May watched Emily stride purposefully toward the house, she wondered if she was looking at the same languid, effusive woman who had warmly welcomed her into her home just a short time ago. This Emily was furious. She walked in quick, short steps, arms swinging like a soldier's, with determination and forcefulness. The soft features, so quick to dissolve into laughter, were now edged with steel. Emily looked like a lady who had had something precious taken from her and was going to retrieve it at all costs.

May stepped into her room and sunk down into the chair, where she laced her fingers together nervously. Someone had told Emily the truth, and the revelation had infuriated her.

Now May wished she had disregarded her mother's advice and gone straight to Nelson and Emily after the Forsythe incident. But no, Margaret had insisted, "Don't say a word. It would only upset them, and besides once he calms down, Captain Forsythe is a gentleman and will say nothing."

So much for gentlemen.

Well, we'll remedy that right now, May said to herself, rising and hurrying across the room and out the door. She rushed down the hall and was just in time to see Emily's door swing shut.

"Emily?" she called, testing the knob. "May I come in?"

"Not right now," a chilly voice called out from far away. "I've got a beastly headache and need to lie down."

"Please, Emily. It's very important."

"It will have to wait."

Dismissed, May turned and went to her mother's room, where she found her inspecting her hair in the bronze mirror she carried everywhere like a good-luck piece.

"Emily knows," was all May said.

Mrs. Fitzgerald looked up at her distraught daughter. "Don't be absurd. How could she possibly know?"

"Captain Forsythe, I would imagine. She's just returned uncommonly soon from her morning calls, and you should have seen the expression on her face. Now she's locked in her room and won't even talk to me."

"That's a bad omen," her mother admitted, as she set down the mirror and glared at her daughter. "Whatever made you decide to go ... go *dallying* with a man you'd known only a few hours? Quite frankly, I'm surprised at you, May-Ling. This isn't England, you know, or France. It's China. Standards are much more rigid here. One false step, and it's social suicide."

May felt her temper soar. "I did not go dallying! As I told you, he tricked me. Captain Forsythe pretended to feel faint so he could get me alone."

Mrs. Fitzgerald shook her head. "Before we go jumping to conclusions, let's find out exactly what our situation is, all right? Lord knows, there are plenty of other reasons for Emily to be upset. Perhaps the cook didn't make her enough sesame sweets, or something equally catastrophic."

"I suppose," May mumbled, and started back to her room. On the way, she noticed Emily's door was now ajar, so she went up to it and knocked. There was no answer, so she gave the door a gentle shove, poked her head in, and called Emily's name.

The room was empty.

When she heard voices, May froze, afraid of discovery. Then she noticed Emily also had left the door connecting her bedchamber with her husband's open, presumably in her haste to confront him before he departed for work.

May took a deep breath, closed the hall door without a sound, and noiselessly walked over to the connecting door to listen, knowing full well that eavesdroppers never hear good of themselves.

"—and she wouldn't even *see* me!" Emily wailed.

Silence, as Nelson collected his thoughts. "Well, if you didn't see her, how did you hear this preposterous story about May?" His calm voice was touched with asperity. "Honestly, I can't believe what you're telling me."

"Believe me, Nelson, it's the truth. After Lady Hertford refused to see me—*refused* to see me, Nelson—I went to Betty Grainger's. She, at least, is still my friend. And she told me what all of Shanghai knows, that our houseguest is nothing more than a common—"

"Don't say it!" Nelson barked. "I've known the Fitzgeralds all my life, and I refuse to believe that of May."

May could visualize his pink face growing darker with anger as he faced his wife, for Nelson was a staunch defender of his friends.

"But her husband committed suicide because of her blatant infidelity, and her story about him still being in England . . . and we believed her."

"Balderdash. A couple of women past their prime are spreading tales about a beautiful young woman." He paused, and May envisioned him smoothing his mustache, like ruffled feathers. "And I'm surprised at you, Emmy, being so quick to believe the worst of old friends."

She ignored his reproach and continued. "But that's not all. Captain Forsythe has been boasting of his new conquest to every man he meets. Just listen when you go to your club for tiffin today. Just listen to the topic of conversation on everyone's lips. It won't be the price of tea, either."

"Well," Nelson said, "I'm sure we can all weather it quite nicely—if it is true."

"But you don't understand. May has to go." Emily was crying now, and her voice shook with emotion. "I'll be ostracized if she stays. No one will speak to me, like poor Mr. Wolders the other day at our party. You have your business and your club, but I have nothing without my friends." She was silent, and when she spoke again, her voice was soft and cajoling. "Do you realize what it's like to be alone here, with no one to talk to, with nothing to do?"

"And don't you understand that I can't sell old friends for a bit of socializing?" Nelson retorted, his voice sharp and exasperated. "I am taipan, and you are my taitai. We are above such pettiness, and don't you forget it. Noblesse oblige."

"May and Margaret must leave, Nelson."

"No. Not until they're ready. I'll not be dictated to by a gaggle of gossiping old hens."

"Then I want to go back to England."

Stunned silence at those grim and final words. "What did you say?"

"You heard me. I want to go back to England, and I'll take Willie with me, of course."

"You will do no such thing."

May shuddered at the coldness in Nelson's voice.

"I've always hated China," Emily went on dismally, "but I've worked hard to make the best of the situation, because I loved you. But if you can't understand what this means to me, then I'm afraid we don't have much of a marriage, do we? And I will fight you with my last breath to leave this heathen place with my son."

Poor, foolish Emily, May thought to herself as she silently backed out of the room and left Nelson and his wife to their battle of wills. She returned to her own room to compose herself before telling her mother what she had overheard.

May went onto the balcony, into the blazing heat, and

shaded her eyes against the white-hot sun inching its way to the top of the sky. Off in the distance, in the Chinese part of the city, May could hear the faint notes of whistles, drums, and bells and smell a hint of incense and camphor wood on the morning air. She breathed deeply, and the scents were overwhelmed by the flowers from the garden below.

The dull clop of hoofbeats caught her attention, and she looked down to see Willie and Abbott come walking up the drive on their Mongolian ponies. Both man and boy were protected against the sun with wide-brimmed hats and long sleeves and gloves, but dark rings of sweat curled beneath their arms, and their white faces were shiny. Abbott was chattering away to Willie, and May found it curious that the pale man only seemed at ease with children and art objects, but not with other adults, especially women.

Willie. As May watched the child's round, upturned face gazing rapturously at Abbott, she knew Nelson would never give up his son. Never.

She withdrew before the man and boy below saw her and went to find her mother.

"We have to leave Shanghai," was Mrs. Fitzgerald's pronouncement after she heard what her daughter had to say.

May's mouth went dry. "So soon?"

"A little sooner than anticipated, surely."

"But Uncle Nelson said he would stand by us . . ."

Mrs. Fitzgerald gave her an exasperated look. "You must realize I can't ask Nelson to ruin his marriage just for us."

"No, of course not. I wasn't thinking."

"I'm sure Nelson, being the gentleman that he is, will urge us to stay, but we just can't. And I wouldn't want to have Emily for an enemy under any circumstances."

"You're right, of course."

Mrs. Fitzgerald rose, a glimmer of excitement in her eyes. "Let's go find the Wrights and tell them of our plans."

Nelson had already left for the hong, but they found Emily in the solarium, a sulky, mutinous expression on her face as she sat with a half-empty bowl of sesame sweets within an arm's reach.

"Good morning," Mrs. Fitzgerald said heartily.

"Good morning," Emily muttered, without smiling.

"Well, I have some news for you," Margaret announced. "May and I will be leaving for Paoting within the week."

Emily's eyes widened hopefully, then narrowed in suspicion. "But I thought you would at least stay a month—at least that's how long my husband said you were staying. Why have you changed your mind?"

"You know me, I could never stay away from my home for that long," Margaret said, "and, besides, May is anxious to get back, too. Aren't you, dear?"

"Yes," she agreed, taking her mother's hint. "I'm longing to see my home again."

"Of course," Emily said, beaming. "Nelson will be *so* disappointed. Are you sure I can't dissuade you? You know we both enjoy having you so much."

"Our minds are quite made up," May said.

"Nelson will be so disappointed," Emily said again.

On the contrary, May thought to herself, he will be pleased, because harmony will once again be restored to his house, and he will not lose his son. But he will pretend to be disappointed, so we can all save face—Emily, Nelson, Mother and I.

"That was clever," May said to her mother as they climbed the stairs back to their rooms.

"What purpose would be served by confronting her? This way, Emily thinks we still think highly of her, and you are saved the embarrassment of defending yourself."

"I wonder if Uncle Nelson will believe your story?"

"He most of all," her mother replied.

The two women confronted Nelson on the verandah when he came home at three-thirty that afternoon, looking hot, tired, and cross. The man barely had enough time to pour himself a drink before May and Margaret appeared.

"Nelson," Mrs. Fitzgerald said, "we have something to tell you."

He leaned back in his chair, then said, "Yes?" When she told him that they would be leaving, he seemed surprised. "So soon?"

"We appreciate your hospitality," May said, "but Mother and I are anxious to get back."

Nelson looked from one to the other with a cool, speculative look. "When did you plan to leave?"

Mrs. Fitzgerald told him.

"How will you go, by steamer, to Tientsin?"

"No," May said in alarm, remembering how her father had died, "not that way."

"Don't be absurd," her mother chided her gently. "Steamer is the only practical way. A houseboat up the Grand Canal would take weeks."

"Well," Nelson said, raising his glass to them, "we've enjoyed having you both, even though it was only for a short while. And you're always welcome here. You know that."

"Thank you, Nelson," Mrs. Fitzgerald said, unaware how soon they would be forced to hold him to his word.

He smiled. "You two are marvelous women, just marvelous." Then he downed the rest of his drink and rose to find his wife, to tell her there would be no more nonsense about returning to England with Willie.

May sat in the folly, her eyes closed, listening to the hum of bees and hummingbirds as they went from blossom to blossom in search of sweet nectar. It was so quiet here, so peaceful, and only now and then would the sounds of the city—footsteps, hoofbeats, rolling wheels—intrude. She could hear the high-pitched voice of the lawn amah singing to herself as she scoured the grass for any twigs or stones that would offend the taipan's feet or the feet of his family as they strolled. Every once in a while, the water would splash, and May envisioned a carp breaking its glassy surface and arching into the air to catch a dragonfly.

As she sat here, May found her thoughts turning to Robin, and she felt the old, familiar ache in her throat. She thought of their stolen afternoons and shivered in spite of the heat. If it hadn't been for Nigel . . .

Oh, what was the use? Robin was gone, thanks to her, and now she had to accept a life without him.

"All my fault," she murmured to herself, "all my fault."

"Aunt May?" a voice said at her elbow.

Her eyes flew open to find Willie looking at her, his face long and dejected with betrayal.

"Yes, Willie?"

"Is it true, what my mother says, that you're going to leave Shanghai?"

May nodded. "My mother and I must go back to Paoting."

His dark eyes filled with tears as he bravely tried not to cry. "But why? Who will tell me about the different dragons, and the princess who rides her fiery chariot across the sky?"

Willie had been spending almost every evening in May's room, eating almond cakes smuggled up from the kitchen under cover of night. Then they would sit cross-legged on the floor, while May told the child Chinese fairy tales and myths she had learned long ago, at her own amah's knee. For the last few nights, May had been telling him about different types of dragons—those that lived in the mountains and others that lived in the sea—until the boy couldn't keep his eyes open any longer. Later, May would accompany him back to his room and tuck him in bed, after brushing cookie crumbs from his chin, so Miss St. John would find no evidence of his nighttime foray.

May put her hand on his shoulder. "I'm sorry, Willie. I'd stay if I could—you know that—but you'll have your father and Mr. Abbott for company until I come to visit you again."

"You won't come back!" he cried, his face crumpling.

"Yes, I will. Please don't cry."

"You won't! Miss St. John says the Chinese cut off people's heads. They'll do that to you, Aunt May. I know they will!" He tore himself away and ran back to the house, leaving May to curse the pinched-face governess under her breath.

"Willie!" she called, but he didn't stop or turn around. She watched him bolt across the verandah and disappear inside, and she felt powerless to help him. She just hoped he would understand, and forgive her.

When all the adults gathered for dinner that evening, Nelson had an interesting bit of news for them.

"Claus Hummel's daughter has disappeared."

May and her mother exchanged looks, recalling the buxom blonde standing near the azalea bush, with a flock of men around her.

Emily turned pale and set her fork down. "Oh? What happened?"

Nelson shrugged. "No one seems to know for sure. She went walking in the park with a friend, then excused herself because she said she wanted to talk to someone she knew. The friend continued to listen to the band, but when the fraulein didn't return, she went to look for her. She was nowhere to be found."

"No one saw anything?" Mrs. Fitzgerald demanded.

"No one," Nelson replied.

"Have the police been notified?" May wanted to know.

"Of course. As soon as anyone was aware of her disappearance. The consuls are all working on it as well, but it doesn't look promising."

Mrs. Fitzgerald's smile was grim as she said, "What's one more woman missing in Shanghai?"

Emily was aghast at her offhand manner. "Margaret! How can you say such a thing?"

"What could have happened to her?" May wondered aloud.

"Claus is very wealthy," Nelson said, sipping his wine. "Someone could be holding her for ransom."

"How horrible," Emily muttered.

"On the contrary," Margaret said, "that's one of the best things that could have happened to her."

While both Nelson and May knew what Margaret meant, Emily was obtuse. "Why, whatever do you mean?"

"I'll tell you later, Emmy," her husband said, then dabbed at his lips with his napkin. "This is the second European woman to disappear this year."

"When something is in short supply, the price is very high," Margaret said, her voice cynical.

Emily's eyes widened. "Margaret! You don't mean—!"

"Oh, Emily, don't be such an innocent! Of course that's what I mean. Some Chinamen have ... unusual tastes."

"I'm going to be sick," Emily declared, rising.

Nelson looked up at her. "Please, dear, no vapors at the table."

She glared at him as she turned and flounced out of the room.

Nelson seemed to unwind further without his wife present. "I wouldn't be surprised if the Dutchman had a hand in the fraulein's disappearance."

"Alexander Wolders?" May said, recalling how he had comforted her the day of the disastrous party. "Surely his activities are only rumors."

One of Nelson's shoulders rose in a shrug. "Talk flies thick and fast, but no one has ever caught him at it—unfortunately." His lip curled in derision. "The man should be shot just on principle." Then he calmed down, adding, "And, as for my other news, misfortune has befallen another one of Sunday's guests."

"Who?" May asked.

"Joseph Forsythe. Captain Forsythe."

The two women froze and exchanged glances, but Nelson didn't appear to notice as he crumbled a roll. "He was having a few drinks with friends in the Shanghai Club when Alexander Wolders came storming in and—for no reason at all—hit him and sent him flying across the room."

"Good heavens!" Margaret exclaimed in perfect imitation of Emily.

"He didn't say why he struck the captain?" May asked.

Nelson shrugged. "Not a word. He just turned and walked out, leaving the man with a broken jaw and a bruised back where he crashed into some tables on his way down. I'd be curious to know why Wolders hit him."

So, he had not let the captain escape after all, and May felt absurdly pleased.

When dinner was over, Margaret looked at her daughter and said, "Come, May-Ling, we've got plans to make and packing to do."

And they went upstairs to plan their journey into China.

A week later, May and her mother were standing on the deck of the *Hanover*, sailing down the silt-filled Hwang Pu

River, away from Shanghai and toward the China Sea.

"I'm glad that's over with," Mrs. Fitzgerald said with a sigh of relief.

May knew what she meant. She could still see the Wrights on the dock, Uncle Nelson watching them with a strange look on his pink face, one arm around a sullen Willie, who refused to smile or even wave good-bye, and Emily crying noisily and waving her handkerchief like a banner.

"I think Emily's tears were tears of joy," Margaret added, reading May's mind. "She certainly wasn't sorry to see us go."

May leaned on the railing and studied the low green fields in the distance, which lined the river on both sides. "I used to like Emily, but after what happened, I don't think I can ever feel kindly toward her again."

"What do you mean?"

"One expects loyalty from one's friends."

"True. But in a way, I can't blame her."

"What, Mother, defending her, are you?"

Margaret smiled faintly. "Oh, she's silly and vain, and she annoys me a great deal, but I try to understand her." She paused to finger the coral pendant she wore. "You see, she has to live in Shanghai long after we're gone. But, judging by all the invitations she received once it became known that we were leaving, I'd say Emily's social status was restored."

"I'm glad Nelson stood by us at least."

Margaret scowled. "Yes, but I wonder how long he would have resisted Emily. She may act flighty, but she's got a core of steel, that one."

"Nelson is taipan," May said simply. "I'm sure he would have resisted her very well." Then she added, "I'm going to miss Willie terribly. Last night, I passed by his bedroom door, and I heard him sobbing."

"Oh, May . . ."

"It nearly broke my heart, but what could I do?"

Margaret placed her hand on May's arm, and her eyes were understanding. "I hated to leave the lad, too, but you know we had no other choice."

"I know."

"You and I both know people come into your life and pass out of it as quickly as a typhoon sometimes. It's something we must all accept, Willie included. It's part of growing up."

Her mother's words made her think of Alex Wolders. She had never seen him again after the party that Sunday, and she doubted if she ever would. She was on her way to the interior, and he doubtlessly would return to his Javanese woman in Macao or his opium smuggling or whatever else he did to earn his reputation. A shaft of disappointment struck her, for May was half hoping he would be waiting at the dock to say good-bye. She had even watched for him among the throng of Europeans and Chinese, but no lanky figure in a rumpled white suit towered above them all, no cool, candid gaze met hers. May didn't even know why she should feel such acute disappointment, for she wasn't sure she even liked the man.

"What are you thinking?"

Her mother's voice snapped May back to the present. "Oh, nothing . . . I was just wondering about our itinerary, that's all."

"When we dock in Tientsin, I thought we'd stay with the Liptons."

May scowled as she sought to match the name to faces. "Do I know them?"

Margaret shook her head. "No. I met them just last year, but already we're great friends. Avery is with customs there, and his wife Leticia is charming. I usually stay in the English concession when I'm there on business."

"And then we'll go south, to Paoting?"

"By Peking cart."

May thought of the springless, two-wheeled conveyance, and she winced. It was not going to be a comfortable journey. "Peking cart? I thought they'd have a train to Paoting by now."

Her mother gave her a dubious look. "And risk violating their gods?"

"Pardon me. Peking cart it must be."

"You'll adjust," Mrs. Fitzgerald said brutally. "Now, if

you'll excuse me, I'm going to our cabin to check on a few things. I hope the steward remembered all of our bags."

She bustled off, leaving May to stand on deck, contemplating the passing coastline and her shipboard surroundings. The *Hanover* was packed with a motley group of Europeans and Orientals of all occupations and ages, but no one spoke to the Fitzgerald women, because, May suspected, her mother had dressed Chinese once again, donning a soft, flowing ch'ang-fu that fastened on the side with decorative braid closings and fell over a skirt.

"I don't want to talk to any of you anyway," May muttered to herself before going to the cabin to join her mother.

Mrs. Fitzgerald was rummaging through a trunk as May entered. "The heat is going to become unbearable in a couple of hours, so why don't you take off that ridiculous dress and that suit of armor underneath it and get into something cooler?" She bent over, digging even deeper into the trunk. "I had this made for you in Paoting."

She lifted out a ch'ang-fu of cool, white, embroidered cotton, much like her own.

"It's beautiful," May gasped, coming closer to inspect it. But she drew away, knowing that the instant she put on the garment, her former life would begin to reassert itself. "I don't think so, Mother. Not yet."

"When you're ready, it will be here." And Mrs. Fitzgerald folded it, put it back, and closed the trunk.

The first day of their voyage was uneventful as an excursion down the Thames, and the two women drifted between the deck and their cabin. Aside from the captain, who touched his cap and smiled now and then, no passengers approached them or attempted to make conversation, so May and her mother kept to themselves.

"And how is Weng Ta-Chung?" May asked that night, as they lay in their narrow bunks and tried to sleep in the hot, stuffy cabin.

"Oh, he's fine," her mother replied from below. "I don't see him as much as I did when your father was alive, except for a few business transactions now and then. But he does visit once in a while. His son did well on his examinations and is a high government official now, with his own house, a very grand affair on the other side of the city. I'm surprised Weng hasn't gone to live with him."

"And how does Ah Sin treat her daughter-in-law?" May asked, thinking of Weng's diminutive virago of a wife.

Margaret chuckled. "I wouldn't wish Ah Sin on any bride. She even sent her daughter-in-law back to her own parents once because she wasn't sufficiently respectful to her!"

"I'm glad I'm not Chinese," May said, "to have a mother-in-law rule my life like that."

Mrs. Fitzgerald instantly rushed to their defense, as May knew she would. "You're being unfair. The English do the same. Why, if your father and I had stayed in England, his mother would have made my life a hell on earth. She ruled that family with an iron fist."

May recalled Nigel's mother, a straight-backed, silver-haired queen who always rose at five o'clock every morning, rain or shine, to ride alone on horseback once around the estate. Nothing May ever did had quite pleased her mother-in-law.

"Is Weng's old mother still alive?"

"The laughing buddha?" Margaret said. "Oh, yes, she's ninety-five if she's a day, but she can still set Ah Sin to trembling with one glance."

May smiled to herself in the darkness.

After a few minutes, her mother said, "May? Are you still awake?"

"Yes. I was just thinking how fortunate we were—are—to have a friend like Weng Ta-Chung."

"Weng has been good joss," her mother admitted. "His acceptance of us certainly hasn't hurt. I'm in a rather precarious position, being a European woman living alone in a Chinese city. It's a good thing most people know me."

The lifelong friendship between Timothy Fitzgerald and the jade carver had always astounded May, and, as she was growing up, she never tired of hearing how the Irish merchant had befriended the struggling artisan, encouraging him, selling his jades to Englishmen. Later, when Weng's father died and the man was distraught because he couldn't afford to buy his poor father a coffin, let alone the lavish funeral of Chinese custom, May's father had paid for both. Weng Ta-Chung had never forgotten and repaid his benefactor a hundred thousand times, watching out for the safety of his wife and daughter when the restless Timmy Fitz went wandering.

Soon, the green-eyed child became a common sight in the jade carver's house, in his workroom constantly, following him through the market, learning the different pieces of jade and how to recognize them by sight and touch.

May smiled to herself. The heathen Chinese could teach Emily Wright a few things about loyalty . . .

"Mother?"

No sound from below except heavy, rhythmic breathing.

May turned over on her side and closed her eyes. There were still many things she wanted to ask her mother about Weng and Paoting, but they would have to wait until tomorrow.

The next day, as May was dressing, she spied the white ch'ang-fu lying atop the other clothes in her mother's trunk. She hesitated, her fingers seeking to couple hook to eye on her corset, then she continued her work, until each hook and eye were secure and she could feel the whalebone stays girding her ribs like iron fingers. After slipping her dress over her head, she closed the trunk with a decisive click. She wasn't ready yet.

As she left their cabin and crossed the deck to find her mother, May came up behind a cluster of passengers trying to see through the light mist that enveloped the boat.

"I think it's disgraceful," one of the women said angrily to her companions, "an Englishwoman wearing Chinese clothes. Just look at her, bold as you please."

May knew they could only be discussing her mother, for she could see her standing at the rail on the far side of the ship.

"Poor thing," a man was saying in a high, nasal voice. "She's one of the ones who has been here so long they go native. No fortitude. Weak-willed."

"And she acts as though it's beneath her dignity to talk to the likes of us," a second woman added with a sniff.

May just stood there for a moment until one of the trio noticed her. The woman started, her face first coloring in embarrassment at being caught, then growing sullen and defensive.

Without a word of retort, May just smiled sweetly, inclined her head, and went to join her mother.

"Good morning," she said, slipping her arm through Margaret's.

"Oh, good morning, dear. Did you sleep well?"

"As well as can be expected in a bunk that's two feet wide."

Her mother's smile was faint, and May could tell that she was preoccupied about something. Lines of worry scored Margaret's forehead and cheeks, making her look twice her age, as did her startling black hair, so artificial and hard against her white skin.

"I do hope this fog clears," she muttered.

"With any luck we'll reach Tientsin safely," May added, trying to reassure her.

Both women fell silent. All May could hear was the slapping of the waves against the hull, for even the strident voices of gulls were still this morning.

Suddenly she said, "Has the Black Dragon House changed?"

"Not the house, but some of the people in it," her mother replied, glancing at her. "Your amah is no longer with us."

"Julie?" May's head snapped round in alarm. "What happened? Did she die? Why didn't you tell me sooner?"

Margaret tried to keep her face still, but her mouth twitched. "For one thing, you haven't exactly been curious about your home during these last two weeks, and, secondly, I never heard from you while you were in England, so I assumed you didn't care."

May withdrew her arm, suddenly irritated. "You never could resist needling me, could you?"

"Just stating the truth, my dear. Anyway, Tzu-Lieh left about six months after you did. 'No can stay without young missie,' she said, and off she went. I assume she went back to her village, because I never even heard from her after that. Rather ungrateful, if you ask me."

May had been looking forward to seeing the plump, jolly nurse she had called "Julie" because she couldn't pronounce "Tzu-Lieh," the woman who had taught her Chinese and how to use chopsticks so she could pick up a single grain of rice with them.

"And I've got a girl, too," her mother added. "She's Eurasian, and her name is Dinah Quo. I paid two hundred taels of silver for her."

May stared, her mouth agape. "A slave girl? You bought a slave girl?"

"Well, it was either buy her or have her sold off as a concubine to some lecherous old mandarin. Her father was French, and her mother was a 'mist and flower maiden,' to put it delicately. Both didn't want her, so I bought her."

"But you've always deplored one person owning another, Mother," May protested.

She shrugged. "Dinah's free to go whenever she wishes. I paid for her, but I don't own her. I just thought living with me was preferable to a worse fate. In a few years, I'll find a suitable husband for her, but right now, I'm enjoying her company." Then she added, "I think you'll like her—I hope you'll like her."

May said, "Look, the fog is beginning to lift."

When the *Hanover* chugged around the piece of land that jutted out into the Yellow Sea like a mandarin's jade fingernail shield, May put away her corset and dress and put on the white ch'ang-fu and skirt. The minute the material fell down her body in a gentle sigh, she felt free. May next combed her hair into a sleek chignon and secured it with a hairpin of deep blue lapis lazuli. She looked at herself in the bronze mirror and scowled. The high, narrow collar framed her face, making it appear more oval, but, unlike her mother, she resembled nothing more than a European dressed Chinese. There was nothing inconspicuous about her.

But she had to admit the clothes were comfortable and certainly cooler than the corset and whalebone stays.

As she joined her mother on deck to the accompaniment of more disapproving stares, May suddenly felt her spirits lift.

Margaret beamed with pleasure. "Welcome home," she said.

The Liptons were waiting for them when the steamer docked in Tientsin, and May warmed to them instantly. Avery Lipton was a kind, rough-hewn man with a salty tongue, and his wife Leticia was a wisp of a thing who admonished him good-naturedly for his profanity.

Their home was a modest, neat cottage, tucked away in a corner of the English part of the city. It was a plain house, but Leticia had made it homey-looking by adding a flower garden out front and hanging white curtains in the windows. A marmalade cat, serenely watching their approach as it washed its whiskers, completed the scene.

May and her mother spent an enjoyable two days in the Liptons' company. Since their two children were in English schools, Leticia spent her days tending house, visiting with other Englishwomen in the city, and trying to help bewildered newcomers adjust to their new life. She also sewed clothes for the orphans at the Catholic mission and taught them lessons twice a week.

Avery was an agent for several firms in England, and, unlike Nelson and Margaret, who sold goods for export, his main purpose in coming to China was to open new markets for English goods.

"Holy hell," he said to them one night after supper, "with the way these North China winters are, you'd think they'd welcome the chance to buy some good, warm English wools instead of wearing cotton jackets."

"Avery . . ." Leticia began with a shake of her head. "Must you always swear?"

He just smiled and draped his heavy arm over his wife's slender shoulders. "You know I can't help it."

Trade was always the main topic of conversation, and

May was surprised to discover the Liptons weren't interested in hearing news of England.

When she mentioned this, Avery said, "Damn it, our life's here in China now."

His wife glanced at him and just shook her head. Then she added, "Avery and I believe in looking to the future, not the past. Oh, we get homesick once in a while, especially when we get a letter from the boys, but we can't waste our time being homesick, now can we, when there's so much to be done?"

May quite happily could have remained with such warm and outgoing people forever, but her mother was like a racehorse at the gate in her eagerness to get to Paoting. On the morning of the third day, a pair of Peking carts waited to take them on their half-day journey.

CHAPTER FOUR

As the carts rolled out of Tientsin and inched their way across the edge of the North China Plain toward Paoting, May watched the flat, monotonous landscape pass by from the open rear end of the second cart. The scene was a panorama of brown, shimmering fields, occasionally relieved by a splash of green against a cloudless, hot-blue sky. Sometimes she saw a village pop out of the ground, a few buildings clustered against a grove of trees, or a farmer prodding his reluctant oxen on this straight line of road that seemed to disappear into the horizon.

Just as May looked back, not forward, so were her thoughts on the past, not the future. London and Robin . . . Shanghai and Captain Forsythe . . . they haunted her, refusing to go away. She only half-listened to her mother chatter on about Paoting, but she didn't dare hope that her life would be different there.

After a half-day passed, when May thought her bones had been permanently shaken out of their joints, signs of civilization suddenly appeared everywhere—people, buildings, streets—and a short time later the cart stopped abruptly.

"We're here," Margaret announced excitedly, leaping out of the cart with the agility of one Willie's age.

May moved slowly, almost reluctantly, as she took her mother's expectant, outstretched hand to steady herself before jumping down. Then she looked around at the Street of the Arched Bridge.

As she expected, it hadn't changed. All the houses were hidden behind high walls, to shield them from the noise and activity outside, and in the distance, May could see the gentle hump of the camelback bridge that gave the street its name.

But she couldn't remember it ever being this crowded and noisy. A farmer shouted at their driver to move his cart to make room for his own vehicle, while a rakish-looking young man leading a tame piglet on a leash gave May a lingering glance. Two housewives only a few steps away were shaking their fists and berating each other at the top of their lungs, their rapid screeches drowning out the supplications of a blind beggar woman seated outside the gate to the House of the Black Dragon.

"Shall we go in?" Mrs. Fitzgerald said impatiently, after tossing a coin into the beggar's bowl.

May nodded.

The smiling gatekeeper flung the gates open wide with a flourish, and much bowing, as his mistress and May walked into the yard. May noticed her mother's palanquin off to one side, propped up against the wall, and she could hear the soft nickering of a pony in the shed that served as a stable.

Then they approached the intricate, carved red screen that barred the door from evil spirits, and once they walked around that, they confronted the door itself, with its writhing black dragon painted above and around it, each scale outlined in thin lines of gold, its eyes glowing and fierce, its nostrils flared.

May stopped to stare at it, her mouth dry. How that beast had frightened her when she was a child, prowling through her dreams, stalking her. Now it seemed more benevolent and welcoming than frightening.

"Come inside," her mother said gently, realizing the enormity of this moment for May. When Mrs. Fitzgerald saw that there was no one to greet them, she picked up a hammer and beat the brass gong that stood to one side to announce visitors.

Instantly, there was the scuffle of feet, and three servants appeared, their round faces startled and eyes alarmed.

May smiled and stepped forward to greet their "Number One boy," Han, and his two sons, T'ing and Lien, who had served the Fitzgeralds since May could remember. All three men smiled and bowed in return.

"Missie May-Ling," Han said in his soft voice. "Our house that has been waiting will now rejoice at your return."

She bowed. "My heart is happy to be among old friends once again."

"I should sell the lot of you miserable slaves tomorrow," Margaret bellowed, taking charge once again. "When I return from a long journey, I expect food and a bath awaiting me. Go fetch Cook. Tell her honorable mistress and esteemed eldest daughter have returned and demand food and tea at once." A stream of dire warnings continued to flow from Mrs. Fitzgerald's lips until the trio vanished.

May smiled at her mother's display. "Still intimidating the servants, I see."

"I have to get something for the 'squeeze' they put on me," her mother replied. "Otherwise, I'd be ruined."

Both women were startled when a sweet voice said, "Welcome home, honorable mother," from the doorway at the end of the foyer.

May turned around just as a Eurasian girl of no more than eighteen entered the hall, knelt down before Mrs. Fitzgerald, and began to touch her forehead to the floor.

"Please, Dinah," Margaret reproached her. "You know I don't approve of the kowtow."

"Insignificant slave wishes to please mother," the girl replied, continuing until she had touched the floor three times. Then she rose and bowed.

"It would please me even more if you didn't kowtow. You will cause me to lose face before my daughter, who is English and prefers English ways."

"So sorry," Dinah murmured, bowing her head in dejection.

"This is my other daughter, Mrs. May-Ling Monckton. I

hope you two shall be as sisters. In fact, it would please me if you called each other that."

"Dinah," May said.

The girl bowed again. "Esteemed eldest sister."

Even in a roomful of beautiful women, Dinah would stand out like a diamond among lumps of coal. Taller than most Chinese, her body was both straight and gently curved beneath the thin silk of her blue and gold ch'ang-fu. Dinah's Chinese mother had given her that glossy, straight black hair and those upturned eyes as dark as mystery, while her French father had doubtlessly contributed the creamy ivory skin and sweet, lilting voice. As May studied the girl's small upturned nose and straight mouth, she couldn't help thinking that Dinah resembled a jungle feline with unsheathed claws.

And she made May uneasy. There was something too frankly presumptive about her gaze, a boldness that belied her self-effacing words, and she had a watchful air about her.

Don't be absurd, May scolded herself. You don't know the girl and have no reason to dislike her. Give her a chance, before you go forming an opinion based on a first impression.

May glanced at her mother, and a pang of jealousy seared her. Dinah and Mrs. Fitzgerald were looking at each other with exclusive affection, leaving May to feel left out, like a beggar child peering in at a rich man's feast.

"Dinah, see what's keeping our tea, and have our baths ready. Eldest sister and I are going to unpack."

The girl looked horrified. "No, honorable mother, you must let Dinah unpack for you."

"Nonsense, child, we shall manage superbly. Now, be off with you and do as you're told."

Dinah bowed and backed out into the hall, then disappeared.

"Well," Mrs. Fitzgerald said expectantly. "That is my slave girl."

"She's very beautiful," was May's only comment.

"She was a terrified, half-starved child about to be sold as a concubine when I bought her. And she's quick. I've been teaching her my business, and she's been a great help to me.

She often hears about items for sale before I do." Margaret sighed, "Yes, she's been a great help to me." Then she added, "Of course, she can't match your expertise with jade, but she's learning."

May just smiled, but said nothing.

"Well, shall I take you to your room?" Then she went sweeping out of the hall, only to stop and turn at the doorway when she noticed May wasn't following. "Well, are you coming or not?"

May nodded and followed her.

In sharp contrast to the Wrights' villa and other European homes in Shanghai, the House of the Black Dragon was orderly, sparse, and devoid of bric-a-brac. While small compared to some of the other houses on the street, it was still large enough to have four wings with a garden courtyard hollowed out of its center.

May felt curiously at home in these rooms, where chairs and tables of rosewood were lined up against walls or positioned at right angles to one another in the Chinese manner, and beautiful rugs in deep, wine colors graced the floors.

The two women climbed stairs to the upper floor, which contained May's bedroom and a few empty ones used only for storage now. They walked down the hall and stopped before the round moon door covered by a curtain.

"Your room," Mrs. Fitzgerald said with a flourish.

May hesitated at the doorway, then went inside. A spacious bed with a carved canopy was the room's dominant feature. It made her recall the countless nights she had cried herself to sleep behind the heavy silk curtains, and a great sadness touched her. The only other furnishings were four chests containing each season's clothing, and a small, rickety bookshelf her father had built to hold her precious books from England. The sadness left her as she knelt to read the titles, most of which were faded or completely worn away by insistent, eager fingers.

"I thought you would have thrown them out," she said, smiling.

"Whatever for?" her mother asked, puzzled.

May shrugged as she rose and stopped as a glimmer of metal caught her eye. It was a bronze mirror that her father had hung over her bed to frighten off evil spirits by showing them their own horrible reflections. May had hung a similar mirror over Robin's bed, and he had chuckled tolerantly when she explained its purpose.

"He said nothing evil would ever happen to us," she murmured to herself.

"What did you say?" her mother demanded.

"Nothing, Mother, just talking to myself."

"Oh. Well, after the trunks are brought up, and you unpack, you can bathe. Then we can eat, and perhaps Dinah will play the lute for us. She's a very talented girl." And without another word, she turned and left. May listened as her mother's footsteps echoed down the hall; then she sat on the edge of the bed, buried her face in her hands, and cried.

Later that night, after dining on crisp roast duck, noodles, and steamed bread eaten to the melancholy strains of Dinah's lute, May returned to her room, where she read Robert Browning by lamplight until the rest of the house grew still.

Usually, the poetry soothed the ache inside and brought Robin back to her as clear as a temple bell, but tonight it had no effect.

"It's this house," May said, glancing around as she rubbed her arms to ward off a chill.

She rose, now restless and troubled and not knowing why, moving like a wraith to the window. She opened the latticed panels lined with tough oiled paper, and instantly a warm night breeze touched her skin.

The scene below was eerie tonight. The full moon, a white wafer hanging high in the sky, made fanciful puzzles on the floor as it seeped through the paper. In the garden below, with its grotesque rocks and gnarled wood set among the bushes and walkways according to Taoist principles, something harsh and expectant waited. It was easy to believe the ghosts of evil spirits walked tonight.

May shivered and returned to bed, where she lay on her

back, her head pillowed by one arm. She should have stayed in England, she knew that now. She should have weathered the scandal until the storm lost momentum and blew itself out. That's what her solicitor had told her to do, but George had been half in love with her himself and had wanted her to stay for his own selfish reasons.

But no, she had to run halfway across the world to Shanghai, which had proved to be no safe harbor either.

Now she was finally back in the house of her childhood, but it was not quite what she had expected. She had hoped to feel differently, to be at peace, to accept, but she still felt disturbed. Watching Dinah and her mother tonight, May found herself thinking, Dinah is more like her daughter than I. The thought stung her, but at the same time she could accept it. If she had alienated her mother, it was her own fault, because she was the one who had left, she was the one who had turned her back on China, a cardinal sin to Mrs. Fitzgerald.

Everyone she had ever loved had been taken from her—her father, Nigel, Robin, and now her own mother.

Not everyone, she reminded herself resolutely. There was still Weng Ta-Chung, and she made up her mind to visit the jade carver tomorrow.

"Where are you going?" Mrs. Fitzgerald asked, when May appeared for breakfast the following morning dressed in her white ch'ang-fu.

"I am going to visit Weng Ta-Chung," she replied, entering her mother's bedchamber on the first floor.

Mrs. Fitzgerald looked like a Manchu princess this morning in dark mulberry silk and white jade, as she sat cross-legged among silk cushions scattered everywhere. She had always received visitors on the k'ang, a hollow stove-bed of brick that was heated in the winter, and it was here that she and the family usually took their meals.

May suppressed a smile as she thought of Nigel's formidable family, and what they would have thought of a woman receiving guests in her bedchamber.

"And where is your slave girl this morning?" May asked,

parting the heavy silk curtains embroidered with mandarin ducks and seating herself on the k'ang.

"Don't be pert," her mother snapped. "Dinah's eaten, and she's doing an errand for me."

May helped herself to steamed bread, while wrinkling her nose at her mother's bowl of rice. "How can you eat rice so early in the morning?"

"I'm used to it. Here, have a peach, instead. They're delicious."

As May ate, her mother said, "Will you be needing the chair this morning?"

"I thought I'd walk and become acquainted with the city again."

Margaret's face grew set. "I wouldn't, if I were you. The streets aren't as safe as they used to be, and I don't want you ending up in a brothel somewhere."

"As you wish."

"And why don't you wait until Dinah gets back and take her for company?"

"No!" May replied with such vehemence that Margaret's eyes widened.

"Why not?"

Because Weng belongs to me, and I'll not share him as well with Dinah, May thought rebelliously. But she said, "I haven't seen Weng in years, and I'd like our first meeting to be a private one, if you don't mind."

This seemed to satisfy her mother, who murmured, "As you wish."

At first, May was going to keep the curtains of the palanquin closed all the way to the jade carver's house, but as the chair made its way through the streets, the sounds and smells seduced her, and she found herself drawing back the curtains to observe the China so different from Shanghai. As she passed through the town's outskirts, she watched a group of scrawny beggars clothed only in strips of rags station themselves at a rich man's gates to embarrass him into being more generous, while a trio of stoop-shouldered students filed by with scrolls and writing materials tucked under their arms.

Then May's chair joined the procession of people, donkeys, and oxen entering the city through the south gate.

As they approached the marketplace, the men carrying the chair were forced to slow down, giving May even more time to satisfy her curiosity. There were vegetable merchants and weavers out today, their wares spread before them in the streets, and barbers shaving their customers right in the road. The "tap-tap-tap" of the coffin-maker's hammer rose above the din of the streets, while the sharp, bitter odor of hot dye overpowered the stench of animals and humans alike.

May smiled as she passed a pair of giggling girls who were staring into a box she knew contained intimate pictures of men and women guaranteed to bring the roses to any respectable Englishwoman's cheeks. "Typical heathen filth," as Emily Wright would say. And, at the end of the marketplace, a poor devil wearing a heavy wooden collar called a cangue was frantically beseeching indifferent passersby to feed him, since he couldn't reach his own mouth because of the block of wood around his neck.

"Why," May thought, as no one stopped to help the criminal, "he's going to starve to death."

She shivered, as she wondered what his offense was, but she knew better than to stop to feed him herself.

She arrived at the jade carver's house a little past eleven o'clock. It was a modest dwelling, past the bustling marketplace and—like Robin's house—close to a park, where two old men seated in the sun still whiled away their afternoons playing Chinese chess or fantan.

If the servant who showed May in was amazed at the sight of a barbarian woman—and an unaccompanied barbarian woman, at that—he didn't show it. But, then, he was used to the ways of the foreign devils, and nothing they did surprised him anymore.

He bade her wait while he trotted off, then reappeared minutes later, and motioned for her to follow. The two of them moved through the house until they came to Weng's workroom, a tiny area filled with birds of all types in bamboo cages.

The room abruptly came alive with rustlings and twitterings as they sensed an alien presence. Wings beat against bamboo, and the silence was split by indignant caws and hoots and whistles. May strolled around, marveling at the collection of canaries, macaws, pigeons, and finches, the males with their brilliant plumage outshining their drab mates.

"Welcome to this miserable hovel, esteemed daughter of one who is dear to me."

May whirled around to face Weng Ta-Chung. She resisted the impulse to fly into his arms, for she knew such a display of emotion would offend the man. So, instead, she honored him by kneeling and kowtowing. "Good day, honorable master of jade. You do this insignificant woman a great honor by granting her an audience."

As he padded noiselessly into the room, the birds quieted at once, and their agitated rustlings ceased.

"It has been much too long, my daughter." There was great warmth behind the man's words, and his eyes twinkled from within, although he and May never touched in greeting.

"Rise," he said with a faint smile. "We shall drink tea, and then we shall talk."

As they stood facing each other briefly, May stared at her mentor, trying to recapture something that had been lost. Weng, whose unlined face made him seem younger than his fifty odd years, now appeared shorter than she remembered, but his high, shaved forehead and waist-length queue were the same, and he still radiated that blessed sense of tranquility and peace, like a glowing coal in the center of his soul.

Why do your heathen gods give you peace, May wondered, while mine do nothing for me?

Before sitting down to tea, May paid her respects to Weng's old mother, the laughing buddha, then to his wife, Ah Sin, who eyed her coldly. May knew Weng's wife had never approved of her husband's association with the Fitzgeralds, but she was a wise and obedient wife and had kept her tongue all these years.

When they sat down, Weng said, "You must tell me about your country," as he sipped the strong, bitter tea.

"I thought I found happiness there," she replied. "I even married while I was in England."

He smiled. "And rightly, too. The beautiful daughter of a noble house must marry and provide many sons."

The words caught in her throat as she said, "I have not been blessed."

"I see. Well, then we must pray to Kuan Yin for your fruitfulness."

It's going to take more than Kuan Yin to accomplish that feat, May thought bitterly. But she said, "My husband is dead, so that is impossible."

Weng just stared at her, his dark eyes sorrowful. "A husband's death is like a broken mirror. Bad joss. But may your widowhood be as virtuous as your honorable mother's."

No, May said to herself, anything but that.

She changed the subject, and they talked into the early afternoon about the town and the countryside, of the rice crop that had failed last year and the bandits that had ridden down from the hills to pillage the neighboring villages. Finally, when the teapot was empty, Weng rose and beckoned May to follow him, for he had his work to show her.

They returned to his birds and the workroom, and the jade carver went to a cage and gently lifted out a plain brown peahen that trembled between his fingers.

He stroked her head and back with one finger, and then said to May, "Why did you return to the Flowery Kingdom, my daughter? Were you not happy among your own people?"

"I was very happy there, for a while, but not at peace. There were those who would do me harm. I returned to the land of my birth to put my troubled soul at ease, and, once I do that, I shall return to my people."

The jade carver was silent for what seemed like an eternity. Finally, he said, "When I was a young man, there was a very beautiful maiden in my village. I desired her, but her family was gentry, and there was no chance of my offering for her because I was very, very poor. But nothing could stop me from spending every hour dreaming of her. Then one day my parents informed me that they had chosen my bride."

"Ah Sin?"

He nodded. "I, of course, respected my parents' wishes and married her, although my heart and mind were always on my lost love, much like these caged birds dream of freedom."

"But you and Ah Sin have been married—happily married—for years."

"A sage who lived at the beginning of recorded time once said, 'Sometimes we look to the mountains on the horizon when we should be looking at the pebbles near our feet.'"

May smiled slightly. "Thank you for sharing his wisdom with me."

"Now, for the jades."

May felt an excitement grip her as the jade carver brought out his latest works, a shallow fluted bowl of spinach-green jade, carved so delicately that it turned transparent in the light. She held it, letting her fingers caress it, letting its beauty overwhelm her. Then Weng handed her a camel carved out of yellow soapstone and some smaller carvings of cicadas, and on each, the workmanship was painstaking and faultless.

Suddenly the man grew reflective, and May could almost hear his thoughts fly to another time and place. She waited until he returned to the present.

"Esteemed daughter," he began. "Your father once did a great service for me that this insignificant mortal could never hope to repay in twelve lifetimes. I promised my brother that I would care for his family as if they were my own."

"And you have, master of jade."

"There may come a time when I am powerless to do so," he murmured softly, his eyes dark with regret. "I am only a poor, insignificant jade carver, and there are many enemies of the foreigners now, and they are growing every day."

May's heart stopped for an instant, then started in a great rush. "But Mother and I have lived here all our lives. Everyone knows us and that we mean no harm."

"Even as the seasons change, so do people. There are many who are angered by the foreign devils. They gather in the streets and inns to speak among themselves. They speak of the devils who come to them preaching of strange gods, telling them to forsake their revered ancestors to follow this one god."

"Missionaries," May said in disgust.

Weng nodded. "The hate is beginning to fester and spread, and one day I fear I shall not be able to keep my promise to my brother to protect his family."

May felt cold all over.

"But I have many brothers, all sworn by an oath to protect each other." Weng's voice dropped to a whisper. "You must promise me, my daughter, on the grave of your revered father, that you will keep my secret locked within you, telling no one. It is death for me if you do not."

"You have my word."

"There is no way you can recognize members of our brotherhood by some outward sign, for we wear none, lest we are discovered. But there is a way, and only one way, to recognize a brother."

May leaned forward expectantly.

"If you are in danger, and there is a person who may save you, you must ask that person this question: 'Where have you come from?' He must then answer, 'I have traveled far.' You must then ask, 'From Peking, in the north?' If he is a Son of the Celestial Phoenix, his last reply will be, 'From the south, where the phoenix dwells.'"

Weng repeated the series of questions and answers, then made May repeat them until she had them memorized.

"But wouldn't a member of your brotherhood question the reason a foreign devil knows their secret?" she demanded.

He shook his head. "A Son of the Celestial Phoenix is sworn by blood to protect anyone who knows our secret words, be he a foreign devil or Chinese. The bond is like iron between us, and brothers do not initiate others without good cause." He was silent, then said, "Remember, you must tell no one, otherwise there will be much bad joss on both our houses."

"I have promised on the grave of my father."

Weng smiled and nodded.

Later, in the palanquin headed back to the House of the Black Dragon, May mulled over the words the jade carver had taught her, and prayed she would never have to use them. She knew a little about secret societies, especially the White Lotus, which had tried to force the British out of Hong Kong early in the century. But she never had dreamed she would ever be initiated into one.

"This has been an eventful second day in Paoting," she murmured, leaning back on the cushions.

And it wasn't over yet. When May arrived back at the house, she found a strange woman standing in the yard. She carried a baby in her arms and held another child securely in her free hand, while still another clung to her skirts and an older girl stood nearby.

"Good afternoon," the woman greeted her with a hesitant smile, as May stepped out of the palanquin. "You must be Margaret's daughter, May. I'm Harriet Hammond, and this is Evelyn," the older girl, "Jane," clinging to her mother's skirts, "Sarah," in hand, "and baby John."

May smiled at them all. "Oh yes, the missionaries. How do you do?"

Harriet Hammond had once been as pretty as porcelain, but was now faded, like a delicate lace curtain left too long in the sun, and her face was hardened by too many disappointments. She was a walking madonna with all her blonde, blue-eyed children, who were so unnaturally silent and somber they made May uneasy.

She addressed herself to Evelyn, the oldest. "Why don't you take the other children and find Han? He'll take you to the kitchen and give you all cookies."

Without a word, Evelyn took the baby and pried the others loose from her mother. As she was about to disappear, her mother scowled at her and said, "Don't any of you have tongues in your heads? What do you say to the kind lady?"

"Thank you," three wee voices intoned, as they all scurried into the house, leaving Harriet and May alone in the yard.

Harriet shook her head. "Sometimes I wonder if I shall ever teach them manners."

"They're just children," May said, starting back to the house.

"But never too young to learn manners, as my husband Nicholas always says," she insisted.

As they entered the house, Mrs. Fitzgerald greeted them with a warm smile. "So, you two have already met. Splendid. Now, I'll just introduce you to Nicholas, and you'll have met the entire Hammond family."

A blond, broad-shouldered man stepped forward, reached out for May's hand, and enthusiastically shook it. "I'm delighted to meet you, Mrs. Monckton. Margaret has told us so much about you."

May had not been expecting Nicholas Hammond to be so good-looking, but, she reminded herself, why shouldn't a handsome man choose the religious life if that was his desired vocation?

Finally, she found her tongue. "I'm pleased to meet you, Mr. Hammond."

Then Mrs. Fitzgerald ushered everyone into the parlor, where Lien was serving tea and almond cakes.

"What church do you represent?" May asked, as they seated themselves and Margaret began pouring.

"The Church of the Divine Redeemer," Nicholas replied in his deep resonant voice, his eyes lighting in pride and fervor. He reached over to squeeze his wife's hand. "We have a church in the city, and we just finished building a new spire for it. It's rather grand, and we hope you'll come to services with us."

A tall spire that no doubt offended Chinese gods with its insolence, May couldn't help thinking.

"And we have many new converts," he added, still looking at his wife, who would not return his look of complicity.

May suspected Harriet no longer shared her husband's enthusiasm for hardship and deprivation. "Are you sure your converts aren't more interested in filling their rice bowls than in worshiping Christ?" May challenged him.

Nicholas blushed and looked a little disconcerted. "I know their people call them 'rice Christians,' but I personally believe they are sincere."

"Then you don't know the Chinese," May replied.

Nicholas just smiled politely and set out to convince her that she was wrong, speaking of the enthusiasm the converts displayed, but, as he droned on, May couldn't help but recall Weng Ta-Chung's words about the devils who came to urge the people to forsake their ancestors to follow one god.

She, for one, was glad when tea was over and the Hammonds collected their somber children and left.

On the morning of her third day in Paoting, May awoke with a headache. She unwisely chose to ignore the dull throbbing just above her eyebrows and instead bathed, dressed, and joined her mother, who was already in state on the k'ang, eating her morning rice to the clicking of chopsticks.

Mrs. Fitzgerald squinted at her daughter. "Are you feeling well? You look a trifle pale."

"I have a beastly headache," May confessed, seating herself and pouring a cup of tea. "But, other than that, I'm fine."

Her mother then asked her what she thought of the Hammonds, and May just shrugged as she reached for the steamed bread. "They seemed sincere, but misguided, and those odd children . . ." She shivered. "They looked like they're fed sermons for breakfast."

"They're not as lively as Willie, I'll grant you that," Mrs. Fitzgerald agreed, "but they're really quite pleasant, once you get to know them."

"What are your plans for today?" May asked, seeking to get off the subject of the missionaries.

"Dinah's told me she's heard of a merchant who's got some fine *blanc de chine* porcelain to sell, pieces dated from the eighteenth century. I've known the man for a long time, so I won't have to use Mr. Yee on this deal."

"Mr. Yee?"

"My comprador. Don't look so surprised. I've had to use one ever since your father died, especially with the younger merchants. You know how the Chinese are about women. They'd never let me in the door, even to sell me something."

"Times *have* changed," May muttered. "Is he selling figures or bowls?"

"Figures, including two of Kuan Yin."

May's mouth twitched in the semblance of a smile. "Kuan Yin, goddess of mercy. Weng told me to pray to her for a child."

Mrs. Fitzgerald was uncharacteristically silent as she scooped up the last grains of rice from her bowl. "What else did you and he talk about?"

May hesitated, recalling what Weng had said about the Sons of the Celestial Phoenix. Tell no one—no one. There was a time when she would have told her mother without a moment's hesitation, but now there was Dinah Quo to consider. How did she know her mother wouldn't tell the girl about the secret society, and what if Dinah told someone else, someone who could harm the jade carver?

"Well," Margaret said impatiently. "You must have talked about something after all these years."

"We had a warm reunion, and Weng showed me many new pieces he had done," May replied and told her mother everything else they had discussed—except the Sons of the Celestial Phoenix.

"Shall we go?" Mrs. Fitzgerald said, rising. The tiny jade figures attached to her belt tinkled musically with every step.

"Just let me finish my tea," May replied, draining her cup. She started to rise, then sat down again abruptly as a sudden pain shot through her knees.

"What's the matter?" her mother demanded.

"My knees are just stiff, that's all." May braced herself against the k'ang and rose. "There. I guess I'm just not used to sitting cross-legged anymore."

"You're hardly doddering."

"I'm fine now, really. Let's go."

"Good. I wouldn't want to risk losing those porcelains."

Later that morning in the merchant's splendid house, May's headache became a hammer beating against an anvil, making it painful for her to even open her eyes, and now her elbows and knuckles were beginning to ache as well.

Please, she silently begged her mother as they sat across from the merchant, let's go home.

But Mrs. Fitzgerald and the merchant droned on, discussing the appalling taxes, the soaring price of wheat, and even the new bridge being erected in the memory of an old virtuous spinster who had dedicated her long life to helping beggars and orphans.

Get on with it, can't you, was May's silent plea as the pain shot through her head afresh.

But her prayer was not to be answered, for it took the merchant and her mother another hour to get to the subject of the *blanc de chine* figures. Once they did, however, negotiations moved rapidly, and May nearly sobbed with relief when the haggling came to an end.

The "click-clack-click" of the abacus beads sounded like pistol shots to May's brain, as the merchant did his rapid calculations, and Mrs. Fitzgerald handed over her entire string of coins.

"There!" Margaret said in triumph when the figures were wrapped and placed before her. She looked relieved and self-satisfied, like a grouse that has just evaded the hawk.

The women left the merchant's house with the precious pieces of white porcelain cradled in Margaret's arms. May had offered to carry one of them, but her mother wouldn't hear of it. It was fortunate, because, if May had been carrying one, it would have been dashed to the ground when she stumbled and fell on the way to the palanquin.

"By the sword of Lu Tung-pin!" Margaret exclaimed. "What's wrong?"

May remained on all fours, stunned for a moment as the weakness washed over her and the tremors began to wrack her body in wave after wave.

"I . . . I don't know. My head is splitting, and I ache all over."

Mrs. Fitzgerald tucked the porcelains under her arm protectively and put her free hand to May's head. "You're burning up. Can you get into the chair? I'm sending for Dr. Gates as soon as we get home."

May managed to rise, with much assistance from her mother, and stagger to the palanquin. The ride home seemed to take forever, and, just when she was ready to scream, hands were reaching out to help her into the house. She wobbled like a gouty old man, for every step sent white hot fire searing up her ankles, then to her knees.

May felt herself nearly dragged up the stairs by sheer physical force, then gentle hands were removing her robes. She flopped down gratefully onto the bed with a soft groan, but even the silk cushions couldn't soften the ache in her bones.

"Am I going to die?" she cried out as the darkness began to overtake her. "Did I come back to China to die?"

No one answered her.

She felt like she had fallen to the street from the top of St. Paul's Cathedral, and every bone in her body was splintered and shattered. But at least she was alive—she had to be to feel pain so agonizing even the roots of her teeth and hair throbbed.

And then the hallucinations began. She imagined Robin was lying next to her, loving her again. Then he became cold, oh, so cold, and when she turned to warm him, his chest was spattered with blood. May awoke screaming, and some strange man with gray, thinning hair and sad eyes was holding her head and commanding her to drink.

She drank and slept and dreamed some more, vague, unremembered dreams that left her drained and trembling.

When May next opened her eyes, the pain had disappeared, leaving her weak and wrung out. She could barely lift her hand off the bed without great effort, or even turn her head more than an inch.

But I'm alive, she thought and recited a little prayer of thanks.

"You're awake," a voice said from the doorway.

She waited until the speaker entered the room and walked into her field of vision, which was still a little fuzzy and blurred. All May could manage was a movement of her lips that she hoped would pass for a smile.

The gray-haired man was instantly sympathetic. "Ah, still a little weak, I see. Well, that's to be expected. Your eyes troubling you? We'll just have to keep the room dark for a while. You've had a nasty fever, but I think we've beaten it."

Then he added as an afterthought, "I'm Dr. Chad Gates, by the way. I regret we had to meet under such unpleasant circumstances."

"How do you do?" The words came out as a whisper, but the effort left her feeling drained and exhausted.

"You've had a bout of dengue fever," the doctor said, "and probably won't be yourself for another week or two. We can't rush these things, you know. You must take time to get your strength back, or you may never completely recover."

May could sense him moving around the room, but she kept her eyes closed and just listened to his quiet, soothing voice drone on and on.

"I'm giving you a sleeping draught now. You'll have to eat nothing but broth for a few days, and then I'll come back at the end of the week and see how you are."

May just smiled, and when he held her head and told her to drink, she did as she was told and soon drifted off to sleep.

Five days later, when she was feeling stronger and able to sit up in bed, Dr. Gates returned, as promised.

"I see my patient is doing much better," he said, after entering and greeting her.

"Yes, thank you," May replied. "At least I can talk without exhausting myself."

"Splendid," he said.

"Thank you for saving my life."

"There were moments when we despaired of you. But you're young and strong."

Then he examined her, pronounced her fit, and said, "I would rest for a few more days and perhaps sit out in that garden and get some sun on those pale cheeks."

"Sunlight is bad for the complexion," May reminded him with a smile.

"Oh, yes. Dear me, I had quite forgotten."

"Mother has told me so much about you. She thinks quite highly of you."

He smiled. "And I think quite highly of your mother. She's given my work so much financial as well as moral support. I couldn't begin to repay her."

"Tell me, Dr. Gates—"

"All of my friends call me Chad."

"Chad, then. How did you happen to find yourself in China?"

He pulled up a chair and sat down. "My life is a very long and boring story."

"I doubt that. I'd like to hear it, if you've got the time."

May learned the doctor came halfway around the world from a place in America she had never heard of called Rhode Island, and he had first practiced in Hong Kong, where most of his patients were Europeans. But he wanted to do more for the Chinese, so when the great famines swept through the north, wiping out entire villages, he headed inland to try to help in some way.

As he told of his fight to get money to fund his hospital—badgering wealthy relatives, churches, merchants in Hong Kong—May studied him with interest. Dr. Gates was of medium height and as sturdy as whipcord, with an indefatigable air. May could imagine him doctoring patients all day, spending half the night with a woman in labor, then getting up at dawn to do it all over again. He had a bony, homely face that inspired trust, but his gray eyes were so sad, and May suspected that Chad Gates had never acquired the physicians' detachment concerning death.

He ran his fingers through his hair in an attempt to straighten it. "So that, my dear lady, is my story."

"You're to be admired, Chad."

He blushed an unfortunate shade of red. "You embarrass me."

"Forgive me. That was not my intention. May I ask you a question?"

"Of course."

"How did you meet my mother?"

He blushed again as he told of meeting Margaret Fitzgerald for the sole purpose of getting money for his hospital.

May suppressed a smile. "And did she throw you out?"

"Oh, no . . . she was most kind." His sad eyes managed to twinkle. "She invited me to stay for dinner, then gave me the money I needed. She even brings medicines from Tientsin for my hospital. Your mother is a great lady." He looked down at his hands and added, "I hope she will retain her generous nature, even under the influence of Missie Sly-Eyes."

May stared at him. "Missie Sly-Eyes?"

"Dinah." The doctor blushed. "I'm sorry. I shouldn't have said anything to you, but I seem to have some difficulty keeping my dislike of her to myself."

Missie Sly-Eyes, May thought to herself. That is appropriate.

She ran her hand over one of the pillows. "Do you believe in disliking someone on sight, Dr. Gates, without rhyme or reason, without even knowing that person?"

He grew thoughtful. "I suppose it has happened to me on occasion, although many times I've found my original impression to be erroneous, once I got to know the person better."

"I know it sounds foolish and petty of me, but that's the way I feel about Dinah. There's something about her that leaves me cold, although she's never done anything to me or said anything that should give me cause to mistrust her. But I do. It's so irrational. However, I have noticed a subtle change in Mother since coming back to Paoting."

"In what way?" Dr. Gates demanded.

"Until we came here, Mother was always solicitous for my welfare. Now it's as though Dinah is her main interest, not I." May shrugged helplessly. "I don't know. Perhaps I am just jealous. I returned to China to . . . escape from something unpleasant in England, and, instead of finding a refuge, I find I'm replaced. That sounds so childish and petty, doesn't it?"

"No, it's understandable because I found myself in a similar position when Margaret bought Dinah."

May's brows shot up in surprise.

"I see I have startled you," he said with a wry smile. "But your mother and I had become quite close over the years, and we'd even been talking of marriage." He looked at her. "You seem surprised."

"It's not that," May assured him hurriedly. "It's just that Mother never said a word to me, and she's always so enshrined Father's memory that I find it hard to believe she would consider marrying anyone again."

"Well, time heals all wounds," he said optimistically, "and what I say is true. Was true," he amended, his eyes growing sad once again, "until Missie Sly-Eyes came along." He shrugged and spread his hands futilely.

"Then what happened?"

"She just cooled. Margaret stopped helping me at the hospital like she used to and became all-absorbed in Dinah."

"But Mother has always been like that. I think her porcelains and jades mean more to her than people, and, with Dinah helping her with the business . . ." Then May said, "Did you confront her?"

Dr. Gates assured her that he had.

"And what did she say?"

"Only that she didn't know what I was talking about. She seemed most offended."

May sighed. "It is very puzzling." She looked up at the doctor. "Well, as one dispossessed person to another, shall we become allies?"

Dr. Gates' eyes twinkled. "Yes, we shall."

The sound of someone at the door caused them both to fall silent, and May was thankful they did when she saw Dinah part the curtain and step inside. May felt her dislike even more strongly, now that she knew the doctor distrusted Dinah as well.

"Good morning, eldest sister," she said sweetly, ignoring Dr. Gates. "I have come to nurse you, as our mother commands." And she set the tray she held down and advanced with a bowl of hot soup. "I will feed you."

"Thank you, Dinah, but I am perfectly capable of feeding myself," was May's crisp reply, as she hauled herself into a sitting position with pillows at her back.

But she could barely lift her arms to take the bowl, and a flash of triumph flitted across Dinah's face, as she steadied the shaking bowl with her own hands.

"Better let me feed you," she said.

"No," May insisted, her lips pursed. "Dr. Gates can feed me, and you may leave."

Dinah's eyes darkened in hostility when she saw they were allied against her. "As you wish, eldest sister." As she handed the bowl to the doctor, it somehow tipped, splashing the hot liquid down the man's trousers.

"Oh, so clumsy of me," Dinah exclaimed in horror as the doctor sprang to his feet with a yelp of pain. "I clean, bring more soup." And she made an attempt to dab at the sodden trousers with a napkin.

"Just leave us!" May barked, her anger draining what little energy she had left.

Dinah backed out of the room, bowing and murmuring profuse apologies.

"Are you burned?" May asked when she was sure Dinah was out of earshot.

Dr. Gates shook his head, but his face was pale with pain. "The material protected me somewhat. I doubtlessly will have a few blisters tomorrow." He finished mopping up the spill, then gave May a significant look. "You realize, of course, that we three are now at war."

May nodded. "Dinah does seem to have thrown down the gauntlet. But I will not be obliged to her for anything. That pretense of feeding me was calculated to make me feel helpless, and I will not tolerate it. Now Dinah knows where she stands with me as well."

"Dinah was merely trying to be helpful," Margaret said later, long after Chad had left.

May looked up at her mother, standing over her with arms folded belligerently. "I won't be treated like an invalid by Dinah or anyone else."

Margaret's eyes narrowed in suspicion. "You don't like her, do you?"

"To be honest, no."

"Why?"

"I can't explain why. There's just something about her that makes me uneasy. I don't trust her."

"It's Chad," her mother said. "He's been talking to you about Dinah. I can tell. And now he's turned you against her."

May looked up at her. "It's not anything Chad has said," she insisted. "I formed my opinion long before talking to him."

Her mother pounced on that like a triumphant cat. "Then he *did* say something to you." She stalked around the room. "I have half a mind to give him a good talking-to about this."

May sighed and rubbed her forehead. "It won't do any good."

"You're just jealous of Dinah," Margaret said. "You never did like sharing your father or me with anyone else, even when you were little."

May said nothing, for she knew her mother spoke the truth.

"You're acting like a spoiled and spiteful child, May-Ling, and I won't have it. I've tried to make allowances for you, considering what you've been through, but I won't have you bickering with Dinah. If you can't get along, I'll—"

"—send me back to England?"

"Of course not," her mother snapped. "But I'll tell you right now that you two had better get along, my girl, because Dinah is staying, whether or not you or Chad like it."

"Please, Mother, I'm tired," May said, leaning back against the pillows and closing her eyes, hoping her mother would leave. "Do you know what's the most difficult part of all this?"

"What?"

"No matter what I do, I always take second place—first to Father, then to China, and now Dinah."

Her mother's eyes flashed fire, and she appeared to grow in stature. "That's absurd. You're fabricating a fiction, and I refuse to play a part in it." And she turned on her heel and stormed out in an angry tinkling of jade, leaving May to stare up at her own reflection in the bronze mirror, and wonder what tomorrow would bring.

CHAPTER
FIVE

The days disappeared one by one, and, before May realized it, she had been in Paoting for a month. When she wasn't resting to recover her health, she visited the jade carver's house, Dr. Gates' hospital, and the Hammonds, although the children were beginning to fray May's nerves with their silent, accusatory presences. She and Dinah avoided each other as much as possible, and an uneasy truce had been declared between them.

May found her thoughts turning to Shanghai, and she wondered if Nelson Wright's company was still thriving, if Emily's social status had been restored, and whether or not Willie still remembered her with bitterness. As if in answer, she received a letter from Emily on the first Monday in June.

It was as chatty and effusive as the woman herself, discussing card parties, the weather, and lamenting the lack of eligible women in Shanghai. Actually, the letter said nothing of substance, and Emily had been careful to skirt the issue of May's departure. When she finished reading, May put the letter away with a dismal sigh.

The following day she went out into the courtyard, seated herself by the dragon-eye tree, and proceeded to cull through a box of small jade pieces her mother had given her to sort and catalog. She spent the entire morning examining each piece, identifying it, and writing down the information in a ledger for future reference.

So absorbed was she in her work that she didn't even glance up when a long shadow fell across her lap. "I'm almost through, Mother," she said absently.

"You wound me deeply, Mrs. Monckton."

At the sound of Alexander Wolder's low, lazy voice, May started and jerked her head up in surprise. "Mr. Wolders! Whatever on earth are you doing here?"

He smiled down at her from his great height. "My travels often take me away from Shanghai, Mrs. Monckton."

May stared at him and couldn't help but notice the change in his appearance and manner. He wore a wide-brimmed hat, and his white suit had been exchanged for a khaki belted jacket with many pockets, tight-fitting whipcord breeches, and heavy leather boots that stopped just below his knee. He looked even taller and leaner than she remembered, but his eyes were still cold, and May found herself wondering just what it would take to warm them.

"Please sit down." She jerked her hand in the direction of the stone bench. He thanked her, removed his hat, and seated himself. "You must forgive me," she added. "You took me by surprise. You're the last person I'd ever expect to see here."

His eyes flicked over her, and she felt her color deepen at the intensity of his scrutiny. "You're looking well, Mrs. Monckton. I would say China suits you."

"Suits me? It nearly killed me."

He scowled. "Killed you? What do you mean?"

May told him about her fever, and added, "I'm lucky to be alive, so the doctor says."

"I'm pleased to see you've recovered." Then he glanced around the courtyard. "The House of the Black Dragon . . . everyone knows the two English missies who live here."

"I would suspect so," she replied. "We've been here for years and have never meant anyone harm."

Wolders looked at the objects spread out before her. "Are those jades? I was told you're an expert."

"I have some knowledge," she replied, wondering what else he had heard about her. She picked up a piece and handed it to him. "I'm cataloging them for Mother. They're tomb jades."

The man's eyes narrowed and turned even colder. "Tomb jades? Stolen from Chinese tombs?"

May's chin rose an arrogant notch and her voice became sharp. "My mother did not steal them."

"I wasn't accusing your mother of thievery, but whoever she's dealing with may not be as scrupulous." He held the piece up to the light and examined it. "This, I believe, is placed on the deceased's tongue before burial, is it not?"

Her brows arched in surprise. "I'm surprised you know that. Most Europeans don't."

Wolders just grinned as he handed it back to her. "I have some knowledge."

May was silent for a moment, then said, "My mother doesn't question the honesty of the merchants. She buys what they sell."

"Perhaps it's time she did."

They stared at each other like combatants, cold blue eyes holding fiery green ones, neither looking away.

Finally, May rose, folded her arms and turned her back to him. "I resent your implication that we are dishonest, Mr. Wolders. I think you should leave now."

"Not until I've done what I came here to do."

She turned around, suddenly curious. "And what is that?"

"I'll tell you when you stop being angry with me."

May sighed and relented. "All right. I owe you that much, after what you did to Captain Forsythe."

Wolders's mouth twitched. "So you heard about that, did you?"

"Yes. And if I weren't a woman, I would have done it myself. Thank you." She became brusque once again. "Now, come, what are you here for?"

He reached into one of his pockets, drew out a small scroll. "You read Chinese, I presume?"

When she replied, "Of course," he handed her the scroll. "This will explain my presence in Paoting."

May uncapped it and unrolled the paper, squinting at the columns of Chinese characters that filled the page. Her lips moved silently as she read, then she looked up at him in alarm. "This is an official summons from a mandarin I've never heard of. Why does he want to see me, and why are you his courier? You have a lot of explaining to do, sir."

Wolders shrugged, and his face was unreadable. "I don't know. I'm not taken into the mandarin's confidence. I was hired to deliver the summons, escort you to him, and take you back to Paoting when he's through with you."

Her voice held a trace of scorn as she said, "So, you work for the Chinese, do you?"

"For a fee. I do a great many things, if someone can pay for my services."

May started pacing around in tiny circles, her brow furrowed as she reread the scroll. She glanced over at Wolders once or twice, as though trying to catch him off guard, but she wasn't successful.

She stopped. "Why should a mandarin hire you all the way from Shanghai when one of his own couriers could have delivered this?"

"He didn't hire me from Shanghai. I have been in this area for a few weeks on . . . other matters." He laced his fingers around one knee. "Perhaps he felt a fellow Englishman would be less intimidating and more persuasive."

"Well, he was wrong, because I'm not going," she insisted, suddenly afraid.

Wolders's voice was deceptively low and lazy. "I wouldn't advise you to ignore a summons like that."

She stared at him as her heart began to pound in her throat. "And if I refuse?"

"You'll find a group of bannermen at your front gate one morning, and they will be most unpleasant."

May felt as though she were suffocating and turned away so he wouldn't see her tears.

"I'm not your enemy, you know," Wolders said softly,

rising and coming up behind her. "Do you believe I'd let any harm come to you after rescuing you from the likes of Captain Forsythe?"

She looked up into his eyes, which were devoid of cunning for all their coldness. "No."

"All right, then. Trust me."

"I suppose I shall have to."

Wolders stared at her. "Are you feeling well enough to make the trip? It would be by horseback and take about two days."

"I've recovered from the fever," May replied, her shoulders slumping in resignation.

"Good. Can you be ready to leave tomorrow morning?" When she looked at him in alarm, he added, "I have my orders to bring you to the mandarin as soon as possible."

"What shall I tell Mother? She's bound to ask questions."

"Just tell her the mandarin wishes to avail himself of your expertise on jade, that's all."

"Mother is not stupid. She'll see through that in an instant."

"Let me do the talking."

They found Mrs. Fitzgerald in her storeroom, kneeling on the floor amid the boxes and crates, gently packing the statues of Kuan Yin for shipment to Shanghai. She was muttering to herself and failed to hear them enter, so May had to announce their presence.

"Mother, we have a visitor."

"Oh?" When she glanced up and spied Wolders, her brows shot up in surprise. "Why, Mr. Wolders!" she exclaimed, rocking back on her heels. "Whatever are you doing in Paoting?"

He smiled broadly at her. "I'm here on a combination of business and pleasure, Mrs. Fitzgerald." And he proceeded to explain his presence at the House of the Black Dragon.

As she read the scroll, Margaret's face darkened, and she wrinkled her brow. "A mandarin wants to see May-Ling? Why?" She looked from one to the other. "What did you say his name was?"

"T'chuan Hsi Lo," Wolders replied.

Mrs. Fitzgerald fingered the lavender jade beads that hung from her neck like small grapes. "I think I remember him. He came here right after you left, May-Ling. He seemed like a fair man, and everyone loved and respected him—not like the mandarin we've got now," she added scornfully under her breath.

May glanced sharply at Wolders. "This mandarin held office here, in Paoting?"

"Years ago," her mother replied, rising and shaking the dust from her robes, then wiping her hands together. "But you know these mandarins are shuffled from one city or district to the next. Just when you get used to one, there's another one to take his place." She was silent for a moment, as though thinking of something. "How long would you be gone?" When Alex told her two days, she gave a small, "Humph."

"T'chuan's summer residence is not far from here," Wolders explained.

"Still, I find it odd."

"What, mother?" May asked. "What do you find odd?"

"I find it odd that he should want to see you, May-Ling, considering that you've only been in China for a month."

"Why so, mother?"

Margaret Fitzgerald folded her arms and stared straight at Alex. "You said he wants to consult May-Ling about some pieces of jade?" Then she looked at her daughter. "I'm not denying that you know a lot about jade, my dear, but there are many Chinese who are even more knowledgeable. Why, he could consult any number of his own countrymen."

May flashed Wolders a triumphant look.

"I don't really know why your daughter was summoned," Wolders said to Mrs. Fitzgerald.

Suddenly the older woman put on her Chinese face by narrowing her eyes into slits. "He doesn't want her for himself, does he? May's not going to vanish like that poor Hummel girl in Shanghai, is she?"

May made an indignant noise, while Wolders tried to keep from smiling. "No, Mrs. Fitzgerald, I can assure you he does not want your daughter. You have my word that no harm will come to her while she is with me."

Margaret slid her hands up the sleeves of her robe and stared at the two in silence, her face unreadable. Finally, she said, "Mr. Wolders, will you excuse my daughter and me for a moment?" When he nodded, she said, "May-Ling, will you come with me?"

May did as her mother requested and followed her into another room several doors down.

By the knitting of her mother's brows, May knew she was displeased. Margaret demanded, "Is he serious about this?"

May nodded. "You read the summons."

Her mother took a deep breath. "I don't exactly like the idea of you going off alone with a man of Wolders's reputation," she said. "Why, he could . . . never mind."

"Mother, I can't ignore the mandarin's request."

Mrs. Fitzgerald's brow furrowed in concentration, then her face lit up. "I shall go with you. At least there will be two of us."

"You have merchants coming," May pointed out. "You might miss a rare piece."

"Yes, that's true. Well, you'll just have to send this mandarin a note of polite refusal because I'm not allowing you to go."

Suddenly May grew fearful. "I don't think we have any choice but to trust Wolders. If I ignore the summons . . ." She spread her hands futilely. "There's no telling what the mandarin might do. We all might be in danger."

The two women regarded each other for the longest time. Finally May smiled and put her hand out to touch her mother's arm. "I trust Wolders, Mother. God knows why, but he does seem like a man of his word. He did save me in Shanghai, and rescued me from Captain Forsythe."

"But, May, this is an entirely different set of circumstances. You would be *alone* with him, and I don't have to tell you that you are an attractive young woman."

May blushed and dropped her arm. "Somehow, I don't think he would take advantage of me."

Her mother sighed. "All right. I must be mad, but I'll agree to this." And they walked back to where Wolders stood waiting.

"When do you plan to leave?" Mrs. Fitzgerald demanded.

"Tomorrow morning."

"All right. Then I insist you spend the night with us."

Wolders smiled. "I appreciate your hospitality."

A shadow appeared in the doorway, and a sweet voice said, "Mother, there is a trader from Peking here to see you."

"Ah, splendid!" Mrs. Fitzgerald said. "Come, Dinah, let us see what he has to offer. You'll excuse us?" And she swept out in a rattle of beads.

As Dinah followed, she glanced back over her shoulder at Wolders.

May caught the glimmer of frank interest in the man's eyes. "And who is that?" he asked, when the two women were out of earshot.

"Dinah, mother's slave girl," May replied. "And she's not for sale. Now, if you'll follow me, I'm going to show you to your room."

Wolders couldn't keep his eyes off Dinah all during dinner that evening. May grudgingly had to admit her enemy was especially alluring tonight in a red silk robe that barely skimmed her body and with her magnificent raven hair dressed in an ornate Manchu manner. And the girl possessed a sensuality that went beyond her gently curved body and inky eyes. It was a quality that disturbed most women, but made men reckless.

Although May had taken great pains with her appearance tonight, selecting a jade-green silk robe embroidered with fine gold thread, and wearing her hair loose about her shoulders, she felt positively dowdy next to Dinah. Why had she even bothered, she wondered, for she wasn't engaging in any contest for Wolders's interest.

Finally, when dinner was over and both her mother and Wolders were begging Dinah to play her lute, May pleaded exhaustion and asked to be excused. She rose and left the room, unaware that Wolders's eyes followed her until she disappeared down the hall.

Once back in her room, May dressed for bed and opened her book of Browning poetry. She read for a while by lamplight, but somehow the plaintive strains of the lute intruded, keeping Robin away. May snapped her book shut, put out the lamp, and slipped into bed, but she was wound up as tight as a spring, and her body refused to sleep.

She wondered if Alexander Wolders would find his way into Dinah's room tonight. Well, let him. It was no concern of hers whom he slept with.

May rolled onto her back with a sigh, then finally fell asleep.

The next morning, she awoke at daybreak to the mournful coo of a dove in the tree outside her window.

May was feeling rebellious this morning, as she washed and dressed and went downstairs to breakfast. Had she really agreed to accompany Wolders in answer to the mandarin's summons? Yes, she had, for there he was, ahead of her, being served by a gracious Dinah.

May nodded, resisting the impulse to ask him if he had slept well, and throughout breakfast they exchanged meaningless chitchat. After they finished eating, Wolders left to gather horses and supplies, while May went to change into her traveling clothes. An hour later, she went out into the yard, where Wolders was saddling their mounts, two dusty Mongolian ponies sturdy enough to climb the Himalayas.

He stared at her, from the conical hat and white scarf hiding her flaming hair to knee-high brown cloth boots. If she lowered her head and hid her hands up the sleeves of her blue ch'ang-fu, no one could tell she was European, let alone a woman.

"You look like a Chinaman." He appeared startled, as though May had surprised him in some way.

"We Fitzgeralds always dressed this way when traveling into the interior," she explained, then asked which pony was hers.

"The dun."

May went up to the friendly little fellow, who was peering out from beneath his shaggy, matted forelock, and she stroked the animal's velvet muzzle. "What's his name?"

"Attila."

"Attila the dun. Clever."

He grinned as he tugged at the saddle girth one last time. "I knew you'd appreciate my wit. And this fierce-looking creature is called Dragon."

"He looks like he's half asleep."

"He's only pretending," Wolders insisted, slapping Dragon's rump and raising dust. "He's really the fastest pony in China."

May gave a snort of derision as she began checking her own gear, making sure the saddle was secure.

Suddenly Wolders turned to her, his face serious. "Do I dare ask if you can shoot a rifle?"

She curled her lip in disdain. "Of course. I'll have you know I'm an excellent shot. My father taught me about guns. Are you expecting trouble?"

He came around and slid a rifle into the case attached to the saddle. "One should be prepared for anything. There are only two of us, and, since we'll be riding by mountains, there's no telling if bandits will attack."

May looked him up and down. "Perhaps it would be prudent for you to dress Chinese as well. You look so very English, so why call attention to yourself?"

He confessed that he had never thought of it.

They turned at the sound of tinkling jade to see Mrs. Fitzgerald come striding through the yard toward them. "Well, are you two ready to leave?"

Wolders nodded. "We'll be on our way."

"Now remember, Mr. Wolders, I'm holding you responsible for my daughter," she warned him again, practically shaking her finger under his nose. "If anything happens to May-Ling . . . "

"Don't worry, Mrs. Fitzgerald. I've given you my word."

"I still don't approve of this venture, but I suppose

there's nothing I can do about it." She so resented not being in control of the situation and was determined to let everyone know it.

"No, there isn't," Wolders replied with a smile.

"Well, see that you take good care of her, or, by the sword of Lu Tung-pin, you'll answer to me!"

Then she hugged May tightly and released her.

"Good-bye, mother," May said, giving her a peck on the cheek. When she was mounted astride Attila and passing through the gates, she glanced back to wave at her mother and saw Dinah standing in the doorway and looking like a cat with cream on its whiskers.

They left Paoting and traveled southward through a landscape that May knew by heart—flat land and grain fields broken only by the majestic Tai-hang Shan Mountains to their right.

"The fields look dry," she said to Wolders.

"There will be a famine this year," he predicted. "Thousands will die."

May could think of no reply, and, after riding in silence for the rest of the morning, Wolders stopped, rose in the stirrups, and said, "It's almost noon, and there's a village over there where we can rest and get something to eat. The horses could use some water, too."

The two of them rode into the village, stopped, and dismounted under a small grove of trees, and few people took much notice of them. A young woman plucking a chicken in her doorway glanced at them, then returned to her task, while the acrid odor of singed feathers made Attila sneeze. Another woman hanging noodles out in the sun to dry spoke sharply to a group of children who stared curiously at the two strangers before scampering behind the houses.

Wolders wandered off to buy food, and May took it upon herself to tend to the ponies. By the time his lanky figure came striding back, she had them unsaddled, watered and was rubbing them down with a cloth she had tucked into her pack before leaving Paoting.

He stopped in his tracks and stared at her, a look of amazement on his face.

"What's the matter?" she asked, giving Dragon's dusty rump a final swipe.

"You didn't have to do that."

May said, "I know, but I wanted to. Surprised?"

"Yes and no."

"My mother never could abide a helpless woman, so she taught me to take care of myself."

"I can see that."

Wolders then seated himself on the ground, leaned against a tree, and handed her a paper cone filled with parts of crisp roast duck and two small bowls filled with rice. "It feels good to get out of the saddle."

May agreed as she sat down and began to eat, stripping away the fatty skin from her duck. "My legs feel like jelly." She was silent for a moment, then said, "Have you always lived in China?"

"All my life," he replied, with something like pride in his voice.

May's curiosity got the better of her. "Did your parents emigrate here, like mine?"

He nodded. "My father was a Dutch trader operating out of Canton, and my mother was English."

"She was a merchant's daughter?"

He nodded. "She was the only child of a prominent family. Her father—my grandfather—had great plans for her, and was quite incensed when she thwarted those plans for an advantageous political marriage to run off with my father. I don't think they ever spoke after that. I never met my grandfather, actually, and both my parents are dead."

May expressed her sympathies and said, "Your parents must have loved each other very much to risk angering your grandfather."

He shrugged. "They always seemed besotted with one another."

"That's all that counts. I suppose you've been to England to meet your mother's family."

"I went to school there for a few years and spent my summers at the ancestral manor, which I stand to inherit, since old Uncle Clarence never married and is childless. It's a monster of a house called Dudleigh Hall that stands high on a cliff in Cornwall and faces the sea. On a quiet night you can actually hear the waves crashing against the rocks below from every room in the house."

May sighed rapturously. "It sounds delightful. How can you be so . . . so cavalier about it?"

"Delightful?" He looked at her as though she were mad. "It was abominable, that's how I can be so cavalier about it. I used to call it 'Deadly Hall.' I was forever getting lost in a maze of dark, paneled rooms that were always chilly and damp, even in July. That's how the whole country was, cold and damp, and forever in a fog. I'd go to bed with the cursed mist outside my window and wake up to it. I even got myself thrown out of school just to get sent back home to China in disgrace, and I'll never set foot in England again," he declared with great finality. "Never."

May pictured a frightened child running a gauntlet of suits of armor down a long, dark, paneled gallery, and her heart went out to the man.

"What would I do there?" Wolders demanded. "Be caged in London during the winter, pretending a pack of boring people were interesting, then spending the summer at Deadly Hall, slowly going out of my mind, listening to the sea."

His words stung her, erasing any sympathy she might have felt. "Not all Londoners are boring," was her indignant reply, as she thought of Robin and his literary friends.

"Perhaps not. But I'd rather die young running opium than creaking away in a rocking chair with a cat in my lap."

"I'll take the rocking chair," May said, scooping rice into her mouth with her fingers.

Wolders smiled mysteriously. "Would you now?"

"Give me the quiet life," May declared.

"I see. A husband and a house in the country overrun with dogs and children."

May hung her head, her appetite snuffed out. "Don't you think we should be going?"

"What's the hurry? I haven't finished eating yet and neither have you."

"I'm not very hungry." And she rose and went to saddle Attila, leaving Wolders to wonder what he had said to cause the light to die in her eyes.

They left the village and chose a road that wasn't as well-traveled, passing through more rippling fields of corn and wheat. On the way, Wolders pointed out a sacred temple inhabited by a holy man reputed to be one hundred years old and a place where an entire town had once stood, until it was destroyed by two powerful feuding families. Later that afternoon a screaming, howling wind rose out of the south, raining dust that stung and blinded both ponies and riders, so that they were forced to seek shelter in a farmer's old shed for a few hours until the wind subsided.

Once they were back on the road, Wolders said, "Did you love him?"

May stiffened. "Who? My husband?"

"No, the . . . other man."

So he knew about Nigel and Robin. She shouldn't have been surprised, for he was bound to hear about her sooner or later, along with the rest of Shanghai.

Her eyes filled with tears, but she brushed them away before they could fall. "I loved him very much. Robin—that was his name—used to say I was like an exotic plant that needed careful gardening. And he was a very, very good gardener."

"I see. And what would you have done if your husband hadn't killed him?"

"That's a very personal question."

"I know, but you don't have to answer it."

Irrationally, May felt compelled to talk. "I would have asked Nigel—my husband—for a divorce."

Wolders whistled. "He sounds too proud to let you go."

"He was. In which case I would have left him for Robin

anyway, but at least I would have given him an honorable alternative."

Wolders startled her by bursting into laughter that caused both ponies to fling back their heads and snort in alarm. May fought to control Attila, and when she had him calmed down, she said, "If you'd stop laughing, perhaps I could see the humor in this conversation."

"You're a fraud, Mrs. Monckton, a beautiful fraud."

She bristled, her eyes snapping fire. "Explain yourself, or I'm turning around and riding back to Paoting."

Gradually his laughter subsided, but his eyes still twinkled. "All this talk of growing old from the safety of a rocking chair . . . you're deluding yourself. You crave adventure as much as I. That's why you came back to China."

"That's absurd! I came back to China because I had no money and nowhere else to go. It was purely a matter of necessity, of survival."

"I don't believe it. If you wanted to stay in England that badly, you would have found a way. I know I would, if I had been in your situation. A month or two cloistered away in the country at a place like Deadly Hall, or visiting friends in Paris until the scandal died down—there were ways."

"You're wrong!" she sputtered.

"Am I? And I suppose living with a man without benefit of clergy, as my mother used to say so delicately, is the height of convention."

May was shaking with indignation. "You're insufferable, and I regret ever agreeing to this."

"I'm only being honest with you, as I suspect few people have."

She said nothing, just set her jaw and stared straight ahead. Despite Wolders's attempts to cajole a few words out of her, she kept silent, and he finally just shrugged and ignored her until twilight, when they arrived at an inn in the middle of nowhere.

It reeked of ponies and mules, and she wrinkled her nose in distaste. "We're staying here?"

Wolders jerked his head toward some trees away from the smell and noise. "Not inside. There, by the trees."

"I don't know," May said dubiously, looking all around. "I don't relish being murdered in my bed."

"There's more of a chance of that happening if we spend the night inside." He was already dismounting and leading his pony over to the watering trough. "Don't worry. I promised your mother nothing would happen to you, and I mean to keep my word."

Nothing did happen that night.

Wrapped in a blanket, with her saddle for a pillow, May reclined on the hard ground, pretending to sleep. She waited, alert, but Wolders made no move toward her, and after an hour she fell asleep in spite of the animals' restless noises and the raucous sounds coming from the inn.

Much later, a sense of danger jolted her awake. Her eyes flew open, but she kept herself from starting as she strained to hear any intruder. There was an unnatural stillness, as though an army were waiting for the order to charge. The animals were quiet in the inn yard—not a whicker or wheeze among them—and the inn's boarders had caroused themselves out, like gutted candles. Looking up, May could see a few stars through the branches, which were even blacker than the night sky.

Something moved, and she tensed, ready to roll and whirl out of harm's way. Then her darting eyes spied a familiar figure, arms folded across his chest, as he leaned against a nearby tree.

Wolders, standing in a patch of moonlight that had managed to seep through the leafy boughs overhead, was watching her intently. He looked spectral in his light-colored clothes, with the light polishing his hair to silver, and judging by his furrowed brow, some struggle was raging within him.

Suddenly, he moved away from the tree and walked softly toward her. May squeezed her eyes shut and forced herself to breathe slowly, even though her heart was thudding in her chest.

After what seemed like hours, Wolders whispered, "Damn!" and May heard the sound of footsteps walking away in resignation. When she opened her eyes just a crack, she saw him angrily fling himself down on his blanket and turn his back toward her.

May unwound, and her whole body went limp with relief. How could she and her mother have been so foolish to believe that a man like Wolders could be trusted to keep his distance? She shuddered, as she wondered how long she would be safe from him.

The next morning, she jumped when Wolders shook her awake, and they mounted and rode out of the inn yard to the accompaniment of the sun rising in a glorious orange sphere, its coming heralded by the trumpeting of a rooster.

They continued south, and May noticed that the Tai-hang Shan Mountains loomed high and forbidding now, like dragon's teeth, and the land itself was beginning to roughen. There were few fields here, just a dry, dusty plain dotted here and there with poor villages.

May glanced at Wolders and said, "Tell me about Mandarin T'chuan. How did you come to work for him?"

Wolders glanced at her, his eyes alight with laughter. "Curious, aren't you? I told you, there are many things I do for a fee. I onced trained the mandarin's bannermen in English military methods." He shook his head at the memory. "They were in sore need of training, too. Each man would always close his eyes just as his rifle fired, which, as you can imagine, is no way to hit a target. But I soon turned them around. T'chuan is no fool. He may be a civil mandarin, but he knows the value of a good army. I happened to be visiting him on other matters when he hired me to bring you to him."

"And he didn't tell you why he wants to see me?"

He shook his head. "I take my money, and I don't ask questions, but I suspect you'll soon find out. T'chuan's estate is just a few miles to the east. We're almost there."

The mandarin's country estate, with its dazzling, red-tiled roofs and white marble terraces, took May's breath away, for it was even more magnificent than the Monckton country house in Surrey. Once inside the gates, they were greeted by a retinue of servants, who took their ponies and ushered them up terraced steps to a small antechamber, where they were offered plum wine.

May accepted a basin of water to wash her face and

hands, which smelled of leather and horse. Wolders watched her take off her hat and scarf and shake her hair free, but he said nothing.

The servants, however, gasped and whispered among themselves, one of them pointing to May's hair.

When the travelers were through, three more servants appeared and led the way to the reception chamber, a vast, austere room where footsteps made hollow, echoing sounds before dying. It contained only a long table, decorated with a solitary, foot-tall carved ivory buddha seated on a turquoise throne that caught May's attention instantly.

There was T'chuan, standing with his back toward them as he stared out at a garden scene purposefully framed by a window. May suspected he had struck this pose so she would notice the coral button on his cap, which signified that he was a mandarin of the second-highest rank, and be awed and intimidated. She decided she was dealing with a shrewd man and should tread carefully.

When he heard them enter, he turned and said in English, "Ah, my friend, you have brought her."

May was dumbfounded. "You speak English!"

He smiled as he came toward them and bowed. "I am the product of a diligent missionary."

May stared in spite of herself. T'chuan had the lithe, muscular body of a soldier, with a narrow, tightly belted waist, and, because he was Manchu, he wore no queue. The mandarin's fingernails were also trimmed, as though he were a man of action who had no use for long-nailed indolent hands.

"Sir, you must forgive me, but I am eager to learn why you summoned me here," May said.

He frowned, his mouth drooping. "The Yinglish are so impatient, wanting to know everything right away. But sometimes what we wish to know is revealed to us slowly, and we must be patient. First, we shall dine," he commanded.

May sighed in resignation, for she realized T'chuan would not be rushed.

The meal was a banquet, a feast for the eye and palate, served in bowls of paper-thin porcelain and eaten with jade chopsticks. It seemed to stretch on for hours, and no sooner did May finish one course than a servant appeared with another to set before her. After the last bowl was whisked away, and May thought the mandarin was finally going to reveal his reasons for summoning her, he rose and invited them to tour his gardens, which, May discovered to her dismay, were several and extensive.

Finally, when May's patience was ready to snap, he said, "Now I will have Ming-sheng tell you why you are here."

"Ming-sheng is a Manchu princess and his favorite concubine," Wolders whispered to her when he saw her puzzled look.

What did the mandarin's concubine have to do with her, May wondered, as the woman entered. Even though her face wore the white paint and red lip color favored by Manchu women, Ming-sheng put even Dinah to shame, with her regal, sensual air and the confidence of a cherished favorite. She strode toward them with great purposefulness on unbound feet, her soft silk robes swishing lightly with every step. May suspected Ming-sheng could persuade a man to do anything she wanted, so great was her beauty and power.

The concubine smiled, bowed, and, after customary courtesies were exchanged, T'chuan gave her permission to be seated. Then she stared at May as intently as a judge and only looked away when T'chuan commanded her to tell her story. She began in a light, flutelike voice that was both hypnotic and commanding.

"I am the number one daughter of a noble house far to the north. My grandfather was a prince of the Imperial family, and our line is long and distinguished. We are Manchu," she added, raising her proud head a notch.

"I had a brother, younger than I. We were the only children of my honorable father and his wife, although I have several sisters by my father's concubines. My only brother was spoiled, and a spoiled son is like a rotten apple. He grew more spoiled as his years increased. He stole and lied. Then one day he committed the gravest sin of all."

A hush fell over the group, and May leaned forward eagerly, falling under the woman's spell.

"He violated the tombs of our sacred ancestors for profit."

May gasped, for she was well aware of the riches royal

tombs held, from jades and bronzes of unbelievable age to priceless porcelains.

"My father died of shame when Win-Lin's crime was discovered, and dishonor now stains our once-noble name like blackest pitch."

May said, "What happened to your brother?"

Ming-sheng's dark eyes smoldered. "He disappeared. Win-Lin never returned to burn joss papers at our father's funeral. I have sought him throughout China to bring him to justice." She bowed her head submissively in T'chuan's direction, and the gesture was as physical as a touch. "My lord has most graciously aided me in my quest to find my brother and restore honor to my house once again. It is a monumental task for one so insignificant as I, but I have made a sacred vow to have my revenge. However, Win-Lin is as wily as the ghost fox and flits just out of reach, taunting me."

Wolders said, "Ming-sheng's brother has taken up with the Europeans who bought the tomb treasures. The mandarin tracked him down to Canton before he was transferred to another district."

May glanced around, suddenly suspicious as alarm bells began ringing in her head. "And just what does all of this have to do with me?"

T'chuan said, "I have reason to believe that Ming-sheng's miserable dog of a brother has been dealing in stolen goods through your mother, Margaret Fitzgerald."

May felt herself turn white, and she had to clutch the table for support. "That's absurd."

"Speak Chinese so Ming-sheng can understand," the mandarin commanded sharply, and May repeated herself.

"T'chuan has spies everywhere looking for Win-Lin," Wolders explained. "They traced him to Paoting, but just when they thought they had him, he eluded them again."

"We must have your assistance," the mandarin said. It was not a request.

May shook her head in disbelief. "My mother would never do such a thing. Never." She looked across at the three faces for reassurance, but there was none, not even from Wolders.

"All the mandarin asks is that you do nothing more than

watch whom your mother deals with, and, if you see anyone suspicious, contact me, because I will be nearby. That's easy enough, isn't it?" he said smoothly.

May rose, turned her back to them and folded her arms to keep them from shaking. "I don't meet my mother's dealers, and I can't be by her side every minute. And besides," she added, whirling around, "you're asking me to spy on my own mother. I won't!"

Wolders rose and towered over her, his face dark and menacing. "Will you excuse us?" he said to T'chuan and Ming-sheng. Then he grasped May's arm, propelled her out of the room and into an empty antechamber.

May was so furious she was shaking. "You didn't appear very surprised to hear what T'chuan expects of me."

"What's that supposed to mean?"

"I think you knew all along why he wanted me here. And then you lied to me, by pretending you didn't. You'd never lie to me—isn't that what you said on the way here?" she reminded him bitterly.

He had the grace to look uncomfortable. "All right. I did lie to you. But would you have come if I told you the truth?"

"Of course not."

"Well, then . . . the end justified the means."

She tossed her head and started for the door. "I'm going back to Paoting right now."

Wolders reached out and grasped her wrist. "Will you please listen to me?"

She tried to pull away, but he held her fast, and all she could do was glare up at him, her nostrils flaring in anger.

"That's better. Now, the reason you are going to help T'chuan is because he could be a valuable ally to Britain someday."

"What do you mean?" May said softly, suddenly still.

"I mean he's a progressive fellow and pro-British, as you have seen. There are many Europeans—merchants, missionaries, and their children—who now enjoy T'chuan's protection in this province. But Ming-sheng has a great deal of influence, and she could change that if you don't agree to help." He tilted her chin and looked deeply into her eyes. "You don't want any deaths on your conscience, do you?"

"You fight dirty, Dutchman," May replied, pulling away in misery, because she realized he spoke the truth.

"I know, but I've got to be brutally frank with you. Look, I'm not saying T'chuan will massacre anyone. What I am saying is that it's a difference between him preventing a massacre someday or doing nothing should one occur."

"So now you're saying it's my patriotic duty to spy on my mother, is that it?"

"Something like that."

May's eyes narrowed as a thought struck her. "Are you working for the British? Are you a spy yourself, Dutchman?"

Wolders's broad grin was disarming. "Me? Work for the British? Don't be absurd. It's against my principles, and besides they could never afford my services." He hesitated. "But come, will you help us?"

"Absolutely not."

Before she could move, he grasped her by the shoulders and shook her. "What do you think this is, some child's game we're playing? When I first met you, I thought you were an extraordinary woman. But I can see now that you're as selfish as the rest of your sex." And he flung her from him and started to walk away. Then he stopped and turned. "Well?"

May felt as helpless as a criminal wearing the cangue. "I'm going to walk in the garden. I have to think."

Wolders watched her step out into the deepening darkness. He felt confident that he had not misjudged her, and he knew what her answer would be when she returned.

When May stepped inside an hour later, three pairs of expectant eyes followed her every step.

"All right," she said in resignation. "I'll do what you ask." As Wolders grinned and unwound in relief, May brought him up short by adding, "But I must have my guarantees."

He was wary again. "And what are those?"

"No matter what happens, my mother will not be harmed or prosecuted, whether or not she is involved with Win-Lin."

"I can't make promises," Wolders said.

"Then I cannot help you."

May saw the look that passed between T'chuan and his concubine. He said, "You have my word."

"I must have the Dutchman's as well."

T'chuan leaped to his feet, furious. "Stubborn woman! I could have you tortured for your insolence."

May didn't flinch. "Those are my terms."

"I'll do what I can," Wolders said, relenting.

The tense moment passed, and the four of them became congenial once again. Both Ming-sheng and her lord were restrained in their thanks, but May sensed the excitement they shared. The mandarin insisted that they spend the night, and rooms were readied in minutes.

May's troubled mind kept her from sleeping that night, even though she had soaked in a steaming tub fragrant with rose petals and listened to the soothing strains of Ming-sheng's lute, which reminded May of Dinah, although the former's playing was much more skillful. Now, as she watched the moon rise through the windows, she wondered if Wolders and T'chuan were off on a cloud in one of the estate's opium rooms.

"Typical," she snorted, as she rolled onto her side and made a pillow of her arm.

But Alexander Wolders continued to haunt her troubled thoughts, keeping sleep away. She recalled the previous night at the inn, when he had looked down at her with blatant desire in his eyes. And it had been desire—she was not so naive as to misread the signs. What would she have done if he had tried to touch her? She was grateful she hadn't been put to the test.

Thinking of the man made her too uncomfortable, so she turned her thoughts to what she had been told about her mother, that Margaret Fitzgerald was somehow connected with the unscrupulous Win-Lin and dealing in stolen goods. The very thought sickened her.

She and her mother had had their differences over the years, but May staunchly refused to believe that her mother would ever do anything dishonest, especially against the Chinese, whom she thought of as her countrymen. No, Wolders, T'chuan, and the Manchu concubine were wrong.

Then May willed herself to sleep, because she wanted to be refreshed for the journey home.

The next morning, their ponies were saddled and ready for them, and, after taking their leave of T'chuan and Ming-sheng, May and Wolders started back to Paoting.

"You're still angry with me, aren't you?" Wolders said when they had ridden in silence for two hours.

May refused to look at him. "How do you expect me to feel? You've asked me to play Judas to my own mother."

A hurt look passed across his face as he reached out and put a conciliatory hand on her arm. "Please don't act this way. I haven't asked you to play Judas, I've just asked you to report any suspicious comings and goings at the House of the Black Dragon."

May shook him off, nudged Attila's ribs with her heel, and rode a short distance away from him. Wolders let her ride by herself for another hour, before urging Dragon forward until he caught up with her.

Finally, May relented and spoke. "What will Ming-sheng do if her brother is found?"

"Have him put to death," was Wolders's curt reply.

May shivered in spite of the blazing heat. "Her own brother?"

"A brother gone bad, who has disgraced her family and their ancestors. You more than anyone should know how the Chinese revere their ancestors."

May was silent as she reflected on the truth of what he said.

"And," he added, "Manchu women aren't like their Chinese sisters. They have more freedom, and if they're firstborn, like Ming-sheng, they have much power."

"Why isn't Ming-sheng with her family?" May wanted to know. "And why isn't she T'chuan's taitai?"

Wolders' grin was insolent. "Is your English sense of morality outraged?"

"Don't be silly," she snapped. "What I meant was—"

"I know what you meant. From what I understand, T'chuan already had a wife when he met Ming-sheng, and she had to choose between marrying a powerless man or becoming the concubine of one who could help her fulfill her sacred vow to find her brother."

May shook her head. "That's absurd."

"No more absurd than marrying for money or a title," he pointed out.

May shook her head. "You're always defending them. You're as bad as my mother with her China passion."

"China's the only home I've ever known," he said gruffly, as he scanned the horizon. "Let's go this way. I think I know a shorter route back to Paoting."

And they turned their ponies to the northwest, unaware of the danger that awaited them.

CHAPTER SIX

It was late afternoon when May reined in Attila and ran her shirtsleeve across her damp forehead. Her mouth tasted dry and gritty, like sand, while her knees ached from gripping the saddle for hours.

"Can we stop and rest a while?" she begged, letting the reins go slack. "I'm exhausted."

Wolders, himself red-eyed and slouching in the saddle, quickly assessed the area from their high vantage point. "I see a city over there. We can find an inn yard to spend the night and be back in Paoting by noon."

"Anything to get out of the saddle," she replied, nudging her pony's ribs with her toe.

Attila and Dragon picked their way down the hill, dislodging a shower of rocks and pebbles and sending up a cloud of dust in their wake. May could see the town now, but paid scant attention to it, for after a while, Chinese towns looked as similar as a string of paper dolls to her, with their groves of trees and walls and suburbs. All she could think of, as they drew closer and closer to the main gate, was food and a place to pillow her head, where she could empty her mind of its burdens and let her tired bones sleep.

Just as they were approaching the gate, Wolders reined in Dragon and cautioned May to stop. "Did you hear that?"

"Hear what?" May demanded.

"A noise. It sounded like a gunshot."

May looked around in alarm and shook her head. "I didn't hear anything."

Wolders relaxed. "I must be imagining things."

They started their ponies again, drawing closer to the gate so that it towered over them ominously. Wolders halted the animals a second time, his eyes narrowing in speculation.

"What now?" May whispered.

"Something is very odd here." The man was on guard now, like a panther scenting the enemy. "Have you noticed how quiet everything is, no bird twittering, no dogs barking? And we haven't seen a farmer plowing his fields for miles."

May glanced around nervously, the hairs on the nape of her neck rising. "You're right. Perhaps there has been an epidemic here, cholera or typhoid."

Wolders reached down and slipped his rifle out of its scabbard. "I don't like the looks of this."

Before they could move, an explosion rippled through the air, like the crash of a gigantic dam bursting, and the ground quaked beneath their ponies' hooves, causing the animals to squeal in panic. Momentarily stunned, May and Wolders watched as the city gates creaked open, and a few people trickled out, stopped, and stared at them.

Wolders raised his hand, smiled, and greeted them in Chinese.

"Fank-wei!" one of them screamed in reply and sent his pitchfork singing through the air, to fall ineffectually on the ground not five feet from Dragon.

"Ride!" Wolders jerked Attila's bridle to turn the startled pony in the opposite direction, then brought down his hand on its neck with a stinging slap.

Squealing in indignation, the dun sprung forward as if struck with a red-hot poker, momentarily catching May off guard so she almost tumbled off backward. But she caught herself in time and leaned forward over Attila's neck like a Newmarket jockey. Within seconds, she drew alongside Wolders, and the two ponies raced for their lives.

"Follow me!" Wolders shouted.

May needed no urging. She risked a quick glance back over her shoulder, her eyes bulging in fear at the wall of ragtag peasants swarming out of the city, like enraged hornets eager to strike at anything that moved. But, although the farmers chased them as fast as they could, they were no match for Attila and Dragon, who flew as though their hooves had wings attached and surged effortlessly ahead of the crowd.

She turned and settled back into the saddle again, confident that they would soon outrun the mob, but her elation was short-lived, for suddenly a shot rang out behind her and echoed horribly on the air.

May saw Wolders flinch, drop his rifle, and clutch his side, which turned scarlet between his fingers. Dragon, smelling blood and bewildered by the sudden slackening of the reins, started to veer off to the right while slowing down.

"Alex!" May screamed, clutching at Dragon's bridle and pulling him back into line.

"No use," Wolders cried with a shake of his head. "Save yourself."

In a split second, May knew their only chance of survival lay back in the city, where houses could shield them from the mob and buy them precious time. So, ignoring Wolders's plea to save herself, she turned the ponies in a sweeping arc away from their pursuers, yet back into the city and down the closest deserted street. Her eyes darted at walled houses and locked doorways as she desperately searched for a place to make a stand, for Wolders was about to topple out of the saddle any minute. Risking another glance back, she was heartened to discover the mob was beginning to thin out, as the farmers became exhausted and, one by one, dropped by the wayside.

"Hang on," she called to Wolders and sent the ponies racing around a sharp turn and up a narrow street. Miraculously, the enraged cries grew faint, then died. They had lost the mob and gained a few precious moments.

As they broke free of the streets and into an open area

toward the far side of the city wall, May saw their salvation, a pagoda rising magestically above the treetops. She felt wild and dizzy with triumph, and in the midst of despair she felt herself laughing.

"The pagoda!" she shouted. "We're almost there."

An ashen Wolders nodded and, with superhuman effort, pulled himself erect in the saddle for their last mad dash to safety. As they came careening up to the pagoda's door, May pulled Attila back on his haunches and was out of the saddle before his forefeet touched the ground. She pulled her rifle out of its sheath, grabbed the ammunition bag, then slapped the pony on the rump so he ambled away from the pagoda. May turned her attention to Wolders, who was on the verge of toppling out of the saddle.

May nearly collapsed under his weight. "Don't give up now, for God's sake!" Then she shouted, "Go!" over her shoulder to Dragon, who wasted no time racing after his companion.

Wolders managed to steady himself enough for May to get an arm around him. Then they went teetering toward the door, like a pair of Shanghai sailors on shore leave.

Once inside, the incense-scented darkness momentarily blinded May after the afternoon brightness outside, but her fumbling fingers found the door's lock and drew the bolt home with a comforting click. Then Alex lost consciousness again, and she eased him to the floor.

"Welcome, travelers," a soft voice said behind them.

May jumped and whirled around, her fingers finding the trigger instinctively, and, as her eyes became accustomed to the darkness, she could discern a robed figure standing before her, with soft, flickering lanterns and incense burners behind him.

His smoothly shaved head and gray robe identified him as a Buddhist monk, and May suspected he must be the pagoda's caretaker and priest.

"Have you traveled far?" he inquired innocently enough.

May stared at him, as Weng's words came back to her. "Yes, I have traveled far," she replied.

"North, from Peking?"

May swallowed hard. "From the south, where the phoenix dwells."

The monk smiled and darted forward to lift Wolders. "How can I aid you, my sister?"

"You can hide us," May replied, as they each took one of Wolders' arms. "If you don't, we shall be killed."

The monk nodded. "What I have feared has come to pass. The farmers have risen against the mandarin—a most cruel man—burning his yamen and freeing the prisoners from the jail. That was the explosion you heard a while ago. The farmers are enraged and will not listen to reason."

May felt strangely calm in this softly lit holy place. Its overpowering scent of incense was sweet and slightly cloying, and the bronze buddha stared benevolently down at them from the other side of the room. The temple was hushed and devoid of worshipers, and May, for one, was thankful.

Wolders groaned and cursed as they helped him up the stairs leading to the second of the pagoda's thirteen levels, and May felt the sweat rise on her face, from fright and exertion. She glanced back at the buddha, its gold-leaf finish glowing softly in the lantern light.

There was no time to even think, for she became a creature of instinct, a jungle beast concerned only with survival. While Wolders staggered against one wall and slowly sunk unconscious to the floor, May pulled off her hat and scarf with trembling fingers and shook her hair free.

The monk drew away, as if burnt, his placid face suddenly hostile and ugly. *"Fank-wei!"*

"Yes, I am a foreign devil, but the Sons of the Celestial Phoenix have sworn to protect me. Otherwise, how would I know your secret words?"

The monk hesitated as a loud knock broke the pagoda's stillness. The mob had found them.

May swallowed hard, then knelt to stanch Wolders's wound with her scarf. "Well?" she demanded, looking up. "Will you violate your sacred oath to help one protected by your brotherhood? Or will you let them have us?"

117

The knock came again, louder and more insistent, while May awaited his answer.

"I will help you," the monk said flatly.

"Thank you." May licked her parched lips. "I sent our horses running off, so their tracks should look as though we rode past this temple. Do you think the farmers will try to search here?"

"They may," the monk replied. "I will try to dissuade them." And he turned and trotted down the steps, leaving May to crouch beside Wolders and contemplate her next move if the monk was not successful.

She held her breath as the monk muttered profuse apologies for his tardiness while unlocking the door, and she heard the angry chorus of voices demanding to know if the foreign devil and his Chinese companion had come this way.

The monk spoke so softly May couldn't hear his reply. She narrowed her eyes as she stared at the serene face of the buddha, while an icy bead of sweat ran down her neck. Time stopped, every second dragging into an hour, while May's legs ached and her finger waited, curled around the trigger. She crouched there, praying for any sound, yet at the same time fearing it, for the only sound she would hear would be the footsteps of the peasants as they poured into the temple to search the upper levels. When found, she and Alex would surely die—quickly, if they were lucky. She had never thought much about death before, except to wonder once or twice what it would be like, and she tried not to think of it now. May risked a glance at Alex, his face so peaceful, with a shock of dark hair falling onto his forehead. She reached out and swept it back, a gesture she found oddly comforting. Could she bring herself to shoot him before the mob descended on them? She closed her eyes and cringed.

And then she heard it, the sound of a door being closed and footsteps—solitary, soft footsteps—making their way across the temple floor.

The monk stopped at the foot of the stairs and looked up at her. "They are gone."

May's bones seemed to turn to water, and she breathed a shaky sigh of relief. "They believed you?"

"I am a holy man," he said simply. "They would have no reason to believe I would lie. I sent them on the trail of your horses. It will be some time before they realize they have been tricked, and perhaps they'll grow tired of their search and go home. And perhaps they will come back here and search. That is just the chance you must take."

May rocked on her heels and drew her hand across her forehead. "Thank you. We are in your debt."

"May?" she heard a feeble voice call.

Looking down she saw Alex watching her. He said, "What happened?"

"The mob came to the door, but the monk persuaded them we were not here," she explained.

Then she knelt beside him, but her heart sank when she saw her scarf was dark crimson with blood. "Your wound will have to be cleansed and dressed. Now, if I were a sensible female, I'd have a petticoat to tear into bandages." And she burst into tears.

"Pull yourself together," Wolders said brutally.

She sniffed and took a deep breath. "Sorry."

The monk helped her remove Wolders's jacket and shirt, which she rolled up and used to pillow his head.

"I hope the bullet didn't hit anything vital," she murmured, as the monk began pulling away the scarf to examine the wound.

"If it did, I wouldn't be talking to you now," he replied, before going as limp as a rag doll.

The monk trotted off to find water, while May stopped the bleeding as best she could. He reappeared a few minutes later, carrying a jar of water and some clean cloths. The benign face was tight with mistrust, yet calm with a certain resignation, as he soaked the cloth in water and handed it to May, who proceeded to sponge Wolders's face. But she had to look away when the monk began to dress and cleanse the wound, for all she could think of was the day she had found Nigel and Robin.

Bright lights danced before her eyes, and, as she felt herself falling, cruel fingers bit into her shoulder and the monk said, "Drink," handing her another vessel.

She took it and drank deeply until the searing plum wine caused her to choke and cough. But the faintness passed, and she felt strong again.

"What is your name?" she asked the monk.

"My name is of no consequence," he replied.

"But I wish to know to whom we owe our lives."

"I do not wish to be known to you beyond this time and this place."

"I will always remember what you did for us whether I know your name or not."

"Then I choose not to give it to you."

"As you wish."

When the monk finished, he rose and said, "I have done all I can. Now I will go to find food, for you must be hungry after your ordeal."

"May you be repaid a thousandfold for each kindness you have shown us," she said, looking up at him.

His eyes narrowed. "How you came to be favored by the Sons of the Celestial Phoenix I do not know, nor do I wish to know. But I have taken an oath to protect my brothers. Otherwise, I would have surrendered you, *fank-wei* woman."

May shuddered as he disappeared down the stairs in a flurry of soft footsteps.

"Are we safe?" Wolders demanded in a weak voice.

May turned, wondering how much he had overheard about the Sons of the Celestial Phoenix, but he said nothing, and she assumed he had just regained consciousness.

"You're awake," she said. "Are you in much pain?"

"I can bear it," he replied, but his white face belied his words.

May hugged her knees. "I think Dr. Gates's hospital isn't far from here, but I'm sure Attila and the fastest pony in China are halfway back to Paoting by now. And even if we did have horses, you can't ride—not in your condition."

Wolders reached up to touch her arm, and she was stunned to see the defeat in his eyes. "You'd better go on without me."

"Nonsense," May snapped. "I don't want your death on my conscience."

"May, I'm serious. You've got no other choice. I'll only slow us down."

"I can't accept that." And she rose and left him, fearing he might be right.

Hours later, when the last light had faded from the sky and May worried whether the monk himself had fallen prey to the mob, he returned with more food and water, which a famished May and Wolders ate gratefully.

"It's dark now," the monk told them, "and the city is quiet. The rebels' ardor has cooled, and I suspect they are having second thoughts about what they have done, for they have all gone back to their farms. I had the good joss to find a pony and cart. But you must hurry."

"Can you walk?" May asked Wolders, while she helped him back into his jacket.

He looked across at her. "Take the cart and go."

She shook her head and sat down again.

"May . . ."

"Are we going to sit here all night arguing, or are we leaving?"

"Damn you," he muttered, heaving himself to his feet.

After quickly tying her hair back again, and tucking it out of sight beneath her hat, May and the monk each took one of Wolders's arms and assisted him down the stairs and past the buddha, who had certainly worked some magic tonight. When they reached the door, May clasped her hands together and bowed to the monk. "Again, a hundred-thousand thanks."

"Do not thank me, *fank-wei.*"

"I will burn papers for you," May replied. Once outside, she shouldered the rifle and helped Wolders into the cart, which was strewn with a thick layer of hay.

He sunk down into it with a gasp, then a grateful sigh, and May walked around to the front, relieved that he was being so compliant. She was pleased to see a pony hitched between the traces instead of a mule, for, while the latter were more surefooted, they were also more temperamental, and

May couldn't afford the luxury of an animal that might stop in the middle of the road just when she needed speed.

She laid the rifle across her lap, gathered the reins and waved one last time to the monk as the cart rattled off. He did not wait to see them go, but turned and walked back to his pagoda, without so much as a backward glance. May, however, would remember him for the rest of her life.

Pointing the pony in the direction of the north star, she set him on the road, clearly illuminated by the full moon suspended low in the sky. The only sound was the clatter of wheels and the dull thud of hoofbeats. The monk had been right. Everyone was behind doors tonight. It was as though the initial flush of rebellion had paled, and now more sobering second thoughts had taken their place.

As they rode away from the town, and the miles ran into one another, May's eyes were never still. She peered back to see if they were being followed, to the sides for any sign of bandits riding down from the hills, and ahead for danger lurking. No one—it was as though she and Wolders were the only two people in the world, and she was sure of him only because he groaned whenever the cart's wheels bounced into ruts, jarring both driver and passenger.

Any thoughts of sleep were crowded out by desperate thoughts of survival, even though it seemed she had been traveling half the night. Finally, when the pony stumbled, May realized she had to stop, or the animal would drop, and she really would be in jeopardy. So she turned off the road to where a stream beckoned, a silver ribbon in the moonlight.

She let the pony drink its fill, then tied it to a shrub, where she prayed it would stay. Then, with a weary sigh, she climbed into the cart, her rifle clutched in her hand.

May held her breath and listened. The man's breathing was regular, but ragged, and, when she touched her hand to his forehead, she found it hot and dry. Since there was no light, examining his wound would be futile, so she just lay down beside him and slipped her shoulder beneath his head.

Suddenly, he stirred. "Java?"

"No," May whispered. "Go back to sleep."

"Must be. So soft." Then he dozed off fitfully.

What had Emily said about him keeping a Javanese

woman in Macao? Well, she thought wryly, at least he hadn't called her Dinah.

May curved her body against his and fell asleep instantly.

The snorting of the pony jerked her out of sound sleep, and she instinctively felt for the rifle, then disengaged Wolders before rising and jumping out of the cart. May looked around in panic, but not even a cricket stirred.

God, was she tired! Her stomach was making grinding noises, so she tried to appease her hunger with water before starting off again.

After driving for what seemed only minutes, the landscape suddenly appeared familiar, as though May had turned the pages of a book and happened upon a favorite illustration. She stood up and gave a gasp of recognition at a cluster of buildings that looked suspiciously like Dr. Gates's hospital. The temptation to slap the reins against the pony's flanks and send it into a gallop was great, but she thought of her cargo and resisted.

"Aiyah, Dutchman," she said quietly. "We made it."

The cart stopped before the hospital door, just as the eastern sky turned warm-rose, and a sleepy-eyed servant carrying two buckets on a pole stared at them blankly.

"Fetch Dr. Gates," May said, her head spinning so fast she had to hold it to steady it. The servant went scurrying inside, and a minute later returned with the doctor, wiping shaving soap from his face with a towel, his eyes alarmed.

"May! What on earth—!"

He reached up just in time to help her down. "There's a man inside the cart. He's been shot. He may be—" her voice broke "—dead, for all I know."

"Take missie inside," Dr. Gates said to the servant.

"I'm all right," she insisted, just before the darkness engulfed her and she fell forward in a faint.

May slept the entire day sprawled on the hospital's only bed, oblivious to the crowded, noisy ward downstairs. When she finally woke, just as the sun was sinking into a flaming sky, she found her mother seated on a stool at the foot of the bed.

"By the sword of Lu Tung-pin. What happened to you?" were the first words out of Margaret Fitzgerald's mouth.

May yawned and rubbed her eyes. "I'll tell you later. How is Wolders? Is he—?"

"No, he's not dead, but by all rights, he should be. Chad's downstairs with him now. He says Mr. Wolders will live, if he stays off his feet for a while. And you'll tell me what happened this instant."

May told her what had happened as they passed through that town. "One of the peasants had a gun, and he used it."

Her mother closed her eyes and shook her head, then she said, "Chad said he was very lucky."

May told her how they had hidden in the pagoda and were aided by a monk, but she omitted the part the Sons of the Celestial Phoenix had played. That was still between Weng and herself, and she resolved to thank him at the first opportunity.

"Where is Wolders now?" she wanted to know.

"I told you, downstairs in the men's ward, sleeping on a floor mat like the rest of the Chinese." She fingered the jade bracelet she wore. "Do you want to see him?"

"No," May grumbled, "I just want to go home."

"I've got a cart waiting."

May rose, pulled her unkempt hair back into a tidy knot, then splashed water on her face, while her mother watched.

Mrs. Fitzgerald said, "Well, what did the mandarin want?"

"T'chuan had a marvelous collection of art objects," May replied, avoiding her mother's direct look, "and he wanted some advice on how to sell it to the English, that's all."

"What did he have? I might be interested. Perhaps Nelson would, also."

May told her about the ivory buddha on the turquoise throne, and Mrs. Fitzgerald's face brightened at the prospect of such an acquisition.

"He will contact me when he's ready to do business," May said. "Now, shall we go?"

"Yes. Dinah will have dinner waiting. She'll be so disappointed Mr. Wolders won't be joining us."

May sneezed from the strong smell of carbolic acid that filled the air. "Perhaps Chad will let her come here and nurse him back to health."

Mrs. Fitzgerald gave her a withering look as they left the room. "She's such a compassionate girl. Dinah would like that, and I'll have to suggest it to her."

When they arrived at the House of the Black Dragon and sat down to the dinner that Dinah had ordered for them, May endured her mother's chatter and Dinah's polite silence. Later, she excused herself and went up to her room, where she immediately changed and slipped into bed.

But her thoughts kept her awake. She kept seeing Wolders in the pagoda, lying there, his pale face tight with pain but still relishing the danger and excitement of the moment. She had to admit she had been drawn to him, but danger had a way of bringing even bitter enemies closer together. Now she had her treacherous emotions under control once again and could keep her distance.

Was Alexander Wolders merely an unscrupulous adventurer, selling his services to the highest bidder, as he insisted, or was it only an act to throw people off guard, so he could work secretly for the British government?

She wondered, as exhaustion claimed her once again, and she slipped away into comforting sleep.

The next morning, May went to Weng Ta-Chung's house to tell him of her narrow escape. She found the jade carver in his workroom, seated cross-legged in a puddle of sunlight and meditating over the block of white jade before him. May stood silently in the doorway, watching the serene brow furrow in concentration and the long fingers reverentially probing the stone to reveal its secrets. She felt a sudden outpouring of love for this man.

"Esteemed master of jade?" she called softly from the doorway. "Forgive this unworthy one for interrupting you."

Weng smiled ever so slightly. "Welcome again to my poor home, my daughter." Then he beckoned to her. "Come join me. See what I have here."

May came forward and seated herself across from him. "You are beginning a new carving?"

He inclined his head. "It is beautiful, is it not? Snow jade streaked with red fire. But a most difficult piece. I have been studying this stone for weeks, and it still has not revealed itself to me. Tell me, what do you see here, hiding in the stone, waiting to be set free? A horse? A dragon?"

May studied the stone, touched it, and suddenly smiled. "I see two carp, swimming. The white jade is their bodies, and the red their fins and tails."

Weng smiled broadly. "The student has surpassed the teacher." Then his face darkened in a scowl. "The mandarin wishes me to carve a lion, but I do not sense a lion here. Carp, yes, but not a lion."

"A man must do what he has to do."

"True, my daughter," Weng agreed. Then he studied her as he had studied the jade. "You look greatly troubled, and I would say your stay in the Flowery Kingdom does not suit you."

"I have come to thank you, and the Sons of the Celestial Phoenix."

He was instantly alert, his eyes hardening to coal as May told him of her escape. "I am pleased my brothers were able to assist you, but I had not expected this so soon."

May swallowed hard. "There is something else I must tell you, something that has been troubling me." And she told him what T'chuan and Wolders expected her to do.

"The Manchu princess will not rest until her family honor is avenged," Weng warned her. "I have known your esteemed mother and father for many, many sunrises. Many of my people have frowned on that friendship, including my own wife, but I have come to know them as well as I know myself. Your mother would never consort with such men, my daughter."

"But what if she has been . . . corrupted?" May nearly choked on the word.

"Your first duty is to your parent," he replied firmly. Reading her mind, he added, "I cannot give you peace, as much as I would like to grant you such a gift. You must seek it within yourself."

"In that case, I may never find it."

"You shall. One day."

On her way home, May happened to notice a young girl sitting in the street and playing with a chipped, red-clay water buffalo. The sight of the clay figure, with one leg missing, forced May to recall a similar toy given to her one year on her birthday by Tzu-Lieh, her amah.

She hadn't thought of her nurse since the *Hanover*, when her mother told her the woman had gone back to her own village, but now May was overcome by the desire to find "Julie" and talk to her about so many things, especially about her father. Perhaps Han or one of his sons would know where the nurse had gone.

When May arrived back at the house, she found Han in the kitchen, preparing tea.

"Han," May said, "whatever happened to Chen Tzu-Lieh? My mother told me she went back to her village. Do you remember the name of her birthplace?"

The servant's brow wrinkled in concentration. "The amah did not go back to her village. She went to Shanghai, to live with her niece, who works in a textile factory there."

May's mouth fell open. Shanghai! Tzu-Lieh was in Shanghai all the while, and she had never known it. May thanked him and went to find her mother.

She was surprised to discover her seated on the k'ang and sewing, a disdainful occupation she had always happily relinquished to their Chinese sewing lady. May didn't announce her presence, but watched her mother in silence from the doorway. Mrs. Fitzgerald looked old and tired, with an unaccustomed vulnerability that brought a lump to May's throat.

They won't harm you, no matter what you've done, was

May's silent, fierce promise. Not T'chuan, not Wolders, not the British Empire.

Margaret Fitzgerald glanced up. "Oh, there you are."

"You're sewing," May said, entering and seating herself on the k'ang. "What are you making?"

"Jackets for the Hammond children."

"Jackets? It's only June, for goodness sake. Aren't you getting a little ahead of yourself?"

"It'll be winter before you know it," her mother replied briskly, as she stuffed some wadding up the sleeve. "The poor little mites. Nicholas and Harriet do their best on what the mission sends them, but it's so hard. They use most of their funds for the Chinese and barely have enough left over for themselves."

"I have a feeling you do more for those children than make them jackets, mother."

She shrugged. "And what if I do? We Europeans have to stick together. There are so few of us here. There," she said, standing the blue cotton jacket to the side. It was so stuffed with padding that it could stand by itself. "That ought to keep them warm." As May watched, her mother began to embroider a circular symbol in red thread near the collar. "My trademark," she explained.

"I heard something interesting just now from Han," May announced, and repeated what she had been told.

"Shanghai?" Mrs. Fitzgerald looked up from her sewing. "That is a surprise. She told me she was going back to her village."

"I thought I'd write to Emily," May said. "Perhaps one of the European families hired her to care for their children, since Tzu-Lieh speaks excellent English."

"Why this sudden interest in your old amah?" her mother demanded, glancing up without missing a stitch.

May shrugged. "I was very close to her. She practically raised me, remember?"

"I've heard Mr. Wolders is better," her mother said suddenly.

"Is he?" May's voice was flat with disinterest.

"Why don't you ride out to see him?"

"I don't think I will, mother."

"Why? Are you angry with him about something?"

"Yes, but I'd prefer not to say why."

"Well, since Dinah has gone to visit him, would you like to visit the Hammonds with me this afternoon?"

May bit off her comment about being second-best and instead said, "I'd like that very much."

Later that day, as they walked to the mission, May and her mother passed the joss house, an impressive temple, where large numbers of Chinese came to worship and burn silver papers to their gods for good fortune.

Mrs. Fitzgerald stopped and touched May's arm. "Isn't that Nicholas, preaching?"

There was Nicholas, his arms spread wide in supplication and a Bible in one hand, as he stood on the top step of the joss house, right next to a painted wood carving of Chu Jung, the god of fire. Hammond's face was flushed and his eyes blazed with religious fervor, and May had to admit that, if she had been standing in St. Aedean's pulpit back in Surrey, he would have her hanging breathlessly on every word, convincing her that salvation was at hand.

"Nicholas is brave," May said, "preaching to them at the doors of their own temple."

"He's quite fearless," her mother agreed. "He came to China to save souls, and save souls, he will."

Whether the Chinese like it or not, May thought.

The Chinese thronged around the steps were obviously more interested in entering the joss house than in Hammond's sermon, but were too polite to elbow their way past him.

Then May heard Nicholas speak, as they drew closer, and she stared in amazement.

"What's he trying to do?" she whispered to her mother. "Why isn't he using the converts to interpret? He can't even speak Chinese well, and he's making a fool of himself."

"I think his sincerity surpasses any language barrier," Mrs. Fitzgerald said in his defense.

Suddenly, the crowd burst out laughing, for Nicholas's last reference to Christ in Chinese came out decidedly bawdy and blasphemous, but, when his next statement insulted Chinese gods, the laughter died abruptly.

"I think he's in trouble, Mother."

The tolerant, benign mood of the crowd was wiped away like a cloud across the sun. Smiles were replaced by scowls, and a rumbling rippled through the onlookers. But Nicholas Hammond, unmindful of the turn in mood, plunged right on.

Without warning, a sharp, shrill cry rose, and an object came flying out of the crowd, to hit the missionary in the face, cutting him off in midsentence.

"By the sword of Lu Tung-pin! He's been shot!" Margaret cried, turning white.

May clutched her mother's arm to hold her back as Nicholas came staggering down the steps, passed none too gently from man to man.

"I think it was only a tomato," May said, relieved.

"Oh, dear."

Nicholas was livid. "Fools!" he screamed, shaking his fist at the dispassionate Chinese, who now ignored him to stream into the joss house. "I come to save your poor heathen souls, and this is how you repay me?" And he wiped the red pulp from his cheek as he turned, his handsome face dark and angry.

Why, May thought, he looks as though he'd kill them all, if he could.

Nicholas started when he saw the two women, and instantly his entire manner changed, turning him into the benevolent, kindly man May first met.

"Ah, Margaret," he said, trying to compose himself. "And May. Did you enjoy my sermon? I must confess, I wasn't very well received."

"Your Chinese is atrocious, Nicholas," Mrs. Fitzgerald said with a shake of her head. "You should take one of the converts to translate for you."

Hammond colored, then said, "The people disapprove of the converts, and some are downright abusive toward them."

"That's because they think the converts have abandoned their own gods in exchange for food. You've said yourself that other Chinese call them 'rice Christians.' "

"I know, but that's silly," Hammond said as the three of them started walking back to the mission. "The converts have accepted Christ as the Supreme Being. They have forsaken their heathen ways for the salvation of their immortal souls."

May thought the man dreadfully ignorant of the Chinese, but it was pointless to argue with one so blinded by his own faith.

"Is this the first time the people have been antagonistic toward you?" Margaret demanded.

Nicholas was silent for a moment. "Yes, yes, it was. Usually, they just listen politely, or laugh, and wander off. But this was the first time anyone has been openly hostile to me. It's most distressing."

May felt a shiver of forboding caress her shoulders. China, the slumbering dragon, was beginning to awaken, and Heaven help them all when it finally woke, roaring and breathing fire. Today it was a tomato hurled through the air, and tomorrow . . . ?

They rounded a corner, and the mission came into view, two buildings and a small church with its arrogant spire.

"Oh, look," May said, "there's Dr. Gates's pony."

"Baby John is sick," Nicholas said, his voice tight and strained. "Dr. Gates came to examine him."

"Oh, no," Mrs. Fitzgerald said in alarm. "Nothing serious, I hope."

"I don't know. He's in a great deal of pain."

When they walked in the door, Harriet was waiting, her arms curiously empty without the baby. After a while, one got so used to the children clinging to her that one noticed their absence even more acutely.

"Is John all right?" Nicholas demanded, going to his wife and taking her hands.

She wiped her brow wearily with the back of her hand. "Dr. Gates is with him now. Good day, Margaret . . . May," she added absently, before noticing her husband's spattered coat. When she did, her eyes widened in alarm. "Nicholas, what happened?"

"Something that's never happened to me before, my dear. Someone threw a tomato at me."

Harriet's hand flew to her mouth. "Nicholas!"

He smiled reassuringly. "It's all right, my dear. How can I complain of a rotten vegetable when our Lord suffered the agonies of crucifixion? No, I welcome these tests of my faith."

Harriet didn't look as though she welcomed such tests, but the sound of footsteps on the stairs made them all look up to see Dr. Gates descending, his face calm and satisfied.

"How is he?" Harriet demanded, her worn face not daring to show a glimmer of hope.

"I think he'll be fine," the doctor replied, wiping his hands in a towel. "He's sleeping peacefully, and I think his stomach won't trouble him again."

Harriet sighed in relief. "Thank God! If you'll excuse me, I'll make some tea." She dragged herself off toward the direction of the kitchen.

"Thank you for saving my son," Nicholas said, shaking Dr. Gates's hand. "It's selfish of me to say this, but I'm humble and grateful the Lord didn't take him to Him this time."

"So am I, Nicholas," Dr. Gates said, "so am I."

"Now, if you'll excuse me as well, while I go change . . ." And Nicholas left the three of them alone.

Mrs. Fitzgerald sniffed the air. "What Chinese concoction did you use on the child, Chad?"

He looked sheepish as he ran his hand through his thinning hair. "I never could fool you, Margaret. Herbs, if you must know, burned next to John's stomach." The doctor shook his head. "I came to China to bring the miracles of modern medicine to a supposedly backward people, and sometimes they teach me a thing or two."

"You have an open mind, Chad," May said. "I admire you for that."

He seemed touched as he thanked her. Then he added, "By the way, I released Alexander Wolders this morning."

"Is he better?"

Dr. Gates shrugged. "I think he should have stayed for

another week, but he said he had someone who could take care of him, so I had no other choice."

Then Harriet returned bearing a tray filled with cups and a teapot, and they all sat down to tea, after giving thanks for John's recovery and his father's escape.

"I'm worried," Chad said later that evening, when the three of them had returned to the House of the Black Dragon and were dining.

"What about?" Mrs. Fitzgerald asked.

He ran his fingers through his hair. "The attack on Nicholas and on May a few days ago."

May chose some green grapes from the fruit bowl. "Alexander Wolders and I happened to be in the wrong place at the right time. Our attackers were rebelling against their mandarin, not the foreign devils."

"But the Chinese did attack Nicholas today, and I've heard from some medical colleagues in the north that some missions there were attacked last week."

Mrs. Fitzgerald stirred and her jades tinkled. "Do you think we're in danger, Chad?"

He shrugged as he sat back in his chair. "Margaret, I honestly don't know. But the signs are there. Perhaps you should be ready to leave on a moment's notice, and go to Shanghai to stay with your friends."

"Leave?" she snorted. "Never."

"Margaret, Margaret . . . " he said with a shake of his head.

"Chad, I only left Paoting once, and that was before I knew you, during the famine of 'seventy-eight. I'll die here, and that's the way I want it."

May looked from one to the other. "You two are upsetting me with all this talk of dying in China. I, for one, will be eager to leave in the wink of an eye."

The doctor studied May for the longest time. Finally, he said, "China hasn't gotten into your blood yet, has it?"

"No, and it never will."

"You mean there's nothing that could induce you to stay?"

"Nothing."

"And no one?"

"No one," May answered with great finality. "Not even Mother."

"I see."

"Speaking of staying . . . " Mrs. Fitzgerald said. "I don't think you should ride back to the hospital tonight, Chad."

"Are you inviting me to stay, Margaret?" His voice had an intimate, teasing quality May had never heard the man use before, and she sat up in surprise.

"Yes, I am," her mother replied. "I'll have one of the servants prepare a room."

May could see her company was no longer desired, so she stifled a yawn. "It's been an exciting day. I think I'll retire."

After good nights were said, May rose and crossed the room. Before leaving, she glanced back over her shoulder to see her mother and the doctor leaning toward each other, their heads almost touching, and thoughts of China, or leaving, forgotten.

May awoke to darkness, her senses sharp and alert. Something had pulled her straight out of a deep sleep, some noise, some animal foraging, perhaps. She sat up and listened, but she heard nothing.

Just when she was about to lie back down, she heard the unmistakable crunch of gravel below her room. Someone was walking in the garden.

It was too late for Han or Lien to be about, for they went home to their families at the end of the day. Perhaps it was Dinah, returning home late from nursing Wolders outside Chad's hospital somewhere.

May scowled, rose, and padded silently in bare feet to the balcony. She could see the stars twinkling like diamonds on blue velvet, and she glanced around the courtyard, so silent and eerie in the moonlight.

Then she heard it again, that scraping sound like soft footsteps on hard gravel.

She tensed and listened.

Then she heard her mother's voice, low and secretive,

but audible, below her. "Come quickly, before we awaken someone. You mustn't be seen."

This was followed by hurried footsteps, then silence so still, May wondered if she had imagined the entire scene.

She smiled to herself as she suddenly realized whom her mother had met in the courtyard. So she had been right about Margaret Fitzgerald and the doctor after all.

She turned, entered her room, and went back to sleep.

CHAPTER SEVEN

The next morning, May was startled to find only Dr. Gates downstairs at breakfast, so, after greeting him and seating herself, she asked, "Where is mother?"

"I don't know," he replied with a smile. "Tea?"

"Yes, please." May peered under all the dishes until she came to the fried eggs Cook prepared especially for her. Out of the corner of her eye, she glimpsed Dinah passing by in a soft swish of silk, so she called out, "Dinah, where is my mother this morning?"

Dinah stopped, all honey and politeness, her dark eyes bright with laughter. "Our mother has not yet risen. I don't think she feels well, so I am taking her tea."

"Strange," May murmured, frowning. "She seemed well enough last night."

"Perhaps I should examine her before I leave," Dr. Gates said. "Several villages have come down with a strange fever I've never seen before, and it's better to be safe than sorry."

May shot him a surprised look, and blurted out, "But weren't you two together last night?" Then she turned scarlet. "Oh, I'm sorry. I didn't mean—"

The doctor also blushed, cleared his throat, and looked away. "Quite all right, my dear."

With a puzzled frown, the doctor excused himself, rose, and went to find Margaret, while May watched him, equally perplexed. If her mother hadn't been with Chad last night, who had she met secretly in the courtyard? "You mustn't be seen," Mrs. Fitzgerald had warned. May pushed her plate of food away, suddenly not hungry, as the feeling of uneasiness gripped her once again.

She pressed her fingers to her temples and tried to dismiss last night from her thoughts, but like uninvited guests at a party, they refused to be ignored.

Dinah reappeared and asked, "Is something troubling you, eldest sister?" Her smile was solicitous, but May sensed the ever-present laughter behind her eyes.

"No, Dinah," she snapped. "Nothing is wrong."

Dinah inclined her head and left.

I shouldn't let her irritate me so, May told herself, with a sigh, and looked up as Chad entered the room.

"There's nothing wrong with your mother," he said. "But she's puttering around that storeroom of hers like a woman possessed. Doesn't look like she's had a wink of sleep, either."

May felt her spirits plummet. "When Mother gets some new items in, she often loses herself in her work. She'll stay up half the night, trying to decide who to sell to and for what price."

Chad smiled. "She's a remarkable woman, your mother. I know China would never be the same for me without her."

May looked up at him. "I think there are many people who feel the same way."

"Well," he said, "I must be getting on my way. Several patients of mine are expecting babies today, and I have been asked—no, commanded—to examine one of Mandarin Ki's concubines, so I really must be going, however reluctantly. Thank you for your hospitality, and tell your mother I'll be seeing her soon."

"I will." May rose and walked him to the door, then went to find her mother.

She found her in the crowded upstairs storeroom, rummaging through box after box, as though desperately looking for something.

"Aren't you going to eat any breakfast?" May asked gently from the doorway.

Mrs. Fitzgerald jumped, and her head jerked up. "No, I'm not hungry. Food is the least of my concerns."

Her hair straggled down her shoulders in untidy strands, and May was surprised to see dark circles beneath her mother's eyes. Her face looked haggard and drawn, and her mouth pulled into a hard line.

"Chad had to go back to the hospital," May said.

"Will you please leave me alone? Can't you see I'm busy?"

May refused to be offended or leave. "At eight o'clock in the morning?"

"You know I work day and night. Now, if you'll just go . . ."

May was silent for a moment, then she said, "What are you afraid of, mother?"

"Not a thing," Mrs. Fitzgerald replied without so much as a pause.

But May noticed how her mother's back stiffened ever so slightly, and she wondered if she spoke the truth.

"Are you sure?"

Margaret whirled around, bristling like a hedgehog. "By the sword of Lu Tung-pin! I already said there was nothing wrong, so will you stop annoying me?"

May gave up and wordlessly turned to go.

"Send Dinah to me," her mother called after her with the urgency of an opium addict demanding his pipe.

"Yes, your majesty," May murmured, trotting off down the stairs. When she found Dinah, hunched over her desk and practicing calligraphy, she relayed her mother's message, then went back to her own room, wondering for the thousandth time why she ever had come back to China.

Several weeks later, May was faced with an empty afternoon, and she decided to stroll among the many shops that lined the streets of the marketplace. Perhaps her browsing and poking would be fruitful and yield a puzzle box or toy monkey for Willie, and a pretty glass-bead necklace for her to wear. The thought cheered her as she attached a string of coins to her belt and set out on foot for the city.

No sooner did she get inside the gates when a familiar voice said, "Lady Jade want to buy slave?"

May stopped and stared at the tall thin figure lounging in the alleyway. "Alex!" she exclaimed in surprise.

She just stood there a moment, blushing and uncertain, as he regarded her with that enfuriating smile. Then she decided she was pleased to see him after all, so she smiled back and bowed.

When he winced, she asked, "*Are* you all right?" He did look thinner and paler and not quite well enough to be out of Dr. Gates's care.

"I'm a little sore," he admitted, "but I'll live."

"You're sure you're all right?"

Wolders nodded, his eyes filled with amusement. "Your concern is both touching and bewildering, considering you never once came to visit me in the hospital, while I was lying at death's door. Not very devoted, are you?"

May stepped back and stared at the ground, embarrassed. "I was angry with you," she admitted. "And besides, I understood Dinah Quo was a very capable nurse."

"So that's it," he said with a smile. Suddenly, he became all seriousness once again. "Do you have anything to report?" he asked, carefully watching her face.

May thought of last night and debated whether she should tell him the truth, but her face betrayed her at once, taking the matter out of her hands.

"Something has happened," Wolders said softly.

Her reply was too hasty. "No, nothing."

His eyes narrowed. "You're a terrible liar, May. Your face is as transparent as glass."

"I'm telling you the truth. Nothing happened."

Wolders took her chin in his fingers and tilted her head so she had to look into those cold, calculating eyes. "I don't believe you."

She jerked away from his touch. "Believe what you wish. It's of no consequence to me."

"It will be easier for your mother in the long run if you

tell me the truth," he said, tightening the thumbscrews.

May was silent for a moment, then surrendered. "Oh, all right. I overheard my mother talking to someone last night." And she told him what they said.

"You heard her mention no names?"

She nodded belligerently.

"Did you see what this person looked like? Was he Oriental?"

"It was dark, and they were standing beneath the balcony. None of the merchants ever come in the evening. At first I thought it was Dr. Gates and Mother meeting for an assignation, but I later learned they were not together."

Wolders smacked the side of the building with the flat of his hand. "This could be what I've been waiting for. I know it's Win-Lin. It's got to be."

"Why don't you just ask my mother?"

He gave her a skeptical look. "You think she would tell me the truth?"

"Probably not." May was gripped by unreasoning fear. "What are you going to do?" she demanded, putting a hand on his arm.

"You needn't look like the world is about to end. I promised no harm would come to your mother, and I'm a man of my word."

"What will you do now?"

"Get back on Win-Lin's trail. I know he's here in Paoting, but for how long is anyone's guess." Then he patted her shoulder and turned to go.

"Alex," May called after him. When he stopped and turned around, a questioning look on his face, she said, "I'm glad you're all right. I sincerely mean that."

He looked surprised at first, then saluted her and entered the crowd, towering above the Chinese like a solitary cattail among swamp grasses.

May went trudging back home, any enthusiasm stifled by a strong feeling of dread that sat knotted in her chest and would not go away.

Two days passed before it occurred to May that Dinah was missing. At first she thought they had just been bypassing each other, but, after a search of the house proved fruitless, she began to wonder. Dinah's lute stood mute on its stand in the corner of the parlor, and her calligraphy brushes were all clean and put away brush end up in their jade holder. The house was completely cleansed of her presence, as though someone had swept each room clean.

"That's odd," May muttered to herself and went to find her mother, who turned up in the storeroom once again, cataloging her latest acquisitions.

"Good morning, Mother," May greeted her.

"Good morning, May-Ling," she replied absently, without looking up, her pen clenched between her teeth.

"Where's Dinah? I haven't seen her for the last two days."

"Don't tell me you miss her." Now she did look up, her eyes devoid of expression, as she took the pen from her mouth. "Your sudden concern is odd, considering the fact that you don't particularly like her."

"I haven't seen her, and I was just wondering where she was, that's all." May couldn't resist asking, "Has your pretty slave run away?"

Her mother's look was frigid. "That was uncalled for."

May looked at her feet, but did not apologize.

"I've sent her away for a while," was her mother's explanation.

"Might I ask why?"

"With so much animosity toward her, Dinah wasn't very happy here. She begged me to let her go away, so peace could once again be restored to our house. So I agreed to let her go for a few weeks."

May felt her temper skyrocket. "Oh, no, Mother, I'll not take the blame for this. I have been doing my best to get along with Dinah, and, while we can never be friends, we were living quite peacefully with one another. So her accusation that I have been hostile to her is quite untrue."

Mrs. Fitzgerald crossed her arms and glared up at her daughter. "You've been resentful of Dinah ever since you came here."

"I'm sorry. No matter how hard I try, I can't warm to her. Lord, I've tried, but we're like oil and water."

"Dinah says she has tried to make herself more likable to you, but you refuse to bend or even offer her a crumb of kindness."

"Is that what she told you?"

Mrs. Fitzgerald nodded slowly. "The poor girl was so upset that she had failed to make you like her."

"Why, that conniving little witch!"

"Conniving witch! I'll have you know it's Dinah who feeds the beggar woman sitting outside our gates. The woman went blind doing fine embroidery, and, if it weren't for that 'conniving witch,' she'd probably starve."

May just whirled on her heel and stormed out of the room, her face burning as though she had been struck. She hurried to her room, stripped off her robe, and slipped into her ch'ang-fu and trousers. She had to get out of this house and talk to someone before she exploded. But who? The Hammonds? No, she really didn't feel comfortable with them, and Nicholas would probably deliver her a sermon on the Christian virtue of charity. Dr. Gates was too far away and too busy, and Alex was off somewhere chasing the elusive Win-Lin.

That left Weng Ta-Chung. Of course. Just the thought of his serene presence was like a soothing balm to her tumultuous emotions, and May felt better.

When she passed her mother on the stairs, the two women didn't so much as glance at each other, but went their separate ways in stony silence.

As May left the house and melted into the crowd, she automatically slipped her hands up the sleeves of her ch'ang-fu. Head bowed, she wondered why she stayed here, suffering her mother's caustic tongue and overbearing manner. Perhaps now was the time for her to swallow her pride and ask her mother for money to go back to England, although what she'd do when she got there was anyone's guess. It was July now. She could be in England for Christmas . . .

Her last Christmas had been spent with Nigel's family, buried deep in the snowbound Surrey countryside, surrounded by relatives and lavish gifts. But her real holiday came a week later with Robin, one stolen afternoon, bright and precious as the solitary star on Robin's scrawny little tree. They had spent the afternoon curled up in his brass bed, while black and brown snowbirds pecked for food on the icy window ledge outside. When she had returned to Nigel late in the afternoon, he'd asked how she had enjoyed the play.

How effortless it had become by then to look him in the eye and lie.

May stopped in the middle of the street, suddenly dazed, as one who has just come out of a dream. People jostled her, and one man swore when she didn't move out of his way fast enough.

Robin, she cried silently, the pain of loss stabbing her afresh. There was no one to turn to anymore, no place to run.

She glanced around and realized she had walked right by Weng's street, so she turned and retraced her steps. When she came to the jade carver's house, she was surprised to find a crowd gathered outside the entrance. Puzzled, May joined them and listened.

"Why is everyone gathered here?" she heard a man ask, craning his neck to see over the tops of heads.

"The police were here just a few minutes ago," another man replied.

May felt herself go cold.

A woman with a squalling infant in her arms said, "There's been a murder here."

"That is true. The jade carver's mother was killed."

"Do they know who killed her?"

"Her own grandson."

Exclamations of shock rippled through the crowd, until someone said, "That's not true. I saw them take away the jade carver himself."

At those words, May hurled herself forward, pushing people aside in her frenzy to reach the door. Then she flung herself against it, beating at it with her fists and screaming until it opened and a pair of hands pulled her inside the dark foyer.

She faced T'ai, Weng's son and the only member of his family to be really civil to her. He was a faithful replica of his father, except he was shorter and more muscular, with slightly protruding ears and slanted eyes that seldom seemed to blink, a most disconcerting feature. His expression was also more shrewd and worldly than serene, and May suspected he was more suited to the political world of officialdom than the spiritual, contemplative life of his father.

May bowed and greeted him. "T'ai-Lung. I am pleased to see you once again, jade carver's son. I hope your house prospers and all are well within its walls."

His voice was soft as he replied, "I greet you with much gladness after your long absence. May-Ling Fitzgerald."

"Only son," May said eagerly. "What has happened here? Is what the crowd says true?"

The young man bowed his head. "My esteemed mother told me the police awoke her this morning. They found venerable grandmother dead in her chamber and esteemed father bending over her with a knife in his hand."

May could only stare at him in horror. When she found her tongue, she said, "But there must have been some explanation."

T'ai shook his head. "The police led him away without letting anyone speak to him. I just arrived myself and was on my way to the jail to learn what I can."

"Enough!" a hoarse voice commanded from the doorway, and May looked up to see Weng's virago of a wife descend on them like a malicious Chinese devil. She made no attempt to hide her animosity now. "Our family's bad joss is no concern of yours, *fank-wei.*"

May's chin rose a stubborn notch. "We have always been friends of the jade carver and his family."

"You try to disarm us by wearing our clothes and speaking our tongue, but you are still bad joss. I told my husband the barbarians would bring shame on our house one day, but he refused to listen." Her eyes narrowed even further. "Do you know the penalty for murdering a parent, barbarian?"

May barely whispered the words, *"Ling che."*

Ah Sin nodded, her eyes filling with tears that hardened them into obsidian. "My husband will be cut into a thousand pieces that will never come together in the afterlife."

"But there will be a trial . . . they will have to prove

Weng killed his mother, and anyone who knows him knows he would never commit such a horrible crime."

T'ai's voice was flat and resigned, as he said, "The police found him with the dagger in his hand. They could have executed him immediately for such a crime."

"But he must be given a fair trial!" May wailed.

"His fate is sealed," Ah Sin said. "If we bribe the executioner, perhaps he will put opium in my husband's food before he dies, so he will not feel each stroke of the sword."

"Or perhaps he'll plunge the dagger into his heart first, so he will not suffer," T'ai added, his voice unsteady.

"Something will be done," May said, whirling around.

"You can do nothing, barbarian! Nothing!" Ah Sin's voice was a raucous caw that pursued May into the street.

May ran like she was running for her life, weaving through clusters of people, dodging carts and palanquins that lumbered across her path, and leaping like a steeplechaser over baskets that seemed to spring out of the ground. Her breath was coming in painful gasps that burned her lungs as she flew down the narrow streets. Occasionally her voice would bark out a warning or a curse at some pedestrian who had the misfortune to wander in front of her.

May rounded a corner, and the House of the Black Dragon loomed just ahead. She flung herself through the gate screaming, "Mother!"

Suddenly, Han and Lien appeared to stare curiously, while the jingling of jade heralded her mother's approach.

"By the sword of Lu Tung-pin! What on earth is wrong?" She shooed the servants away and pulled May into the parlor.

"Weng is going to die," she babbled. "The police . . . killed his mother . . . *ling che.*"

Mrs. Fitzgerald grasped May by the shoulders and shook her. "You're not making any sense. Control yourself."

May gulped in air until her knees stopped trembling and her thoughts were more coherent. "I went to Weng's house to visit him. His wife and son told me . . . told me that Weng is accused of killing his own mother." And she told her mother the entire story as related by T'ai.

Mrs. Fitzgerald fingered her pendant nervously, her face growing progressively bleaker as May's story rapidly unfolded.

When she finished, her mother didn't say a word.

"Mother, we've got to *do* something."

Mrs. Fitzgerald stalked around the room, her brow furrowed in concentration. "The situation looks hopeless, May-Ling."

"I know, mother, I know."

"If we were in England, he might have a chance at a fair trial, but in China, justice is a capricious thing. Men have been executed on the mere suspicion of committing a crime."

"Perhaps we can bribe the jailer to let us see him," May suggested.

"That's a possibility." Margaret was deep in thought for a moment. "We may even bribe the jailer into letting him escape."

May's eyes lit up with hope. "Do you really think so?"

"We'll just have to take many taels of silver, that's all, many taels of silver."

Mrs. Fitzgerald moved quickly and returned with two sacks ladened with silver. "We must be careful not to tip our hand too early. And we'd better take Mr. Yee with us. We mustn't offend the jailer with our femaleness."

They moved with great urgency, walking in quick, short steps to Mr. Yee's house.

"Mother," May said, "I wonder who did kill Weng's mother—and why."

Mrs. Fitzgerald looked at her. "If we knew the answer to that, the jade carver would be a free man." She shook her head. "Weng Ta-Chung, I can't believe it . . . your father's old friend."

"Please don't talk as though he were already dead."

Margaret Fitzgerald just looked at her daughter.

May had never seen a prison before, but she recalled tales her father had told about the crowded, foul-smelling places, where maggots infested wrists and ankles scraped raw by heavy iron manacles. She thought of the gentle jade carver in such a place, and her eyes filled with tears of anger and frustration.

When the women had their audience with the jailer, they let Mr. Yee do the talking, while they stayed inconspicuously in the background. May watched as the jailer shook his head repeatedly.

Mr. Yee, who had three wives and always looked harried, came back with bad news. "He will not let you see him, missie."

"Go offer him more silver," Mrs. Fitzgerald said firmly, turning the man around and giving him a little push.

Again the two conferred, and again Mr. Yee returned with bad news. "Although he regrets having to refuse such a generous offer, he cannot allow the English missies to see his prisoner, because Mandarin Ki has forbidden it, under pain of torture and death."

"Ah, that explains it," Mrs. Fitzgerald said. "Well, let's be on our way. We're not going to make any progress here."

May balked. "Please, mother. Offer him more silver . . . offer him the *moon* if you have to, but we must talk to Weng."

Her mother dug her fingers into her arm. "There is nothing more we can do. The man will not be bribed, and that's the end of the matter. Now, come quietly like a good girl before we all join Weng."

Subdued, May followed her mother and Mr. Yee out of the prison, and the three of them started back. After the comprador parted and went back to his three wives, the Fitzgerald women found their way back to the House of the Black Dragon. May's spirits were as black as the mythical beast itself, and she couldn't keep the tears bottled up any longer.

"Oh, stop sniveling!" her mother snapped. "I'm trying to think."

"What's there to think about? Weng's going to die for a crime he didn't commit."

"There's something odd here." Mrs. Fitzgerald's eyes narrowed as she toyed with her pendant, and she looked even more Chinese than ever. "The jailer said the mandarin had

LADY JADE

given orders that no one should see Weng. I wonder why he's taken such a personal interest in this case. Has Weng ever offended the mandarin, do you know?"

May shrugged. "Not that I know of. Wait! The mandarin wanted him to carve a lion out of a chunk of white and red jade, but Weng couldn't see a lion in the stone and was going to carve something else instead. Do you think that could be the cause?"

"A piece of jade?" Mrs. Fitzgerald scoffed. Then she grew thoughtful. "What we perceive as insignificant may be of the utmost importance to the mandarin. Yes, it's possible."

"Well, what are we going to do?" May was very nearly at her wit's end.

"We're going to seek an audience with Mandarin Ki and plead for Weng's life," her mother said. "Your calligraphy is better than mine, so you will write to him."

May spent the next two hours before Dinah's desk, painstakingly writing the Chinese characters to her mother's dictation, informing the mandarin that the two English-women of the House of the Black Dragon were requesting an audience with him, concerning the fate of the jade carver. When the scroll was completed and dried, May rerolled and tied it. Mrs. Fitzgerald summoned one of the servants, gave him enough silver for bribes and more for his "squeeze," then sent him on his way.

Then they waited.

The boy returned three hours later, triumphant. The scroll had been delivered to one of the mandarin's high court-iers who had promised to deliver it into the mandarin's hands personally—after relieving the boy of most of his silver.

"Now all we have to do is wait," Mrs. Fitzgerald said.

Their reply came the following day, after May had spent a sleepless night tormented by the thought that the man who had been like a father to her was caged like an animal.

"And they call us barbarians," was her last thought as the moon waned in preparation for the sunrise, and she fell asleep at last.

She awoke with a jolt to find her mother bending over her. "What is it?"

"The mandarin will grant us an audience tomorrow afternoon at two o'clock."

"A whole day?" May wailed, rubbing the sleep from her eyes. She thought of Weng in his cell again, and shivered.

"Let's be thankful we got an audience at all, shall we? Now, why don't you get some more sleep? You look like you could use it. Then we can ride out to the hospital to discuss this situation with Chad. Perhaps he can put this fiasco into its proper perspective."

"Yes, Mother, I think that's a good idea," May said, rolling onto her side and burying her head in the pillow.

Mrs. Fitzgerald patted her on the shoulder and left the room.

May knew her mother suggested seeing Dr. Gates only because it would keep her mind occupied, and she was touched by her mother's concern and thoughtfulness, which she had seen precious little of since coming to Paoting.

But May found herself wanting to talk to Alex, not Dr. Gates, and the thought surprised her. She could picture him as he listened, his tall frame lounging in the doorway, his blue eyes narrowed in speculation.

She shook her head, disgusted with herself. "I must be mad to want to trust the man who would destroy my mother," she muttered, quite mad. And she fell asleep again, against her will.

"Dr. Gates, do you know where Alexander Wolders is?" May asked him when she and her mother rode out to the hospital later in the day.

The doctor shook his head. "I haven't the remotest notion, May. After I patched him up and he healed, he thanked me and disappeared. I haven't seen him since."

"I need to speak to him," she said, "so if you happen to see him . . ."

"I'll tell him you're looking for him." Dr. Gates ran his hand through his hair. He had just delivered two babies, extracted a tooth, and stitched a gash, but his enthusiasm and energy were undiminished. "So, Margaret. Tell me about this audience you're supposed to have with Mandarin Ki."

Mrs. Fitzgerald sipped her tea. "I don't know Mandarin Ki at all. He's new in Paoting. I used to know his predecessor quite well, until he was transferred. A most enlightened man. What do you know about Ki, Chad?"

The doctor's homely face grew thoughtful. "I'd be careful of him. I don't think he's receptive to our barbarian ways. I know I get no cooperation from him as far as the hospital is concerned, and I plead with him monthly for money. I think he rather enjoys watching me beg. Of course, he doesn't forbid his people from coming here, but he won't lend any financial support, either, and he has no scruples about summoning me day or night when one of his concubines is ill."

"Wonderful," May muttered, her hopes plummeting.

"I think you should be careful," he advised again.

Mrs. Fitzgerald said, "How do you suggest we handle our interview, then?"

"First of all, dress English, if you can. He might take offense at your trying to look Chinese?"

Margaret wrinkled her nose in distaste. "I suppose I could wear that gauze dress I bought in Shanghai."

Dr. Gates glared at her. "And I wouldn't try to intimidate him either, Margaret. Don't overpower the man, or threaten him."

"Oh, Chad . . ." she scoffed. "Credit me with some common sense."

"I credit you with an uncommon amount of sense, but I know you. You're bound to let your tongue run away with you. Now is not the time to say what's on your mind."

"I was never a diplomat, Chad."

"I know. Then let May do the talking."

May watched them both. "A great deal depends on this audience—Weng Ta-Chung's life."

The doctor looked across at her, sitting with her head propped up against her hand and looking pale and dejected. "Don't worry, my dear, everything will turn out all right."

But May was far from convinced, so she said, "I'm going outside," rose, and left the room.

Dr. Gates found her sitting under a tree, watching two young girls tossing a ball to each other to amuse themselves while their mother or father was inside the hospital. May didn't look up, but she sensed the doctor's presence there, because she said, "Why do I feel so alone?"

"This is a lonely country," he replied, seating himself next to her. "I've felt it myself. There are millions of people here. They seem to be everywhere, these puzzling Orientals, and yet we foreigners are truly alone. Your mother, and you, too, May, whether or not you realize it, are unique." His eyes took on a dreamy, faraway look. "I remember the women of my youth, spirited things waiting to have their courage tested. But I doubt if even they could survive China. I even asked one of them to join me, and she had the good sense to refuse."

"Good sense?" May questioned gently.

He nodded. "Oh, I couldn't blame her. It was asking too much . . . too much."

May smiled. "I'm glad you're here, Chad Gates. And, if Mother had a lick of sense, she'd marry you tomorrow."

He chuckled. "I couldn't agree with you more." Then he grew serious again. "Never think you're alone, May, because you're not."

"I'll try to remember that," she said, wondering where Alex Wolders could be.

The following day, at their midday meal, Mrs. Fitzgerald said, "I think we should take a gift to Mandarin Ki—not an obvious bribe, you understand—but a gift."

"What did you have in mind?"

"This," she replied, handing May a box.

Inside was a white jade plaque engraved with the twelve signs of the zodiac.

May was so overcome, she could only shake her head speechlessly.

"Well," her mother demanded, "what do you think?"

"Oh, mother, not your wedding gift from father."

"The gift must overwhelm him, and this is the grandest item I possess."

"You would do this for Weng?"

"As I've always said, a life is worth more than an object, no matter how beautiful or valuable," Margaret said in exasperation.

Then the two women got dressed, entered their palanquins, and in the blink of an eye were being set down at the entrance to Mandarin Ki's yamen, where his official duties were performed.

"Courage," Mrs. Fitzgerald whispered, squeezing May's hand as they walked up the steps with the others seeking an audience today.

Once inside, they were ushered into a splendid chamber to the reverberation of gongs and much bowing of minor officials and supplicants, who hovered around the mandarin seated on a dais.

May took one look at Mandarin Ki, and her heart turned to lead. If she was expecting another T'chuan, she was deeply disappointed. This mandarin was soft, and his waist would never tolerate the brutal cinching of a belt. His fingernails were long, curved, and protected by jade shields, so his servants probably had to dress him every morning, and, where T'chuan was hearty and vigorous, Ki was almost torpid. May's overriding impression was one of decadence and decay. She could easily imagine this man taxing his people to the point of starvation or personally attending a prisoner's interrogation and execution. One look at his eyes, filled with hatred, and May shivered.

Among the many officials that filled the noisy crowded room, one courtier seemed to enjoy a most favored status, for he was at the mandarin's elbow, whispering in his ear. The beak-nosed courtier reminded May of a parrot perched on a pirate's shoulder, but this parrot, she suspected, was close-mouthed and ingratiating.

Suddenly he picked them out of the crowd, snapped his fingers, and motioned for them to approach the dais. May felt her knees grow weak, but she did as she was told, letting her mother make the first move. She and her mother bowed from the waist, but did not kowtow.

"You may speak," Parrot Man said.

"Your excellency," Mrs. Fitzgerald began in Chinese. "This insignificant woman thanks you a thousand times for granting us an audience. As a token of our esteem, we bring you a gift, unworthy as it may be of your greatness." And she handed the zodiac plaque to Parrot Man, who transported it to the mandarin.

His eyes lit up as they rested on it, but he dismissed it with a wave of his hand. "Truly insignificant," he said, "but worthy of one of my concubines."

"We have come to plead for the life of a prisoner," Mrs. Fitzgerald began, and a hush fell over the room.

"Which prisoner?" Parrot Man screeched.

"The jade carver, Weng Ta-Chung."

"Ah, I am afraid that is quite impossible," the mandarin said.

"True, he is accused of killing his mother."

"The most heinous of crimes," Ki replied.

"He would never kill his mother," May spoke up, her voice shattering the silence.

"And who is this insignificant woman?" the mandarin demanded. "She speaks without permission."

"She is my daughter, May-Ling, and you must forgive her rude behavior and impetuous tongue," Margaret said.

"So I see." His eyes wandered over her flaming hair and down her tall, straight figure, causing May to flinch. "And you dare dispute the fact that my police found the jade carver with the knife in his hand?"

"I have known the jade carver all my life, and I know he would never kill his mother," May said flatly.

"My men saw him with their own eyes."

"Do you see the magician's serpent when it is nothing but an illusion?" May challenged, ignoring her mother's abrupt motion to be silent.

The mandarin's eyes narrowed into dark slits, as his parrot leaned forward and whispered something into his ear, and May's heart sank with the realization that she had no doubt overstepped her bounds.

"What would you have me do?" the mandarin demanded.

"Spare the jade carver," Mrs. Fitzgerald replied.

"But, even if he did not kill his mother, he is still my enemy."

This announcement caused May and her mother to exchange startled looks. "How is that, your eminence?"

The mandarin said, "It has come to my attention that Weng Ta-Chung is a member of a brotherhood dedicated to overthrowing the Manchu dynasty. Therefore, he is against me, and I cannot allow him to live."

Mrs. Fitzgerald turned pale. "There must be some dreadful mistake."

"There is no mistake."

Mandarin Ki and his courtiers stared at the two Englishwomen as intently as chess players, waiting for the next move.

"Then there is nothing more for us to say," Mrs. Fitzgerald said dismally, squaring her shoulders and preparing to leave.

Suddenly, Parrot Man leaned over and whispered in his master's ear. They carried on a long conversation, with quick glances at May, who strained to catch any snatches of conversation, without success.

Finally, Ki said, "Perhaps there is something that can be done for the jade carver. Perhaps we can strike a bargain, as you barbarians say."

"What sort of bargain?" Margaret regarded them with suspicion.

"I cannot grant the jade carver his life," the mandarin said. "That would be comparable to letting a viper live in my house. But I can guarantee him a merciful death."

"What do you wish in exchange?"

The mandarin's eyes lit up and he stared straight at May. "I am attracted to your daughter."

May felt herself grow white, while her mother started, like one caught off balance.

"You want my daughter's life in exchange for the jade carver's?" She glowered at them both. "I cannot permit it."

Ki smiled, showing all his teeth. "I would not be so barbaric as to take the life of one so beautiful. She will join my other concubines. A barbarian woman would be . . . a novelty."

Mrs. Fitzgerald shook her head and planted her feet firmly on the ground, girding herself for battle, as though she would fight them all barehanded. "I cannot give you my daughter, even for the life of the jade carver."

The mandarin's eyes grew hard and hostile, and he and his courtier had a hurried conference once again. When they finished, he was smiling.

"Twelve cycles of the moon, then. If your daughter agrees to become my concubine for that time, the jade carver will be granted a painless death. He will be dead before his sentence is carried out. That is the best I can do for a traitor."

May felt three pairs of eyes fasten on her, one calculating, one predatory, and the other frightened. She realized she was expected to say something, but her throat closed and no sound came out.

Twelve cycles of the moon. One year.

Finally, she squeaked, "I . . . I must have time to think."

"I expect your answer within seven days," Mandarin Ki said and dismissed them with a wave of his hand.

The women bowed, then turned to go. May's knees wobbled and would barely support her as she and her mother walked out of the chamber followed silently by Parrot Man. When the doors closed, the courtier stopped them.

"You insignificant women realize that the mandarin has bestowed a great honor on your house. The noblest families from throughout the province send him their most beautiful and talented daughters." He looked May over as though she were a prize horse. "Although you are not small and dainty, you might please my master."

Anger contorted Mrs. Fitzgerald's face, and for a moment, May feared her mother would strike the courtier. But she said nothing.

"I realize the honor," May told him. "I will consider the mandarin's offer carefully."

"Consider very carefully," he warned. "The mandarin could easily see that you both join the jade carver." And he whirled on his heel in a swish of his robes, as he padded off to provide further counsel for his master.

"Let's go home," May said dully. "I have to think."

"Think!" her mother exclaimed. "What is there to think about? You're going to join Dinah as fast as you can. You can't even be thinking of such a proposition, May!"

"Please, mother, we'll talk about this later."

She thought of the mandarin's jade-shielded fingernails and his corpulent body, and she wondered what it would be like to share his bed. One year of hell, stretching into an eternity, just so Weng Ta-Chung would die quickly. May felt like she was drowning.

CHAPTER
EIGHT

S he knew what she had to do without even thinking twice about it.

Her mother, however, was strangely silent on the subject of the mandarin's proposal, and May thought this odd, for Margaret Fitzgerald was never one to hold her tongue, having always been forthright. When May tried to broach the subject, her mother interrupted her immediately, muttering excuses and bustling off to Paoting or the hospital, not returning until late at night, and disappearing before May rose in the morning. Her mother was obviously trying to avoid her at a time when May needed support and counsel more than ever, and this hurt her deeply.

On the morning of the third day, May confronted her mother as she sat on the k'ang, waiting for Han to serve her breakfast. Mrs. Fitzgerald looked like a black dragon herself this morning, wearing an inky robe that made a dramatic foil for the carved malachite necklace resting on her chest. There was a dark, fierce look to her mother's face that May knew all too well.

"We have to talk, mother," she said.

Mrs. Fitzgerald gave an impatient wave of her hand. "Not now, May-Ling. Tonight."

"I've decided to accept Mandarin Ki's offer."

She showed no surprise. "We'll discuss it tonight," was

all she would say. Then Han and Lien appeared, quickly ending all conversation. "Ah, this looks delicious," Margaret said, uncovering several dishes. "Won't you join me for breakfast?"

"Only if you'll listen to what I have to say."

"I really don't have the time. I'm to meet Mr. Yee in twenty minutes to look at some jade pieces. Would you care to accompany us? I would appreciate your expertise."

May felt like screaming, "No, mother, I have more important things to think about." And she whirled on her heel to leave. But her mother's voice stopped her at the door.

"Wait, May-Ling!"

She turned, a mutinous expression on her face.

"I know you're thinking that I don't care what happens to you," her mother began as she filled her rice bowl. "But, despite what you may think, I do care about you. I promise we shall discuss this tonight."

May sighed. "I suppose I'll just have to wait."

"I would appreciate it. I do have my reasons," she added.

May suddenly thought of something. "I don't want Dr. Gates to know until . . . I'm gone. Or the Hammonds."

"They should be told."

"No. I don't wish them to know."

"As you wish," was her mother's curt reply as she returned to her breakfast.

Dismissed, May went out to the courtyard, to be alone with her thoughts.

She spent the afternoon sitting cross-legged by the dragon-eye tree, unmindful of the hot sun beating down on her bare head or the whistling of the temple pigeons as they flew home to roost.

Her thoughts were mostly of the jade carver, locked away in a crowded, infested prison, unable to see the sun or feel the cool jade beneath his fingertips. In a sense, they were both condemned, but May suspected Weng was accepting his fate with more stoicism than she could muster.

She smiled ruefully to herself, and she began to view her year with Ki as retribution for the deaths of Nigel and Robin, weighing so heavily on her conscience.

May pressed her fingertips to her temples to ease the pressure building there and wondered where Alex Wolders was at this moment.

"Well, my friend," she mused bitterly. "You will not need me after all to help you find Ming-sheng's brother."

A feeling of hope caused her to sit up straight. Perhaps Alex could find some way of freeing Weng and saving her from Mandarin Ki. Then she slumped down in dejection as she realized it was a wild, improbable scheme, one better suited to a Ouida novel than reality. About the only course of action Alex could take would be to prevent her from going to the mandarin, and her gift of a peaceful death to Weng would be forfeit.

May sighed, closed her eyes, and counted the hours until her mother came home.

Later that day, when May walked into the parlor, she was startled to find Dr. Gates and the Hammonds with her mother, and all of them were staring at her with bleak faces. She turned on her mother in a rage. "You told them, after I told you not to."

"I thought the situation called for a conference," Mrs. Fitzgerald said dryly.

"My dear May," Dr. Gates said, his sad eyes bereft. "How could you mean to keep this from us?"

"Yes," chimed in Nicholas, rising to take her hands, his eyes shining with fervor. "We are the only Europeans in Pao-ting, and we must stand together against the heathen Chinese."

May found his comfort oddly cold, and she pulled away. "But there is nothing to discuss. I am going to go to Mandarin Ki for twelve cycles of the moon."

"An entire year?" Harriet gasped in shock. "May, you can't mean that! You would become a Chinaman's . . ." She could not finish the sentence.

May felt her face turn scarlet. "Yes, Harriet, yes I would, to save a friend."

Now it was Harriet's turn to blush, and she looked away in embarrassment.

"May," her mother said, placing a hand on her arm. "I wonder if you've thought this through."

"Mother, I have thought of nothing else day and night for the past six days."

"But have you considered what is going to happen to you once your year is up—if Mandarin Ki even lets you go free?" She paused so her words could penetrate, before continuing. "What white man will ever want you, once he hears that you've been a Chinaman's concubine? Unless, of course, you run back to England, or perhaps France, where they may be much more tolerant of such matters. But you know yourself how one's past tends to catch up with one."

May stared at her, arms folded in hostility. "I'm beyond feeling like damaged goods, mother. I was treated horridly in England, and I survived quite nicely, thank you." Then she added, "Just what do you propose I do?"

"Go to Tientsin and stay with the Liptons," was her mother's reply. "If you're not here, Mandarin Ki cannot take you."

"But you're overlooking the most important point," May wailed, "and that is Weng Ta-Chung. It's not a simple matter of the mandarin desiring me—I could escape that very easily by going to Tientsin as you suggest. The real issue is Weng's fate. If I don't submit to the mandarin, Weng will be cut to pieces while he's still alive, for a crime he didn't commit."

Harriet murmured, "Oh, God!" and covered her face with her hands, while Dr. Gates shook his head sadly and looked away.

"But May," Nicholas pointed out, with his charming smile, "he's only a heathen Chinese. He knows his life is worthless to his own people."

She gave him a look of such contempt, his steadfast gaze faltered. "Weng is my friend. He is like a father to me, and that explains how I can feel this way about a 'heathen Chinese.'"

"Oh, May," Mrs. Fitzgerald said gently, "I know how much Weng means to you, but—" She spread her arms in despair. "There's nothing you can do for him now."

"But there is!" she cried. "Aren't any of you listening to me? I can give him a peaceful death."

They all stared at her in silence.

"And what if I did go to Tientsin?" she continued through tears of frustration. "Do you think Mandarin Ki would let any of you escape his wrath? Have any of you noticed the policeman standing outside our gate? I doubt if he's talking to the beggar woman about embroidery."

"I've seen him," her mother said. "I don't underestimate Ki for an instant. But we are British subjects, and he will not risk our government's wrath."

"Don't be so naive, mother," May snapped. "The House of the Black Dragon could burn down tomorrow with you in it. Ki would claim it was an accident, and no one would be the wiser."

"Oh, I have a few aces up my sleeve yet," Margaret replied ominously.

Suddenly, May felt the walls beginning to close in on her, and, if she didn't leave the room, she knew that together, everyone present would break down her resistance with their persistence and cool logic. And it was imperative for her to win this battle.

"Oh, what's the use?" she muttered, throwing up her hands and escaping to the peacefulness of the courtyard.

She had been sitting there in semidarkness for ten minutes, crying softly into her handkerchief, when one of the shadows moved and came toward her.

"Well, Chad," she said, addressing the figure. "Where do you stand? In shock and disgust with the Hammonds, or determined to do what's best for me, like Mother?"

"We all care about you," he replied heavily, sitting next to her on the stone bench and taking her hands in his. "I would give my life to keep you from Mandarin Ki, May, but—God help me—I can understand why you must do this."

"Thank you. That's a great comfort to me. I just wish Mother would understand, that's all."

She could see him run his hand through his hair. "Oh, I think she does, May. Your mother is so used to controlling every situation, she thinks she can prevent the inevitable. Unfortunately, none of us can win in this instance. Ki is too powerful, and there are seemingly no alternatives."

"You know, Chad, all my life has been spent running away. I ran from China to England because I thought life would be better there. And then, after . . . after what happened to my husband—as I'm sure Mother has told you—instead of facing up to it, weathering it, I came running back to China." She looked at him through the darkness. "I'm tired of being a coward, Chad. I'm tired of running."

He leaned over and kissed her on the forehead. "You call yourself a coward, but I think you underestimate yourself. I see a courageous woman, and Weng must be proud to count you as a friend."

"Courageous?" May scoffed. "I'm frightened out of my wits."

She wondered if she should tell him about the Sons of the Celestial Phoenix, then decided against it. Weng had told her to tell no one, and Chad was better left ignorant of such matters for his own safety and well-being. What he didn't know, he couldn't reveal, even under torture.

May swung her legs, kicking up pebbles with her toes. "There is one thing I find most puzzling. Why does Ki desire me? I'm ugly, by Chinese aesthetics, so I would think someone like Dinah would be more to his taste."

"Ah, but you are English and represent all he despises," the doctor pointed out.

"So he will take even greater pleasure in abusing me," May said quietly, all hope extinguished, like a candle flame pinched between the fingers.

Dr. Gates sighed deeply. "I'm afraid so, May."

A familiar robed figure appeared silhouetted against the lantern-lit doorway. "Chad? May? Are you out there?" Mrs. Fitzgerald called. When Chad answered her, she added, "Come inside. It's getting late, and dinner will be getting cold."

When Friday dawned bright and clear to the cooing of the mourning dove outside her window, May said to herself, I am a Fitzgerald. I will not bend or break. I will endure this somehow. She bathed and put on her white dress and took one last look at her room. The sight of her pale, drawn face in the bronze mirror over the bed was nearly her undoing, but she took a deep breath, turned, and went to join her mother downstairs.

If May expected her mother to be disturbed by her departure, she was shocked to find Margaret Fitzgerald as unflappable as ever, as though her daughter were leaving for the marketplace, not a mandarin's harem.

"Aren't you taking anything with you?" were her mother's only words.

She shook her head. "Let Ki clothe me. I shall be his responsibility soon."

Mrs. Fitzgerald's brows rose. "Are you sure you want to go through with this? It's not too late to change your mind." She was strangely quiet, then said, almost to herself, "A year is an awfully long time."

"It's past discussion."

"Yes, I suppose it is. Well, let's be on our way, shall we? We mustn't keep the mandarin waiting."

She rose in a tinkling of jade, and May followed at her heels as they wound their way through the house, so curiously silent.

"Where are the servants?" May asked.

"Oh, I gave them the day off," she replied.

"Do they know I won't be coming back for a while?"

"I believe they've heard rumors to that effect."

May felt a sudden rush of helplessness course through her. "Doesn't anything move you? Can't you say something?"

Her mother whirled around, dark eyes snapping. "You made your choice. I've no tears for you."

May was so stunned at her mother's callousness that all she could do was just stand there, gaping.

Slow footsteps shuffling through the door caused May to look up to see Dr. Gates walk around the red lacquered screen and enter the foyer.

She smiled a bittersweet smile. "Have you come to say good-bye to me, Chad?"

His homely face was devoid of expression as he put down his Gladstone bag and reached into it. "In a manner of speaking, May."

Out of the corner of her eye, May saw a figure leap out of the shadows, but, before she could move out of its way, her arms were pinioned to her sides, and she was pulled into a prisoning embrace.

She knew who it was by the feel of his hard body, even before the familiar, lazy voice said, "I'm afraid you're not going anywhere, Mrs. Monckton."

"Alex! Let me go this instant." And she tried to kick his shins, without success.

When she saw Dr. Gates open a brown glass bottle and pour some of its contents onto a cloth, she turned into a thrashing wildcat, but she was as helpless as a rag doll against Alex's strength.

"Don't fight us, May," he whispered in her ear as Chad advanced on her and pressed the cloth to her face, covering her nose and mouth with professional efficiency.

"Judas!" was her muffled cry as the numbing, sweetish scent of chloroform quickly worked its way to her brain and imprisoned her senses one by one.

Gradually slipping down into the darkness, her last conscious image was of her mother looking across at her, a look of satisfaction on her face. And May's last conscious thought was that she would never see Weng again.

May awoke to a windowless darkness so absolute there was not even a hint of light anywhere, not a crack under a door, or through a board. She was lying on her back, her body thoughtfully pillowed by silk cushions. She looked around as she sat up, but no sickness assailed her, for Dr. Gates had been very considerate and precise in his administration of the anesthetic. She shook her head to clear it, rose slightly, wobbled, and reached out, feeling her way around like a blind person. Using her hands as eyes, she traversed the length of the room and determined it was about twelve feet long and very narrow, possibly a mere eight feet in width. May sniffed the air, surprised to find it was not stale, as she would have expected, but fresh and sweet.

Her palms brushed cool, rough brick, broken by smooth

wood that must have been a door of some sort. But it was fitted so precisely, it was virtually seamless.

"Please let me out!" she cried, pounding on the door. "Mother, do you hear me? You must let me out this instant."

The sound of her voice bounced off the walls and echoed back at her, but never left the room.

May sunk down to the floor, as she realized she was a prisoner in a closed room somewhere, but where had they taken her? The hospital? She couldn't recall any such room there. The mission? That was a possibility, but she wondered how they had ever transported her limp and lifeless body past the policeman.

She held her head in her hands in dejection, as she realized too late they had all conspired to keep her from going to the mandarin. She should have known better than to trust her mother to accept the situation so passively.

"You fool," she chided herself dismally.

May perked up at the sound of a key turning in a lock, and, when the door swung open, a flash of light blinded her momentarily. Before she could rush toward freedom, the door shut, and, when she looked up, Alexander Wolders was towering there, a lamp in his hand that cast angry, ominous shadows across his face, hollowing out his cheeks.

He looked like Satan himself, with dark brows furrowed over icy eyes. "Why didn't you tell me, May? Why didn't you trust me to help you?" he said, furious.

She rose and stood up to him, her wrath matching his. "I didn't tell you because you did precisely what I was afraid you'd do. You're going to make sure I don't keep my part of the bargain, aren't you?"

He nodded wordlessly.

"No, please." She clutched his arm. "You must let me out of here. I've got to go to the mandarin, or Weng will suffer so much before he's finally allowed to die. So much."

"I'm sorry, May."

She stared at his implacable face. "Alex, please. I'm begging you to help me get out of here."

"No. We're going to keep you here until it's over. Then

Ki will no longer have any hold over you, and we'll be able to get you to safety." He was silent for a moment, then added, "I'll not see you degraded, May."

"You've no right to tell me what to do."

He looked down at her, his brows raised incredulously. "Do you actually think the jade carver would want you to go to Ki, even to spare him?"

"He would never have to know. His jailer would put opium in his food, and then the executioner would send the sword through his heart first instead of . . . of at the end."

"You're so trusting and innocent," he said with a shake of his head. "Do you really think Ki would keep his word?"

"I would watch the opium being administered," she said, "just to be sure."

"But then Weng would know of the bargain you had made. If I were he, that would hurt me more than the executioner's sword."

May never felt more helpless in her life, except perhaps when she realized Robin was lost to her forever. "Where are you holding me?" she demanded.

"You'll learn that all in good time."

She rubbed her arms. "Am I to be fed bread and water, then?"

"Your every need will be met," he reassured her wryly. "But I wouldn't try to escape, if I were you, unless you want to spend the next few days tied hand and foot in the corner there. Or the doctor would have to drug you again, and we would regret that."

She swore at him and struck out, but he was too quick for her and grasped her wrists, rending her powerless.

"Don't, May. It's futile."

"You're despicable."

"Call me any name you wish, if it will make you feel better, but I will not let you out. The sooner you accept it, the sooner we shall all be able to come through this crisis." He smiled. "Now, I'm going to leave you the lamp, and I'll be back later with food and blankets, although I don't think you'll be cold tonight."

She heard the key turn in the lock, and the door opened a crack. "Are you ready, Alex?" her mother's voice called.

"Yes," he replied, dropping May's wrists.

Before he could back out the door, May slipped past him as quick as an otter, but her visions of freedom were cut off as Alex's long arms reached out, grasped her, and flung her away with all his strength. May went staggering back and crashed against the wall so hard it knocked the breath out of her.

"I'm sorry I had to do that," she heard him say as he disappeared out the door, "but I did warn you."

He did return some hours later with food and blankets as he had promised, but this time he found a subdued May sitting in a corner, her knees drawn up to her chin. Tendrils of hair hung down around cheeks wet with tears, and she didn't move when he entered, or even look up at him.

"I've brought you something to eat."

"I'm not hungry."

"Perhaps not now, but maybe later."

"What time is it?" she sniffed, still refusing to look at him.

"Seven o'clock."

"So Mandarin Ki knows I'm not coming."

Wolders set the covered bowls on the floor, while keeping an eye on her. "This morning, your distraught mother went to the yamen claiming her daughter had disappeared. She accused the mandarin of spiriting you away against your will before you even had a chance to consider his offer. She threatened to contact the British consulate in Tientsin if you weren't returned immediately. Ki, of course, swore he hasn't seen you."

May finally looked up at him. Her voice was bitter and cutting as she said, "You two have thought of everything, haven't you?"

He smiled slightly. "We have. Now Ki's men are scouring the countryside for you, and he assumes you've run away without your mother's knowledge, so he doesn't suspect her."

"I hate you."

"If you think I'm enjoying any of this, you're mistaken, but I'd rather have you hating me than being the brunt of Ki's bizarre tastes." Alex's voice changed, as he said, "He enjoys cruelty, May. I could tell you stories about what he does to his women . . ."

She squeezed her eyes shut and said nothing. Finally, she heard him say, "Good night. I'll see you in the morning."

And he left her.

Alex returned three times the next day to bring her food and listen to her implore him to set her free. But each time, he listened attentively to her arguments, and then he shook his head and left. May tried anger, tears, gentle pleading, but nothing moved him.

As she became more desperate, she decided there was only one course of action open to her.

When she awoke on the third day of her imprisonment, stiff and sore in spite of the cushions, her eyes spied the covered porcelain bowls that had contained her supper from the previous evening. She jumped to her feet, went over to them, then deliberately dashed one to the floor. She heard the fragile tinkle of breaking glass, and, when she gingerly ran her finger over its jagged edge, she smiled in satisfaction, for she had a weapon at last, crude as it was.

She waited for him.

The instant May heard the familiar scraping of the key in the lock, she felt her way along the wall until she came to the door, then flattened herself next to it. She could feel her heart flutter wildly as she gripped the smooth weapon in her fingers.

The door opened, and a shaft of light split the darkness, revealing Wolders's familiar silhouette.

May slashed out, heard his cry of surprise mingled with pain, as the lamp went flying from his hands, and she tried to push past him to the door. But he blocked her way, the door slid shut, and the telltale click, which was like a death knell, foiled her.

"Let me out!" she screamed, beating the door with her fists.

Light abruptly flooded the prison as Wolders struck a match and lit the lamp.

"You're an inept assassin, May," he said. "I would have expected more efficiency from you, such as aiming for my throat."

Her face to the wall, she murmured, "I didn't want to kill you."

"I know."

She turned to see his arm hanging limp at his side, his shirtsleeve cut and bloodstained. "It's just a scratch," he assured her, seeing the look of fear on her face. "But, really, this must stop. You're not going to defeat us, you know. Even if you managed to get past me, you'd still have Chad and your mother to contend with. And they would stop you."

She sighed as she sagged against the wall, feeling utterly conquered. "All right. I won't fight you anymore."

"Good," he said gently. "But you still have to stay here."

"Until Weng is executed?"

"I'm sorry."

"Has he . . . ?"

Wolders shook his head. "But he has confessed to murdering his mother."

May heard a great rushing in her ears, and the walls seemed to shiver and dissolve. Wolders was at her side in an instant, his good arm supporting her around the waist. "You're sick. I'll get Dr. Gates."

She leaned against him for an instant, now grateful for his strength. "I'll be all right." Then she said, "Ki had him tortured. That's the only way Weng could be made to confess to something he didn't do."

"Don't think about it."

"Is that supposed to comfort me?"

He sighed. "It will soon be all over."

She leaned her head on his shoulder and closed her eyes. "Oh, God, I wish it were."

* * *

Her wish was answered later that afternoon. When Wolders appeared, his face was so white and grave May knew what had happened before he even said a word.

"No, Alex," she whimpered as she went to him.

"I'm sorry, May." He held her in his arms, her face pressed against his shoulder until her sobs finally subsided. Then he tilted her face up and kissed her, gently at first, and then with greater urgency, leaving May giddy and light-headed. When she made an attempt to move away, his arm dropped down to her waist to hold her fast.

"No, Alex, please," she whispered, stiffening in panic as his questing fingers found her hairpins and pulled them out one by one until her hair hung loose and free about her shoulders.

"It's like a curtain of fire," he murmured in wonder as he stroked its silkiness.

"So help me, I'll scream."

"I don't think so, Lady Jade," he replied, his lips wandering down her wet cheeks to rest in the hollow of her throat.

Then he made short work of the buttons down the front of her dress, and when she felt his hand against her bare breast, coaxing the familiar fire to rise and consume her, she knew she was lost, for she hadn't been loved in so long.

"Damn you," May muttered in surrender, as she drew him to her and found his mouth again.

Later, he said he was sorry.

May lifted her head from his shoulder and whispered, "Why?"

"For not asking your permission first. Not very gentlemanly of me."

She traced a long scar on his chest with her fingertip. His body was lean and hard and scarred in several places—a warrior's body—but his loving had been skillful and unexpectedly gentle.

She leaned over and kissed him. "Don't concern yourself."

"You love like an Oriental courtesan, Mrs. Monckton."

Her eyes had a sly look as she murmured, "Am I better than Java?"

He smiled lazily. "Demon. You're better than anyone."

She laughed and hid her burning face behind a curtain of hair.

"How could your husband ever let you slip away? He must have been a fool."

When she told him, in a trembling voice, why she and Nigel had grown apart, the pity on Alex's face was almost too much for her to bear.

"You see?" she bitterly accused, drawing away from him, to sit up and hug her knees. "Even you would react in the same way."

He reached out and pulled her back. "I am not Nigel. You would be more than enough for any man, May Monckton."

"For some men, a woman isn't enough. They need a son to inherit, to carry on their name."

"Then, they are fools," he said. Alex sat up and looked around. "We had better get dressed, as much as I hate to. You're not safe from Mandarin Ki yet."

When they emerged from the room, May's mouth dropped when she saw where she was.

"Why, this is my mother's room!" she sputtered, looking around at the k'ang, with its familiar silk bed curtains. "I never left the Black Dragon House."

She examined the hidden chamber carefully and discovered why she had never noticed it in all the years she had lived here. First of all, it was covered by a large, heavy tapestry, but, even when that was pulled back, all that was revealed was a brick wall. But May suspected the wall swung out to reveal the wooden door beneath it when a secret lever was pressed.

Alex said, "Your mother told me about it when she came to ask for my help restraining you. She didn't think she and the doctor could subdue you alone, and the servants couldn't know, because their tongues would surely wag and word would get back to Ki. It seems as though your father had this priest's hole—for want of a better term—built at the same time as the house. I think he originally stored treasures in it, but he thought he could use it to hide his family in case of an uprising."

"That sounds like Father," May said with a shake of her head. "I never knew."

A noise at the door made her look up, to see her mother and Dr. Gates standing there.

"I'll never forgive either of you for doing this to me," May said through pursed lips.

"Someday you will," her mother replied with easy confidence.

"We did it for you, May," Chad said, his gray eyes sad. "There was nothing that could be done for the jade carver. I'm so sorry."

"I must go to his funeral," May said, taking a deep breath to ward off the sudden tears.

"Out of the question," Alex said. "Ki thinks you're gone, but if you should be seen, he will know he has been duped, and we shall all be in grave danger."

"So, even that is to be denied me."

"I'm afraid so."

"Well," May said, "what are you going to do with me now?"

Her mother replied, "You're to go to the Liptons in Tientsin and stay with them for a while. You'll be close by, and I'll be able to visit you on my business trips there."

May gave her a skeptical look. "And how am I to get there?"

Alex bowed with a flourish. "At your service, as always. Here's what we have to do to elude the mandarin's police."

And he outlined the plan with the efficiency of a general planning a major battle.

That same morning, May, dressed in her mother's robes and wearing her mother's jades and a black wig quickly made for the occasion, went out to the gate to drop a few coins into the beggar woman's bowl and to be seen by the policeman still stationed across the street. He glanced at her, assumed her to be Margaret Fitzgerald, then concentrated on breaking up a fight between two boys.

When May went back into the house, she told them, "It worked. He wasn't even suspicious."

"Good," Alex said. "Now, get on the pony and Dr. Gates will accompany you to the eastern wall of the city. I'll be waiting with a cart."

He helped her to mount her mother's pony, and then she followed Chad through the gates, not bothering to look back at her mother or wave.

They rode through the suburbs unaccosted, and a half-hour later, there was Alex and the cart waiting for them as promised.

As May dismounted, Dr. Gates put his hand on her arm, his homely face remorseful. "I hope you didn't mean what you said back there, that you would never forgive me for my part in this deception."

She did not smile. "I'm still furious with you and Mother, Chad, but I know you were only considering my welfare."

"Thank you, May," he said, leaning over to kiss her on the cheek.

Without looking back, she climbed into the back of the cart, out of sight and shielded from curious eyes, while Alex took the reins and pointed the mule in the direction of Tientsin.

They arrived, hungry and exhausted, in that city just as darkness was about to swallow the sky. They went immediately to the Liptons, who were so startled to see them that Avery instantly broke into a stream of profanity. His wife, after chiding him for his blasphemy, urged everyone inside to the drawing room of their cottage, and, after May introduced Alex to the curious couple, she spent the next hour telling them why she was in Tientsin.

"Holy hell!" Avery bellowed. "What in Heaven's name is going on out there?"

"Avery, don't swear," Leticia admonished him, then rose

and said, "Supper should be ready any moment, and I'm sure our guests will want to retire after their long journey."

So they all sat down at the table, and May continued between bites of Leticia's hot, savory stew. What she didn't know, Alex supplied, and, when they finished, it was past eight o'clock, and May could hardly keep her eyes open. She excused herself and retired.

She thought she would fall asleep instantly, after the exhausting activities of the last few days, and the cart ride from Paoting to Tientsin, but she found her senses wide awake and alert. The cottage was hushed and still, so she rose and paced her room.

She had to think about Weng Ta-Chung now. No matter how she tried to put it out of her mind, images kept flashing through her brain in rapid succession—Weng being led to the square where morbid spectators clustered to watch his execution . . . the executioner's sword poised for the first cut . . .

"No!" May cried in anguish, closing her eyes, but the images kept coming unbidden.

She felt numb all over, as she sat on the edge of her bed and rocked back and forth, hugging her pillow and crying silently. Then she became very calm, and the images stopped.

At least Weng was now at peace, his suffering over.

And she had been saved from Mandarin Ki.

Finally, she sighed and slipped into bed, where she cried herself to sleep.

The next morning, Alex presented May with a startling proposal. "I don't think you should stay here in Tientsin. I think you should go back to the Wrights in Shanghai."

May stared at him as she picked at her breakfast. "Shanghai? Have you forgotten the reason I left? I doubt if the Wrights would welcome me with open arms."

"I think they will," he said. "That entire episode should have blown over by now. And besides, if they are as good friends of your mother as they claim to be, they won't turn you away."

May ignored his barb and shook her head. "I don't know. Mother wanted me to stay in Tientsin."

"I don't think that would be wise," Alex countered with his exasperating logic. "Tientsin is not that far from Paoting, and Ki has a long arm. What's to stop him from sending assassins here, should he find out how we duped him? Nothing. And your friends the Liptons would be especially vulnerable. No, May, I still think you should go to Shanghai."

"But I have to tell mother."

He shook his head. "I'll tell her when I return to Paoting."

"All right. I'll think about it."

She spent the entire day thinking about Shanghai and reluctantly decided that perhaps Alex was right. The last thing she wanted was her mother or the Liptons harmed by a vengeful Mandarin Ki. No, the further she removed herself from Paoting, the better off everyone would be. Why, she could even search for her former amah, Tzu-Lieh, there as well. And as for the Wrights, she would just have to trust her faith in them as friends to accept her back into their home once again.

The following day, while packing for her trip, May searched through her bag, but no welcoming hard leather binding offered resistance to her fingers. She had left Robin's book in Paoting. May bit her lip to keep the tears of consternation away. Now her last tie to the past was gone as well.

Finally, her bags were packed, Alex purchased her ticket, and by ten o'clock May was waving good-bye to Avery and Leticia and stepping into the rented carriage beside Alex.

She had guessed he would not be accompanying her to Shanghai, but she couldn't resist saying, "You're not going to Shanghai?"

"No, May, I'm not," he replied as they drew away from the Liptons' cottage and headed toward the docks.

She looked down at her hands folded demurely in her lap, feeling oddly disappointed. "Why not?"

"I still have work to do for T'chuan. A great deal of work."

"Well, it looks as though I needn't have worried about helping Ming-sheng," May said. "I'll be of no use to you alone in Shanghai."

Alex glanced across at her. "Who is to say Win-Lin isn't in Shanghai?"

May's eyes widened as she looked back at him. "I thought he was last seen around Paoting. That's why you wanted me to watch Mother."

"He was, but he doesn't seem to be there now, as far as I can tell. But Shanghai is the perfect place to sell stolen goods. You never know, he could even try to sell some to Nelson Wright or one of the other merchants." Alex got a faraway look in his eyes. "The man could be anywhere, he is so elusive and clever. Compounding the problem is that I really don't know what he looks like, except for a description Ming-sheng gave to me. I have the feeling he's got an accomplice, also, or even several." He was silent for the longest time, and May could almost hear him thinking about Win-Lin and what he would have to do to trap him. Without taking his eyes off the road, Alex said, "Take care of yourself in Shanghai, May. I know you're used to going by yourself where you please, but remember that Shanghai isn't Paoting. And, whatever you do, don't go into the Chinese city without a man to protect you."

"Are you worried about me, Alex?" she asked lightly.

He glanced over at her. "No. You're capable of taking care of yourself. But just don't take any foolish risks."

She laughed uneasily. "Whatever do I have to fear in Shanghai? I'll be staying with the Wrights."

"Fraulein Hummel was staying with her father."

May shuddered, and her smile died.

As the docks came into view, she said, "I'm worried about Mother and Chad. Do you think they will be safe from Mandarin Ki?"

"I'm sure they will. Your mother has convinced him she's ignorant of your whereabouts, and the doctor is popular with the people because he heals them. I don't think even Mandarin Ki would risk their wrath."

May placed her hand on his arm. "Alex, see that no harm comes to them, if you can."

His blue eyes held hers as he nodded.

In a matter of minutes, they were on the noisy, crowded dock, so like Shanghai, and May was getting ready to walk up the gangplank into a waiting ship.

Once again, the unknown loomed before her, as forbidding as the Rock of Gibraltar. Her comfortable world had been shattered, and she felt like she had just burned her last bridge behind her and was watching the smoke rise in the distance.

"I think you should go or the ship will leave without you," Alex reminded her when she hesitated, waiting until all had boarded.

Suddenly, May blurted out, "I don't want to go to Shanghai. I want to go with you."

If she had expected the pleasure to warm his cold blue eyes, she was to be disappointed, for he scowled and said, "Do you always offer yourself to men you barely know?"

She felt as though he had struck her. And then the initial hurt was replaced by anger so fierce she could feel its heat all the way up to her eyes.

"You self-righteous bastard," she said between clenched teeth. "It wasn't I who sought you out in my mother's house. And, if you'll recall, you just took what you wanted, as though I were some spoil of war. And, because I responded to you in the passion of the moment, you have the audacity to turn around and call me a—"

His hand shot out and iron fingers encircled her wrist. "I'm sorry, May, I didn't mean that the way it sounded."

She shook him off with a strength she didn't think she possessed. "Don't touch me. You're no better than Captain Forsythe after all."

Alex moved closer to her, seeming taller somehow, as he blocked the sun. "I can't let you go like this."

She clenched her hands into fists. "Will people never forget I was unfaithful to my husband?" She felt her eyes burn with tears, but she refused to cry in front of Alex.

177

When he spoke, he inclined his head, and his voice was low and soft. "I did not mean to imply that you were a woman of easy virtue, May. I meant it was a warning to beware of men like me, men you don't know."

"Oh, I see. Warning me off for my own good, are you?"

"Something like that."

"Men," she sputtered, moving away from him as though his nearness repulsed her. "You're all alike. I hate you, and I don't care if I never see you again."

And she turned on her heel and went striding up the gangplank like a queen.

Once on board, May went directly to her cabin to calm herself. A half-hour later, she went back out on deck, and when she looked back at the docks, she was startled to see Alex still standing there, a featureless figure from this distance, but Alex nonetheless.

CHAPTER NINE

When May arrived in Shanghai, feeling much like an orphan in her soiled dress, with her battered bag in hand, she stood on the dock for a moment, trying to decide whether to go to the Benton and Black godown or the company's business offices in the hong. She decided Nelson would probably be in his office rather than the warehouse itself, so she hailed a rickshaw passing by and instructed the driver to take her to the hong.

Everyone knew the Benton and Black hong. The multistoried building was located at the far end of the Bund, and every traveler to Shanghai passed it eventually. As May walked in the door, she was greeted by a din of voices, all belonging to people with something to sell and eager to talk to the taipan.

Tobias Abbott, as pale as she remembered, spied her immediately. "Why, Mrs. Monckton!" was all he said, his mouth agape.

May smiled and raised her voice so he could hear her. "Good day, Mr. Abbott. Is Nelson about? I'd like to see him, if he's not busy."

He nodded and motioned that she should follow him, ignoring the black looks of those passed over, as he led her on a winding course to Nelson's office. Nelson, seated at a huge polished oak desk, was busy scribbling his signature on a sheaf of papers and didn't so much as glance up.

"Abbott, I thought I made it perfectly clear that I did not want to be disturbed for any reason," he growled in his precise way.

"You mustn't blame Mr. Abbott," May said. "I asked to see you."

His head shot up. "May! What in the devil are you doing in Shanghai? You're supposed to be up north, with your mother." And he rose and came around the desk to take her hand.

"I'm in desperate need of your help," she said, suddenly afraid he might refuse her.

"Please. Sit down, and tell me what this is all about. Would you like tea, or something stronger?"

"Tea would be fine, thank you."

As Abbott disappeared in search of tea, Nelson stared at her, his pink face alight with curiosity. "I must say, you've given us quite a shock. There isn't trouble in Paoting, is there? Your mother is all right . . . "

"When I left, she was fine." And May told him what had happened, from Weng Ta-Chung's imprisonment to her own escape.

Nelson turned a deeper shade and snorted indignantly when she mentioned Mandarin Ki's proposition, but he made no further comment as he listened attentively to her story with his particular habit of looking down at her.

He shook his head when she finished. "I've warned Margaret time and time again something like this was bound to happen. She's lived among these people for too long, and she trusts them, when they're not really trustworthy."

Abbott returned with tea and offered to pour when he saw how unsteady May's hand was. Then he left.

"Mother's still there," May said, gratefully sipping the strong, sweet brew. "To tell you the truth, Uncle Nelson, I don't know if she's all right, or if Mandarin Ki has harmed her."

He dispelled her misgivings with a reassuring, "I doubt that. She's a British subject, and don't you think this Ki person doesn't know it. He wouldn't like his city divided up with concessions, like Tientsin, I'm sure. No, your mother is safe."

May took a deep breath to steady herself. "I have come to ask a favor of you and Emily, Uncle Nelson."

He put a halt to her words with an upraised hand. "You don't even have to ask, May. You're welcome to stay with us as long as you like."

She felt herself blushing, and she forced herself to look beyond Nelson's eyes to the bare wall behind his head. "After . . . after my last visit here and what happened, I wasn't so sure you—or Emily, for that matter—would want me in your home again. I feel rather like an albatross trailing a cloud of bad luck with me wherever I go."

For the first time in her life, May saw Nelson actually look embarrassed, he who was usually so cool and in command of himself. "Oh, I rather suspected that you and Margaret knew that we knew the real reason you left for Paoting so abruptly. That quick departure was all to save face, wasn't it?"

She nodded. "Mother and I didn't want to come between you and your wife."

He smiled, genuinely touched. "Yes, that is like Margaret to be concerned about others. Well, that unfortunate incident was months ago, and I can assure you the citizens of Shanghai have short memories. Besides, Captain Forsythe has been shipped off to India, so I'm sure we'll not be hearing from him for a long, long time."

"But I must earn my keep, Uncle Nelson," May said emphatically, broaching an idea she had on the steamer. "Perhaps I could help you at the godown, or help Emily in the house."

He chuckled fondly. "Dear May. Comprador Wu and Abbott have such absolute control of Benton and Black that I wonder sometimes if they even need me at all! And, as for Emily, she's even got a servant to wash her hands for her if she so desires. I'll not hear of you 'earning your keep,' as you put it. No, you are to be our guest once again, and we'll both be delighted to have you."

May thanked him, then added dubiously, "Will Emily

really welcome me, after . . . after the Captain Forsythe incident? I couldn't bear to have her angry with me, or cause her embarrassment."

Nelson leaned over and patted her hand. "Don't you worry about a thing, May. I'm going to take the rest of the afternoon off, and I'll take you to the villa myself. Emily will be delighted to see you again, and I know Willie will be beside himself."

May smiled across the desk at him, but deep inside she rather doubted that Emily would be as elated to see her as Nelson insisted. She just hoped Emily wouldn't make her stay too unpleasant.

In the garden, Emily was entertaining several ladies May recognized from the disastrous lawn party, and she rose and came forward as the carriage pulled up the drive and Nelson handed May down.

I never should have left Tientsin, May said to herself as Emily bore down on her with the resolve of a ship putting into port.

"Why, good heavens! It's May." Emily wore a bright smile that was actually warm and welcoming as she drew May to her and hugged her.

Nelson tapped his toe nervously. "Emmy, my love, May has had her share of excitement in Paoting and is looking forward to some rest. I've invited her to stay with us for as long as she wishes."

"Why, of course, Nelson, whatever you say."

Nelson snapped his fingers and Number Six boy scurried to his side. "You've had an exhausting journey, May. Why don't you go to your room and freshen up a bit, then Emily and I will be waiting for you in my study."

May thanked him, still stunned by Emily's unexpected welcome, and she followed Number Six boy into the cool house. She glanced back to see Nelson put his hand under his wife's elbow and start walking with her out to the verandah, away from prying eyes, where he could speak to her in private.

"Aunt May!" a familiar voice shrieked.

She turned around in time to see Willie come flying

down the stairs, his expressive face incredulous with delight. Just as he reached her, he pulled himself up short, as though she would disappear if he touched her, but, when May smiled and held out her arms to him, he fell into them readily.

"Aunt May, you've come back. The Chinese didn't cut off your head after all. I'm so glad."

"So am I, Willie," May said, tousling his dark curls.

He drew away from her, but still held her arms as he wriggled like an impatient puppy. "What was it like, where you lived? Did you eat bird's nest soup? Abbott was going to let me try some, but Mama said it was disgusting, and—"

"Master William!" a gray, censuring voice reproached him from the top of the stairs. "Such outbursts of emotion are hardly seemly in a young gentleman of your station."

And Miss St. John, as stiff and pinch-faced as ever, walked down the stairs with one hand on the bannister.

"Yes, Miss St. John," Willie muttered, hanging his head and stepping away from May.

May felt her old dislike for the woman flooding back. "There's nothing wrong about displaying honest emotion, Miss St. John."

The woman gave her a tight, patronizing smile. "I realize there are different schools of child-rearing, Mrs. Monckton. I am merely following Mr. Wright's express wishes concerning the deportment of his son." She extended an imperious hand to the boy. "Come, Master William. It's time for our nature walk."

She nodded briefly at May, and the child and his governess walked out the door.

May imagined that Miss St. John could make even the natural beauty of trees and shrubs gray and dull to anyone. She sighed and went up to her room, hoping that Emily's welcome had been sincere.

Twenty minutes later, after washing her face, resetting her hair, and slipping into a fresh dress, May felt sufficiently restored to go down to the study.

She took a deep breath to compose herself, knocked, and entered.

"May, you poor lamb!" Emily rushed over to her and

took her hand. "Nelson told me all about that wicked, wicked mandarin and what he wanted you to do." She shuddered delicately. "Thank heaven for your mother's presence of mind to do what she did."

May decided Emily could be spared the truth of that entire situation, so she just said, "I can't thank you enough for offering me refuge. I would have had nowhere else to go."

"You're welcome to stay with us for as long as you wish," she said generously, her brown eyes calm, and May wondered what had brought about this sudden change.

Suddenly, Emily blurted out, "My guests!," excused herself, and rushed out of the study.

May seated herself on the divan, where Alex had calmed her hysteria on that fateful afternoon when it looked as though her world were going to come to an end again. "Thank you, Uncle Nelson. I wasn't quite sure if Emily would be so welcoming to me."

He smiled a smile of pleasure at still another situation resolved to his liking. "I think you'll find that my wife has changed since you saw her last. Emmy's become more secure and confident, and she is beginning to assert herself as taitai." Then his face clouded. "But I'm worried about Margaret. You said she remained in Paoting? Why didn't she come with you?"

"She insisted there was no danger to herself, and she and Alexander Wolders concocted this scheme and—"

"Alexander Wolders?" he said sharply, his blond brows scowling. "What was he doing there?"

Caught off guard, May could only shrug. "I don't really know, Uncle Nelson," she lied. "He did once tell me he did a great many things for a fee, for anyone willing to pay."

Nelson gave a snort of derision. "If that doesn't sound like Wolders . . . "

"Mother enlisted his aid to get me away from Mandarin Ki. He helped me to escape from Paoting."

"Well, I'm glad he did something commendable for once in his life," he said, rising. Then he added, "Is there any way you can communicate with your mother?"

May hesitated, then replied, "By letter, I suppose, and pray she receives it."

Nelson looked down at her. "Don't worry, May. Margaret Fitzgerald can take care of herself." Then he said, "You're sure Wolders didn't say why he was in Paoting?"

"Positive. Why is it important for you to know?"

One corner of his mouth turned up in an enigmatic smile. "It's always important to know where a man like Alexander Wolders is at all times."

May stared at him. "Why, Uncle Nelson, whatever do you mean?"

He chuckled as he headed for the door. "Someday I'll tell you. And in the meantime, you are our guest. The house is yours . . . the servants are at your disposal. You may do whatever you like, or nothing at all, if you prefer."

Then he bid her good day and left.

Once back in her room, May discovered her clothes had been put away for her, and she had the entire afternoon stretching out before her. From the verandah, she could see Emily and her guests white as milkweed puffs against the green lawn, and, off in the distance, Willie on his "nature walk" being lectured to by Miss St. John on the merits of some nondescript shrubs at the far end of the property.

If she were his governess, she'd take him to the Chinese city, to a joss house and to a teahouse, where they'd sit sandwiched between the Chinese themselves, eating steamed dumplings and sipping tea. That was the type of "nature walk" Willie should have.

May smiled and shook her head. "Now you sound like your mother."

At that moment, she realized just how much she missed her mother, with her Chinese clothes, tinkling jades, and overbearing manner. She couldn't escape from this swinging of her emotions—one minute affection, then impatience—and May was worried about her. How she wished her mother had come to Shanghai with her.

And where was Alex, she wondered, back in Paoting by this time, or elsewhere, looking for Win-Lin?

Instantly, she chided herself for even wasting a fleeting thought on him. May felt her cheeks grow warm, as she recalled his humiliating last words to her on the Tientsin docks and how she hated him for spurning her.

True, she did not meet the rigorous moral standards of a society that decreed she keep up the pretense of a happy marriage when only the dry husk of one remained, leaving her to wilt in an emotional desert. But, by the same token, neither was she some wanton flitting from one man to the next. May had loved Robin. Surely that counted for something.

But for Alex to break down her defenses, then to cruelly condemn her for surrendering . . . The thought sparked her hatred and fanned it afresh.

May crossed her arms and walked over to the balcony, where she could look down at Shanghai. How could she have been so foolish to think he cared for her even a little? Men like Alexander Wolders regarded women as something to use, then discard.

As she leaned against the balustrade, she took a deep breath and let it out in a long, dismal sigh. Well, she would not make the same mistake twice.

Another matter that preyed on her mind was Nelson's cryptic statement about Alex: "It's important to know where a man like Alexander Wolders is at all times." And she still wondered why he had said it.

Then she went off in search of letter paper to let her mother know that she had arrived safely in Shanghai.

May spent her first week trying to put Paoting behind her, but it was no easy task and required her utmost concentration. But by the end of her fourth day back, her dreams were no longer haunted by Weng's death and Mandarin Ki, and she felt her heart begin to grow light once again.

If she had been worrying that she would not be accepted by Emily's tightly knit social circle, her fears were groundless, for Shanghai took its cue from Emily. She accepted May this time, therefore they would accept her also. How different the city seemed from her first visit, how open and warm, instead of hostile and cold.

Emily graciously took her under her wing and introduced May to the indolent life of the British taitai. They rose late every morning, enjoyed a leisurely breakfast, then spent the early afternoon making calls. The two women made sure they returned to the villa by three-thirty, when Nelson arrived from the hong, and amused themselves by playing croquet, taking tea, or reading before supper. Later in the evening, there were even more calls to make, or people returned their calls, filling the villa with light conversation and the scent of perfume and cigars.

It was after one such afternoon round of calls that May remarked to Emily, "You and Nelson seem to know everyone in Shanghai."

She nodded, as she sat back in the carriage and contemplated her vast social power. "It seems that way, doesn't it? We know the Bradburns and the Taylors, the Sweets and the Andersons." Emily rattled on more names and ended with, "Certainly we know everyone in the English community, especially other merchants. But then, all we Europeans stick together."

Her statement gave May an idea. "Emily," she began hopefully, "do you remember my amah, Tzu-Lieh?"

Emily brightened. "Tzu-Lieh. Of course I remember her. She used to accompany you and your mother here on visits. She was your maid, wasn't she?"

"Yes, and one of my mother's servants told me she was in Shanghai, and I was wondering if perhaps your friends might know where she is, seeing as how you know everyone in the city."

"Oh, I doubt if they would, May. It's been years since I've seen her. Why, I can't even remember what she looks like."

"You never know," May said, persisting. "It seems likely to me that she would seek work caring for children, since that's what she did best. And, since she speaks English so well, I should think an English family would be eager to hire her."

Emily was silent for a moment while she considered May's words. Finally, she said, "I suppose it wouldn't hurt to make inquiries, if you really want to find her."

"I do," May replied.

"All right, we'll start tomorrow."

And so the search began. Whenever Emily and May made their calls, Emily always asked if the lady of the house had hired an amah to care for their children. But their search proved futile, until they visited Mrs. Anna Cooper-Smith.

She was a childhood friend of Emily's who had married a junior bank clerk and accompanied him to China, where they lived in a small, nondescript house miles away from Bubbling Well Road, both in distance and social standing.

"Anna married for love," Emily whispered, as though that explained the cramped quarters and threadbare furniture.

Mrs. Cooper-Smith was a dark, pretty woman who, judging by her preoccupied stare and the unmistakable trace of alcohol on her breath, had not yet come to terms with her reduced circumstances.

May thought of Harriet Hammond and shook her head. She despaired of meeting still another bitterly disillusioned woman, but there seemed to be so many of them in China that she supposed it was unavoidable.

Mrs. Cooper-Smith nearly cried when she saw Emily and threw her arms about her in an embarrassing display of affection. "Oh, Emily . . . dear, dear friend of my childhood. How good of you to take the time to visit me. And you've brought a friend. I do so love company, and there's no one to talk to."

After introductions were made, and she invited them to sit in the parlor, she began talking in a faint voice that was always on the verge of dying. She talked about how much she hated China and how she wished she had never agreed to come out here. Emily gave May an apologetic glance, but listened intently, alternately sympathizing with and scolding her old friend.

"The only thing I have is my Rick," Mrs. Cooper-Smith murmured, staring out the window and tugging at her handkerchief. Then her eyes brightened. "Would you like to see him? He's the most beautiful, charming little baby." And before anyone could say a word, the woman was on her feet, calling, "Julie! Julie, where are you? Bring my precious Rick, will you?" Then she turned. "I just hired the most fabulous Chinese woman to nurse him. She really is a treasure, and she speaks English far better than I." Her face crumpled. "I do so hate speaking to these people and not having them understand me."

As soon as she heard the familiar patter of footsteps on the stairs, May was on her feet, her eyes wide in disbelief. "Chen Tzu-Lieh!" she cried, when her plump amah suddenly appeared, cradling a baby in her arms.

Tzu-Lieh stopped in her tracks the instant she spied May, and her mouth dropped. "Little Ah Ling. Can these old eyes be deceiving me?"

May rushed forward, engulfing baby and nurse in her arms, laughing and crying, while she hugged them both, speaking rapid Chinese. "Tzu-Lieh! I can't believe my eyes!" Then she held her at arm's length, relieved to find her amah as round and jolly as ever.

Tzu-Lieh was crying with joy as she touched May's cheek, murmuring, "My little May-Ling," over and over.

As Rick started wailing, May turned to Emily and Anna, who was watching her with a mixture of surprise and politeness. "Tzu-Lieh used to be my own nurse," May explained. "She was like a mother to me."

"Oh, she was here all the time!" Emily exclaimed. "Why didn't you tell me you hired a new nurse for the baby, Anna?"

"I just hired her last week." Then Anna turned to May. "You both must have so much to talk about, so why don't you go into the garden?" A bitter smile twisted her mouth. "Surprising a place like this has a garden, isn't it? But it's quite private there, and we won't disturb you."

May and Tzu-Lieh left Rick in his mother's care and went out into the garden, which was so small it could hold only five people comfortably. As they sat there, May found herself chattering away about her former life in England and was dismayed that her old amah did not share her enthusiasm and seemed somewhat reticent and distant, even when asked about her own life in the past seven years.

"Tzu-Lieh," May asked. "Is something wrong? You haven't heard a word I've said."

The amah touched her hand. "I will always love you, my

daughter, but I have a new child to care for now. We must both let go."

Tzu-Lieh was a fiercely loyal woman, and she had been loyal to the Fitzgeralds, earning her the nickname "Fierce Temple Lion" bestowed on her by Timmy Fitz. She always watched May with a guarded eye when she was a baby and later was always quick to dispense ancient words of wisdom to the headstrong girl on the threshold of womanhood. But now, May could see the amah had loyalties to a new family and child, and she felt absurdly jealous.

"I understand," she said sadly. "One can never recapture the years that fly by like birds going south."

The round, jolly face smiled back. "It pleases me that you have grown into a beautiful woman and that you remember your old amah. I am proud to have raised you as I would have raised my own. But my life is different now, and we have grown apart."

May swallowed over the lump in her throat. "Can I at least visit you then?"

"If my mistress allows it."

As they rose and went back inside the house, May felt disappointed. She had expected Tzu-Lieh to bring back the past for her, but the Chinese woman was wisely looking toward her own future and wanted no part of the past.

As she and Emily went back to the villa, May wondered if she even should try to see her amah again.

At the end of her third week in Shanghai, May thought she was going to go out of her mind, and this is what she told Nelson one morning at breakfast.

"Uncle Nelson, I'm bored. I need something to do."

He looked at her across the table, his eyes widening slightly in surprise. "Why, I would have thought Emmy would be keeping you hopping, doing all the things women usually do."

May dismissed them with a wave of her hand. "Oh, visiting is fine for Emily. She thrives on the social whirl. But I need something to *do*, Uncle Nelson, something constructive.

I'm tired of sitting on lawn chairs and discussing the heat and the races."

"Hmm," he murmured, sensing an upcoming tempest and wondering what he had to do to avert it. "Well, May, exactly what is it you would like to . . . er, *do?* You must realize, of course, that there is very little for a woman to do in Shanghai, other than what Emmy does."

May leaned forward, her elbows on the table and her eyes shining in excitement. "I want to go to work for Benton and Black, Uncle Nelson."

He choked and sputtered, his pink face turning mauve. "Work? Doing what?"

"In the godown, identifying art objects that come in."

"Between Wu and Abbott, I think we've got all the expertise we need. Wu brings me the objects, and Abbott is very knowledgeable. You know that."

"True, but even they needed my help interpreting the symbolism of the designs on the boulder carving. And I could do much to free the men for other work."

Nelson dabbed at his lips with his napkin in a graceful gesture. "The godown is no place for a woman, May. The men are a rough, rowdy lot. They like to spit and swear. Occasionally, a fight breaks out and someone gets hurt." He shook his head. "The men just wouldn't like working with a woman present. You'd be a most disturbing influence, my girl."

"Please reconsider. I will stay in the office and keep out of the men's way."

He was silent for a moment as he stopped to consider. Then he shook his head. "I'm sorry, May, it's out of the question. And I know Emmy would not approve, either."

May refused to resort to tears or blandishments to win him over. She took a deep breath and plunged on. "Try to see this situation from my point of view. It's been three weeks since I arrived in Shanghai, and Mother still hasn't answered my letter. I don't know what's happening in Paoting. For all I know, Mother could be locked away in that horrid jail awaiting execution, like Weng."

All he said was, "I sympathize with you, I really do."

May placed her hands on the table and leaned forward. "I resent your not taking me seriously, Uncle Nelson. I must have something of substance to do, or I shall go out of my mind."

"I promise I will think about it."

"My expertise could save your company from making costly mistakes," she pointed out.

He perked up at once, ever the astute businessman. "Yes, that is true. Sometimes it is nigh impossible for us to tell an original from a two-hundred-year-old copy."

"I can tell."

Nelson gave a sigh of surrender. "Well, I'll see what Abbott and Wu have to say about the idea, and, if they agree, we shall find something for you to do."

May inclined her head and thanked him.

"I'm not promising anything, mind you," he warned. "My comprador must agree."

When Nelson returned home that afternoon, May could tell by the grim expression on his face that the comprador did not agree.

"I'm sorry, May," Nelson said bluntly, ignoring her disappointed pout. "I'm afraid we don't think the godown is any place for a woman."

"I think you are all making too much of this," she insisted.

"It's in your best interests," was all Nelson said, before scurrying off to his study, his refuge from all women.

Undaunted, May tracked him down. "If I can't go to the godown, perhaps there are some pieces you could bring here for me to appraise."

He whirled around, half-exasperated and half-admiring. "You may not realize it, but you and your mother are very much alike. You both have that stubborn streak and that determined way of hammering away at a man until you get what you want."

May just smiled. "Well?"

He drummed his desk top with his fingertips. "Perhaps you're right. I could bring home some pieces for you."

"It would be a sort of proving ground for me," she said.

Nelson chuckled. "My dear May, I am well aware of your formidable knowledge, as well as your formidable charm. You have no need to prove anything to me. You are a Fitzgerald, after all. However, Wu and Abbott may need further convincing."

"But you are taipan," she sweetly pointed out.

"I may be taipan, but I also fancy myself a democratic despot, if there is such a thing."

"All I ask is a trial," she said, extending her hand. "Do we have a bargain then, Uncle Nelson?"

He looked at her hand, then dubiously shook it. "I have a feeling this is one bargain I'm going to regret making."

So, true to his word, Nelson began bringing home objects for May to appraise. Within a week, she revealed a supposed T'ang pony to be a later copy and urged Nelson to buy an ancient bronze incense burner being used as an ash tray by one of his ignorant English friends.

"What are you doing about larger items, like vases and such?" she inquired. "You can't very well bring those home to me."

Nelson's eyes narrowed, as he sipped his drink. "Why do I have an uneasy feeling that I'm about to be drawn and quartered?"

She gave him an exasperated look. "Well, if you want to transport vases from the godown to the villa and risk damaging them . . . Or, if you still insist on letting my knowledge go to waste . . . "

He laughed. "All right, May, out with it."

"I really do think I should work in the godown. Would your comprador really resent my presence there so much?"

Nelson set down his glass and folded his arms. "Wu travels much of the time, arranging deals for the company, so you wouldn't see much of him, I suppose. But, as I've said, when the junks come in, there are strange men milling about."

May recalled her first day in Shanghai and the sailors' catcalls as she went ashore.

"I would stay out of their way," she said.

He just sighed. "You're a damn fine-looking woman, May. You don't have to do anything to attract men."

She blushed, for she had never heard Nelson Wright speak this way before, and at the same time she knew his words to be true. She never invited attention, it just seemed to come unbidden when she least desired it.

"Just give me a chance, Uncle Nelson. I promise, if I cause any trouble with the men, I'll stop going to the godown and will stay home with Emily and try somehow to keep my sanity."

He was silent and reflective for the longest time. Finally, he relented. "All right. We'll start you tomorrow. But I'm going to hold you to your word. Any trouble with the men, and you'll have to stay at the villa."

May thanked him from the bottom of her heart, confident that everything would run as smoothly as she planned.

"You're going to do what?" Emily demanded, as she reclined on the divan, her hand poised somewhere between her mouth and a dish of sweet almond cakes.

"I'm going to work in the godown," May explained, "helping to appraise and catalog the pieces that come in."

"But why ever would you want to work, especially in this heat?" She fanned herself furiously, finding the punkah's quiet coolness inadequate. "Women working . . . how absurd! Why should a woman work when there's a man to provide everything she wants or needs?"

May wanted to say, because I am bored to the point of madness by your indolent life, but all she did was shrug apologetically and reply, "Oh, it's just living so long with my mother, I suppose. Her habits tend to grow on one."

Emily gave a little shake of her head. "And my husband agreed to this scheme of yours?"

"After much badgering on my part, I must confess."

"I have grave doubts about this, May, grave doubts."

May explained the terms of her arrangement with Uncle

Nelson, how she would have to give up working at the godown if there was any trouble whatsoever.

"That was wise of him," Emily commented. "When do
you start?"

"Tomorrow."

Emily looked disappointed. "What a shame. I was going
to visit Clara Dufresne tomorrow afternoon. You remember
her from the party, don't you, the French attaché's wife
whose daughter had to be sent back to a strict aunt in Paris
because she had taken to frequenting opium dens? Well, it
was a shocking scandal, and . . . "

May felt her attention start to drift like a boat cut loose
of its moorings, and, while Emily chattered on and on about
the wicked Mlle Dufresne, her thoughts were on tomorrow
and her first day at the godown.

The next morning, she rose and dressed while Emily was
still sleeping, and, after breakfasting with Nelson, joined him
in the carriage that would take them to the godown. When
they arrived, they found Tobias Abbott waiting for them, a
slightly rebellious expression on his pale face.

"I'm turning you over to Abbott," Nelson said. "He will
show you how business is conducted at Benton and Black."

And he left.

"This is highly irregular, Mrs. Monckton," Abbott said
stiffly, escorting her to the back office where she had first
interpreted and appraised the white-jade boulder carving.

"I know, Mr. Abbott," May said, "but, since my being
here is a fait accompli, shall we try to make the best of it? I
have no wish to make enemies of yourself and Comprador
Wu, or to somehow usurp your authority. I merely wish to
share my considerable knowledge, to make a contribution."
She turned her most appealing smile on him, for she knew she
must win over this shy, somber man, or she would lose her
one bid for sanity.

Strong emotion and frankness seemed to embarrass him,
for he cleared his throat and busied himself with some papers
on the desk. "Here is some paper and a pen." And he thrust
them at her, then hurried out before May could say a word.

She stared at them, sighed, and sat down, wondering when he would bring her an object to interpret.

Just when she was wishing she had joined Emily in her visit to Mlle Dufresne's mother, Abbott appeared at the door.

"A junk has arrived from Soochow with a load of lacquerware. Come and see."

May rose and eagerly followed him, her pulse racing in excitement, as she trailed after Abbott through the warehouse. The sight of a beautiful woman in the midst of this male bastion caused every man to stop and gape for a second as she passed. But the men seemed to accept her presence after the initial shock, and May breathed a sigh of relief.

A crate was already open, and Abbott went through it, tenderly lifting out each piece for May's inspection.

"I'm sure all of these pictures mean something, but I don't know what," he admitted.

May knelt right down on the floor by his side. "Yes, yes they do." And she proceeded to tell him just what the designs meant. Then she rose and said, "I must write this information down for Uncle Nelson."

By the time she had examined the six pieces of lacquerware, it was time to join Uncle Nelson for tiffin. Abbott escorted her back to the hong, and she and Nelson adjourned to the Shanghai club for their midday meal.

"So, how was your morning?" he asked across the table.

"Wonderful, just wonderful," May replied, beaming. "I've identified designs on several pieces of lacquerware for you."

He smiled, again giving her the impression that he was looking down at her from a great height. "Well, I must say, you're positively glowing, May. There's a sparkle in your eyes that I haven't seen in a long time."

"I feel useful, Uncle Nelson. Men have always been given the freedom and opportunity to bury themselves in their work, so why shouldn't women?"

"Work is so common, but beautiful women are not. They should be placed on a pedestal, to be admired, like a Ming vase or a T'ang jade."

Nigel had felt that way about her, and May had once

felt that way about herself, being content to bask in his accomplishments. But she was beginning to change since returning to China, and she realized for the first time that she needn't fear it.

May said, "As you said once, I guess I'm just a Fitzgerald after all."

"That would be the only explanation," Nelson said. "But, I'm sending you back to the villa now. You've had enough for one day, I think."

"But I've really just begun!" she protested.

He held up his hand. "No 'buts,' my dear. Tomorrow you can work your fingers to the bone if it makes you happy. Wu is due back from Hong Kong, and who knows what he'll bring."

Later that night, when the entire villa was silent and dark, May listened for the three light taps on her door.

When they came, she opened it to reveal Willie in his nightshirt, his cherubic face screwed up in anticipation. "Good evening, Aunt May," he said, bowing from the waist. "How was your first day at Papa's warehouse?"

"Quite exciting," she replied in a whisper. "But why don't I tell you out on the verandah, while we share our almond cakes?"

"Splendid!" he whispered back, tiptoeing across the room to the French doors.

As part of their clandestine ritual, Willie poked his head out, looked right, then left, and, when all was clear, he motioned May forward. She extinguished the lamp, plunging the room into darkness, then followed Willie out onto the verandah with two pillows and a linen napkin bulging with cookies.

They sat down, divided the spoils evenly between them, and commenced talking, being careful to whisper, for, although Willie's parents and the censuring Miss St. John had rooms on the other side of the villa, one never knew how far one's voice would carry on the night air. They had escaped the hawk eye of the governess, at least for a little while.

Since the moon was out tonight, May didn't have to talk

to a shadow, and, when she finished telling Willie about her day, he took his turn to tell her about his.

"Miss St. John took me to the park again today for a nature walk," he said, emitting crunching noises. "She has been taking me there every day, and I thought it was very odd."

"Why is that?" May wanted to know.

"Because she's a frightful one for the schoolroom and books, don't you know? Then suddenly we're taking more nature walks. I became very suspicious."

May suppressed the urge to laugh at his grown-up manner of speaking and said, "Oh?"

"Yes." Willie nodded gravely. "Very suspicious. Then today I found out why." He leaned over to whisper in May's ear. "Miss St. John has a gentleman friend."

May's eyes started out of her head. "Miss St. John? A gentleman friend? No!"

"I know it's difficult to believe," Willie commented with a wisdom that went beyond his years.

"That's unkind, Willie," May chided him out of habit, for verbalizing what she herself had been thinking. "Look," she said suddenly to distract him and to keep him from dwelling on his governess, "do you see all those stars in the sky?"

Willie went right up to the verandah railing and leaned over, so he could look up. "That's called the Milky Way."

May rose to stand beside him. "The Chinese call it the Silver River."

"Why, it does rather look like that," he said.

Suddenly, he stiffened and clutched at May's hand. "Aunt May," he whispered urgently, "there's someone down there, watching us."

She snapped to attention immediately, her eyes scanning the trees and shrubs near the walls, while her hand instinctively gripped Willie's. "Where? I don't see anything."

"There!" His voice was a dry, hushed whisper, as he pointed to a spot past the gardens and near the trees. "It's a man. I saw him move in the shadows."

They watched together for several minutes, but not a tree limb stirred, not a shrub rustled.

"Come, Willie, it's getting late. Let's go inside," May urged him, feeling vaguely uneasy and not knowing why.

"But, Aunt May, I did see someone there, I truly did." Then his round eyes grew even rounder. "Perhaps it was a ghost."

She tousled his hair and smiled down at him in the darkness. "You said it was a man. If it were a ghost, it would take the form of a fox. Have you forgotten what I taught you already?" She paused. "Perhaps it is Miss St. John's gentleman friend after all, hoping to catch a glimpse of her."

The exasperation in Willie's voice was evident as he said, "I rather doubt that, Aunt May. And, even if that were true, he should not be trespassing on our property. I shall speak to Papa about this tomorrow morning."

May envisioned the furor this would cause, so she said, "And betray me, Willie? Your parents would not be pleased to learn I've been filling your head with strange things when you should be sleeping."

His head hung in dejection. "All right. I'll not say a word."

"I shall tell your father myself," May promised, "but in such a manner that I won't give our little secret away. I'm sure there's some simple explanation for it. Now, let's get back to bed."

"Something odd happened to me last night," May announced to Nelson over breakfast the following morning.

"Oh?" he said, raising his brows.

May added a generous splash of milk to her tea. "Yes. I couldn't sleep last night, so I went out on the verandah for a breath of fresh air. I could have sworn I saw a man standing in the shadows, watching the house."

Nelson snapped to attention, his face dark. "A stranger? Inside the walls?"

May nodded. "I could have been mistaken, of course, for, even though there was a moon, he kept to the trees and shadows." Suddenly she felt rather silly under Nelson's skeptical scrutiny. "Perhaps I was just imagining things."

"Could you tell if he was white or Oriental?"

She shook her head. "I couldn't even tell if the figure was a man or a woman. All I saw was someone standing there."

Nelson stroked his mustache. "This is nothing to take lightly, May, especially since there have been several houses burglarized lately. I'll have more guards patrol the property from now on. Thank you for bringing this matter to my attention."

"It's probably just my imagination," she said apologetically.

"In Shanghai, one must always be very careful," he replied, a faraway look in his eyes.

When May arrived at the godown, she found Abbott and the comprador waiting for her.

"Good morning, Mr. Abbott," May said. "And Mr. Wu."

"Good morning, Mrs. Monckton," Abbott said with a rare smile.

The Chinese merely bowed wordlessly, his face expressionless, and May couldn't tell whether he approved or disapproved of her. But his opinion really didn't signify, for he was only Nelson Wright's middleman, nothing more.

May, however, felt she must also win him to her side to make her task easier, so, while Abbott spoke pidgin, she used Wu's own tongue. "Taipan Wright tells me you have just returned from Hong Kong."

"I often travel for the taipan," he replied. His voice was deep and strangely hypnotic, without the singsong quality of most Chinese.

"Judging from what I've seen, the gods are with you."

Wu smiled briefly. "My success or failure rests on my noble house." Then he excused himself and went striding off.

"He's an odd fish," Abbott said, watching him disappear out the door, "but then I find all of these Chinese strange."

His statement didn't surprise May, for she knew this to be the typical attitude of most Europeans toward the Chinese. "He must have a family . . . children."

The pale man made a face. "I suppose. You know, I've never even asked him."

May said nothing as she entered her office, went to the desk, and began leafing through papers. Despite Abbott's reluctance to discuss Comprador Wu, she could not dismiss him from her thoughts so readily. There was something about him that piqued her curiosity.

"Well," said Abbott, "shall we get to work?"

May spent most of her morning interpreting designs, had lunch with Nelson at his club, and returned to the godown. She didn't see the comprador until it was nearly time to go home to the villa.

"Comprador Wu," she began, looking at the man intently. He was, on closer inspection, younger than she had originally supposed, but perhaps she had thought him older because of his voluminous robes. His queue was long, and his hair was covered by a black cap that fitted his skull tightly.

Despite his round, forgettable face, there was something familiar about him, and May couldn't put her finger on it.

"What province do you come from, Comprador Wu?" she asked, suddenly curious.

He gave her a blank stare. "You must pardon this insignificant individual, but I find such personal questions offensive."

May blushed and looked away, making a great pretense of straightening her skirt to cover her embarrassment. "Of course. I do not wish to offend you either. Forgive this insignificant woman for her bluntness."

He bowed silently and padded off, as though he could not wait to remove himself from her presence, leaving May even more curious than before.

"Your comprador is an enigmatic fellow," she informed Nelson, as their carriage eased its way through the crush of rickshaws and pedestrians on Nanking Road.

"Wu?" His tone grew guarded. "He wasn't forward with you, was he?"

May brushed aside his suspicions with a laugh. "No, Uncle Nelson, nothing of the sort. If I'm to work with him, I would like to know a little more about him."

"Such as?"

"What city does he come from, does he have a family . . . ? "

He shrugged. "I can answer those questions myself. He comes from Soochow, and he has no wife or children. All I know is he's a damn good comprador—probably the best in Shanghai." Then he moistened his lips and said, "I wouldn't be too curious about Wu. We all work well together, and we just accept it. It doesn't do to be too curious about these fellows, you know."

"Yes, Uncle Nelson," May said meekly.

She was silent all the rest of the way back to the villa.

When May walked in the door, Emily was pacing the foyer, a letter in her hand.

"A letter," she announced unnecessarily, waving it under May's nose. "It's from your mother."

May's heart leaped in anticipation, as her trembling fingers took the envelope. She excused herself, clutching it as she skipped up the stairs to her room. She didn't think until afterward that Emily might have thought her rude for not opening it right there, but she didn't want to share her only news from Paoting in weeks with anyone right now. When she reached her room, she parted the mosquito netting and threw herself on the bed, then slit the letter open with her finger.

"My daughter," it began

I hope your anger has worn thin by now over the deception we had to play on you, but I'm sure you realize we had no other choice. We did what we thought was best for you.

I cannot go into any details, but suffice it to say that all is well and nearly back to normal here. Chad is well and sends his love, as do the Hammonds.

I was furious when I heard Alex had taken it upon himself to send you to Shanghai. I wish he hadn't. I maintain you were safe enough in Tientsin, and then I could have visited you. I don't know when I'll next be in Shanghai.

Oh, yes. I attended Weng's funeral. I know the circumstances of his death do not guarantee him a place in his afterlife, but I somehow feel St. Peter will open our gates for him. It was most odd, but his son

T'ai was not there. I wonder why. But it was the kind of funeral your father would have wanted for his old friend.

> *Do give my love to Nelson and Willie and Emily,*
> *Your Mother*

May brushed away the tears when she read about the funeral, then fled from her room, and quietly slipped down the back stairs that led to an outside door where she could move about unnoticed. She knew Emily was going to interrogate her about the contents of the letter, but she couldn't face anyone right now. Then she was running through the garden, to lose herself in the grove of trees where the stranger had stood.

She leaned against a tree to catch her breath, feeling stifled in the scalding Shanghai sun. As she glanced across at the villa, she noticed she was about level with her room and she realized she must be standing in the exact spot where Willie claimed to have seen the man last night.

May examined the ground and noticed the grass was crushed, as though someone had been standing there for a long time.

And she noticed a bit of red, like a spot of rust, right near her left toe.

She reached down to examine it more closely, her brow furrowed in concentration. It was a small carnelian button, carved in the shape of a phoenix.

CHAPTER TEN

M ay turned the button over and over in her fingers as she stared at it stupidly.

"So there was someone here last night," she murmured to herself, now convinced Willie hadn't been imagining things.

But surely it was mere coincidence that the lost button was in the shape of a phoenix, and hadn't Weng himself told her that the members of the Sons of the Celestial Phoenix wore no outward sign of their affiliation, lest they be discovered? Yet, in the heat of a Shanghai afternoon, May was chilled to the bone.

Why would a member of the brotherhood be on the villa's grounds at night, watching as silent as a shadow?

May slipped the phoenix button into her pocket and strolled across the lawn back to the villa, wondering whether she should show Nelson her discovery, to prove she had not been imagining an intruder. She decided it was not important for him to know about the button.

The instant she walked in the door, Emily pounced on her. "What did your mother have to say? I trust it wasn't bad news."

May forced herself to smile brightly. "No, of course not. Whatever gave you that idea, Emily? Mother says that everything is fine. I'll let you read the letter, if you wish." And she held it out to her.

She blushed and retreated. "No, that's all right. I was just curious, that's all."

May went back up to her room, slipped the phoenix button and her letter into a bureau drawer, waited for nightfall, and hoped that the watcher in the shadows would come again.

Much later, when the Argand lamps were extinguished and the villa was dark and still, May went out onto the verandah in the warm night air that smelled of rain and the river. She had told Willie not to come tonight because she was too tired, although she almost relented when his face grew long and miserable. But she did not want him here this time.

May stood at the railing, gripping its hard, rough surface until it bit into her palms, while her eyes scanned the moonlit scene below. She could see the small, bright lights of Shanghai in the distance, a mirror image of the star-strewn sky.

The night was noisy, with the persistent clacking of crickets and the bass strummings made by frogs. Now and then, the rhythmic clopping of hooves grew loud, then dimmed, as a solitary carriage passed by the villa on its way down the street. But there were no light footsteps or the scrapings of an intruder scaling the walls, then dropping to earth with a soft thud.

May took a deep breath and knotted her fingers together. This waiting was probably pointless. No one was going to come, and, even if they did, would she risk confronting them?

She thought of Alex's warning: "Be careful when you're in Shanghai." And here she was, disregarding him already, with typical Fitzgerald stubbornness.

The minutes slipped by into what seemed like hours, and May's neck felt stiff with tension. She reached up to massage her knotted muscles, and a soft sigh of impatience escaped from her lips.

She snapped to attention as the crickets and frogs fell mute abruptly. May strained to catch the slightest sound as her eyes darted over every tree near the wall. Had one of the shadows moved, or was it some trick of the darkness? She couldn't tell.

May was ready to whirl around, rush through the deserted house and across the lawn, but Alex's words flashed through her mind once again, and she paused, scolding herself for being so reckless and impulsive. How could she be sure the person who lost the carnelian phoenix button was a member of the brotherhood, or even a friend? She had no intentions of being found the next morning with her throat slit.

Then the spell was broken by whistling and the tramping of feet. She stepped back behind a column, to watch Nelson's night watchman swing his lamp in an arc, the light forcing its way into any hiding places.

No one was there.

May turned and went back to her room, more disappointed than relieved. When she finally fell asleep, her dreams were filled with red phoenixes, flying majestically through the air toward the south.

It rained the following day, a sheet of water that drummed relentlessly on the roof and sent steam rising from the thirsty earth. May didn't accompany Nelson to the godown that day, but imitated Emily by sleeping well into the late morning. She thought she might visit Tzu-Lieh, then decided against it, spending the rest of the afternoon and evening reading and playing with Willie, once he was released from Miss St. John's care for the day.

When the following day dawned bright and well-scrubbed, she resumed her duties at the warehouse. Tobias Abbott surprised her when she walked in the door, by declaring he had missed her yesterday, and his pale cheeks actually turned pink when he said it. May considered it a triumph that she had caused him to express what he felt, instead of bottling it up inside.

"And where is Comprador Wu today?" May wanted to know, as she seated herself at the desk and spread her papers out before her.

"He's off again, as usual," Abbott replied, unconcerned.

"The good comprador is away more than he's here, isn't he?"

Abbott shrugged as he unwrapped a package. "That's his way. He just disappears for days—sometimes weeks—on end, but, when he returns, he brings back the most beautiful things." He held out a small, exquisite rose quartz statuette. "This is just an example."

May held it up to the light as she took it from him. "She's Tien Mu, the goddess of lightning," she told him. "And she is beautiful."

"Some collector in France or England will pay handsomely for it. Many people don't appreciate Chinese objects like we do, Mrs. Monckton, but someday I expect they shall."

"Perhaps, Mr. Abbott, perhaps."

Suddenly Tobias swallowed hard and turned even paler. "I wish you would call me Tobias . . . and come to the park with me on Sunday, to listen to the band."

May looked at him, and really saw him for the first time as a man, not as Nelson's griffin. She wondered why she had never noticed his eyes were a pleasant hazel shade and his jaw surprisingly strong for one so passive. There was an air of kindness and goodness about him that demanded those qualities in return—qualities May wondered if she even possessed.

"We really do have a lot in common," Tobias added hopefully.

May tried to be kind. "Yes, we do have much in common, and I will gladly call you my friend. But," she said, avoiding his eyes by staring at the statuette, "I think it's only fair to tell you that I still have . . . ghosts to lay to rest."

"I see." And he turned away to busy himself with another package. "Forgive me for being a fool to think that you would . . . be attracted to me."

May recognized his attempt to move her to pity, but she refused to let herself feel sorry for him. "I do like you, Tobias, I do—really."

"But not as a suitor."

"I'm sorry," was all she could say.

"Well . . . " he muttered bleakly, suddenly all brisk and businesslike. "Let me know when you've written that description, will you?"

As she watched him hurry from the office, she thought, pity is not love, Tobias, and one day you shall learn the difference.

When May returned to the villa, she felt inexplicably morose. Tobias's sudden infatuation with her was most disturbing, and she hoped it wouldn't interfere with the way they worked together. Well, she thought, as she trudged up the stairs, perhaps a long, leisurely bath and a nap would refresh and put her in a better frame of mind.

She entered her room, was nearly suffocated by the steamy heat, and went to the window to shut out the sunlight. As she started to undress, May noticed a plain white envelope propped up against the Argand lamp. Frowning, she picked it up, read her name scrawled there, and opened it.

All the note said was: "Once again, I am sorry for what I said to you on the Tientsin docks. Will you forgive me?—A.W."

Alex! She felt suddenly lightheaded and had to reach for the table to steady herself. When the dancing lights stopped passing before her eyes, May reread the note. Then she examined it to see where it had come from. Paoting? Tientsin? No, since it had only her name on it, the note must have been hand-delivered by a messenger. That meant Alex was somewhere in Shanghai.

May flopped down into the chintz chair and pulled out her hairpins until her hair fell to her shoulders. His words on the docks came back to her, but this time they had lost their sting. She read the note for a third time, and the ghost of a smile touched her mouth. Well, he said he was sorry. Her resolve to remain angry with him suddenly melted, like snow before sun.

She shrugged and tried to put him out of her mind, but found that he would not be dispossessed. She recalled not their passion in the hidden room, but other aspects of his life that he had revealed on the way to T'chuan's estate. There was the child sent to his uncle's draughty Cornish castle every summer, when he longed to be in China's brilliant heat, and the adventurer who smuggled opium and sold his services to the highest bidder, just for the sheer excitement of it.

She also remembered their first meeting on the Bund, when he had saved her from serious injury or even death, and, later, when he rescued her from Captain Forsythe's advances at that disastrous party. And she also wondered why he had bothered to take part in her mother's efforts to keep her from Mandarin Ki. She flattered herself to think he had been concerned about her.

"And he did apologize," she murmured to herself. Nigel had never apologized to her for anything.

May rose, then summoned the maid to draw her bath water. She had so much to think about.

The days wore on, and May threw herself more vigorously into her work, spending longer and longer hours at the godown. And, as she fell into a routine, she began to grow bolder and more aggressive.

She usually remained hidden in the office, out of sight of the men, and Tobias would bring her the objects to evaluate and describe. But on this Tuesday morning, she finished with a T'ang jade bracelet and Tobias was nowhere to be found, so May impatiently left the confines of the office and went wandering through the warehouse until she came to some boxes stacked against one wall.

She stopped a passing workman and had him open one for her, then she knelt down and gently brushed away the sawdust that cushioned the enclosed object. When she lifted the piece out and looked at it, she felt all the blood drain from her face and heard a great roaring in her ears.

It was the fluted jade bowl, the one Weng had carved, the one she had held up to the light in his workroom just as she was doing now.

What was it doing here, in the Benton and Black godown?

A hundred thoughts and suspicions, all of them wild and horrid, flashed through her mind simultaneously, but she surprised herself by rising, walking over to where Tobias was supervising the loading of bolts of silk, and saying quite calmly, "Tobias, I have to see the taipan right away."

He stared at her, startled by the strange look on her face. "Of course. I'll summon a rickshaw to take you to the hong right away."

Nelson was at the hong, busy at his desk when May interrupted him, still clutching the bowl wrapped in paper.

"May," Nelson said pleasantly, rising and offering her a chair. "Is there some problem at the godown? Not tired of working already, are you?"

She unwrapped the bowl with trembling fingers and showed it to him. "Where did you get this, Uncle Nelson? I found it in one of the crates just a few minutes ago."

He looked truly bewildered. "Why, I don't know. Wu picked it up somewhere, I suppose. Why do you ask?"

"This bowl belongs to Weng Ta-Chung. He carved it. He showed it to me one day in his workroom." May leaned forward, her green eyes wide as she said, "What is it doing in Shanghai?"

Nelson's eyes never left her face, as his fingers drummed on the desk top. "I don't know, May, but I'm certain there is a logical, plausible explanation for it." Then he smiled to put her at her ease. "What is *your* explanation for it?"

May took a deep breath. "It might have been stolen."

Alarm flashed across Nelson's face, and he turned a deeper shade of pink. "Are you accusing my comprador of thievery? That's a serious accusation."

"No, of course not." But that's exactly what she meant.

"Weng's widow could have sold it, you know. I don't doubt she'll need the money now."

"That's possible."

"Anyway, I shall have a talk with Wu as soon as he comes in." His words were soothing as he sought to put this problem to rights and smooth the wave that threatened to capsize this particular boat. "I'm sure you'll find there's a perfect explanation for this." The sound of footsteps by the door caused them to look up. "I've been expecting him, and I suspect that's Wu now."

May turned in her chair to see the comprador enter, his hands hidden up the sleeves of his robes and his face a mask. "You wished to speak to this insignificant one, Taipan?"

"It's about this bowl, Mr. Wu," he said, poking at the jade piece with his finger. "Mrs. Monckton was curious as to where you got it."

The comprador flicked a glance at the bowl and then met May's gaze. "That was purchased from a merchant in Hangchow on my last trip there."

May said, "It was carved by Weng Ta-Chung, my teacher, who is now dead."

He bowed. "The death of a friend brings a thousand and one sorrows."

May had to tread very carefully, lest she insult the man and make an enemy. "I was wondering how it came to be in Shanghai when I last saw it in Paoting."

"I do not know. I buy what I am offered. I do not ask questions to offend the one who sells to me."

Nelson cleared his throat. "Well, perhaps in the future, Mr. Wu, you should question your purchase a little more carefully. That will be all."

The comprador shot another glance at May, bowed, and left.

"There," Nelson said with a satisfied smile. "I told you there was a simple explanation for it."

May felt it was not really an explanation at all, but she would not get any further with her questioning, so she just smiled and said, "Yes, Uncle Nelson. A simple explanation." She rose and took the bowl. "Thank you. I shall go back to the godown now."

"I'll see you at half-past three, then."

"Yes. See you then."

A simple explanation? May ran her fingers along the bowl's fluted ribs, her brow furrowed in concentration as the rickshaw sped back to the godown. After Weng's death, Ah

Sin could have sold his last remaining pieces, but might she have wanted to keep them as remembrances of her husband? She discounted that the moment she thought it. Ah Sin had always been a pragmatist, like most Chinese, and not given to sentiment. It was possible the bowl had been sold. She and Uncle Nelson had no reason whatsoever to doubt the comprador's word.

She hugged the bowl to her, thoughts racing ahead. May would write to her mother. Margaret Fitzgerald was certain to know about the bowl, or else she could find out for her.

"Well?" Tobias wanted to know when she walked in and reluctantly put the bowl back.

May said, "Mr. Wu had a simple explanation for it." And she told him what it was.

"That certainly makes sense," Abbott replied in his off-hand manner, as he rummaged through another crate to produce a vase. "This should be the last one for today," he said, handing it to her.

May took the vase back into the office, and Abbott trailed at her heels. "The Dutchman is back in Shanghai," he said.

May whirled around crashing into Tobias and nearly dropping the priceless object. "Alex? Where?"

He moved away from her, flustered by sudden contact. "One of the aides to the English counsel told me he saw him."

"Where?" May demanded again, trying not to betray herself, and failing miserably.

Tobias shrugged. "Booking passage on a ship bound for Macao, I think he said."

Back to Macao. Back to Java.

May set the vase gently on the desk before she replied. She managed to keep her voice level as she said, "Would you mind hailing me a rickshaw again? I'm not feeling well, and I think I had better get back to the villa. Tell Nelson I've already gone, won't you?"

When May returned to the villa, she found an agitated Emily pacing the length of the foyer and fanning herself.

"Thank God you're home!" she sighed in relief, her hand

to her chest. Then she leaned over and whispered, "My husband didn't come with you, did he?"

"No," May replied with a puzzled frown. "Emily, what is the matter? Why all the secrecy?"

"Because Alexander Wolders has called to see you. He's in the solarium now, and you know Nelson would be furious to find him here."

May's heart gave a queer little lurch. "Alex? Here?" Tobias had said he had gone to Macao.

Emily's head bobbed up and down. "Will you please find out what he wants and make him leave before Nelson gets home?"

"Of course," May said, hurrying off.

Her heart was racing out of control as she rushed into the sun-drenched room and saw him standing there, his back to her as he watched a dog streak after a large white cat.

When he heard her footsteps, he turned, his look one of polite inquiry and reserve. "Good day, Lady Jade. You're looking well."

Again, she hesitated. The urge to fly into his arms was overwhelming, but something—her own pride, the fear of being rebuffed again, as she had been on the Tientsin docks when they parted—made her hold back to see what he would do first.

He sensed her reluctance and mistrust, so he crossed the room and before she realized what he was doing, he reached for her hand, kissed it, and returned it to her side.

May laughed, the tension broken. "Such courtly behavior from an adventurer," she said with a shake of her head.

His cold blue eyes twinkled. "I'll have you know I can be quite gallant when the occasion warrants it." Then he suddenly grew serious. "You received my note?"

May looked at him and nodded.

"And do you accept my apology for my thoughtlessness that day?"

"Yes."

Alex looked like he was about to speak, then changed his mind.

Before another awkward silence could descend, May

said, "Forgive my atrocious manners. Won't you sit down?" When they were seated across from each other, she said, "I'm surprised to see you. I had heard you were in Macao."

He smiled. "My business there has been completed, so I returned to Shanghai."

"How is mother . . . and Chad?" May asked, twisting her fingers together.

"We'll talk about them later," he said. "What's this I hear about your working at Benton and Black?"

"Yes," she replied and explained what she did in the godown every day.

Alex leaned back in his seat and regarded her with an unfathomable expression. "So China's finally cast its spell on you after all. I knew it would in time. This country has a quality that just beckons to people like us, and your mother."

She bristled and sat up primly. "Nothing of the sort. I just needed something to do, that's all, and Nelson graciously allowed me to catalog some items for him."

"You should put your knowledge to use, not waste your time going to lawn parties and gossiping with other women."

May raised a brow. "I'm surprised to hear you utter such a statement, Alex."

"I merely appreciate the unique," he retorted.

Then he fell silent, and May realized it was not because he had nothing to say, but because he was on his guard, listening. He leaned forward and whispered, "Is there somewhere we can talk in private?"

"The folly?" May suggested.

He shook his head. "Away from here." When May's face looked blank, he said, "I know a place—that is, if you're not afraid to be alone with me."

"Don't be absurd," she replied cooly as she rose.

He stood up and retrieved his hat from the table. "You are quite fearless, Mrs. Monckton, to be seen with me."

"I think you rather enjoy your reputation," she accused, and he just smiled mysteriously in return.

As they left the solarium, May noticed the foyer was deserted, so perhaps Emily hadn't been eavesdropping after all. She found her in the parlor, arranging flowers in a vase and trying to contain her curiosity.

May did not ask Emily's permission to leave with Alex. She just said, "I'm going out with Mr. Wolders, Emily," leaving no room for discussion.

Emily turned white and looked as though she were suffocating, but all she said was, "Don't stay out too late, dear. You know how Nelson is."

"I shall guard Mrs. Monckton with my life, Mrs. Wright," Alex said with a mocking bow.

Emily didn't know quite what to say, so she just blushed and gave them a brief wave as they departed.

"Where are you taking me?" May asked, when he handed her into a rickshaw.

"A very private, beautiful place," he replied, not looking at her as he stepped into a second one. "I go there whenever I need to refresh my spirit, or just to think."

His words moved her, but she could think of no suitable reply, so she just kept still.

They traveled up Bubbling Well Road, heading west, away from the busier parts of the city, and May's curiosity was piqued. Finally, the rickshaws stopped before a mansion that made even the Wright villa look like a cottage.

Set behind gates of delicate wrought iron and guarded by massive stone dogs, the mansion gleamed bright-white against the hot-blue sky. It had the requisite number of pillared verandahs, but the major influence of the building was Dutch. May could see white-uniformed groundsmen bustling about, trimming the lawn, washing windows, pruning plants.

"What is this place?" May asked, as Alex handed her down.

"It belongs to my friend Soon Sebastian," Alex replied. "He controls every fan-tan table and gambling den in Shanghai."

May stopped at the foot of the stairs, gave Alex a wary look, her old mistrust of the man flooding back. "Why have you brought me here, Alex?"

He gave her an exasperated look. "Your faith in me is overwhelming, May," and he gave her a little shove.

When they reached the doors, he rang the bell and when a servant appeared, all Alex said was, "To the garden."

The man bowed and indicated they should follow him.

May did so, her curiosity getting the better of her once again, and she passed through dark, cool corridors. When the servant came to the French doors, he bowed and held them open for them.

As soon as she stepped back into sunshine, May's eyes widened in delight.

The mansion was built around a center court, in the Chinese manner, but the trees and ornamental shrubs were arranged so skillfully that the house was barely visible. There was an arched bridge so tiny only one person could stroll over a reflecting pool fringed with white lotus, and May could barely count the profusion of exotic flowers that grew here, scenting the air with their potent incense and startling the eye with vivid splashes of orange, yellow, pink, and red against darkest green.

And everywhere there was blissful silence, as though the garden had been purposely purged of birds and even insects that would make the slightest noise to disturb the meditator.

May smiled in delight. "This is incredible, Alex," she whispered.

He smiled. "There used to be a peacock here once, and he was beautiful when he strutted and fanned his tail. But his screams disturbed the silence, so he was banished to the back lawn."

"I can see why."

"I call this my Eden. Soon Sebastian owes me a small fortune, but I agreed to forget the debt if he agreed to let me have the run of this garden."

"I feel as though we're the only people in the world."

"That reminds me," he said softly, as his cold eyes grew warm and tender. "I haven't greeted you properly yet." And he took her chin in his fingers and tilted her face so he could kiss her, gently at first, then with a growing hunger.

She locked her arms around him and abandoned herself to his embrace. When they parted, breathless, she murmured, "Someone will see us."

He gazed into her eyes, and shook his head. "No one will see us. And would you care if they did?"

"No," she whispered back.

"I didn't think so." Alex tucked an escaped tendril of hair behind her ear. "Come sit down," and he led her over to a stone bench.

"What happened after you left Tientsin?" she asked.

"I returned to Paoting," he replied. "Your mother and the doctor were fine, and the policeman was no longer stationed outside the gates. I stayed with your mother for a few days. It gave me the perfect opportunity to observe her and see who came to trade with her, but I don't think Win-Lin was among them."

May felt herself stiffen and draw away. "Wasn't that dishonest, using her that way?"

"Yes, but the end justified the means in this case." He looked up at the sky. "I came to admire your mother a great deal. She is a charming woman, with spirit, and I hope she's not involved in this affair."

May said nothing. The very serenity and stillness of the garden made the spoken word seem harsh and intrusive by comparison, and May felt the inclination to talk gradually disappear. But she found her other senses blossoming like the flowers that surrounded them. As she looked at Alex, she became intensely aware of him. The silver in his hair was brighter, and his long, straight nose more defined. She admired the sensuous curve of his mouth, and suddenly longed to feel its warmth against her own.

The spell of the garden was like a potent drug, and she wondered fleetingly if this was what an opium addict experienced as he drew on his pipe.

When she reached out to run her fingertips down the back of his neck, where his hair curled slightly at the ends, Alex turned his head, and his eyes held hers.

"I would like to love you now, right here."

May's clothes suddenly seemed too hot and weighed heavily on her skin. "Why don't you, then?"

Alex caught his breath, and his eyes seemed to darken to sapphire, as he watched her undo the buttons down the front of her dress, and, when she reached for his hand and drew it to her breast, he smiled slightly in triumph.

"Over here," he said, rising and leading her to a grassy alcove, sheltered by ornamental trees.

This time, May did not resist, and within minutes the garden was filled with the sounds of their pleasure, which somehow did not intrude on the silence.

Later, May stretched languidly, gently dislodged Alex's slumbering head from her shoulder, and rose to her feet. She listened, but no servants came to disturb them, and she could actually believe she was in some sort of primeval paradise.

"What a pagan place," she thought, half listening for the wind-tossed voices of the ancient Chinese gods from out of the beginning of time.

Without quite knowing why, she stepped boldly out of the shelter of the branches and into the reflecting pool, where she bent down, cupped her hands together, filled them with water, and let its coolness trickle down her white, burning skin until it ran back into the pool again. When she finished bathing, she turned and found Alex already in his trousers, propped up on one elbow and watching her.

May blushed and concealed her breasts with her hair, then walked back to him. Without a word, she slipped into her undergarments while Alex just watched her perform this feminine ritual.

She tossed her hair, reached back and began winding it into a knot from memory. "Will you pluck out any leaves?" she asked.

"Why?"

May smiled at his naivete. "I must eliminate any evidence for Emily to find."

He kissed her bare shoulder as his fingers pulled a dried leaf from her hair. "All she has to do is look at your face for evidence."

"Does it show?"

He nodded with a wicked grin.

"Then I'm doomed," she said with a hopeless sigh, as she pulled her dress over her head. "Uncle Nelson will lock me away in the attic for sure."

Alex laughed, as he himself finished dressing. Then he

glanced up at the sky. "It's getting late, and I have to get you back to the villa."

"Thank you for bringing me here."

"We shall come here again," he promised. Suddenly he said, "I have rooms at a boarding house run by a woman named Zetta—Shanghai Zetta. If you're ever in trouble, or need help, that's where I can be found."

A sudden chill caressed May's arms, as though a cloud were passing over the sun. "You sound so ominous. Why would I ever need help?"

"I hope you never do," he replied. "But you'll know where to find me, just in case."

Then they left the tranquility of the garden and reentered the bustle and noise of Shanghai.

Later, after Alex left her at the villa's doorstep, and May entered, she found a grim-faced Nelson waiting for her. "Emily tells me you've been with Alexander Wolders," he said, not pleased.

"Yes. Why?"

He pulled at his bushy mustache. "I wouldn't, if I were you, May. It's not seemly for a respectable woman to be seen keeping company with Wolders."

For an instant, May's color deepened as her temper flared. "I see nothing wrong with the man."

Nelson gave her his most exasperated look. "Don't get testy with me. I'm only telling you this once, for your own good. Wolders is persona non grata among the English community, and you would do well to avoid him. Do I make myself clear?"

May sighed. She was, she reminded herself, the Wrights' houseguest, subject to the laws of the household, and, if Alex was off limits, so be it. "Yes, Uncle Nelson," she said in resignation, then excused herself and went up to her room.

CHAPTER
ELEVEN

The next morning, when May went to the godown, she found herself unable to concentrate on her work, for her thoughts were filled with the previous day.

Alex had come to call on her. If she closed her eyes, she could transport herself back to Soon Sebastian's garden, with its serenity and beauty.

His words came back to her. "I come here whenever I need to think or refresh my spirit."

May was intrigued by this contemplative side to Alexander Wolders, which was so at odds with his reckless adventuring ways. She wondered if he had fully intended to reveal so much of himself to her.

But, despite his reputation, she enjoyed his company, and Nelson's decree that she should not be seen with him rankled her.

A voice from the doorway jolted her back to the present. "I said, where do you want this?"

May's head jerked up, and her eyes focused on a short man standing in the doorway. He was one of the workmen, someone she had never seen before, dark and stocky with a heavy beard and red, wet mouth.

She stiffened. "What do you want?"

"I was told to bring this to you." And he set down a small box on the desk. As he left, he gave her a sly glance over his shoulder and said, "The name is Dawes, ma'am."

"Thank you, Mr. Dawes," May said coldly, not liking him.

She reminded herself to speak to Tobias about letting any of the men come back here again, for she wanted to remain as inconspicuous as possible. She must not disrupt the men, Nelson had said, otherwise it was back to Emily in limbo.

Tobias, who had long forgiven her for refusing him, came sauntering in, took one look at her face, and said, "Is something wrong? You look quite shaken."

May gave him a wan smile as she put the jewelry away. "Oh, I'm just preoccupied, that's all. I worry about my mother."

"And Alexander Wolders, I suspect," he said gently.

Her eyes darted up to meet his, startled by discovery.

"I thought so," he said, his pale face filled with hopelessness and misery. "Don't look so surprised. I may be quiet, but I'm not insensitive."

"I never thought you were insensitive, Tobias."

"No, you've always treated me kindly, and, for that, I thank you." He was silent for a moment, then he cleared his throat. "Why are women always attracted to the bounders, like Alex Wolders?" he mused. "And they never give a decent fellow a chance?"

Even as she shrugged and said, "I don't know," May knew the answer. Men like Alex either sent a woman soaring or plummeting, never letting her settle on safe, dull middle ground. She thought of Emily, Anna Cooper-Smith, and herself while married to Nigel, each looking forward to days that were all the same, never ignited by a spark of the unusual or the unexpected. May shook her head. Her life had been so dreary with Nigel—she could finally admit that to herself. He had given her everything she wanted, but not what she needed.

"He's not worthy of you, you know," Tobias was saying.

May knew he referred to Alex. "He once told me we were two of a kind. I'm beginning to think he was right."

Tobias looked stricken. "How can you even compare yourself to an . . . an adventurer?"

"You don't know me, Tobias, and besides I don't wish to discuss it any further."

Tobias, ever the gentleman, changed the subject. "Will you be joining us for tiffin?"

She nodded and followed him out of the office. As they walked through the warehouse, the very air vibrating with the sounds of hurried footsteps and boxes slithering across the floor, May had the uncomfortable feeling she was being watched. When she turned her head, she saw Mr. Dawes staring at her intently, his red, wet mouth pulled into a smile. May looked away, a flush coming to her cheeks in spite of all her efforts to look composed.

Tiffin in Uncle Nelson's office provided a pleasurable break for May. The three of them were discussing the business of the day over sandwiches and cold tea provided by an old Chinese woman known only as the "tiffin amah."

This noon, Nelson was in the middle of explaining Comprador Wu's latest coup, when the door to the office burst open and Miss St. John stood in the doorway, her cheeks flushed and her breathing labored, as though she had just run ten miles.

They were all on their feet in an instant.

"Miss St. John!" Nelson exclaimed, rushing over to take her hand and lead her over to a chair. "What is the matter?"

The woman was nearly incoherent. "Master William. It is Master William."

"What about him?" May snapped and shook her shoulder.

"Abbott, water. Quick!" Nelson snapped. Then he said, very calmly, "Please, Miss St. John. You must control yourself and tell us what has happened."

She was gulping air like a fish out of water, her pinched face terrified. "I was taking William for our nature walk in the park, when . . . when I stopped to point out a specific variety of elm tree. And, suddenly, he was gone!" Her voice rose in a hysterical wail. "Gone!"

"Did you look for him?" Nelson demanded, turning white.

"I looked everywhere," the woman sobbed. "He just vanished."

Abbott handed her the water, which she downed gratefully, and, when she came up for air, she continued. "I scoured the park asking everyone if they had seen a small boy. No one had. I walked around in circles for hours, calling his name."

"Did you call the police?" May wanted to know.

Miss St. John gave her a scathing look. "Of course! What do you take me for? They're looking for him now."

May had never seen Nelson look so terrified.

"May, you stay here with Miss St. John," he ordered. "Abbott and I are going to look for him. He's probably wandered down to the waterfront to watch the boats."

"I want to go," May said, not wishing to be alone with the distraught woman.

"No, you stay here. I don't want to have to look for the both of you," Nelson said, as he and Abbott disappeared out the door.

When the pounding of their footsteps died away, the only sounds were the rhythmic ticking of the clock and Miss St. John's sobs. May stood there in silence, her dislike of the woman growing as she wanted to lash out at her for not keeping an eye on Willie, yet realizing it would do no good.

"More water?" she asked, her voice tight and constrained.

Miss St. John's eyes, as gray and cold as her dress, stared at May. "It wasn't my fault," she insisted, her brow shining with sweat. "And if something happens to the little hellion, the Wrights will surely blame me. They'll dismiss me without references, and then what will I do? What shall become of me?"

When May said nothing, the woman looked up at her beseechingly. "I've been a good governess, haven't I? It wasn't my fault that the little brat ran away."

May rose, sickened by the woman's lack of concern for her charge. "I'm going to look for him," she said.

"But Mr. Wright told you to stay here with me."

Without so much as a backward glance, May left the room and went out on her own to look for Willie.

When she emerged from the hong, she stopped, shaded her eyes against the brilliant sun, and tried to get her bearings, amid all the bustle and confusion.

If I were a curious ten-year-old boy, she asked herself, where would I go?

At first she thought of the Chinese city, and she mentally chastised herself for making it so inviting to him, like forbidden fruit. But the Chinese city was a good distance away for a penniless boy to travel on foot, even one as resourceful as Willie, so she must think again. May bit her lip in vexation. Where would he go? Somewhere near the park, no doubt.

Well, the best course of action for her to take would be to hire a rickshaw and scour the neighborhood around the park. Once she hailed one and was seated, she gave the coolie directions, and they went rocking off.

As they went around the park, May's eyes scanning faces, insidious thoughts of disaster threatened to reduce her to a state of panic. What if someone had taken Willie? Nelson was a wealthy man, willing to do anything or pay any price for his son. Worse still, what if they never saw Willie again? May snapped at the coolie to go faster.

As they rounded a corner, May nudged him with her toe to make him turn left, much as she would a horse. The driver obediently turned down a narrow street, easing his way between pedestrians.

Suddenly, out of the corner of her eye, May saw a small figure of a child dart out of a shop and scurry down the street, to disappear.

Willie.

She ordered the driver to go on, but he refused in a stream of Chinese, saying the street was too narrow and the neighborhood too dangerous to make it worth his while. In desperation, May paid him a few extra coins and told him to wait, while she ran down the street, unmindful of the curious and hostile stares directed at her.

"Willie?" she called, "Where are you?"

When there was no answer and no sign of the child, she gathered her skirts and ran on, determination blinding her to the roughness of the neighborhood. As she went running past, eyes peered out at her from upstairs windows and through doors just open a crack.

May felt like she was back in the boxwood maze at Monckton Hall, darting left and right, coming up against a dead end, retracing her steps in her quest to reach the heart of the maze before anyone else. But here the stakes were much higher than the triumph of being first.

She stood there like one caught in the middle of a tug-of-war, being pulled first one way, then the other, not knowing whether to go left or right. Just when she was about to give up entirely and return to the rickshaw, a tall, familiar figure stepped out of a shop doorway down the street and stood there for a moment as if deciding where to go next.

May could have pinched herself to make sure she wasn't dreaming, but she'd recognize Alex anywhere.

"Alex!" she called, waving her arms wildly to attract his attention.

At the sound of his name, his head came up, and his eyes searched the crowd. When he spied her, his face went from incredulity to pleasure, as he crossed the narrow street and came up to her.

"Lady Jade, I didn't expect to see you again so soon. In jeopardy already, are you?"

May didn't know whether to laugh or cry. "You're close to the truth. Willie has run away, and I've been searching for him for hours, and—"

"Easy, May, calm down," he said, his voice soothing and soft. "You're shaking. Now, what's this about the boy being lost?"

She told him in short, incomplete sentences, unmindful of the people jostling them as they brushed past, and, when she finished, Alex said, "Well, let's go see if we can find him, shall we?"

May mumbled her thanks, and together they spent the better part of two hours walking up and down streets, peering into windows and doorways, stopping people to ask if they had seen a small, dark-haired English child recently. May's feet were sore, and her legs ached, but, whenever Alex mentioned calling off their search, she would plead for them to go down just one more street, then another, and another.

Finally, Alex lost all patience with her. "We've got to stop, May," he said firmly. "You're exhausted and are about to drop."

"But we've got to find Willie."

"I'm sure someone has found him by this time, and he's fine." He looked around. "I'm walking you to my rooms. They're not far from here. At least you'll be able to rest before I take you back to the hong."

"But Alex . . ."

"Don't argue with me." And he put his arm under her elbow and forcibly steered her across the street.

In a matter of minutes, they reached a corner and turned down still another street.

"There's where I live," Alex announced.

Alex's rooms were in a rundown boarding house sandwiched between an opium den and a coffin-maker's. May read the discreet card with "foreign mud" written on it—the establishment's only advertisement—and listened to the "tap-tap-tap" of the coffin-maker's hammer, as he worked away to his customer's specifications. The rooming house was run by a fat Frenchwoman with a gold front tooth and frizzy yellow hair, who gave Alex a broad wink and an elbow in the ribs as he and May went upstairs. That, May assumed, was Shanghai Zetta.

Zetta's place seemed frequented by sailors more than any other class of clientele, for May could hear the mournful strains of a sea chanty coming from another room.

Alex read her expression as he unlocked the door. "This ia a palace compared to some of the places I've lived."

And they went inside.

The room, May was not really surprised to discover, was like the man himself. Scrupulously clean, it looked spare and devoid of any personal touches, as though he could pack his life and possessions in one bag and clear out quickly to follow adventure's siren song. But, upon closer inspection, she noticed he did have a few belongings that must have meant a great deal to him.

May picked up an old photograph in a tarnished metal frame. It was of a woman, dark and compelling, with a happy light shining out of her eyes, though she was unsmiling and slightly forbidding.

"Your mother," she guessed at once.

Alex nodded as he walked over to a small table, took out a bottle of brandy, and poured some into a cup.

"And this?" she asked, picking up a cast-iron toy soldier that Willie would covet, its red uniform chipped and peeling.

"A gift from my father on my seventh birthday. I used to collect them a long time ago." He saw her expression and he grinned. "Are you surprised that a man such as myself could be so sentimental?"

"No," she said gently. When her eyes fell on a well-worn violin case propped up against the wall, she added, "But I am surprised at that."

He walked back, handed her the cup, and offered her a chair. "One can't cart a piano around, now can one?"

"You are a man of surprises," she said, sipping her brandy delicately, while he drank from the bottle.

They sat there in silence, neither knowing quite what to say.

May longed for him to take her cup, set it down on the table, and lead her over to the bed, but he made no move to touch her. In fact, there was a coolness and distance about him today that bewildered her. He was not the same man who had taken her to the garden, and May wondered if she had done something to cause such behavior.

Finally, she said, "Will you play the violin for me?"

"Perhaps some other time."

She smoothed an imaginary wrinkle from her dress, so he couldn't see the disappointment on her face. "Have you had any success in your search for Win-Lin?"

Alex shook his head. "I had a few leads, but they turned out to be nothing." He took a sip of brandy and stared at the floor. Then he said, "And how is life among the rich and privileged?" without envy or malice.

"Since yesterday? It's about the same." She ran her finger along the rim of the cup. "I find I'm accepted more than when I first arrived in Shanghai. In fact, my life here resembles the life I had in England, to a certain extent."

His eyes narrowed. "And do you think that's good?"

She looked at him and shrugged. "I don't know anymore. I used to think it was, but now I'm beginning to wonder."

Alex's voice grew soft. "And what has brought about this change, I wonder?"

"I really don't know." May rose and walked over to a window and looked down into a filthy, deserted alley. "But I find myself growing very restless, even with my work at the godown."

Suddenly, he said, "Well, I think it's time we got you back to the Wrights before they send a search party of Sikhs out after you."

May's hand flew to her mouth. "Willie! I'd forgotten all about him."

"I'm sure the lad will turn up," Alex said.

They first went to the hong, where Tobias Abbott glared at Alex, while giving them the news that Willie had been returned by some seamen whom he had talked to down at the docks. He, his father, and a very relieved Miss St. John had gone back to the villa, where, Abbott imagined, Willie would soon regret causing everyone so much concern.

Indeed, May and Alex found this to be the case when they went to the villa.

"How's Willie?" were the first words out of May's mouth when she burst into the parlor.

Nelson scowled at her and flicked a cool glance at Alex. "Never mind Willie. How are *you?* We returned to find that harebrained governess near hysterics again and babbling some nonsense about you taking off to find Willie by yourself. You frightened us half to death, May. How many times do I have to tell you not to go out unescorted? The streets are dangerous."

Emily fanned her flushed face wildly. "All I could think of was that poor German girl who disappeared a few months ago."

"I'm all right," May said, feeling ashamed. "I'm sorry I caused everyone so much concern. Mr. Wolders found me and brought me home."

Emily jumped to her feet, ever the gracious hostess. "Why, Mr. Wolders, I didn't even notice you standing there. Do join us, and stay for tea."

"Thank you for your kind invitation, Mrs. Wright," he said in his low, lazy voice, "but I really must be on my way."

Emily clicked her tongue in disappointment. "You've done such a service for us, you really should let us repay your kindness."

"Mrs. Monckton's safety is payment enough," he replied. Then Alex bowed, bid them all good day, and started out the door.

May watched him from the doorway until he disappeared down the drive and out the gate. She wondered what had brought about the abrupt change in him from yesterday, when he had loved her so passionately in Soon Sebastian's garden. May sighed dismally, as she turned and slowly walked upstairs back to her room. Alex was a moody man, but she had suspected that from the first. His behavior certainly was baffling. She recalled how he had desired her in the hidden room, yet rebuffed her on the Tientsin docks when she had offered herself to him. Perhaps he saw her as a threat to his precious freedom, yet she had made no demands on him, or expected anything more from him.

With another sigh, she decided to look in on Willie.

He was lying on his bed, his eyes red and swollen. "I'm being punished, Aunt May," he said with a sniff. "Papa gave me a caning, and says I can't come out of my room for two days. And I can't ride Tartar for two weeks." And he dissolved into sobs.

May leaned over and tousled his dark curls. "Well, you know, Willie, you gave us all a horrid fright by running off like that, especially Miss St. John."

His tears stopped as he peeked up at her in glee. "Yes, I did, didn't I?"

"That's nothing to be proud of, young man," she admonished him.

"But Miss St. John is an awful prig."

"Whether or not that is true, she is a person with feelings just like you and me."

He said he was sorry once again. Then he stared up at her, his eyes growing rounder. "Have you seen the ghost again?"

"The ghost?"

"You know," he prompted. "The one we saw at night."

May shook her head. "No, he never came back."

Willie's face fell once again, and a dejected sigh escaped his lips. "I suppose I shan't be able to visit you tonight."

"That wouldn't be wise," May said, then left to go down to dinner.

That evening, at the dinner table, Miss St. John was the chief topic of discussion, and it did not bode well for the governess.

"I've got to dismiss her, under the circumstances," Nelson declared, then took a large swallow of wine.

Emily looked agitated and sat straight up in her chair. "But Nelson, we can't do that. Wherever would we find another governess? All the families send their children back to England for schooling, so there isn't a governess to be found." She cocked a brow at him. "Unless, of course, you're proposing to send our son away to school."

"No. I want my son here with me."

Emily sighed in exasperation, and the jewels at her throat twinkled. "Well, then, we'll have to let him have a Chinese amah. Perhaps we can hire Julie away from Anna Cooper-Smith."

"Absolutely not!" Nelson snapped.

May bristled and went to her former amah's defense.

"She was my amah for eighteen years and I don't think she'd be a bad influence on Willie."

Nelson looked from his wife to his guest. "What are you two talking about?" After May explained about Tzu-Lieh, he just shrugged. "It's not that I have anything against the woman, I just don't want Willie to be raised by any Chinese. I'm sorry, that's just the way I feel."

"Well, then, what do you suggest?" Emily cried, slamming her fork down. "Willie must have his lessons. I won't have him growing into a dolt!"

"Since we'll soon be going back to England ourselves, I don't expect it will make that much difference if the boy misses a few weeks of lessons," Nelson replied, all patience exhausted.

Emily perked right up. "Then we really are going back to England? And soon?"

Nelson glanced at May. "We'll discuss it later, Emmy. We don't want to bore our guest. Tell me, May, what were you and Wolders doing together today? I thought I had . . . suggested that you not see him again."

"When I was looking for Willie, I saw him come out of a shop," she explained. "I was frantic, and he offered to help me look for Willie, that's all." She did not tell them about Shanghai Zetta's.

"Well, I suppose you can be excused this time," he said, his pink face relaxing. "But I don't want to have to warn you again."

"I don't seek him out," she retorted, bristling.

"See that you don't," were Nelson's last words on the subject.

His words of warning had cause to go unheeded the following day.

When May awoke that Thursday, she decided that, after all the excitement Willie had caused, she was entitled to a rest. So she made up her mind to go to the Cooper-Smiths' and visit with Tzu Lieh for a while. After a leisurely breakfast, May informed Emily of her intentions and departed.

When she arrived at her destination, she was greeted at

the door by Anna herself, cradling the slumbering baby in the crook of her arm.

"Why, May," she said in surprise and delight, "I was just wondering what to do with myself today. But let's not just stand here. Come in, please."

Anna looked sparkling and alert, and there was no taint of alcohol on her breath today, probably, May suspected, because it was too early yet.

"Actually, I came to visit Tzu-Lieh, if it's all right with you," May said, gently stroking Rick's cheek with her finger and making him wake up and smile for her. "Does she have the day off today?"

Anna's face clouded over as they walked into the foyer. "Oh, dear. I don't know how to tell you this, but Julie is ill."

May stopped and stared at her in alarm. "Ill? What do you mean?"

"About a week ago, I thought she looked under the weather, so I asked her if there was anything wrong, or if she wasn't feeling well. Julie said no, but the next day, she looked feverish, and nearly collapsed while bathing the baby." Anna put her hand to her throat in a distressed gesture. "I couldn't risk having the baby catch something, so I sent her home and told her not to return until she was well."

"And you haven't heard from her in a week?" May asked, suddenly overwhelmed by panic.

Anna bit her lip and shook her head.

"I wish you had let me know sooner," May said, vexed. "Do you know where she lives?"

Anna nodded hurriedly and started walking into the drawing room, with May at her heels. "Yes, yes I do. I have her address somewhere. She lived with her niece before moving in with us," she added, eager to make amends as she came to a desk and rummaged through its drawers. "She had a room upstairs, so she could be near the baby at all times, but I just couldn't let her stay here, being ill and all. So she went back to her niece."

If Tzu-Lieh had still been at the House of the Black Dragon, she never would have been sent away ill. But, May had to remind herself, not every employer was as concerned about her servants as Margaret Fitzgerald.

"Here," Anna said in triumph, as she took a slip of paper out of one of the drawers. "Here is where she is living."

May read it and recognized the street as being located in a poorer part of the Chinese city.

"What are you going to do?" Anna asked, her voice trailing off.

"Go to her and see if she needs medical attention," May replied.

Anna put her hand on May's arm. "But . . . but the Chinese city, May. My husband says it's dangerous for a European woman to go there alone."

May smiled slightly. "It's dangerous for *anyone* to go there alone. But don't worry, I'll find someone to go with me," and she instantly thought of Alex.

"Please do," Anna said.

May nodded, bade her good day, and returned to her waiting rickshaw. Minutes later, they stopped before Shanghai Zetta's just as Alex came walking down the stairs, a familiar figure in his cream-colored suit and wide-brimmed hat, which threw his face into shadow.

"Alex!" May called, relieved that she had caught him just in time.

He looked up, saw the agitation on her face, and asked, "What's wrong?"

She made a desperate motion with her hands as she fought back the tears. "My amah . . . Tzu-Lieh is sick with a fever. I feel terrible asking you this, but will you come with me to the Chinese city, where she lives?"

"Of course," he said without a moment's hesitation. "We'll go by barrow." And he motioned to a driver.

May scowled as she climbed out of the rickshaw and into the barrow, the memory of her first day in Shanghai. "Are these safe?"

Alex grinned. "Of course, they are, if you can keep your balance."

"I don't mean to inconvenience you, but you're the only one I could turn to."

"I'm glad you thought of me," Alex said simply, "and were not so foolish as to try to go there alone."

"I had been seriously considering it," she admitted.

He glowered at her and shook his head.

Her thoughts were on the amah, as the barrow wound its way through the streets of Shanghai. Why hadn't she visited Tzu-Lieh sooner, then perhaps she could have done more for her old nurse. She was angry with both herself and Anna Cooper-Smith for not informing her of the situation. Fevers were nothing to trifle with, as she knew from her bout with that tropical fever she had in Paoting. Why, Tzu-Lieh could be dying.

May banished any such thoughts from her mind as they passed from the European settlements into the Chinese city. The barrow eased its way through narrow streets with bright red chop signs hanging down overhead, past the innocent facades of opium dens, and through open markets, where fresh fruits and vegetables were piled high, some speckled with black flies.

She was not beyond noticing that every once in a while, strange, unsavory-looking men would slowly nod at Alex, and he would nod in return.

"Friends of yours?" she asked.

He smiled slightly. "Men who can be of use to me upon occasion."

He also kept asking her questions about Tzu-Lieh, and May realized it was a ploy to keep her mind occupied, and she was grateful to him for that.

They finally reached their destination, a crowded squalid area where many Chinese who had just come to Shanghai from rural provinces lived before they found work. The barrow stopped, its driver puffing from the exertion. Alex jumped down, then helped May to alight. The house Tzu-Lieh's relatives lived in was of crumbling gray stone, with a black tile roof in such a state of disrepair that a goodly number of tiles were missing, torn off by wind and weather and never replaced.

As Alex took her arm, he said, "Don't worry. I'm sure everything will be all right."

"I hope so," May said, her voice tight and strained.

Then she gathered her skirts, while Alex ordered the driver to wait, and they both went to the door. After he pounded on it several times, a skinny, sullen girl with a mouthful of crooked teeth suddenly appeared.

"Is this the home of Chen Tzu-Lieh?" Alex demanded firmly, in Chinese.

The girl gave them a blank stare. "What is your business with her?"

"She is my venerable amah," May replied. "I understand she is gravely ill, and I wish to see her."

The girl hesitated, unsure. "I shall ask my honorable aunt if she wishes to speak to you. She is very ill."

"This can't be the niece who works in the textile mill," May said, "otherwise she'd be working today."

"I imagine she's one of many nieces and nephews living in this house," Alex said, his eyes scanning the dwelling.

When the girl returned, she opened the creaking door wider and motioned for them to come inside.

"My aunt will see you," she said.

They followed her into a small dark room filled with hostile eyes, all staring, and May was grateful for Alex's strong, comforting presence. There were Chinese of all ages in this room, from a wizened old grandfather sucking on a water pipe to whipcord-thin girls in their teens, with their undernourished children clinging to their legs. As May and Alex bowed to all, she heard someone mutter, *"Fank-wei,"* and heard a gasp of astonishment as they noticed her auburn hair.

When they followed the niece upstairs, May was conscious of eyes boring into her back. Finally, they entered a tiny room about the size of the hidden room at the House of the Black Dragon, and even in the heat of summer, the stone house was chilly.

There, lying on a pallet on the floor and covered by a thin, ragged blanket, was the amah.

"Tzu-Lieh!" May cried with a catch in her throat, trying to rush to her side, but Alex's arm shot out and held her back.

"Does she have cholera?" he asked the niece in Chinese.

The girl's eyes widened in fear, but she shook her head adamantly, and Alex released May to let her go to the amah.

She knelt down, one hand smoothing hair away from her forehead, and the other seeking a pulse in her neck.

At the sound of her name, the amah's eyes flew open, to rest on May with some surprise. "May-Ling," she murmured, the ghost of a smile on her mouth. "You have come to see your old amah."

"Yes, I have come, and I am going to send for a doctor for you right away, and then I'm going to take you back to the taipan's house and care for you myself." She turned to see Alex hand the niece some coins, presumably for a doctor, and send her out of the room.

Tzu-Lieh, who seemed to have shrunk since May saw her last, twisted and turned, her feverish face breaking out in a fresh sweat. "No, not good joss. The doctor can do nothing for me."

"Nonsense," May said briskly. "You have a fever, but I don't think you're ready to join your ancestors just yet."

The woman managed another smile. "My May-Ling, always defying the gods."

Alex knelt down next to May and placed his hand on Tzu-Lieh's forehead, while May reassured the woman with, "This is a friend. His name is Alex." Then May looked at him and said, "Well?"

"I'm no doctor, but I think she's approaching a crisis. If the fever breaks, she'll be all right."

Tzu-Lieh's face broke out in a sweat that glistened on her forehead and cheeks, and she got a faraway look in her eyes, as though she were looking back into the past and fighting to remember something that had happened there.

"Do you remember New Year's Day, the year before the honorable master died?"

May nodded. "We had spread honey on the kitchen god's mouth so he would not tell tales of us when he went up the chimney to heaven. I remember how you let me tie the red papers on the door and throw the dust into the street."

Tzu-Lieh gave a little cackle. "There was no child as bright and clever as my May-Ling. You were like the monkey, quick and clever as the namesake of the year you were born."

May scowled, feeling confused. "But I was born in the Year of the Ox, don't you remember? You once gave me a red-clay water buffalo on my birthday."

The amah's face suddenly clouded, as she fought to remember. "My mind is confused. May-Ling was born the Year of the Monkey. No," she amended, "the other one was born in the Year of the Monkey."

"What other one?" May asked sharply, suddenly alert.

Fear crossed Tzu-Lieh's face. "Nothing. Forget the ravings of a feverish old woman."

"Tzu-Lieh, what are you talking about?"

The amah closed her eyes and turned her head away from May, as her frail body was wracked by violent spasms. Then she began muttering softly to herself. "The scholar is coming tonight, and I can see the excitement in my missie's eyes, as she dons her best silk robes for him. I disapprove, but she will not listen. I wish my master would come home soon and put an end to this disgrace."

May looked over in alarm at Alex, who was frowning and listening attentively. "I think she's approaching the crisis."

Tzu-Lieh continued, her breath coming in shallow gasps. "What I have feared has come to pass. I offer my missie a solution, even though it means the tortures of hell for me. She laughs and tells me she has a plan. The child is a girl, but not as beautiful as my May-Ling."

May swallowed hard as she gently shook the amah by the shoulder. "Tzu-Lieh, whose child?" she demanded, knowing the answer even as the woman stared at her and replied, as lucidly as if she were not feverish, "Your mother's child, of course. Your sister."

May felt numb all over, as though a Taoist magician had turned her to jade, while a wide-eyed Alex rocked back on his heels.

"A sister," May said, shaking her head as if to clear it. She looked at Alex. "I don't remember my mother ever expecting a child. What did she do with it? There were no other children in the Black Dragon House when I was growing up." May turned quite pale, and she felt lightheaded. "Good God! Did my father know, I wonder?" She closed her eyes, and the lightheadedness vanished. "When did she have the child?" she demanded of the amah. "When?"

Tzu-Lieh wet her lips and took a deep breath to gird

herself against the coming tremor. "The year of the famine. You were only eight years old then, so perhaps it is lost to your memory."

Tzu-Lieh coughed and went on. "There was terrible famine in the province, and the master had left us once again. Everywhere there was death. The village streets were filled with starving people. Some tore down their houses to try to sell wood for food, but there was no rice to be had at any price, except for the Christians. Others were even killing their own children to spare them from wild dogs and wolves that dared come down out of the hills into houses. We heard how many were too weak to fight them and were devoured."

Alex reached out and found May's hand, grasping it tightly.

"I have never seen my mistress so afraid," Tzu-Lieh said, "she who is so fearless. Paoting had stores of food, but it was running out and my mistress knew her own supplies would soon be discovered. Her fear for you, May-Ling, and her unborn child made her close the house and order the servants to prepare for flight. Han, his wife and children—the entire household—departed for Tientsin in several carts. There was danger we would be attacked and our ponies killed and eaten, but luckily, we reached the city safely."

May closed her eyes and let her mind drift back in time. Finally, she said, "I think I remember now. Mother and I went to Shanghai. When we arrived, I was taken away from her, and Nelson's first wife had to care for me. She didn't relish the task, and she locked me in the schoolroom for long hours at a time, and when she finally let me out, I was the happiest child in the world." May stared into space. "I don't remember your coming with us, Tzu-Lieh, for if you had, I would not have been treated so cruelly."

"Han's family and I stayed in Tientsin," the amah said, her voice dying to a whisper. "Your esteemed mother did not wish me with her when the baby was born, perhaps because she did not want me to see what would become of it."

May looked down at the feverish face in alarm. "She didn't harm the baby, did she?"

Tzu-Lieh shook her head. "When she returned after the famine was over, she did not have the child with her, but she assured me it was well and safe. We were to resume our lives as though nothing had happened. But I would often see my mistress sitting alone in the garden by the dragon-eye tree, staring into the still pool, and I knew she was thinking of her scholar, and her other child."

"Who was this scholar?" May wanted to know, suddenly immensely curious about a man who could captivate her mother and cause her to compromise her unswerving love for her husband.

Tzu-Lieh took a deep breath. "I do not even remember his name, it was so long ago. All I know is that he passed through Paoting on his way to Peking, to serve at Court. My mistress met him at the house of another merchant, and she impressed him with her knowledge and her beauty. Then he began to call at the Black Dragon House." The amah's waxen face turned dark. "Most unseemly, their being alone together. If she had been Chinese, it would not be tolerated."

"Did he know of the child?" May asked.

"No," Tzu-Lieh replied. "He went away, never knowing."

May looked up at Alex and felt inexplicably sad.

Then Tzu-Lieh's eyes closed, and she murmured, "I am tired now, so tired . . ." And she drifted off into semi-consciousness. May just lifted her and rocked her gently, not wanting to speak anymore and tire the old woman, even though she herself was burning with curiosity.

Where would a child of mixed parentage go, half Oriental, half white, accepted by neither the English nor the Chinese?

Suddenly a thought so astounding came to May that she felt a jolt of shock.

"Dinah!"

Alex stared at her. "What do you mean?"

"Dinah," May said incredulously. "Of course . . . it explains so much. Dinah is my sister!"

Skepticism was written all over Alex's face, but May plunged on. "What if my mother sent for her illegitimate child years later and accepted her as a daughter? That would explain everything!"

"Would it?" Alex asked.

"Oh, yes, yes," May said, remembering so much of her mother's odd behavior where Dinah was concerned. When Dinah called her Eldest Sister in her mocking way, May hadn't even suspected she literally spoke the truth.

Alex ran his fingers through his hair. "Is there anyone who could substantiate this theory of yours?"

"Why, Nelson, of course," she replied. "He let Mother have the baby at the villa. His first wife is dead, but he is very much alive."

Both she and Alex jumped when the thin girl with the crooked teeth suddenly appeared. "The doctor is here," she said in a hushed voice. "He wishes to examine my aunt, so I crave your pardon for asking you to leave."

May nodded. She was reluctant to leave Tzu-Lieh, for there was still much she had to know, yet she didn't want to disturb the sick woman any more than she had to. She looked down at the round face, so waxy and feverish, and a sliver of fear stuck in her heart. What if Tzu-Lieh should die? May reached down to hug the limp pile of bones one last time before rising.

Her eyes darted to the damp walls, then back to Alex. "This place is dismal as well as drafty. I can't leave her here, but on second thought, I don't think Nelson will approve of my taking her back to the villa."

"Surely he could have no objection to such an act of kindness," Alex replied.

May shrugged. "Nelson's unpredictable."

"Then I'll see that she's taken to a hospital as soon as she can be moved." A brief smile lit up his features. "Don't worry, May. I'll see that Tzu-Lieh is well taken care of."

May smiled up at him and put her hand on his arm. "Thank you, Alex." Then with a long, shuddering sigh, she turned to her amah and whispered, "Good-bye, Tzu-Lieh. I will burn silver papers for your recovery." There were tears in her eyes, and she leaned against Alex all the way downstairs, past all those inquiring eyes and out into the street.

All around her, people bustled past, chattering among themselves. There was noise and color and life. May took Alex's arm and let him help her into the barrow.

"A sister. I have a sister." May said the words as though she couldn't believe them, and it seemed to stick to her tongue unpleasantly. "I always wanted a sister . . . someone near my own age, to share secrets with. I suppose every girl does."

"I'm sorry, May," Alex said quietly, his eyes filled with sympathy. "I can see this discovery has been quite a great shock to you."

"Shock isn't the word for it," she replied. "But Dinah . . ." She shook her head in disbelief, then looked at Alex with a wry smile. "We dislike each other intensely, and the sudden discovery that we're related . . ." She shrugged.

"Nothing says you have to like each other just because you're related," Alex pointed out.

May closed her eyes and rested her head back. "I feel as though I've been thrown off a bridge."

"You'll land on your feet," he said. "You always do."

As the barrow sped back to the villa, May tried to visualize Dinah, searching for some resemblances between the girl and her mother that she should have noticed. But there was nothing, no curve of cheek or angle of chin that both women could lay claim to. The ivory skin, yes, but that was about all. Dinah had too much of her Chinese father in her.

Alex sat there silently, giving her time to think her private thoughts. When they finally arrived at the villa, he said, "We're here, May. Will you be all right?"

She nodded and gave him a weak smile. "I shall confront Uncle Nelson as soon as he returns from the hong today."

"Would you feel better if I stayed?"

"I would, but I don't think the Wrights would appreciate it."

He reached for her hand and kissed it. "Are you sure you're all right?"

May smiled and nodded, then she stepped down from the barrow and went inside.

Why hadn't her mother told her, she wondered as she went upstairs to her room? She knew the answer to that even before she formulated the question in her own mind. No doubt Margaret Fitzgerald had thought very carefully about what such news would do to a daughter who revered her father, who was so shaken by his disappearance and presumed death that she grasped at the first opportunity to be sent as far away from China as possible. Even now, she was shaken and angry. The thought that her mother had once been unfaithful to her father left her feeling bereft.

She smiled bitterly to herself. How could she presume to judge her mother, when she herself had been unfaithful to her own husband? She could see how her mother, constantly left alone—deserted—might succumb to the attentions of someone else. She had always been at ease with the Chinese, so how natural for Mrs. Fitzgerald to let herself be seduced by one.

"Oh, Mother," May murmured. "You should have told me. I would have understood. Really."

She went out onto the verandah and stood there until the carriage came rattling up the drive, carrying Nelson Wright home from the hong.

May went downstairs and was waiting for him at the door.

"Uncle Nelson," she said to him, as he came walking up the steps, "May I have a word with you, in private, in your study?"

"Can't it wait?" He looked tired and cross, as he wiped his pink face with his handkerchief.

"No, it can't," she replied.

"Well, I would like to wash and change first."

"It is very important."

He glared at her as he snapped, "Oh, all right, if it absolutely cannot wait . . ."

When they were in the study, and Nelson had closed the door behind him, he turned to May and said with some exasperation, "Now, what is so important that it cannot wait for me to wash and change?"

May clasped her hands in front of her to keep them from shaking. "I've had a most enlightening afternoon. I've just come from the Chinese city, where I visited my old amah, Chen Tzu-Lieh."

"Your nurse? The fat one who used to come to Shanghai with you and who now cares for the Cooper-Smith child?"

May nodded. "She is very sick with fever. In fact, she may even die."

Nelson's face grew impatient. "I hope what she has isn't contagious."

She ignored that and said, "She told me something very interesting, something I had never known before, that I have a half-sister."

Nelson's eyes widened, and he snapped, "That's absurd!"

"The woman thought she was dying, Uncle Nelson. Why would she lie? It was eating away at her, and she felt she had to clear her conscience in case she should die."

He rose and paced the room, glancing at her in astonishment as he pulled at his mustache. May could see him searching for an explanation. "I've never heard such poppycock in all my life, May. The woman must have been delirious or even lying."

"She was feverish," May admitted.

"Well, that explains it. She must have gotten you confused with some other child she cared for. I say, I can't believe you'd even entertain such a suspicion at all. It puts your parents in an unsavory light, don't you think?"

May hung her head.

"I've known your parents for years, girl," he said, furious with her now. "And I will swear to you on several Bibles that neither Margaret nor Tim had any byblows." Nelson wiped a thin sheen of sweat from his face. "I'm astounded at you, May, really astounded that you could even think such a thing of either of your parents. They were in love with each other, and their behavior was exemplary in every way."

"But they were human," May cried and told him what she remembered when she was very young, of coming to the villa and not seeing her mother for days.

"And you think she was giving birth in this house?"

May nodded miserably.

Nelson came up to her and looked her squarely in the eye. "May, you are simply making too much out of this, and you're upsetting yourself for nothing. You must put such wild fancies out of your mind completely. I assure you, you have no sister, Chinese or otherwise."

"How can you be so sure? Tzu-Lieh was so adamant,

Nelson. Why should she lie when she was convinced she might die?"

He was suddenly annoyed with her again. "I don't know the answer to that. The woman was delirious and confused, as I said. She didn't know what she was saying, that's all."

A tiny suspicion began to grow and flower in May's mind. "Did Mother swear you to secrecy? Did she make you promise not to tell me, if I should find out?"

Nelson scowled. "No, May, she did nothing of the sort. She never swore me to secrecy about anything, because there was nothing to swear me to secrecy about." He was becoming agitated again, and May could tell he just wanted her to drop the subject and leave him alone. "I think you have been out in the sun too long. You should go upstairs and get some rest."

She sighed. "Perhaps you're right."

But, when she went to her room and lay down on her bed, nagging doubts began to plague her once again. Could Nelson be lying? But what would he have to gain by not telling her the truth? He insisted that she had no sister, but Tzu-Lieh seemed very lucid and sure of herself. And what did she have to gain by telling May lies?

May's head was beginning to throb, so she mixed herself a sleeping draught, drank it, and dozed off into a deep, dreamless sleep.

CHAPTER TWELVE

The following day, May awoke feeling as though a dark fog was enveloping her from head to toe, and the mood couldn't be shaken, no matter how hard she tried. She had an overwhelming desire to go back to bed and just sleep for days, the same feeling she had had when she finally came to accept her father's death. But she forced herself to wash, dress, and go downstairs for breakfast, even though every movement was slow and sluggish, as though she had stones attached to her wrists and ankles.

Nelson scowled at her as she sat down to breakfast. "Are you all right?"

"Yes," she lied. "I just didn't sleep well."

"Perhaps you shouldn't go to the godown today."

"No, I'll be all right."

Once May arrived at the warehouse and began working, her absorption in her task did make her feel better. As long as she did not think of what Tzu-Lieh had told her, everything was fine.

"How is Willie today?" Tobias inquired. "I understand our morning rides have been curtailed for a while."

May nodded from behind the desk. "He's being punished for his little escapade."

Tobias shook his head. "He really is a good lad."

"I agree. But he's got to learn not to go running off and worrying everyone to death."

"Speaking of running off, you gave us quite a fright yourself."

May thought of Alex and smiled. "I wasn't in any danger."

"Good. Well, I'll leave you to your own devices for a while. I've got to go down to the wharf to supervise the unloading of one of the junks."

"Fine," May said, her mind back on her work.

She continued to scribble away, glancing up now and then to study the design on a Ming vase set before her. She had been writing for what seemed like hours when the acrid, unpleasant odor of sweat caused her to sniff and glance up. Mr. Dawes was lounging against the doorjamb, watching her, an eager light in his eyes.

"Yes?" Her tone was cold and impersonal.

His red, wet mouth split in a smile. "My, you do work hard, don't you? I've been standing here for a good ten minutes, and you never even noticed me."

"May I venture to suggest that the time spent watching me could have been put to more productive use just doing your job?"

He looked injured. "I don't mean anyone no harm. I just heard you were an educated, refined lady with exceptional taste in Chinee art."

May did not succumb to his flattery or smile. "Will you come to the point, Mr. Dawes?"

He moved away from the door and, as he approached the desk, May noticed for the first time that he held a scroll in his hand.

"I bought this painting from a Chinee fella. He claimed it was worth a lot of money, and I just wanted your expert opinion, ma'am." He held out the scroll to her. "There's no harm in that, is there, now?"

May, overcoming her aversion to the man, took the proffered scroll. "I am not an expert in paintings, Mr. Dawes."

When she unrolled the scroll and saw its subject matter, May's face seemed to ignite as she sat there in stunned silence.

"Do you like it?" Mr. Dawes whispered.

May sprung to her feet and flung the scroll at the man's

leering face. "Take your filth and get out of here!" she snarled, advancing on him in a blind rage, unmindful of her own safety.

Dawes just grinned as he picked up his scroll, rolled it up, and backed away. "Wait until you see what I have for you the next time."

When May was alone, she clutched at the desk for support as a feeling of revulsion rose in her throat. Shaking uncontrollably, she found her way to her chair and sank down into it, where she held her head in her hands to stop the waves of nausea. Her face felt cold and clammy to the touch, and she prayed she wouldn't be sick.

In England, a man could be locked in prison for possessing such a picture, but in China such graphic depictions of intimacy were accepted and even considered stimulating.

She sat back, breathing slowly to calm her quaking insides. If Dawes had wanted to upset her, he had certainly succeeded, and May mentally called him every vile name she knew.

The question now was, what should she do about it?

Her mind settled down, and she began to think rationally again. She should tell Uncle Nelson, that was for certain, and he could dismiss the man, and good riddance. But how could she possibly prove what Dawes had done? She didn't have the scroll as evidence, and, even if she did, he could deny it, making her look like just another hysterical woman.

Worse still, Uncle Nelson might refuse to let her come to the godown anymore, thus taking away her only refuge. No, she didn't want that. Perhaps the best course of action was to forget the incident ever happened and to stay out of Mr. Dawes's way.

She would also make certain she wasn't left alone again.

It wasn't as easy as May had hoped. Whenever she went out of the office to fetch another object, even with Tobias present, it seemed Dawes was always nearby, watching her. It was as though, by showing her that picture, he had imposed his will on her and forged some kind of intimate bond between them. She was acutely aware of the man and seemed to sense his presence.

And his words kept coming back to her: "Wait until you see what I have to show you next time."

May was becoming as skittish as a cat on a stove. Every noise outside her office caused her to jump in alarm, every sound caused her to whirl around, eyes wide and poised for flight.

The situation became worse as the week progressed, but she would not stay at the villa, for that would admit defeat. Still, she looked forward to three-thirty, when the carriage came for her, and she and Nelson left for home. Dawes could not reach her there, so she was safe. Or so she thought.

At the villa, Alex continued to insinuate himself into her thoughts. She had never met a man quite like him, and he puzzled her. Men usually were at ease in her presence and quickly bared their souls to such a degree that May often discovered more about them than she wished to know. But Alex was different. Except for the time he told her about his painful childhood in England, he kept his soul well-guarded. Even in the hidden room and Soon Sebastian's garden, when he had taken her with such fierce passion, he had not totally surrendered his spirit in return. May wondered if any of his lovers had ever truly possessed him.

To try to keep Alex out of her mind, she thought of her mother in Paoting. She yearned to hear from her again, especially about the fluted jade bowl and why it had appeared in the hands of Comprador Wu. May had waited and waited, but no letter came.

And there was the carnelian phoenix button sitting in her bureau drawer, which presented another mystery. Did the Sons of the Celestial Phoenix reach all the way to Shanghai? Was the button a warning of some sort?

May shook her head in puzzlement, then went to bed, only to see Dawes' red, wet mouth gaping at her.

"Is everything all right, May?" Nelson inquired of her the next morning, when she joined him for breakfast on the verandah. "You have circles under your beautiful green eyes." He scowled as he smartly tapped his austere boiled egg with the back of his silver spoon. "Your work at the godown hasn't been exhausting for you, has it?"

She laughed as she shook out her napkin and spread it across her lap. "Nonsense, Uncle Nelson, I love my work. I look forward to it."

"Well, something is bothering you. Come, tell your Uncle Nelson."

May sighed and used her standard excuse. "I'm just worried about Mother, that's all." And other people, she added to herself.

"Margaret Fitzgerald is an extraordinarily capable lady who can take care of herself. She has done admirably for all these years. It was one of the reasons your father married her."

May perked up. "Was it?"

He nodded. "Tim was always wandering off somewhere, so he needed someone capable of managing alone. Sometimes your mother would go with him, and other times she'd stay at home."

May shuddered. "To be alone . . . here."

"Oh, there were the servants."

"But to be in China, without your husband for protection or comfort . . ."

Nelson made a face. "I know what you mean. I used to tell Tim he was a fool for doing it, but I don't think Margaret minded so much."

"How long was Father usually gone?" May asked, interested by this other side of her father's personality and his relationship to his wife.

"Usually two months at a time. And then when you came along, your mother stayed in Paoting—at least until you were old enough to travel."

May wrinkled her forehead in a frown. "I have vague recollections of being packed into a cart and seeing strange places."

"I told Tim he was daft for carting a child around, but he just laughed and said, 'It's you who are daft, boy-o. It'll be good for her, you'll see.' "

"I wonder if Mother was ever lonely for my father?"

Nelson was silent and reflective a moment. "I suppose,

for Margaret was head-over-heels in love with him. But she did have you for company. Women tend not to need men when they have a child to nurture. Maternity tends to stifle passion."

May blushed and looked away, for Nelson had never spoken of such matters before, and it seemed out of character with the man's clipped, dry manner.

"I apologize for being so frank, my dear. It's living in China, I suppose. It tends to dampen one's inhibitions a bit."

May suddenly thought of Dawes again. "Uncle Nelson?"

"Yes?"

She made a movement with her hand. "Oh, nothing. Thank you for telling me about Mother, that's all."

He was regarding her curiously, assessing the situation and debating what to do about it with his usual flair. "Your mother and I have been friends for many years, May. If Tim hadn't found her first . . ." He spread his hands and chuckled. "Who knows? You might have been my daughter instead. Margaret Fitzgerald is a headstrong woman who had to come to China. She is free to be herself here, in a way she could never be anywhere else. She is too . . . too"—he groped for just the right word—"*grand* for England or Ireland. She tends to follow her own road, no matter what the consequences to anyone else, even those she loves. I realize that must sound selfish to you, and I don't really mean to present your mother that way."

May felt the old bitterness touch her. "It's very difficult being her daughter sometimes."

"I think it was sometimes difficult for Tim to be her husband."

May caught at this right away, snapping to attention. "What do you mean, Uncle Nelson?"

He brushed her interest aside with an offhand laugh. "Oh, nothing, just talking off the top of my head, that's all. Don't pay me any mind."

But she did wonder, as they finished their breakfast, and the talk turned to more innocuous topics—Willie's escapade, the weather, the price of silk. This was the second time Uncle Nelson had said something cryptic and refused to explain himself. First he had said Alex was a man whose whereabouts should be known at all times, and now this remark about her parents.

Breakfast over, Number Six boy came forward to clear away the dishes, while Nelson rose and went to his study. When he returned with his keys, he and May left for the go-down.

May, as was her custom now, stayed with Tobias whenever possible, lest Dawes confront her again. But this morning, when she arrived at the godown, she found Tobias even whiter than usual, looking decidedly green around his mouth.

"Are you ill?" she demanded.

He nodded dismally. "I ate fish last night, and I don't think it was fully cooked. I suspect I should have stayed in bed today, but there's so much work to be done . . . a shipment of silk coming in, porcelains . . ." His voice trailed off.

"You go home, Tobias. Comprador Wu has returned, and, between us, I think we can keep things running smoothly."

"Thank you," he murmured. "I'll check with the taipan and let him know I'm leaving."

When he left, Comprador Wu appeared, and May explained Abbott's absence. She found she couldn't be too cordial to the man after the fluted bowl incident, but they managed to work well together nonetheless. He padded off to direct the men, while May went to the office to continue writing her descriptions.

It was almost tiffin time when the sudden silence alerted her to something being amiss. The outer warehouse had suddenly grown so still, she scowled and rose from her desk.

"Quiet, isn't it?" a hateful voice said from the doorway.

May stopped, startled to see Dawes there.

"All the men have gone to unload the junks. Except me. So that means we're alone, you and I." And he took a step forward into the office.

May stood ground, glaring at him, while her heart pounded wildly. "Get out."

"Fierce, aren't you? They all act that way—at first. But I figure, since you didn't tell old Abbott about my pretty painting, you must have really liked it. And you must like me."

"I think you're as repulsive as your logic is faulty."

He took another step toward her. "You won't think so—later. I'll have you purring."

Dawes lunged at her, and that's when May screamed. She battered at his outstretched arms, clawing and scratching, while he swore and struggled to grasp her wrists.

"What in God's name—?" And, like a miracle, there was Nelson Wright, filling the room with his presence, as he dragged Dawes away from May and flung him against the wall.

"What in the hell do you think you're doing?" he snarled at the man, a blue vein standing out on his temple. "May, did he hurt you?"

"No, Uncle Nelson, he didn't."

He turned back to Dawes. "You're damned lucky."

Dawes looked affronted. "What's a bloke supposed to do with a judy like her working a few steps away? It's mighty tempting. And especially with her flirting with me every chance she gets, real provocative like."

"Liar," May's voice was filled with disdain.

"You're dismissed," Nelson said. "Come to the hong and collect the wages that are owed you, then get out of my sight."

"A woman like that's got no business working around men," Dawes muttered, "no business at all."

"And I don't want to ever see your face around here again," Nelson called out after him, as he disappeared out the door.

May sunk down into her chair and rested her head in her hands. "Thank you, Uncle Nelson, you came just in time."

"I wanted to see how the business was progressing without Abbott, and it's a good thing I was here." He scowled. "I was afraid this would eventually happen, May."

She looked up at him in alarm. "What do you mean?"

"I was afraid having you here would be a disturbing influence on the men, and that one of them would step out of line someday."

"The other men have been perfect gentlemen—with the exception of Dawes."

"All it takes is one Dawes," Nelson pointed out.

"In a sense, it is my fault," May said, rubbing the back of her neck. And she told Nelson about the time Dawes handed her the scroll.

Nelson turned green. "My God, May! Why ever didn't you say something sooner? I would have had the scum locked up in jail and left to rot."

She gave a lame shrug. "It was my word against his."

"Don't you think I would have believed you?"

"Oh, I suppose I just wasn't thinking straight. I knew if I told you, you'd do exactly what you're going to do now, forbid me to work in the godown, and I couldn't face that."

Nelson stroked his mustache. "I can't allow this to happen again, May."

Fear began to gnaw at her. "What do you mean, Uncle Nelson?"

"I'm afraid I just can't have you working in the godown any longer." When May gave a wail of disappointment, he said, "I'm sorry, but this is the way it's going to be. You're my responsibility while you're here in Shanghai, and I never should have agreed to this in the first place."

"Oh, please let me stay, Uncle Nelson. I'll be all right, really, now that Dawes is gone."

"I'm sorry, May. That was our bargain, remember? We'll have to find something else for you to do."

He was taipan, and his word was law. May knew it was senseless to argue.

She saw her days stretch out before her, interminable mornings and afternoons and evenings filled with inactivity. She could see herself with plenty of time to dwell on Tzu-Lieh's revelation, and the black melancholy descended on her once again.

She wished she were plain and pinch-faced, like Miss St. John. Then the Captain Forsythes and Daweses of the world would chase other skirts.

When they returned to the villa, they discovered a pale-faced Emily reclining on her divan, moaning and thrashing about like one in pain.

"Emily!" May cried, rushing to her side and kneeling to take her hand. "What is wrong? Has something happened to Willie again?"

"The most terrible calamity has befallen us!" she wailed. "My vinaigrette. Quickly!"

Nelson glared down at her. "Emmy, pull yourself together and tell us what happened. I'm not in the mood for histrionics."

She sat up and flashed a sheet of notepaper under his nose. "Miss St. John has run off. With a *man*. She's eloped."

May read the note and handed it to Nelson.

"Can you imagine?" Emily cried. "Not even proper notice. Pouf! The ungrateful wretch is gone, just like that. What am I to do? Willie needs a governess. I certainly can't manage the child by myself." And she fanned her flushed face.

"Willie did say something to me about Miss St. John having a beau, some man she kept meeting on their nature walks in the park," May told him.

Emily's dark eyes snapped in irritation. "Why on earth didn't you tell me?"

May shrugged. "I had supposed Willie told you."

"My son and I seldom have anything to say to one another," she replied, before she realized what she was saying. Then she clasped her lips shut and kept silent.

"This does present a problem." But, even as Nelson said it, his mind was racing ahead, thinking of ways to solve it.

Suddenly, May had an idea. "Why not let me be Willie's governess?"

Two pair of eyes stared at her incredulously. "You, May?" Nelson said.

"Yes. Willie and I get along famously, and I'm certain I know more mathematics and history than he does—enough to teach him for a while, anyway." When Nelson and his wife exchanged looks, May plunged on, in her most persuasive tone. "And I'm sure I'd be a much better governess just by virtue of the fact that I'm quite fond of the child. And besides, since I'll no longer be working at the godown ("I'll tell you why later," Nelson added aside to Emily), I would feel I was doing something useful. I would save you the aggravation of having to hire someone else."

"Nelson?" Emily asked hopefully.

"Hmmm. You make a convincing argument, May."

"I think it's a satisfactory solution for all involved," she said.

"But you must be firm with him," Nelson warned. "Willie can be a little demon when he wants to. And he would have no scruples about using you unmercifully."

"I'm well aware of the pitfalls," May said.

Nelson smiled. "Well, then, you can try the role and see if it suits you."

May smiled at him in wordless thanks. "Shall I tell Willie?"

"No, I shall. Tonight."

Emily was wreathed in smiles, and May suspected that she was relieved to have the burden of caring for her own child lifted from her shoulders once again. "Well, now that that's settled . . . A letter came for you today, May. I put it on the table in the foyer."

That letter, May discovered, was from her mother, and it contained some disturbing news.

> *The climate here is beginning to change toward the missionaries in Paoting and the surrounding villages, becoming decidedly chilly. When I went to buy some porcelains this morning, I noticed several antimissionary posters on several buildings, and I know Harriet is beginning to be afraid. She keeps the children indoors all the time now, never letting them even out to play among themselves, especially since one of their converts was stoned. Without Chad's diligent doctoring, the man never would have lived. I fear it is not going to get better.*
>
> *But don't worry about me. I continue to conduct my business with no interference. Mr. Yee sees to that. And I have my faithful Han, T'ing, and Lien to protect me. Chad, of course, is safe, because he heals them and cures their pain. We both send our love, and I send my regards to Nelson and Emily and—of course—my Willie.*

May's eyes scanned additional paragraphs, but nowhere did her mother mention the fluted jade bowl of Weng Ta-Chung.

"How odd," May muttered in consternation. She had plainly mentioned it in her letter and specifically requested information about it, and yet her mother had refused to acknowledge her request.

Perhaps Margaret Fitzgerald had too many other matters on her mind, May thought in resignation. It was so easy to overlook a request in a letter.

She strolled out onto the verandah, the urge for physical activity welling up inside of her. If she had been in Surrey, she would have ordered her horse saddled and would have ridden for miles, until her arms and legs were stiff and sore. But here, all she could do was pace the verandah and wonder why her mother had not mentioned the fluted bowl.

May sighed and started upstairs for her room, where she would wait for the time when Willie would be told he had a new governess.

Later that evening, after dinner, Nelson called both Willie and May into his study.

"Sit down, son," he ordered.

"Thank you, Papa, but I prefer to stand."

May had to avert her head, so he wouldn't see her smile.

"As you wish," Nelson said. "Now, I've called you here to tell you that, beginning tomorrow, you shall have a new governess."

Willie's face lit up like a beacon. "You mean Miss St. John won't be my governess anymore?"

"That's correct. She has left our employ to get married, and your Aunt May has agreed to take her place."

The child's face was alive with incredulity, then was split by an ear-to-ear grin. "Aunt May? My governess? Oh, Papa, how splendid!"

Nelson remained stern. "You must remember, young man, that I'll have none of your antics any longer. Is that understood?"

"Yes, Papa," he replied soberly, trying desperately not to fidget.

"Very good. We understand each other, then. Run along

to your room. Under the circumstances, I think your punishment can be suspended starting tomorrow morning."

May watched him run off, wondering just what she had gotten herself into.

The following morning, she rose early to go to the schoolroom to examine the books Miss St. John had used, and she managed to discern just what lessons Willie should learn today. She was just finishing the history text when the door opened and a familiar dark head peeked in.

"Good morning, Willie," she greeted him with a smile. "Are you ready to begin your lessons?"

"I must have my porridge first, Aunt May."

She looked at him in mock horror. "I wouldn't dream of depriving a young man of his porridge."

His eyes grew huge and conspiratorial. "But I don't have to study all the time, do I? We shall have time for some fun, shall we not?"

"But of course," May said. "All work and no play makes Willie a dull boy. We do have to get some studying done, and you'll find me a much more exacting teacher than Miss St. John ever was."

"I can't study on an empty stomach. I have to have my porridge first."

"Agreed."

After breakfast, May and Willie plunged into their lessons and May found him to be as she suspected, a bright, intellectually curious pupil who was eager to please. Teaching him was a pleasure, and by tiffin time May felt a great deal of satisfaction in her choice. She felt useful, and her forboding thoughts were kept at bay, until lessons were over and she had some time to sit by herself in her room or the folly.

She began to hate these quiet times, when she couldn't avoid thinking of all that had happened to her since her return to Shanghai. May shuddered when she thought of Dawes, and she tried to shut him out of her mind much as one would ignore a nagging toothache. If it hadn't been for him, she would still be working at the godown.

And there was the puzzle of her half-sister, Dinah. May found herself wondering about her mother and the Chinese scholar who had fathered the child. What had caused Margaret Fitzgerald to search for the illegitimate daughter she had given up years before? Guilt? Loneliness?

There was also the question of her mother's involvement with the concubine's brother, and this made May's sense of forboding grow even stronger, like the strange calm before a roaring typhoon. What if Alex were right? What if her mother were somehow involved with such a man?

May thought of Alex in Soon Sebastian's garden, and she sighed. In spite of her initial mistrust of him, she found herself being drawn to him, slowly and steadily.

"Break away," a voice inside her urged, "before it is too late." But she was afraid she had passed that point long ago.

The next day, Willie did so well at his lessons, May decided to give him a treat and take him out for the afternoon.

When she asked him where he would like to go, he clasped his hands together, screwed up his cherub's face and said without hesitation, "The Chinese city."

May looked at him skeptically. "I don't think it would be wise for us to go there."

His face grew long and dejected. "Now you sound exactly like Miss St. John, Aunt May, and I thought you were my friend."

"I am Willie, and one day we shall go to the Chinese city, but with a man to accompany us and protect us. But for now I think we should restrict ourselves to the park or the Bund."

"Well, let's go watch the ships then. I never get tired of doing that."

Since the carriage was back from the hong, May let Willie ride up front with the mafoo, while she sat in the back. All the way to the Bund, Willie kept chattering excitedly with the mafoo, who listened patiently. When they arrived, they disembarked, leaving the mafoo to unhitch the ponies, while he waited for them to return. May took Willie's hand and joined the people on the promenade.

Strolling beneath the cool, shady trees, May sometimes let Willie run ahead to chase the pigeons, but always called him back before he ran too far. When they stopped to watch the ships, Willie suddenly tugged at May's sleeve. "Aunt May, there's a Chinese man watching us."

She smiled down at him. "I imagine many people are watching us. We make a handsome couple, you and I."

"But this man has been watching us ever since we got here," the boy said, all seriousness. "I think he's been following us."

May felt her blood turn to ice as she slowly turned, pretending to look at the sky. There was a young Chinese man standing not twenty feet away. When he saw her staring at him, instead of looking away, he started walking toward them.

"Aunt May!" Willie called out in distress.

She patted his hand reassuringly. "There's nothing to be afraid of." She hoped she was right.

The Chinese approached, bowed respectfully, and said, "Missie May-Ling?" in Chinese.

"Yes."

"I have been asked to give you this." And he drew a slip of paper from his sleeve, handed it to her, bowed, and started walking away in short, quick strides. Then he was gone, blending into the crowd without a trace.

"What is it?" Willie demanded.

"It's a note," she replied, unfolding it. "I wonder what it says."

It was written in Chinese.

> *Esteemed friend of my father's.*
> *I must speak with you on a matter of grave urgency. You would do me a great honor to call upon me tomorrow afternoon after early rice.*

It gave an address and was signed "Weng T'ai-Lung."

T'ai! Weng's son was here in Shanghai. May stared at the characters, not believing her eyes.

"Well?" Willie demanded, looking up at her expectantly. "What does it say?"

"It's from an old friend," was May's reply, her eyes scanning the crowds for any sign of the messenger.

"Oh, is that all?" Willie moaned. "I thought it was a secret message."

May smiled at him, while a thousand questions flooded through her mind. "No, Willie, it's not a secret message."

"Well, in that case, let's go to the hong and see Papa."

"Yes, let's do that."

The following day, after Willie's lessons were done and May was free for the afternoon, she had Number Six boy summon a rickshaw, and, after telling Emily she was going to do some shopping, she left for the address T'ai had given her.

Thoughts crowded May's mind, as the rickshaw sped on its way. What was Weng's son doing in Shanghai? Did he have any connection with the man she and Willie had seen that night?

But her uppermost thought was, why did he wish to see her at all, considering his formal and somewhat cool reception after his grandmother's murder?

May had been close to T'ai once, when they were still children, but, as they grew, so had the distance between them. She'd noticed that, with each passing year, T'ai had become increasingly absorbed in his own self-interests. No simple life of an artisan for the son of Weng Ta-Chung. T'ai's ambition was to rise through the ranks of China's civil service system and secure a more prosperous life than his father's. And he had succeeded.

When the rickshaw pulled up in front of an elegant home, obviously belonging to someone of wealth and influence, May was taken aback. She had expected some hole-in-the-wall, like Alex's rooms near the docks, but, then, T'ai was high enough in the bureaucratic hierarchy to have influential friends.

She rang the bell, a servant appeared, and, after stating her business, she was shown to a quiet, incense-scented chamber overlooking a small, neat garden dominated by a calm reflecting pool.

She hadn't been waiting more than a few minutes when T'ai himself entered the room.

He bowed. "Friend of my childhood, it was most kind of you to come."

May felt like Weng had returned from the grave to stand before her, and tears sprang to her eyes. "Friend of my childhood, I am surprised to see you in Shanghai."

Though T'ai smiled, the smile was unfathomable as he indicated a chair for her. Then he tugged at a bellpull and joined her. He was dressed in a flowing robe of white, indicating that he was still in mourning for his father. "I am allowed a period of mourning, and my position is held for me until I return."

"I am sorry about the jade carver." May hung her head. "I mourn his loss as much as you do."

He regarded her without blinking. "I heard how you and your honorable mother tried to free him, and I also heard of the great sacrifice you were willing to make on his behalf."

May felt herself blush.

"It was the generous act of a generous spirit. You have no cause to be ashamed."

She stared at him. "You are a high government official, and yet the mandarin gave you no consideration concerning your father. Why? I do not understand."

"Mandarin Ki and I are of opposing factions within our government," he explained. "That is why there was no special consideration for me."

"Your father was not guilty of the crime they accused him of committing," she said. "Ki had no right to do what he did . . . no right."

T'ai's eyes narrowed. "That is why I came to Shanghai."

A servant appeared, carrying hot water and cups for tea, so conversation was suspended while May poured. When the servant padded off, she said, "What does Shanghai have to do with your father's death?"

T'ai sipped the dark brew. "Ki did allow me to see my

father before he died. He assured me on the graves of our ancestors that he did not kill his venerable mother, but that she was dead when he entered the room. He told me he was awakened by her crying out in the night, and, when he rushed to her chamber, he found her nearing death, and a man hurrying from the room. My father debated whether he should chase the man or tend to his dead mother, and he rightly decided to stay with her, although the criminal escaped."

May's eyes were round with horror.

T'ai continued, his voice quivering with emotion. "Father said he got a glimpse of the man's face, and that he recognized him as a man who had come to the house once, to buy some carvings, and that he said he was from Shanghai."

"That's all that brought you to this city? It's such a slender clue. The man could have been from another city."

"No, I have another reason. Shortly after Father's execution, a green-jade fluted bowl was stolen from my mother's home."

May turned white, and her hand shook as she set down her teacup. "I have seen the fluted bowl."

T'ai's eyes widened as he leaned forward expectantly. "Here in Shanghai?"

She nodded and related her discovery of the bowl and what Uncle Nelson told her happened to it.

"That is possible," T'ai agreed. "Many stolen goods find their way to the Europeans. I suspect my grandmother startled the thief, and he killed her, later returning for the bowl when my father was taken away to prison."

"How do you propose to find a man you've never even seen?" May wanted to know. "There must be hundreds of thousands of people in the city alone."

"Yes," he agreed, "but even fewer people trade with the English, so that narrows my search. And since you have told me the bowl has appeared at Benton and Black, that narrows my search still further. In addition, the Sons of the Celestial Phoenix know much and can be most helpful to one another. I will find the man responsible for my father's death, never fear, because I do not work alone."

"And were you responsible for this?" May said quietly, reaching into her pocket and retrieving the carnelian button.

"I see you found my missing button."

"So it was you that night, watching us at the villa. Why didn't you just call at the house?"

"I would never have gotten past the lion who guards your gates, so I had one of my brothers watch you for an opportune moment to deliver my letter."

"You know I'll assist you in any way I can," May declared, rising. "You have only to ask."

T'ai also rose and bowed. "As yet, the mystery is a long way from being solved. There are too many pieces to the puzzle, but soon I may test your love for my father."

"Nothing you could ask me to do would be a difficult test," she said. "I owed your father my life. It is a debt I would gladly repay."

May bowed and departed.

On the way back to the villa, May felt a surge of excitement at these latest developments. She wondered if the man who killed Weng's mother was somehow connected to the elusive Win-Lin. He was supposed to deal in stolen Chinese goods, and the fluted bowl was certainly valuable. But to place Win-Lin in Paoting was to connect him with Margaret Fitzgerald.

May felt her mouth go dry. Had Alex been right then? Was her mother somehow involved with Win-Lin after all? She shook her head, refusing to believe it. There had to be some other explanation.

She was haunted by the question of how the bowl had come into Benton and Black's possession in the first place. Perhaps Win-Lin and Comprador Wu had some sort of arrangement, whereby Win-Lin supplied Wu with stolen merchandise, and Uncle Nelson unwittingly sold it. She shivered. How could she even prove such an accusation against a comprador who served Benton and Black with such efficiency?

May was in a quandary and didn't know which way to turn, and as usual she thought of Alex. Perhaps he could offer her a solution. She shook her head in consternation when she realized she had never even told him about the fluted bowl, what with Willie's escapade and Tzu-Lieh's startling confession driving all other thoughts out of her mind.

Well, tomorrow she would go to Shanghai Zetta's and tell him what she had learned.

The next morning, May told Willie he could have the morning free and his lessons in the afternoon, and she set off by rickshaw to Alex's rooms. Within fifteen minutes the vehicle stopped before the boarding house, and, when May paid the driver to wait and stepped inside, there was Zetta herself, gold tooth and all, swilling her morning beer instead of tea and flirting with a one-armed sailor.

"Is Mr. Wolders in?" May inquired, ignoring the sailor's blatant appraisal.

Zetta threw back her head and cackled. "*Mon ami,* he is upstairs. *Entrez, mam'zelle,* he won't mind."

May thanked her and walked up the stairs, quietly going down the corridor until she came to Alex's room. She knocked on the door several times, but there was no answer, so she twisted the knob and opened the door just a crack.

"Alex? Are you here?" she called, stepping inside.

She smelled the opium, thick and cloying, as it hung in the air, even before she saw the two people lounging on the bed, the opium lamp between them, glowing with a dull ruby at its heart. The woman, clad only in loose blue silk pajamas, had her face averted so all May could see was a curtain of straight black hair. Alex leaned over and whispered something to her, while his hand searched for her breast.

The woman giggled, tossed her head, and revealed her face.

May felt herself turn white. "Dinah!"

At the sound of her name, Dinah froze, wary as a fox, but, when she saw who the intruder was, a slow smile of satisfaction spread across her face. "Alex, see who is here. It is Eldest Sister." Her sweet voice was triumphant and filled with mockery.

Alex could barely raise his head, and his eyes were heavily lidded, as though he was still in the drug's thrall. He squinted and blinked a few times, fighting to see her, but the drug wouldn't release him. All Alex could do was fall back helplessly against the cushions.

"May?" His voice was thick and slurred as he rubbed his eyes, and May felt a sudden pang of pity at the sight of a powerful man shorn of all his strength, as effectively as Delilah had shorn Samson.

Dinah, still smiling sweetly, said, "Won't you join us, Eldest Sister? I don't mind sharing."

May just turned, groping for the door through her tears.

"May!" she heard Alex call after her, louder this time, and he must have been struggling to his feet, because she heard a crash behind her, as the opium lamp tipped over.

But she was beyond his entreaties as she went flying down the stairs, her hand to her throat, unable to breathe.

"Done so soon?" Zetta cackled, and the sailor guffawed as May went running by and fled out into the street.

CHAPTER
THIRTEEN

When May returned to the villa, she immediately went to her room before anyone could see her, locked the door, and sank into the chair. She laced her fingers together to keep them from shaking, but she could not stop the sobs that wracked her shoulders. After what seemed like hours, when she had no tears left, she let herself think about what she had witnessed in Alex's room.

He had been making love to Dinah—her sister—and May could still see Missie Sly-Eyes' mocking smile and hear her words that stung and taunted: "Won't you join us, eldest sister?" But another more pressing thought nagged at her. Where had Dinah come from? The last May knew, Dinah had wanted to go away from Paoting, ostensibly because May had been so hostile to her. Now she was here in Shanghai, looking quite at home in Alex's room. The only explanation that May could think of was that Dinah had been with Alex all along, hidden out of sight, so no one would know they were lovers.

May closed her eyes and rested her aching head against the back of the chair. She couldn't understand why she should feel such deep hurt and primitive jealousy. Alex owed her nothing—he could sleep with whomever he pleased. She was no innocent fresh from the schoolroom, equating passion with love. True, the times they had loved each other, she had desired him as much as he had desired her, but that's all it was—physical desire.

May brought her clenched fist down against the chair's arm. "Yet why does Dinah matter so much to me?" she demanded aloud.

She rose and paced the room restlessly, trying to sort out her conflicting emotions. Could she be falling in love with him? That disturbing thought brought her up short, and May stood stock still for a moment in the middle of the room.

That she found to be even more disquieting than discovering him with Dinah. "Oh, no," she whispered.

Then she unlocked the door, summoned one of the amahs and had her draw a bath immediately. May soaked in the tub for what seemed like hours, then she scrubbed the sweet, sticky scent of opium from her skin and washed it from her hair. But, as she rubbed herself dry, she imagined she could still smell it in her nostrils, and it nauseated her. She would have the dress she wore burned tomorrow.

Alex called the next morning, while May was in the schoolroom with Willie. She told Number Five boy to say that she was not in, for she did not want to see him. The morning after that, Alex called a second time.

May said, "Tell Mr. Wolders I am no longer at home to him. You might even tell the guard not to admit him."

She watched from the upstairs window as he stepped into his rickshaw and disappeared down the drive. Did she imagine the despondent look on his face, the air of resignation, as he jammed his hands into his pockets?

May worried that something she said or did would betray her feelings to the rest of the household, for at tiffin Emily said, "You look ghastly, May. Has Willie been a handful?"

"Oh, no!" she said hurriedly. "He's an angel, and I love taking care of him."

"I know what's wrong," Emily said, as she put her hand over May's. "You need to get out of the schoolroom and do some socializing."

May stared at her blankly. "Socializing?"

Emily nodded. "There's a party at Lady Hertford's tonight, and I wish you'd come along. You haven't been out since you became Willie's governess. I know your mother always thought Lady Hertford a bore, but she knows some interesting people."

May found herself blushing. "After Captain Forsythe, I—"

"Don't worry about that," Emily reassured her. "That was all in the past."

"But what shall I wear? I don't really have an evening gown."

Emily's dark eyes sparkled at the prospect of outfitting May. "Don't worry about such nonessential details. I had a dress made last spring, but the shade of green was all wrong for me. On you, it will be lovely. You're so much more slender than I, and it would have to be taken in, but if the sew-sew amah works all afternoon, it will be ready for you by tonight."

"Oh, I couldn't possibly . . ."

"Please, May, say you'll come. We do so need some fresh faces at these affairs, and so many eligible men will be there."

May relented. "Oh, all right. I'll come."

She submitted herself into Emily's hands, and after tiffin the Chinese sewing woman brought the dress to May's room. She exclaimed over the exquisiteness of the fabric as she smoothed it with her hand, but, when she slipped the dress over her head to try it on, she uttered a cry of disappointment, for the garment only came to her ankles and hung as straight as a curtain.

"This dress could fit two of me," she murmured in dismay.

"No worry, missie," the sewing lady said, taking in around the shoulders, bosom, and waist and letting down the hem.

May spent half an hour being fitted, then went to find Willie, who was feeling neglected and sulky. By the time Nelson came home and they had tea, it was time to dress for the party.

True to Emily's word, the sew-sew amah had performed her magic and padded into May's room, the green dress held as reverentially as a votive offering. When May tried it on, she couldn't believe her eyes. The dress of shimmering silk the color of the fluted bowl was cut low to reveal her snowy throat and the gentle swell of her breasts. She was so used to being covered up to her chin that at first she thought the gown left her indecently exposed. But, she reminded herself, this was the fashion for soirees in Shanghai. Robin had always said the combination of her tall, slender body and full breasts was devastating, so May decided she would be just that tonight—devastating. Perhaps some masculine attention would ease the hurt of seeing Dinah with Alex.

She turned, admiring the way it clung to her tiny waist and gently flared out around her hips for a perfect fit. Even the hem had been let down, so the gown now reached the floor.

After May finished arranging her hair in a heavy coil that rested on the nape of her neck, she stood back to assess herself. Dressing up and the prospect of a party perked up her flagging spirits, and she found herself smiling.

May left her room and hurried down the hall to Emily's chambers. After knocking and hearing Emily say, "Come in," May entered and kissed her on the cheek as she sat before her mirror.

"Thank you, Emily. The dress is beautiful."

"It's you who are beautiful, my dear. The dress is merely a backdrop," Emily said, as she cast a critical eye over May. "But your ensemble needs one final touch." She rose and opened her jewel case and returned with a necklace. "Nelson gave this to me when Willie was born."

She held out a small cabochon emerald set in a plain gold setting, strung on a simple chain.

"Oh, it's beautiful!" May said breathlessly, "but I couldn't possibly wear it."

Emily brushed her objections aside with a simple, "Nonsense. I want you to have it," and fastened it around May's neck. "This can be worn only by someone of singular beauty,

LADY JADE

so I don't know why my husband gave it to me. I need lots of jewels," she added, patting the diamond and garnet necklace that blazed across her chest.

"Oh, Emily . . ." May leaned forward and hugged her. "I can't thank you enough."

The woman had tears in her eyes. "It's the least I could do, May, after treating you so shabbily when you first came here. I want you to know that I was never so ashamed in my life for my part in that entire affair. It forced me to take a long, hard look at myself." She hung her head and looked away. "I saw a shallow, petty, gossiping woman, and I didn't like it. But I've tried to change."

May was at a loss for words at Emily's heartfelt confession. "Let's forgive and forget, shall we?"

Emily nodded, then turned at the sound of someone at the door. "Here's my husband. We can be on our way."

May couldn't remember enjoying a party more than the soiree at Lady Hertford's that evening. Contrary to what her mother had said, May found her hostess to be charming and rather witty, with a knack for choosing guests that could complement one another and provide for a stimulating evening.

But the chief topic of conversation was the theft of some old and valuable diamonds from some woman May had never seen before, a member of the English aristocracy named Viola Winchester who was visiting relatives in China. Every person who engaged May in conversation had an opinion about the theft.

"I say," Emily muttered to May at the first opportunity, "first this German girl disappears, and now this . . ." She shook her head. "We'll all be murdered in our beds next."

May was having such a good time, she almost forgot about Alex and the pain he had caused. She was, however, to be forcefully reminded later that night, when she and the Wrights returned to the villa rather late.

May whispered good night to Nelson and Emily and walked back to her room on tiptoes, lest she wake Willie. She let herself into her room, where a thoughtful servant had left a lamp burning so she wouldn't have to grope around in the darkness. She went at once to the mirror to undo Emily's pendant.

"Did you enjoy yourself?" a familiar voice inquired from the opposite side of the room.

May's heart seemed to stop beating as she started and whirled around. "Alex!"

He was seated in the chintz chair not eight feet away, watching her intently, his head propped up against his hand. He was dressed entirely in black, so he would blend in with the night, and the dark clothing made him look even leaner.

"How did you get in here?" May managed to keep her voice down, so no one would wake, but she couldn't keep from trembling.

His mouth turned up at one corner in a sardonic half smile. "No walls are high enough to keep me out when I want to get in. You should know that by now."

May reached up to pull her hair out of its knot, thought better of it, and let her hand fall. "Well you can leave the way you came in. I have no desire to see you."

He said nothing, but his eyes wandered over her. "I've never seen you wearing an evening gown before. I've seen you in that white gauze, looking like some confection, or in those damn Chinese clothes that make you look like a boy. Or," he added with a wicked smile, "without any clothes at all. But never like this. I must say," he added, his voice strangely husky, "you look like you should be standing in the foyer at Deadly Hall, at the foot of the staircase to receive guests."

She thanked him cooly for the compliment, but said no more.

"Why have you refused to see me for the last two days?"

"I thought that was rather obvious."

"I'm genuinely sorry you happened in on that little scene," he said, his eyes never leaving her face. "I assure you that I don't often indulge in opium—run it, perhaps, but seldom smoke it."

May waved her hand in impatience. "The opium is of no consequence."

A frown of puzzlement formed between his brows. Then he said, "It's Dinah, isn't it?"

"No," she said too quickly, looking away.

"Yes, it is, I can tell. If it didn't matter to you, you would continue to see me, to let me explain, but you're furious with me."

"Why should you care how I feel? You have your Dinahs and your Javas. You have no need of me."

He was on his feet in an instant, but made no move toward her. "I've known a few women in my thirty odd years. Some of them meant something to me, but most of them didn't. We enjoyed each other for the moment, and never expected any tomorrows. I always kept them at arm's length."

"How sad," was all May said.

"I never used to think so . . . until I came to know you."

May's heart seemed to stop, but she kept her emotions on a tight rein, suddenly wary. When she saw him cast a lingering look at the bed against the opposite wall, she said, "So *that's* why you came tonight," as though she had known it all along.

Anger darkened his face. "No, I didn't come here to seduce you. I'll admit that I desired you in the hidden room and in Soon Sebastian's garden." He took a deep breath. "You have a way of just looking at a man, that—well, a man would be a fool not to take advantage of such a situation with such a beautiful and desirable woman."

"I was not entirely blameless," May said.

He continued to stare at her, and finally he swallowed hard, as though it were an effort to speak. "You mean a great deal to me, Lady Jade."

She said nothing as she undid the knot and tossed her head to free her hair. When she spoke, her voice was soft and injured. "If you care for me so much, as you claim, why were you with Dinah?"

"May, don't look at me that way."

"I just want to know why you were with her." She fought back the tears as she asked, "Has she been your mistress long?"

"She has not been my mistress," he corrected her. "It was the opium that caused my desire for her."

May gave him a skeptical glance. "Then why did you smoke that poison at all? You know what it can do to you."

"Only if you let it. Once in a great while, I feel the need for it. The drug deadens the senses, but frees the imagination, until it takes on senses of its own, making things appear to be what they're not. It can be an exciting experience. And, in Dinah's case, I was making love to a faceless phantom."

"You haven't yet explained why she was with you at all."

His expression grew wary. "I can't tell you that—yet. I had my reasons, but they have nothing to do with you. Dinah has been with me, but, except for that one meaningless time, she is not my mistress, and that is the truth."

"Why should I believe you, Dutchman?" she asked.

"Because you don't have a mean or spiteful nature, May. You are honest, and I think you can recognize the truth when you hear it."

There was such a look of torment on his face that she almost surrendered, almost flew to him and put herself in his power. But a nagging, lingering doubt caused her to hold back.

A bitter smile jerked at one corner of his mouth. "Your hesitancy tells me all I need to know. I can see my coming was a waste of time." Then he turned and started walking toward the French doors.

"Alex," she called after him. When he stopped and turned, a question in his eyes, all May said was, "Did you ever take Dinah to Soon Sebastian's garden?"

"No, never." And he disappeared through the doors and into the night.

May followed, watching as he flung a rope over the balcony rail, leaped over it in one light, fluid movement, and started lowering himself down a pillar with the agility of a spider. She went out and heard him drop softly to the ground, jerk the rope free, then sprint across the lawn to the concealing trees and darkness.

"Call him back," a desperate voice urged from within, "before it's too late. Tell him you believe him."

May rushed up to the balustrade, ready to call his name, but she caught herself and fell back, though reluctantly. She clutched at the cold stone railing until her fingers ached and until she knew that he was out of earshot. With a deep sigh, May slowly turned and went back inside, her heart as heavy as if it had been cast in bronze.

The next morning, while listening to Willie recite his history lesson on the Battle of Trafalgar, May found her mind wandering.

Finally, Willie gave an exasperated sigh and said, "You aren't listening again, Aunt May. Come to think of it, you don't look well this morning."

May, who was growing more irritated with people telling her she didn't look well, nonetheless managed a small smile for the child.

"Have you lost your best friend?" he asked.

"You could say that."

"Well, I'll still be your friend."

"I know that, Willie, but this was a grown-up friend."

He grew instantly suspicious. "Not a gentleman friend, like Miss St. John's."

"Yes, Willie."

He turned pale, as he bolted out of his seat and flung his arms around her. "Oh, Aunt May, you won't run away, like she did, will you? I couldn't bear it, if you did."

Small chance of that, May thought wryly, as she gently tousled his dark curls. "I can't promise that I'll be here forever, Willie," was all she said, for she refused to make false promises to the child. He was old enough to know people often grew away from one another to form new friendships and alliances.

Willie grew thoughtful, twisting in her arms. "If you are so unhappy, Aunt May, why don't you join Abbott and me on our picnic tomorrow? We're going to the park to listen to the band, and then we're going down to the waterfront to watch the boats," an activity Willie relished more than eating cookies.

"I don't wish to intrude on your day. Perhaps Mr. Abbott wouldn't want me on your picnic."

Willie beamed. "I'm sure he won't mind. He likes you. In fact, he told me he likes you very much."

When Tobias Abbott arrived late the next morning, his smile of delight told May that he wouldn't mind if she accompanied them on their picnic. She wore a new dark skirt, a white blouse, and a wide-brimmed straw hat with two tails of grosgrain ribbon hanging down the back, casual attire for a stroll in the park.

Willie himself looked quite dashing in his shirt and white shorts, his socks up to his knees.

"I told you Abbott wouldn't mind," he said gleefully as they piled into the carriage that Nelson graciously agreed to lend them for the day.

They rode to the park, where no dogs or Chinese were allowed, found a tiny patch of unoccupied ground beneath a cool, shady tree, and spread the tablecloth that the cook had lent them for the occasion. May unpacked sandwiches and other cold edibles, as well as lemonade for Willie and a bottle of wine for herself and Abbott.

May felt as though she were picnicking on the banks of the Thames with Nigel in the sweet first years of their marriage, watching the Oxford students boating their ladies slowly down the placid river against a backdrop of gothic spires and towers. Perhaps if there had been a child she would be doing that now, settling for a long, dull stretch as a young matron, breeding her way into middle age, like all her sisters-in-law. There certainly never would have been a Robin, or an Alex. "Everything happens for the best, Ling-Ling," her father always said, and May was beginning to wonder if her inability to provide a Monckton heir wasn't a blessing in disguise.

"Is something troubling you?" Tobias inquired gently, ever attuned to her moods.

"I was just thinking about something from the past," she replied, removing the hatpin from her bonnet.

Willie was wolfing down his sandwich, his eyes darting throughout the park, searching for any situation that might give him a few moments of freedom.

When he finished his food, down to its last crumb, he said, "There is a soldier over there, and I think he's an American. Do you mind if I go talk to him, Aunt May? I've never spoken to an American soldier before."

"Well, only if you don't wander off, and, if he doesn't want to talk to you, you come right back, understand?"

"Yes, Aunt May," Willie said, scrambling to his feet and dashing off, running on steam as always.

May watched him approach the soldier, who must have been all of eighteen, and begin talking, his hands clasped behind his back. The soldier smiled down at him and began talking as well. It looked as though Willie had found a friend.

"You have such a way with children," Tobias said.

May started. "One only needs to treat them as people, not burdens, that's all."

Then Tobias was looking at her with a quizzical expression on his face. "I'm not one for fancy phrases Mrs. Monckton," he began uncomfortably, "but I just wanted to say you look especially fetching today."

"Why, thank you. How sweet of you to say so," she replied, the color staining her cheeks a soft rose.

"I mean every word of it." He drew his knees up, clasped one wrist with his other hand, and kept staring at her.

"Tell me about yourself, Tobias," May said, suddenly uncomfortable. "We've worked together in the godown, but I know so little about you."

"There's nothing much to tell," he confessed. "I'm the eldest of nine children in a poor family. My parents own a small shop in London, and I was lucky enough to be sent to school rather than work at an early age. My mother had grand expectations for me, you see. Well, my teacher thought I was a bright, clever lad—too clever to spend my days in a sweat shop—so he contacted this friend of his at Benton and Black. They were looking for bright lads to send out to China, so I jumped at the opportunity."

"So you became Nelson Wright's griffin."

He nodded. "That was seven years ago."

"And what are you going to do with your life?"

Tobias scowled, as though he didn't like the question. "Well, I don't think I'm ruthless enough to become taipan, so—"

"Ruthless?" May said with a laugh. "Are you implying that your employer is ruthless?"

In all seriousness, he said, "Oh, yes. Nelson Wright is quite ruthless when it comes to business. You wouldn't believe me if I told you what he does to competitors." Then he blushed and stammered. "Forgive me for talking out of turn. I realize the taipan is your friend."

"Quite all right," May said. "But go on about yourself."

"Even if I don't make the grade, at least I hope I can eventually rise a little higher in the company. And I'd like to marry one day and raise a family. I suppose every man wants that." He plucked out a stalk of dry grass. "Of course, I couldn't offer a woman a grand life like Mrs. Wright's, with a position in society and all, but we'd be comfortable. I'd see that she never wanted for anything."

"It sounds as much as any woman could hope for, Tobias," May said.

A look of hope flashed across his face, and it looked for a moment like he was going to say something. Then he changed his mind and fell silent. They sat there, just watching the people drift from one end of the park to the other, stopping briefly to exchange pleasantries with friends, then moving on.

Finally he said, "And what comes next for Mrs. Monckton?"

May's brow clouded as she stared at her empty wineglass with its smudged rim. "I don't know, at this point." But she knew what she wanted was not the life Tobias offered.

A long shadow suddenly fell across the tablecloth, and they both looked up to find Alexander Wolders standing there, watching them with anger in his cold blue eyes.

"May, I would like to speak to you," he said.

Before Tobias could open his mouth to protest, May

said, "Of course. Will you please excuse me for a moment, Tobias?"

As May followed Alex across the park to a quiet, unpopulated part, her heart gave a queer little lurch. He looked as though he had been suffering, with his rumpled linen suit and a day's growth of stubble shadowing his jaw. And he didn't look as confident of himself, with his hands jammed sullenly into his pockets and his shoulders hunched over, as though he were walking into the wind.

"So you've set your cap for Death's Head, have you?" he asked.

"Tobias is a kind man, and I count him a friend," she replied, "but that is all."

"He's obviously infatuated with you, like an overeager puppy."

May ran the back of her hand across her brow, and raised her chin. "I like him. He's a very sensitive person, once you break past his shyness."

Alex faced her and grasped May's wrist, his eyes angry. "Is this your way of punishing me for Dinah?"

She struggled to keep her own anger under control. "I am not punishing you for anything. I enjoy Tobias's company, and I shall continue to see him, if I wish."

To her surprise, Alex said nothing and did not release her wrist.

May suddenly asked, "Have you told Dinah we know she is my sister?"

"No," he replied.

"I take it she is still with you."

"Yes."

Her face fell, and she fought to keep back the tears. "Then we have nothing to say to one another." May shook her hand free and turned to go.

"Wait, May. Please." When she turned expectantly, he reached into his pocket and took out a small package wrapped in silk. Before she could object or draw away, he slipped it into one of her deep skirt pockets. "I just wanted to give you something my father once gave to my mother. She didn't know what it meant, at first, but you will." And he was gone, striding across the park grounds with his long, loping gait.

"Alex, take this back!" she called after him, not knowing whether to run after him and risk disapproving stares or to stay where she was.

But he just ignored her and melted into the crowd, leaving her to turn and trudge back to Tobias. When she sat down and looked back, Alex had disappeared.

Tobias looked at her in curiosity, but was too polite to inquire into their conversation. May smiled at him. "Do you suppose it would be possible for us to take a carriage ride around the Bund? I think it would be most refreshing, and I know Willie would enjoy it."

Tobias nodded, then said, "I never thought I'd see the day when Alexander Wolders would be undone by a woman."

May was plainly startled. "Undone? Alex Wolders doesn't care a fig for me."

The pale man rose and managed a smile. "I wish I could agree with you," was all he said, and went off whistling for Willie.

May couldn't get Alex out of her mind as she sat next to Tobias in the carriage. Alex was still with Dinah, so perhaps she had lost him already.

They paraded down the Bund, the white buildings just a blur through her tears. The ponies arched their necks and strutted between Shanghai barrows and rickshaws, and people turned to admire the red-haired beauty sitting there so serenely.

Willie, his knees stained green from kneeling on the grass, leaned over in his seat, craning his neck for any sights.

"Look at that ship!" he cried, pointing at a sleekly outfitted gunboat surveying the harbor.

"It must have been marvelous in the early days," Tobias murmured, his eyes staring dreamily at the harbor. "I've heard it said you could look out over Shanghai harbor and see a forest of clipper ship masts. What an awesome sight!" Then his voice grew wistful. "Can you imagine our fathers and grandfathers building a city like this out of the silt and mud of a swamp?" He sighed. "I think I was born sixty years too late."

May smiled gently at him. "Why, Tobias Abbott, I think you're a romantic at heart."

He blushed. "Yes, I suppose I am."

The carriage sped by the Benton and Black hong, locked up for the day, then moved down the waterfront.

"There's one of our junks down from Soochow," Tobias said. "The men don't usually work on Saturday, but this had to be unloaded at once, so they're being paid extra."

The men were working like slaves, their striped shirts dark with sweat, as they grunted and heaved in the hot, muggy sun. They looked like they were living for the moment they could tumble into the nearest bar for a cold glass of beer and a woman's soft, comforting arm. It was a hard life and a simple one, with a man being judged solely by the work he could do, not by his pedigree.

Suddenly, a familiar face caught May's eye, and she felt the blood run cold in her veins.

There, among the men unloading the junk, was Dawes.

She would have recognized those dark features and that wet, red mouth anywhere. She shivered uncontrollably.

"Is something the matter?" Tobias asked.

"Tobias, what is Mr. Dawes doing unloading Uncle Nelson's junk?"

He looked over at her in surprise. "Why shouldn't he be there? He is employed by Benton and Black. You know that yourself, from the time you worked in the godown."

May ran her tongue over her lower lip. "But I thought Uncle Nelson had dismissed him."

The pale man stared at her as though she were daft. "Let Dawes go? Whyever for? He works like a draught animal, and he does anything he's asked."

"You didn't know?" May asked in a weak voice.

"Know what?"

She told him exactly what had happened with Dawes and his scroll, keeping her language couched in phrases that would prevent Willie from knowing what she was talking about. And she told him what Nelson had done.

Tobias Abbott turned red with anger. "That's despicable. No, I never heard about the incident. Otherwise I would have thrashed him myself and then dismissed him on the spot. And, as far as I know, the taipan never let him go. At least he never said anything to me about it. Of course, there could be some mistake. Perhaps he just forgot to tell me."

May felt puzzled. Why had Nelson told her the man had been dismissed, when in fact, he had not? Why go through such an elaborate charade at all?

When the trio returned to the villa, May discovered that Nelson and Emily had gone out for the afternoon, so her plans to question him in depth about Dawes would have to be postponed. She was sure, however, there was a reason for his being there. Perhaps the man was working without Uncle Nelson's knowledge.

After Abbott left, May was alone with Willie, and they went to the folly to enjoy a cold glass of lemonade and eat sesame seed cookies.

"I had the most interesting conversation with the soldier," Willie informed her, a cookie in one hand and a glass in the other. "He was most kind and not at all impatient with me the way some grown-ups are."

"I am pleased you had a good time," May said.

"I do think I would like to go to the Chinese city to a fortune teller," he said. "Will you take me soon, Aunt May?"

"I've told you before, the Chinese city is no place for an unescorted lady."

Willie stuck out his lower lip in a pout. "You would have me."

May suppressed a smile. "Yes, that's true, but I mean we'd need an adult escort, such as Mr. Abbott." Glancing up, she saw Nelson emerge from the house with a cricket bat in hand, so she said, "I think it's time for your cricket lesson."

"Come along, son," Nelson said. "Let's see how well you do today."

May watched them take up positions on the lawn, with Willie at bat. Finally, after a half hour of strenuous play, Nelson had had enough and came into the folly.

"Whew!" he said, puffing like an old man of seventy. "One does work up a thirst out there in the sun."

He poured himself a glass of lemonade and flopped down across from May. "The child's game is improving. He'll be ready for the playing fields of Eton soon enough."

May smiled absently, wondering if now were the best time to broach the subject of Dawes. "I saw something interesting today."

"Oh?"

She told him about their carriage ride along the Bund and down by the wharves. "I think you should know that we saw Mr. Dawes unloading one of your junks."

"Dawes?" Nelson looked puzzled, his brows knitted in a frown. Then recognition dawned. "Dawes. Oh, yes, the art connoisseur. Unloading one of my ships, did you say?"

Was May imagining things, or did his eyes narrow imperceptibly? "Yes," she said. "I thought you had dismissed him after that incident with me."

"I did," Nelson replied without hesitation, "and I'm going to talk to Wu the first thing on Monday to find out why the man is still working for us. I said I never wanted to see his face in the godown again, and I meant it." He sipped his drink. "You know, sometimes my good comprador takes certain responsibilities upon himself. Perhaps he figured that because Dawes was a good worker, and we're short-handed at the moment, that he could get away with this. Well, I'll see to it that he doesn't."

May rose. "I felt you should know."

"Thank you," Nelson said.

When she went up to her room to think about so many things—seeing Alex in the park and Dawes unloading the junk—May finally remembered the package Alex had given her. She couldn't very well have opened it in front of Tobias and Willie. In fact, she had been reluctant to open it at all, half-fearing what she would find. She took a deep breath and reached into her pocket to draw out something that felt hard through its soft silk wrapper. Her brow knotted in puzzlement as she undid the thin cord that bound it.

She removed a circular piece of pale lavender jade, carved with exquisite open work on the face and with two loops on the back, through which a slender leather belt could be threaded. It was a woman's girdle ornament designed to be worn with a ch'ang-fu. The carving on the front was a wild goose with outstretched wings surrounded by lotus and leaves.

"My mother didn't know what it meant at first," Alex had said, "but you will."

And she did. The goose was the symbol of conjugal fidelity, and the lotus suggested permanence. Alex had given her a love token that some Chinese man had given to his woman as a sign of undying love, just as his father had given it to his mother.

The tears were streaming down her cheeks now, and she felt a mixture of sadness and joy. He was too proud and free to bring himself to say that he loved her, but he had given her something that must have been very precious to him. Alex had not given it to Java, or Dinah, just as he had not taken those other women to Soon Sebastian's garden, his private place—and, suddenly, even Dinah didn't matter anymore.

It would be dark soon, so she couldn't go to Shanghai Zetta's tonight. But there was always tomorrow.

CHAPTER
FOURTEEN

The next day, May thought Willie's lessons would never end, but finally she finished, clapped the books shut, and told him to run along and play, leaving her free for the rest of the day. She then put on a bonnet, went outside and had the guard at the gate summon a rickshaw, to take her to Shanghai Zetta's. She had to talk to Alex, and she would risk Dinah's mockery to do it.

When she arrived there, however, and hurried through the door, a surprise awaited her.

"They're gone?" she said to Zetta.

"*Oui.* Yesterday, the two of them packed up and went God-only-knows-where. But that's the Dutchman for you. Regular gypsy, he is."

"Did he say where he was going?" she pleaded.

Zetta shook her head. "*Non.* He didn't tell me, and I didn't ask." She gave May a searching look. "You seem a woman of quality. Why would you want anything to do with the likes of the Dutchman?"

May ignored her, bid her good day, and turned to leave.

Despair weighed heavily on her shoulders as the rickshaw sped back to the villa. He had lied to her, she thought bitterly, trying to hold back the tears. Even while he had been giving her the jade ornament, he had been planning to run off with Dinah.

Suddenly she felt ashamed of herself, for being so quick to assume the worst of him. Alex was not the kind of man to give a woman a love-token casually. Perhaps it was his way of telling her to have faith in him while he was away, or perhaps he was on Win-Lin's trail again, and he and Dinah had parted company. She would like to believe that was the reason, but why hadn't he left her some word?

May sighed dismally, decided she would trust him—at least for a little while—and prayed he would reappear soon, to explain himself.

If she thought she had more surprises than she could tolerate for a while, she was to be surprised still further, for the following morning's edition of the *North China News* had some information that was totally unexpected.

"Bad news, I'm afraid," Nelson warned her, when she joined him for breakfast on the cool verandah.

May blanched, as she took her seat, and he set the paper at her place. "Not Mother."

He shook his head and stabbed at a column with his finger. May read:

> *A missionary was killed last week in the outport of Paoting. A Mr. Nicholas Hammond, of the Church of the Divine Redeemer, was preaching to an unruly populace when the mob attacked him. The minister was beheaded.*

May's hand flew to her mouth in horror, but she forced herself to read on.

> *The mob then burned the church. According to our sources in the city, they have learned that the missionary's wife and children were not harmed. British officials were dispatched to the city upon learning of this scandalous outrage, but nothing could be determined from talking with Chinese officials there. The few Europeans in the area have*

*been urged to leave until the hostilities subside. The attack
in Paoting is symptomatic of the other troubles in the north.*

The article contained an account of another antimissionary riot further north, but May could read no further. She sat back in her chair, trying to absorb what she had just read.

"Poor Nicholas," she muttered.

"I'm very sorry, May," Nelson said gently. "Those were the missionaries you knew, weren't they?"

She nodded dismally. "It doesn't say anything about Mother or Dr. Gates, does it?"

He shook his head. "Nothing. I assume they're all right, but I'll visit the British Consulate tomorrow just to be certain."

"Thank you. They should have left when they had the chance." She was crying now, unable to control the tears. "First there was the tomato that someone threw at him, and then they beat his converts. The Hammonds should have gone when they had the chance. Why didn't they see this coming?"

Nelson shrugged. "These missionary fellows don't see it our way. It's part of the risk they take, to bring what they feel is the truth to the heathen Chinese." Nelson gave a little snort. "Some of them are just aching for the chance to become martyrs, if you ask me."

"I suppose you're right, but I don't think Nicholas was one of those." May rose. "Poor Harriet. I wonder what she'll do now."

"His wife? Perhaps she'll continue her husband's work," Nelson suggested.

"I doubt it. She wasn't made of the same mettle. I always got the impression she was in China just because he was and would give anything to leave."

"Wouldn't we all," Nelson muttered under his breath. Then he added, "Perhaps they're with your mother, or maybe they went to Tientsin."

"That's possible. They would find refuge with the other missionaries there."

Then May bid him good morning and went back upstairs, all thoughts of breakfast forgotten.

All morning May couldn't concentrate on Willie's lessons. Her thoughts were miles away, dwelling on Alex, then the Hammonds, and back to Alex, always Alex. She felt as though she were stranded on a desert island, alone, the only person on the face of the earth. She found herself sighing and staring into space, while Willie droned on and on, reciting his numbers.

A tug at her sleeve jerked May out of her reverie. She looked down to find Willie staring reproachfully at her.

"You're doing it again, Aunt May," he accused.

"Doing what?"

"Drifting off like that. You haven't been paying any attention to me. I can tell you have something on your mind, and I know how to make you forget what's troubling you."

"And what would that be?"

His dark eyes sparkled. "A visit to the necromancer." Then he proceeded to state his case with the persuasiveness of a barrister. "The fortune teller could tell you what your future held, and, since I'm sure it's going to be fine, that would cheer you."

"Your logic astounds me, Willie."

"What do you say? Shall we go?"

May still felt reluctant. "I don't know, Willie. I don't think your parents would approve."

"Oh, what could be the harm in it?" he demanded, turning on his charm full force. "We would only be gone for an hour at the most. I've heard of a necromancer on the edge of the Chinese city. Abbott told me he went to her once, and she predicted his future quite accurately. I even asked him for her name and address, and he wrote it down for me."

The child had thought of everything, and May could see a budding taipan in the making. "I don't know, Willie . . ."

"Please, Aunt May," he begged. "I've even saved some money to pay for it."

He had, indeed, thought of everything.

"All right," May surrendered. "Find your address, get your money, and let's go."

The fortune teller's house was a good half-hour away from the villa by rickshaw. The woman who answered the door was sour-faced and smelled of unwashed skin and the stale peanut oil that clung to her faded blue robe. She asked them quite disagreeably what they wanted.

"We want our fortunes told," Willie said.

"You have silver?" the woman demanded, and, when Willie dipped into his pocket and produced the coins, she snatched them away with practiced quickness and beckoned them to wait until she had finished with several other customers.

After fifteen minutes, they were ushered into a dark, foul-smelling room that contained only some floor cushions, a green pottery buddha, and a dish of wilted lotus that had been placed before it as a votive offering. May and Willie seated themselves and waited for the fortune teller to get the book and yarrow sticks by which she saw the future.

"You go first, Aunt May," Willie said, ever the gentleman.

May took the sticks, bunched them together, and let them fall into the pattern the woman would read and relate to her. The necromancer screwed up her face and stared at the design for the longest time before replying. "You must not trust one that is close to you. If you do, grave misfortune shall befall you."

May felt her mouth go dry. "Is this person a man or a woman?"

"Man," she snapped.

"Can you read his name?"

She shook her head. "No name. That is all, no more."

"So much for my good fortune, Willie," May said wryly. "Now it's your turn."

Willie took the sticks and imitated May, by bunching them together, then letting them fall. The old woman stared at them from all angles as she scrutinized the configurations.

"The child is in grave danger," she said in a raspy voice. "The configuration does not bode well for him."

May grabbed Willie's hand, for he had suddenly gone pale at his game gone wrong. "Will I die?" he whimpered.

The necromancer shook her head. "Not you, but someone close to you."

May's anger burned like a hot coal. "This is a horrid trick to play on a child!" she scolded in Chinese.

The woman's eyes narrowed stubbornly. "No trick. The sticks never lie. They always tell the truth, whether you wish to hear it or not."

May jumped to her feet and pulled Willie after her. "Come Willie, let's go."

Willie looked on the verge of tears as they climbed back into the rickshaw and started back to the villa. "I'm sorry, Aunt May. I guess this wasn't such a good idea."

She patted his hand. "Don't worry, Willie. The fortune tellers are often wrong."

"But the sailors said that this one often told the truth, that the things she predicts come true. Does that mean we are in danger, Aunt May?"

"I doubt it, Willie. The sticks are just a game, that's all."

But the woman's words had shaken May more than she dared admit. On the one hand, her Western mind dismissed necromancy as poppycock, something the ignorant used to amuse themselves and to blame someone else for their failures rather than doing something about their own situation. But on the other hand, she had known the predictions of many fortune tellers to come true. She had seen it work often enough in Paoting. Once their cook had gone to a fortune teller, who predicted that she would soon be a widow. Within a month, Cook's husband was drowned in a boating accident.

"You must not trust one that is close to you."

A man. That meant either Alex, or Uncle Nelson, or perhaps even Tobias Abbott. And Willie was in danger as well. Why would anyone want to harm the child?

An unexplained feeling of forboding and dread sent shivers up May's arms. She was beginning to wish she had never returned to Shanghai.

They said nothing to each other as they rode back to the villa, though May could see Willie was now worried by the fortune teller's words, but trying hard to keep his fears from her.

"Don't worry," she said with a smile as she reached over to tousle his hair. "I'm sure much of what she said is poppycock."

But the child was not convinced.

As the rickshaw pulled up at the villa's gates, Willie nudged May's arm. "Look, Aunt May. The guard is fighting with someone."

May raised her head to see the guard holding a struggling slip of a girl who thrashed about trying to break his hold. When she turned, and May caught a glimpse of her face, she started, for she recognized Tzu-Lieh's niece, the one who had admitted them to the house that day.

May immediately ordered the coolie to halt, and she stepped down to intervene.

"Let the girl go!" May commanded, her eyes flashing green fire.

The guard returned her challenging look and did not release his prisoner. "She was trying to sneak in. The taipan gave me orders not to let any Chinaman into the grounds unless he says so."

"She came to see me," May retorted, "and I do wish to see her. So, if you would be so kind as to let her go . . ."

Reluctantly, he did let her go, and the girl rushed to May's side and flashed her crooked smile. "A thousand thanks."

May told the coolie to take the curious Willie back up to the house, while she drew the girl aside. "And how is your aunt, Chen Tzu-Lieh?" she asked anxiously. "Is she . . . ?"

The girl shook her head. "My esteemed aunt no longer has the fever, and she wished me to come here to offer you thanks for sending her to the hospital."

"But she is better," May said with a sigh of relief.

"She will return to her duties as amah soon."

May's smile was radiant. "That pleases me and makes

my heart glad. Tell your aunt that I shall see her soon, when she returns to the Cooper-Smiths."

When the girl bowed and departed, May watched her disappear down the street. Then she turned and strolled up the drive toward the house, the necromancer's ominous words forgotten in her happiness that Tzu-Lieh had evaded death.

Perhaps it is a good omen, she thought to herself, as she walked through the door and into the foyer.

If May thought her life would resume its orderly pattern, she was doomed to disappointment, for, no sooner did she try to put the necromancer out of her mind, than T'ai appeared to ask a favor of her.

Early the next morning, finding herself unable to sleep, May went for a stroll on the far side of the grounds, the tree-shaded part where she had first found the carnelian phoenix button. The trees provided cool shade, and the day was not yet blistering, although, judging by the angry glow of the dawn sky, it promised to be a scorcher.

She was just about to return to the house for an early breakfast, when she heard someone softly call her name. Startled, she turned her head just in time to see T'ai jump down from the wall with the agility of a monkey.

May glanced back at the house, to make sure no one had seen him. "T'ai! What are you doing here? If the taipan's guard catches you . . ."

"Missie May-Ling, I must speak with you on an urgent matter."

She glanced at the house uneasily again. "We can't talk here. The guard will see us when he makes his rounds."

"There is a teahouse not far from here on the next street. Will you meet me there as soon as you can?"

May nodded. "I shall have to wait until the taipan leaves for the hong, but then I shall meet you there," and she turned and walked back to the villa.

The hours until Nelson left passed slowly, but finally his carriage disappeared down the drive and through the gates. May asked Emily if she could be excused from Willie's lessons to run an errand for a little while. Emily nodded absently, and May hurried out the door. Within fifteen minutes, she was at the teahouse.

The tiny building was packed with Chinese this morning, as they sat huddled shoulder to shoulder, enjoying dumplings and sweet tea before going off to work. A few of them scowled at May as her rickshaw pulled up to the door, and she caught the words, *"Fank-wei!"* Sensing their hostility, May decided it would be prudent to remain inside the rickshaw until she knew that T'ai was definitely there.

When she saw his stocky figure come striding toward her, she paid the driver and joined him.

He led her over to a secluded table in a garden near the teahouse, ordered tea, and looked around to make sure no one was listening.

"It seemed important that you speak to me," May said. "What is it you wish to talk about?"

T'ai's eyes were emotionless as he moistened his lips and spoke in a low, urgent whisper. He came right to the point: "I must get into the Benton and Black godown tonight."

May's mouth dropped open. "The godown? Tonight? But why?"

"I cannot explain at the present time. All I can tell you is that it is of vital importance for me to get into the warehouse tonight, if I am to unmask my grandmother's murderer and the one who indirectly killed my father."

"Every night it is locked, and there is a watchman on duty," May explained. "He is armed, and he patrols the warehouse. You might be seen."

"You live in the taipan's house. You have worked in the godown, and you must know where a key is kept."

She felt herself blanch. "You want me to get the key?"

He nodded slowly, then fell silent as their tea was served with slow ceremony.

When the man had left, May shook her head reluctantly. "I don't know . . ."

T'ai's eyes narrowed as he fixed his unblinking stare on her. "You do not wish to bring my father's killer to justice?"

"Of course, I do, but . . ."

He rose and slipped his hands up the sleeves of his ch'ang-fu. "I once told you that your love for my father would be put to the test one day. Now is the time. If you will not help me, then I will find a way to get into the warehouse by myself."

May reached out to detain him. "No, T'ai. But I must think. What is it you wish me to do?"

"I wish you to get the key and come with me to the warehouse. There is no one else I can trust."

"You want me to come with you?" She had not expected this, and she suddenly felt apprehension.

He nodded.

"What are you looking for?" May wanted to know, sipping her tea. "You must suspect either Nelson Wright or his comprador, if it's the godown you want to see."

"I cannot say," was his infuriating reply. "I do not know what I am looking for, but I will once I find it. Members of my brotherhood have been most helpful to me in this quest. They have found out certain . . . information that will expose the murderer and bring him to justice. But I do need your assistance."

"You can tell me nothing more?"

"No, you must trust me."

May was silent as she looked out over the garden at the Chinese who were rising to leave and go about their daily business. What could she do? There was no one left to turn to, nowhere left to run. All her life, there had always been a place to run for refuge, or a person to assume control. But now she either had to face the situation and meet it head on or withdraw and flee. She, and she alone, had to decide what to do and suffer the consequences.

Then the words of the necromancer flashed through May's mind. "Do not trust someone close to you." Then she brushed her misgivings aside quickly. Why shouldn't she trust Weng's son?

"All right," May agreed. "I'll help you."

T'ai smiled and inclined his head, pleased with her decision. "Here is what we shall do . . ."

When he finished outlining his plan, May swallowed hard and said, "But I must have Chinese clothes if I am to go with you. I must have trousers and a ch'ang-fu."

"You shall have them. Be at the wall as soon as it is dusk," he said. "The clothes will be thrown over to you."

She nodded. "But you must distract the guard at eleven o'clock, so I can slip through the gates to join you. Then we will go to the warehouse."

"Then we will go to the godown to catch a murderer."

At dusk, May was loitering by the stone wall as he had instructed, and the clothes, wrapped in a tight bundle, came flying over, as promised, and landed just a few yards away. She picked them up and hurried back to the villa, taking great care that no one saw her. She had pleaded a headache, to throw Willie and his parents out of her way for the rest of the evening.

Then she waited.

Getting the key was an easy task, for, although Tobias or Wu usually opened the warehouse every morning, she had often seen Nelson take a spare key on a brass ring from his topmost desk drawer. So, while everyone else was finishing dinner, May slipped into the study, opened Nelson's desk, and took the key.

At ten-thirty, she unbundled the clothes and slipped into the black trousers and tunic that barely covered her wrists and put a scarf over her head to hide her bright hair. She was just about to leave when Alex's jade ornament caught her eye. Without a second thought, she untied her belt, threaded it through the girdle ornament, and tightened it about her waist.

May patted it. "Let's hope you bring me luck tonight."

Then, when she was satisfied that the house was in darkness and everyone was asleep, she crept down the back stairs and out into the muggy night.

As she made her way toward the gate, she could see the guard lounging against the gate, his back toward the villa as he smoked a cigarette, its burning tip red in the night air. Just as May rushed up to the wall and flattened herself against it, the guard jumped to life, as though startled by a strange noise.

"Who's there?" she heard him call out, and then he moved away from the gate.

May waited, then opened the gate just a crack and slipped out, being careful to keep an eye out for the guard, as she closed it soundlessly behind her.

A figure in the darkness grabbed her arm and almost made her cry out, but she breathed a sigh of relief when she saw it was only T'ai. He was dressed all in black as well, making his hard, muscular body look even more threatening. If danger threatened, May felt confident this man could give a good accounting for himself.

"Come quickly," he whispered, motioning for her to follow him.

They disappeared down the street, and a little way off, two rickshaws waited on a quiet street. Nothing was said as they jumped inside and the coolies padded off toward the godown.

For the first time, she allowed herself the luxury of thinking about the consequences of what she had agreed to do. What if they were caught? However would she explain herself to Nelson Wright? She realized that, if they were caught, she might never have the chance to explain anything to Nelson.

But she had to learn if Comprador Wu was somehow connected with the fluted bowl and Weng's death. How, May couldn't fathom yet, but there was no one else to help T'ai except her. She had been willing to become Ki's concubine to insure the jade carver a peaceful death, and now she could certainly let T'ai into the warehouse to find whatever he was looking for.

May felt an odd kind of excitement stirring within her, and she smiled to herself. Alex had once accused her of craving adventure as much as he. Perhaps he knew her better than she knew herself.

Already the first rickshaw had slowed and stopped, and May's driver did likewise. As she stepped down to join T'ai, she glanced around, realizing they were just a street away from the godown.

"It's better to go from here by foot," T'ai explained.

May nodded. "There's a back door near the office I used to use. I think we can get in from there, and hope the night watchman doesn't discover us."

"We shall be very careful," T'ai said.

There were people out tonight—a few rickshaws, a carriage or two, and an occasional pedestrian hurrying home—but no one seemed to pay much attention to them as they walked to the back of the godown. May was relieved to discover the street was dark, deserted, and silent, ideally suited to their purposes. Together, she and T'ai stood for a moment in the alley, making sure they were alone.

T'ai glanced about, and they sprinted to the back of the building, where the door was located. While T'ai stood watch, May's shaking fingers slipped the key into the lock and slowly turned the knob. She motioned T'ai forward, and they slipped through the door like two silent ghosts.

Once inside, they stood in the darkness for a moment, to let their eyes adjust to the lack of light and to see if the guard was anywhere nearby. Nothing. May gradually came to discern huge crates and boxes piled high on top of one another, and even some light came through the windows, so they weren't totally in darkness. The effect was eerie, to find such silence in a place that was bursting with life and sound by day.

"We need more light," T'ai whispered. "I have a candle, but it may be dangerous. One of us will have to hold it, and the other will have to keep watch."

May whispered back, "There's a lamp in the office."

The alien sound of scraping metal caught May's ears, and she put out a warning hand to T'ai in alarm. Her palms were damp from nervousness, and she felt her heart pound in her throat at the prospect of discovery.

When she heard the door open at the other end of the godown and saw the watchman's lantern, she knew what to do instinctively.

"The watchman is making his rounds," she whispered. "Into the office. Hurry!"

She pulled him into the room where she had spent so

many pleasurable hours and motioned for T'ai to crawl under the desk. Then May crouched down beside him and waited.

The seconds seemed like hours to her, huddled there, her every nerve as taut as stretched wire, waiting for sure discovery. Every breath she took sounded like a loud rushing of wind to her heightened senses. Why had she ever agreed to this scheme, she wondered, when she could be safe in her bed at the villa? Because, she thought ruefully, she had to know the truth, and to learn the truth always involved taking risks.

Gradually, the sound of footsteps grew louder and louder, and they could even hear the guard humming to himself for comfort, as he walked through the godown. May could tell he did not expect any unusual occurrences tonight, for his manner was casual and relaxed, without the wary air of one who is on the lookout for trouble. May knew that, after he went through the warehouse itself, he would tour the street outside, and that would give them about fifteen precious minutes to find what T'ai was looking for, then get out fast.

Lantern light flooded the room, and May held her breath, lest he hear her. But the guard only muttered, "Nothing here," and the light disappeared, along with his hollow retreating footsteps.

May glanced at T'ai and breathed a sigh of relief.

They waited until they could hear no sound and the godown was in darkness once again.

"We have to move quickly," May said, scurrying out from beneath the desk and fumbling for the lamp that was always on the desk, for those nights when Tobias wanted to stay late to check records. "We have only fifteen minutes before the guard makes his rounds again."

"That is all the time I need," T'ai replied, lighting the lamp.

"Can you tell me now what we're looking for?" May asked as they rushed into the warehouse, walking through alleys formed by stacked boxes.

"I shall know when I find it," was the man's succinct reply.

May said nothing and followed him as he began examining the boxes, skimming over them, rejecting each one. They spent a good five minutes running through the warehouse, T'ai's eyes scanning boxes hurriedly, but obviously not finding what he sought.

"How do you know what you're looking for?" May demanded in exasperation. "These boxes are sealed, and we could never open all of them to see what's inside."

"I'm not looking for a box," was all he would say.

And then, after they had worked their way through toward the back of the room, May spied what looked like a bundle of blue rags.

She gripped T'ai's arm. "Over there. Let's look at this."

His brow rose in puzzlement, but he followed her as she knelt down by the bundle, neatly tied with hemp.

May felt the blood drain from her face as she recognized what the bundle was. "My mother's padded jackets," she mumbled incredulously at T'ai. "These are the jackets she made for the Hammond children. I remember coming upon her as she was sewing one, and I laughed, because she always hated to sew. What are they doing here, in Nelson's warehouse?"

T'ai knelt beside her. "How do you know your mother made them? Jackets like these are common in China. Perhaps the taipan is exporting them to another city."

May shook her head. "I know she made them. See the red embroidery on the collar? She told me it was her mark." May sat back on her heels. "But what are they doing here?"

T'ai pulled a knife out of his sleeve and began to cut the hemp. "I think this is what I am looking for."

While May watched in stunned silence, he ran his fingers over the fabric, then suddenly stopped. With clean efficiency, he slit the seam along the hem, fumbled through the thick cotton wadding, and drew out a small wrapped parcel.

"What can that be?" May wondered aloud, as he opened it and shook it. A pair of diamond earrings fell into his palm, and settled there, twinkling insolently.

May felt her mouth go dry, and her voice was barely a croak as she said, "Diamond earrings. I know of a woman who had some jewels like this stolen recently. It was the talk of Shanghai."

T'ai just stared at her, comprehension and pity in his dark eyes, but he said nothing.

"I know what you're going to say." May gave an anguished sigh as she sat back on her heels. "What are stolen goods doing in my mother's padded jackets?"

"Let us check the others," T'ai said, the lamplight making his face into a grave shadowed mask, as he proceeded to split open the next jacket.

The second jacket revealed a necklace with more diamonds than May had ever seen together at one time, and in its sleeve was a jade carving of a carp that May suspected was almost a thousand years old.

"This should be in a museum," she said breathlessly, holding the stone fish closer to the light.

"My country's treasures," T'ai muttered bitterly, "all destined for the West."

"I wish we had never found it," May said, fighting tears.

"I wish you never had either," a voice added behind them, blasting the silence to shards and reverberating through the warehouse.

May and T'ai jumped and whirled around to face Nelson Wright holding a pistol aimed directly at May's heart.

CHAPTER
FIFTEEN

May jumped and the necklace fell from her hands onto the floor.

"Uncle Nelson!" she gasped.

He stood there, with Comprador Wu by his side, but there was nothing familiar about him this time. May found herself looking at a stranger, and she realized with a sinking heart that she had fallen into the trap of underestimating Nelson Wright, for, by the merciless glint in his eye, she knew she could expect nothing.

He stared at T'ai, sizing him up and determining he was a force to be reckoned with. "You've brought a friend, I see. Who are you?" he snapped at T'ai.

"My name is Weng T'ai-Lung."

May's voice was strained as she said, "You know about this, don't you?" indicating the necklace at her feet. "You've been smuggling, and Mother's been helping you."

"You always were a bit too clever for your own good," he said, his pink face calm and regretful.

"But why? You're taipan. You have everything you could possibly want."

He shook his head. "Oh, no. I don't have my heart's desire—to leave this hellish land and return to England once and for all."

"You could have gone there any time you wanted. Was there really a need to do anything dishonest?"

"Of course I could have returned to England at any time I wished, but there was a question of living standards, you see. And to live there as I have learned to live here—grandly, extravagantly, richly—requires a great deal of money." His lip curled in a sneer. "Do you think I would lower myself to work as a clerk in the London office of Benton and Black, after heading the entire operation out here? Don't be absurd. I would never tolerate having my wife and son living in some cramped, draughty terrace house in London, after they've been used to the villa. And I can assure you I would never subject my darling Emmy to the snubs of her social inferiors. That would infuriate me."

May fell silent, recalling her mother's words, as they had readied themselves for bed one night. "Nelson's got such a wonderful life here. In China, he's taipan, but in England he'd just be some poor clerk scraping to survive."

"So all that talk of leaving China is finally going to come true," May said. "Mother always thought you were dreaming out loud."

"I never indulge in dreams unless I can turn them into reality. Margaret knows me better than that."

May took a deep breath to steady her shaking insides. "Ming-sheng and T'chuan were right. My mother was a part of your smuggling operation after all."

Comprador Wu stepped forward into the glow of the lamp, and May was startled by the transformation of the nondescript Chinese whose face she never could remember. He was dressed in dark clothing, like T'ai, and he carried a pistol, but gone was his subservient manner. Wu's face was a mask of remorselessness and cunning that May would remember for a long, long time.

"What do you know of Ming-sheng?" he demanded, his eyes narrowed into slits as he stared at her.

And the last piece of the puzzle slid into place.

"You are Win-Lin," she said, astounded at herself for not thinking to connect the comprador with the tomb-robber until now.

Comprador Wu—or Win-Lin—gave her a grave, mocking bow. "How do you know of Ming-sheng?" he asked her more forcefully this time.

May pursed her lips and refused to speak.

"I wouldn't, if I were you," Nelson said. "He can become quite unpleasant."

May sighed, relented, and told them about the trip she and Alex had made to T'chuan's summer residence, where she had met the concubine and learned of her quest for her brother.

"So," Nelson said with a laugh, "the Dutchman has been looking for Win-Lin, and he's been right under his nose all the time."

May's thoughts were racing ahead. "Everything is becoming so clear now. You've been in partnership for a long time."

"Not that long," Nelson replied. "I was the Englishman he sold those tomb treasures to, and we've had a profitable relationship ever since. Win-Lin poses as my comprador, sent throughout China to buy merchandise for Benton and Black. However, if one or two items are stolen and somehow evade Customs . . ." Nelson shrugged.

"But what about this necklace?" May demanded.

Nelson cast a disapproving glance at Win-Lin. "Ah, the necklace. I'm afraid my friend here got a little carried away with his house-breaking activities. But, as you can see, it was a temptation that was hard to resist."

"And Mother helped you? I can't believe she would ever do such a thing."

"Oh, believe it, May, believe it. Margaret was most willing to help us, especially when I produced her long-lost daughter about two years ago."

"Dinah," May said. "So you did know that Mother had an illegitimate daughter."

"You came so close to discovering that secret." There was grudging admiration in his voice. "You weren't far off in your supposition that your mother came to Shanghai to have the baby, because that's exactly what Margaret did. She didn't even risk writing a letter to me, because she feared Tim would find out."

"And did he?" May wanted to know.

Nelson shook his head. "No, I don't think he ever did.

Margaret just appeared at the hong one day, announced that she was going to have a baby, and asked if I would help her conceal it. I was furious with her for being unfaithful to my friend, and when she told me the father was Chinese . . ." Nelson's color deepened at the very thought. "I almost refused to help her, she made me so angry. But I suppose I was half in love with her myself at the time, so I agreed to it." Nelson shifted the gun in his hand and smiled. "Little did I realize what my favor would be worth years later."

"Surely your wife must have objected," May pointed out.

"She wasn't too pleased with the arrangement, for she was a humorless, conventional woman with the morals of the Queen, but she feared me and went along with it. After the baby was born, I promised your mother I would dispose of it by seeing that she was placed in a good home. Your mother was most appreciative. Years later, when Win-Lin and I became partners, I realized I had the perfect means to utilize your mother's full potential."

May wanted to rush at Nelson and hit him with all her strength. "So you blackmailed her into helping you."

"Blackmail? Such an ugly word. No, May, I merely offered to produce her daughter, if she would agree to help us. I think Margaret thought it a fair exchange. She had been besotted with that Chinese scholar of hers, and the thought of having his daughter with her was a tempting offer. Her scruples went out the window easily enough."

She shook her head stubbornly. "Mother would never agree to such a thing, even if it meant never seeing her daughter again."

"Oh, May," Nelson replied with an indulgent shake of his head, "I'm afraid you don't know your own mother as well as you think. Why, I hate to disillusion you further, but she loved that Chinese scholar of hers more than her own husband."

"That's a lie!"

"I'm afraid not. I can't tell you all the times your mother begged me to tell her where I had hidden her Chinese daughter. She even tried to bribe me with her most precious pieces of jade. But, of course, I couldn't reveal the child's whereabouts. Your mother likes to think of herself as Chinese—Heaven knows why—and having a Chinese lover and bearing his child were . . . were an *honor* to her. Can you imagine?" And he laughed. "Many times she regretted relinquishing the child. So, when I finally did offer to send her daughter to her—for a very high price, of course—she was so grateful, she would have done anything." He paused, before adding, "Anything."

May finally believed him, and tears of bitterness stung her eyes. "How could she!"

"Oh, don't be so harsh on her, May. We all have our Achilles' heel."

"And that's how she smuggled the goods, in padded jackets?" May was incredulous.

"Usually," Nelson replied complacently. "But Win-Lin would get the items, give them to Margaret, and she would handle the rest." His voice grew mocking. "Who in Tientsin would believe that one of the most respected English merchants would stoop to smuggling? It was perfect and foolproof. I plan very carefully, you see."

May just stared at him in hostility, and she could sense T'ai beside her, tense as a panther ready to spring, but for some reason he held back. Then he spoke. "You," he said, addressing Win-Lin, "killed my grandmother."

Win-Lin's smile was malicious. "The old woman shouldn't have tried to stop me. All I wanted was the bowl, but she insisted on shrieking and bringing the entire household down on my head, so I was forced to silence her. Most regrettable. I dislike unnecessary violence."

"Then you summoned the police and told them my father had killed her."

"My accomplice did that. I could not afford to be recognized."

May was shaking with rage. "He did that, knowing that Weng would be arrested, and what his punishment would be?"

"It kept the police occupied, so we could get away."

She made an anguished sound and moved to leap at him, but T'ai kept a clearer head and reached out to restrain her.

"We'll have none of that," Nelson warned her. "I'd regret having to shoot you."

The comprador became curious. "And how did you come to know this of me, jade carver's son?"

"With so many hounds snapping at your heels, did you not think one of us would soon find you?" he said in contempt. "You flatter yourself that you are as elusive as the wind, but your days were growing shorter, even before you killed my grandmother and father."

"I hope I'm there when your sister finds you," May added. "Her vengeance will not be harsh enough to satisfy me."

Nelson just shook his head. "No, May, Win-Lin's sister is not going to find him. My comprador and I are going to leave Shanghai and never be seen again. You, however, will be taken care of. I have planned so carefully, as I usually do."

The fear that had been gradually growing inside May since their discovery suddenly blossomed and hit her full force. Staring at Nelson and Win-Lin, who were made even more sinister by the weak lamp light, she realized there was no escape, no hope left. Nelson Wright, her family's old and dear friend, had a gun trained on her and was going to kill her. The necromancer had warned her not to trust a man who was close to her, and, like a fool, she had thought the woman meant Alex.

She could feel the light sweat of fear rise on her skin as her mind frantically searched for ways to escape. But she dismissed them one by one, for they all ended in death.

"How did you know we were here?" she asked, stalling for time, in case the night watchman should come back.

"I've kept a careful watch on you ever since you discovered that damn fluted bowl. Once I saw you meet this Chinaman," he nodded his head in T'ai's direction, "I knew I had better not take any chances. Then, when I saw you slip away tonight, I came to the warehouse to collect the jackets and leave Shanghai. We were pleasantly surprised to find you here."

May couldn't resist asking, "What are you going to do to us?"

Nelson stroked his mustache as though the gesture helped him think. "I have a friend in Hong Kong, a very wealthy man with extravagant—if somewhat perverted—tastes. He loves beautiful women and even has a room where he can enjoy them undisturbed. His last guest was Fraulein Hummel, but she was not sufficiently challenging, and now he is in the market for a new diversion. You, May, shall be that diversion."

The faces around her seemed to flicker like the lamplight, but May steadied herself. "You are despicable."

Suddenly a look of profound regret softened Nelson's features, and he gave a little wistful sigh. "I *am* sorry, May. Why couldn't you have left well enough alone? Then there would have been no need for anything to happen to you. I don't want to have to do this, but you leave me no choice. You do understand, don't you?" And he reached out to touch her cheek, but she drew back sharply and regarded him warily.

When his hand dropped, May said, "If my father's friendship meant anything to you, then let me go."

"Oh, please, May, not that sentimental drivel. You don't really expect me to sacrifice myself for you, do you?"

She said nothing.

Nelson smiled. "We've talked enough." Then he said to Win-Lin, "Bring the coffin."

"How did you abduct the fraulein in broad daylight?" May asked.

"You don't think I'd do it myself, do you? I had someone else do it. They were most efficient." Nelson smiled, then continued. "It's such a pity you were so curious, May. When you found the bowl, you should have let the matter drop, but, no, you had to pursue it."

"So that's why you didn't want me working at the go-down, because you were afraid I'd stumble across your illegal activities."

"One can never be too careful," Nelson replied. "However, Mr. Dawes successfully gave me an excuse to keep you away."

Now May understood. "So even that was all arranged for my benefit."

He nodded slowly. "And very effective."

"You made a mistake by letting Dawes stay on after you told me you had dismissed him," she said.

"A minor one, surely."

Win-Lin's return was heralded by a scraping sound, as he dragged a Chinese coffin across the floor toward them.

"This will be our method of getting you to Hong Kong," Nelson informed her congenially, not taking his eyes off them for a second.

"What about the jade carver's son?" Win-Lin grumbled.

"Take him down to the river and shoot him."

"That would be foolish," T'ai spoke up, his unblinking stare fastened on both men, "especially if you value one who is more precious than life to you."

May had the satisfaction of seeing Nelson caught off balance as he growled, "What the hell do you mean?"

T'ai just smiled enigmatically. "Kill me, and you will learn what I mean."

"He is trying to frighten us," Win-Lin said, removing the cover from the coffin.

"I daresay. Let's dispatch May."

T'ai spoke up again, his unblinking stare focused on Nelson, and there was a deep undercurrent of hatred in his voice. "Your son is called Willie, is he not? I do not make false threats. If I should die, you will never see him again."

A ripple of fear for the child, stronger than her fear for herself, caused May to stare at T'ai in alarm. "What's this? You never said anything to me about Willie being harmed when I agreed to come with you tonight."

He turned his head and looked at her. "I regret having to deceive you, May-Ling, but I had to insure our safety if something went amiss with our plan." He looked back at Nelson and added, "As it has."

"Please, T'ai," May begged. "What have you done with Willie?" Then she answered her own question. "Your friends have him, don't they?"

Nelson's voice split the air like a gunshot. "Look at me, both of you!"

When May turned, she was startled to see Nelson looking pale. "What is this about someone having my son?" When T'ai said nothing, Nelson pointed his pistol directly at May. "He's not talking, so you had better talk for him."

May felt a cold bead of sweat slide down her spine. "T'ai is a member of a secret society called the Sons of the Celestial Phoenix, and its members have been helping him track Win-Lin down in Shanghai." She glanced at T'ai, as if to confirm what she was about to say. "They must have kidnapped Willie and will kill him unless T'ai is released."

Nelson glanced at Win-Lin, who said, "I have heard of this brotherhood. They have many members, and their reach is long. But how do we know they have your son?"

"You have only my word," T'ai said quietly, "and—unlike you—I am a man of my word."

Nelson's white face looked like a bleached skull, all the cunning and bravado gone at the thought of his only son being in danger. His fingers flexed on the gun, as if debating whether to shoot T'ai or take him at his word. But there was doubt in his eyes now.

"Believe him, Nelson," May said.

"Tell me how you kidnapped my son."

"My friends have been watching your residence for days," T'ai replied, his voice echoing hollowly in the stillness of the warehouse. "Tonight, when they saw you leave, they waited, then entered the house through the servants' entrance and crept upstairs to the child's bedroom, which overlooks the garden. They tied and gagged him, and the strongest slung him over his shoulder like a sack of millet, for the boy is small, and weighs nothing. Neither your wife nor the servants heard them."

T'ai paused, and May could see concern and fear for Willie start to override Nelson's well-honed instincts for survival. T'ai continued. "If I do not return to my friends by one o'clock tonight, they will kill your son much the same way my father was executed."

An involuntary gasp of horror escaped May's lips.

"He's lying," Win-Lin said.

"Quiet!" Nelson snarled. "We're talking about my son's life. I've got to think."

"Can you even afford to take the risk?" May's voice rose. "For God's sake, Nelson, will you do as T'ai says?"

Win-Lin kept his eyes on Nelson, as though searching for cracks in his armor. "If we let the jade carver's son go free, he'll have the police and Customs men here before we can leave the warehouse. We'll never leave Shanghai. All we've worked for will be lost."

Nelson ignored him. "All we've worked for means nothing to me without my son." Then he looked at T'ai. "How do I know my son will be set free if I release you?"

"You have my word," T'ai said simply. "When you go back to your residence, your son will be waiting for you, unharmed."

Nelson took a deep breath, like a fox gone to earth who finds itself backed into a corner with hounds slavering at every turn. "I suppose I have no alternative but to trust you, and do as you say."

"Fool!" Win-Lin cried, his round face contorted into a mask of fury. "Would you risk everything on this man's words?"

Nelson suddenly looked old and defeated. "I must do as he says."

"Then I go my own way," Win-Lin said, "and take what is mine."

Nelson just nodded. "That would be best."

Win-Lin said not a word to his partner, just left the circle of lamplight and entered the darkness of the warehouse beyond, and within seconds all that could be sensed of him were soft hollow footsteps that gradually died away.

"Now you," Nelson said to T'ai. He may have been cornered, but he was still taipan. "Go and release my son. I will be waiting for you at the villa. And," he added with a grisly smile, "remember that I have May with me. If you try to send the police here, or try to trick me in any way, she will die. Understood?"

T'ai stared at him for a moment, then nodded his head. Nelson gave him a brief nod. T'ai turned and left them alone.

When Nelson was satisfied that T'ai had actually left the warehouse, he turned to May. "You present me with a dilemma."

May, wound tighter than a piano wire, struggled to keep her arms at her sides without moving. She debated distracting Nelson somehow, then diving for cover while she tried to escape, but she dismissed that at once. She would be dead before she hit the floor.

"You could let me go," she suggested.

He dismissed that immediately. "Oh, no, May, that I cannot do. For, if your friend does not keep his word when we reach the villa, you will die."

"But can't you see it's hopeless? The game is over, Nelson, and you've lost. Surely you can't expect to leave Shanghai with Emily and Willie."

Anger flashed deep in his eyes. "I never count the game lost until the very end, my dear."

They spent the next several minutes staring at each other, with May wondering if T'ai had gone directly to where his friends were holding Willie, or if he was indeed waiting outside for them to appear before apprehending Nelson.

Suddenly, an alien sound—a door being opened cautiously, the soft thud of an arm bumping into a box—caused May to perk up. She held her breath, but Nelson gave no indication that he had heard it, too. It took all of May's resistance to keep her eyes focused on him. If T'ai had returned, she would not give him away.

"To get back to the question at hand," Nelson began, "what am I going to do with you after I get Willie back?"

"If you ever counted yourself my father's friend, let me go, Nelson. Please."

"But Timmy Fitz was so long ago, May," he said with genuine regret. With his free hand, he pulled at his mustache, and she could see he was debating in his mind what to do with her. Finally, he said, "Come to think of it, I don't even want you to come back to the villa with me."

"But what if T'ai doesn't bring Willie with him?"

Nelson shrugged. "That's just one risk I shall have to take. I have nothing to lose at this point. As long as your friend thinks you're alive . . ."

Without taking his eyes off her, Nelson stooped down to pick up the lamp off the floor, and the light turned his face into a grotesque mask.

"You don't want to kill me, Nelson." The words were barely a croak through her dry lips.

"But I'm afraid I'm going to have to," he said. "I'm so sorry, May."

Before he could even raise the gun, a voice barked out of the darkness, "Drop it, Wright, or you're dead!"

In less time than it took May to blink, Nelson blew out the lamp, plunging them in total darkness.

"Don't shoot!" May heard Alex cry out, and, as she instinctively fell to the floor, all around her the air was thick with scuffling and scrambling of feet, a tinkle of breaking glass and smell of kerosene, swearing and more scuffling.

"Everyone stay where you are!" Alex commanded again. "Royce, find a lamp, damn it, before we all kill each other in the dark."

May felt faint with relief, but the cold floorboards against her cheek half-revived her.

"May?" she heard Alex call from somewhere toward her right. "Where in the hell are you?"

"Here," she squeaked. "On the floor."

"Don't move. We'll have a light in a minute."

As if by command, someone struck a match, and there was feeble light in the godown again. When May lifted her head, then started rising on all fours, she heard the hurried sound of footsteps, and Alex was bending over her, his eyes as wide as Willie's in his white, frightened face.

He put his hand on her shoulder and shook her. "Are you all right?" When she nodded, he pulled her head around and kissed her soundly.

Helpless tears filled her eyes. "I've never been so happy to see someone in my entire life."

"I was afraid we weren't in time." Then he helped her to her feet, while her knees wobbled like jelly. She noticed two Sikh policemen holding rifles behind him. Suddenly, a portly man accompanied by a third Sikh came running up to them.

"Wright's got clean away," he said. "Seems he escaped through the back door while we were all groping in the dark."

"Damn!" Alex muttered between clenched teeth. He turned to May. "You wouldn't know where he's gone, would you? And where is his comprador?"

"Wu—who is really Ming-sheng's brother, Win-Lin, by the way—left earlier to try to get away," she replied, taking a deep breath. "I'm certain Nelson's gone back to the villa."

Alex scowled. "Back to the villa? That doesn't make sense. I should think he'd try to get to his junk, which our men are holding."

"T'ai had Willie kidnapped to use as a hostage," May explained, "and, if Nelson doesn't go to the villa, he won't get Willie back."

"You can explain later," Alex said, in command once again. "Right now, we've got to get to the villa, even though Wright's got a few minutes headstart on us." He turned to the portly man. "Royce, I'm going to need Prasad and Khumud. You stay with Mrs. Monckton while I find a carriage." Then he smiled briefly at May, touched her cheek, and was gone, loping through the warehouse.

Royce smiled, bowed, and offered May his arm. "I presume you are May Monckton. My name is Royce, Jeff Royce."

When he saw May's blank look, he said, "I'm with Customs. I realize Alex didn't have time to explain the situation to you, but perhaps I can fill in some of the gaps while we wait outside for him."

They started walking, while the Sikhs fell into step behind them, and they went outside into the cool night air, which smelled of the river and fresh flowers mingling incongruously.

"My men and I—and Alex, of course—have just come

from a junk anchored not far from here. We surprised Wright's men in the act of loading her with contraband about half an hour ago. They did not offer much resistance, I am pleased to say, so no lives were lost. Then we rushed here as soon as we could, while leaving most of our men behind to confiscate the stolen goods." He stared at her. "We didn't know exactly what we'd find, and we certainly weren't expecting you. It was my understanding that only T'ai-Lung would be here."

"He was," May said, rubbing her arms to bring some warmth back into them, "but Nelson had to release him to go get Willie." She quickly recounted how the child had been kidnapped, and the terms T'ai insisted upon for Nelson to get him back.

"I see," Royce said. "We knew nothing of this."

"Neither did I, otherwise I never would have agreed to accompany T'ai tonight." She was silent for a moment, watching the moonlit water shimmering like fish scales in the distance. "Alex works for Customs?"

Royce chuckled. "He doesn't like to admit it, but, occasionally he does work for us—when we can afford him."

May was pleased that he wasn't as disreputable as he would have everyone believe.

Royce continued. "Actually, it was T'ai-Lung who told Alex he suspected Wright would move tonight, and it's beyond me how he knew where the junk was anchored."

May thought of the Sons of the Celestial Phoenix.

Royce's conversation was interrupted by the distant thunder of hoofbeats that reached a deafening crescendo as a carriage pulled by two wild-eyed Mongolian ponies came careening around a corner and down the street toward them, Alex handling the reins like an experienced mafoo. He pulled the animals to a halt before them and tried to hold them in.

Royce, May, and the Sikhs went running across the road toward him. "Where did you find a carriage at this time of night—or morning?" Royce wanted to know. "You mustn't embarrass the department, you know."

"I borrowed it," was Alex's reply. "We haven't a moment to spare. Get in, all of you."

Royce shook his head. "I'm too old for such antics. Prasad and Khumud will be of more use to you. I'll stay here."

Alex saluted him, while the policemen scrambled into the back, and May climbed up in the driver's seat next to Alex.

"Hang on!" he cried, and, as May and the Sikhs clutched at the railings, he lifted the reins and brought them down with a stinging slap on the ponies' rumps.

The lead pony screamed, and the two of them shot forward, breaking into a charge from a standstill, and throwing the passengers back against their seats. Luckily, the streets were nearly deserted at this hour, except for a bleary-eyed gambler with empty pockets on his way home from the fan-tan tables.

Without taking his eyes off the road, which stretched ahead of them free and clear, Alex shouted to May, "Why don't you tell me what happened, if you can?"

Trying to shout over the pounding hooves was an effort, but May talked as fast as she could and within minutes had told him how she and T'ai had gone to the warehouse and found smuggled goods in the padded jackets Margaret Fitzgerald had shipped from Paoting. While Alex listened, May also elaborated on Comprador Wu and his partnership with Nelson Wright.

"That explains a few matters," Alex said.

May glanced at him anxiously. "Do you think we'll get there in time?"

"If these ponies hold up."

When they turned onto Nanking Road, the carriage took the corner at breakneck speed, causing one of the ponies to lose his footing and stumble. A collective gasp rose from the passengers as Alex sawed at the reins, fighting to keep the pony's head up as the animal scrambled to regain its footing.

May heard the policemen muttering in their native tongue, and she wondered if they were praying.

"How did you learn about Nelson?" she shouted to Alex.

"Your mother told me," he replied.

May's head snapped around in surprise. "Mother? But she was helping Nelson all along. I don't understand . . ."

"She came to Shanghai a few days ago to tell me about Wright because she thought you'd be in danger, and she wanted to help catch him. That's why she was so upset when I sent you to Shanghai—right into the lion's den—and why she never wrote back to you about the fluted bowl. She was afraid Nelson was reading her letters. But she's safe. We're both staying at Soon Sebastian's."

May frowned. "So that's why you weren't at Zetta's when I went to tell you about the bowl. And I thought you had run off with Dinah."

Alex risked a quick glance at her, the carriage slowed down, and he turned his attention back to his driving. "We'll talk about Dinah—and other matters—later."

She was silent for a moment, then said, "I suppose Mother will be arrested for her part in this."

"Oh, I think the Crown can be persuaded to overlook her activities, in payment for helping us apprehend Nelson Wright."

May just looked at him. "Thank you, Alex."

"I told you nothing would happen to her, and I'm a man of my word."

May's thoughts then flew ahead, and she wondered if they would apprehend Nelson at the villa. Would Willie be waiting there, too? She shivered in the cool night air that plucked at her scarf and pressed her ch'ang-fu to her arms.

Alex said, "You wore my gift, I see."

She smiled as she felt the ornament on her belt. "It brought me luck." And she hoped their luck held tonight.

The carriage sped down Bubbling Well Road, and May felt like a Roman charioteer as she looked over the ponies' heaving flanks. She craned her neck for any glimpse of the villa through the trees.

"How much farther?" she demanded anxiously.

"We're almost there," Alex replied.

Within mere minutes, the villa's gates loomed ahead,

looking like prison bars in the moonlight. Alex flung his weight back and dragged at the reins, pulling the ponies' heads back and slowing them down. The carriage came to a halt just as the guard appeared, rifle in hand.

"State your business," he challenged them.

"We're Customs men and the police looking for Nelson Wright," Alex replied in a tone that brooked no nonsense.

The guard defered to them instantly, opening the gates for them to pass. The ponies, sides heaving and drenched with sweat after their mad charge, were grateful to be allowed to walk down the circular drive toward the villa, where another pony was grazing on the lawn.

"Nelson must be here," May said.

"He was only about ten minutes ahead of us," Alex said. "There's his pony, so he hasn't left yet."

When their carriage pulled up to the steps, Alex jumped down, reached up for May, and the policemen jumped down after her, their eyes scanning the grounds for any sign of Nelson.

"What do you wish us to do, sahib?" Prasad asked in his low, lilting voice.

"Keep your guns ready and follow me. There may be innocent bystanders about—Mrs. Wright and the servants—and we don't want them harmed in any way. But we must take Nelson Wright," Alex insisted. "Khumud, you go around the back in case he tries to escape that way. Don't shoot unless he shoots first."

His casual reference to the possibility of death frightened May, and she trembled.

Then Alex said, "You stay out here, May," and she bristled in indignation.

"I'll be damned if I will," she retorted, "I'm going with you."

He reached out and his fingers bit into her shoulder. Though she could barely discern his features in the darkness, she knew his eyes were soft with concern when he said, "I don't want anything to happen to you, May. Now do as you're told."

With a noisy sigh, she nodded reluctantly and watched the men disappear into the house, shutting the door silently behind them. She waited, straining her ears for the slightest sound, but all she heard was the mournful cry of a dove in the trees beyond. Then May folded her arms and tapped her foot impatiently as the minutes passed, then she reached out to stroke a horse's neck and was rewarded with a whicker of contentment. Still she waited, and there was nothing.

Finally, curiosity overrode caution, and she started for the door. When she opened it and peered inside, all she could see was the empty, lamplit hallway, so she tiptoed inside. When she rounded a corner, she spied Alex and the Sikhs flattened against the wall, their guns ready.

"What are you doing here?" Alex whispered angrily when he saw her. "I thought I told you to wait outside."

Before May could reply, an unsuspecting Emily came walking out of the sitting room, a look of gentle concern on her face, and she started when she saw them.

"Do you have Willie?" were the first words out of her mouth. "He's missing, and I can't find him anywhere, and Nelson says we're supposed to leave Shanghai tonight, of all times."

"Where is your husband, Mrs. Wright?" Alex asked, trying to keep his voice calm.

Emily turned pale, her dark eyes afraid. "Why are you carrying guns, and why is that policeman with you?" Her hand fluttered to her forehead. "I am so confused . . . what is going on? First my son is missing, and now you people are demanding to see Nelson."

"Please tell me where he is," Alex said softly.

"Upstairs, in our bedroom."

Alex moved swiftly once he learned what he wanted. "May, you stay here with Mrs. Wright."

"But, I want—"

"Don't argue!" And before she could say a word, Alex trotted up the stairs with Prasad following close behind.

Emily turned to her. "Something terrible has happened, I can see it in your face."

May tried to smile reassuringly, as she took Emily's arm to guide her back into the sitting room. "Everything is going to be all right."

"You're lying." Wild-eyed now, Emily grasped May's arms and shook her. "Where is my son? Why do they want my husband? Has Nelson done something?"

May gently pried her loose and lead her to a chair standing among the packed bags waiting to go nowhere. "I'll explain everything later, Emily, when the men return."

Emily seated herself. "First the servants all disappeared, and then this strange Chinese man came to the door with this for Nelson." She reached across at the table and handed May an object wrapped in silk.

Frowning in curiosity, May opened it. Inside was a box of yellow lacquer, and she felt herself go white when she realized the significance of what she held and why Nelson had gone to the bedroom.

Without another word to Emily, May bolted out of the room and took the stairs two at a time, then went running down the hall to the suite, and through a door that had been battered by boots and rifle butts. May saw Alex and Prasad on the balcony, and she knew what had happened.

She crossed the room and tried to run out, but a grim-faced Alex reached out to hold her back. "Don't, May. He's hanged himself from the balustrade."

Her hand flew to her mouth in horror, and she felt sick. "Oh, God." When she regained her composure, she said, "With the cord in this box?"

Alex looked at it and nodded. "That would explain this note we found."

May took the piece of paper he handed her and read, "My freedom for your son, but your life for my father's," was all it said.

May looked at Alex. "T'ai."

"I would think so."

May reread the note, at last understanding the full extent of T'ai's vengeance. He had played the cruelest cat-and-mouse game of all, leading Nelson to believe that if he returned to the villa, he would have his son back. But, when

Nelson arrived, all he found was the yellow lacquer box with a silk rope coiled inside, an invitation to die with honor, by his own hand.

May wondered how Nelson felt when he read it and realized that he had been offered hope, only to have it jerked away at the last moment. She fancied he just smiled in resignation, then did what had to be done.

Weng Ta-Chung was avenged at last.

"We have to tell Emily," May said with a sigh of distaste, not relishing the task that lay ahead.

"We'll do it together," Alex said.

After telling Emily and sitting with her until her hysterics subsided, May led her upstairs to her own bedroom, where she mixed Emily a sleeping draught and made her drink all of it. Then she waited by the bed until Emily drifted off into a fitful sleep.

May managed to shuffle back downstairs, where she found Alex waiting for her. "Emily's sleeping," she said.

He suppressed a yawn. "She could use it."

May smiled ruefully as she sank down to seat herself on the steps. "So could I." She could barely keep her head up. "Where are the Sikhs?"

"Cutting Nelson down."

May sighed. "What do we do now? There's still no sign of Willie."

Alex seated himself next to her. "We wait, Lady Jade."

She rested her head on his shoulder. "I want to see Mother. We have so much to talk about . . . so much."

"You mustn't think too badly of her. She did try to get out from Nelson's grasp several times, but he always threatened to take Dinah away. Then, when you arrived, she tried to break away again, but this time, Nelson sent Wu—or Win-Lin—to Paoting to persuade her. That's when she made Dinah leave, for her own protection."

May sat up as a thought came to her. "That's who Mother must have been talking to one night when I overheard her in the courtyard. And I thought she and Chad were having an assignation."

"And then," Alex continued, "when she sent Dinah away, she made you think you were the cause, so you wouldn't ask questions or become suspicious."

May pulled off her scarf. "And I believed her."

"Oh, yes," he said, reaching out to draw her head back against his shoulder. "Your mother and I had a long, enlightening talk. Did you know Dinah was part of Nelson's scheme?"

May's head bounced up. "How could she be? She is my sister."

"That's my point. She's not your sister. Your real sister was in a Taoist monastery near Hangchow."

"Was?"

"She died some years ago—drowned in a flood—effectively cutting off Nelson's plan to send her to your mother. So he needed a substitute, and that's when he hired Dinah. Your mother, never having seen her child for years, accepted Dinah as her daughter."

"How do you know all this?" May asked with a suspicious frown.

"When I first met Dinah, and she, ah . . . expressed an interest in me, she once let it slip that she was going to make a great deal of money soon. This piqued my curiosity, mercenary that I am. When I told her I was coming to Shanghai, she wanted to come with me, and I felt it was not because of my charm alone. There was something in Shanghai she wanted. I suspect she didn't quite trust Nelson."

"That was a wise move on her part," May said.

A strange expression came over Alex's face, and he hugged her. "I never meant for you to know we were at Zetta's together," he said softly. "When you happened in on us and I saw the look on your face, I thought I'd go out of my mind, because I knew I had hurt you again. And then, when you refused to see me, I thought I had lost you."

He looked down at her, and May thought, how very vulnerable he looks, and how afraid.

"I don't want to lose you ever again," Alex said gruffly.

"You won't."

He smiled and continued. "Then, when we went to see

your amah, and she told us about the child, everything seemed to fall into place. When you claimed Dinah was that child, I began wondering why she had suddenly reappeared after all these years. Then I wondered if someone hadn't put her up to it. When I confronted her, and threatened her with jail, she was quick enough to confess."

"And where is she now?" May wanted to know.

"She's probably back walking the streets of Shanghai, which is where Nelson found her in the first place. Your mother made up her French-Chinese background."

May rose to her feet and rubbed her arms, which had suddenly become cold. "Where are Willie and T'ai?"

"I'm sure they'll be here shortly."

She smiled. "I took Willie to a necromancer once. She said he would be in danger, but he would not come to harm. God, Alex, I hope she was right."

Then she started telling him about Nelson's occasional forays into white slavery, and Tzu-Lieh's recovery, but the sound of footsteps outside the door cut her short, and she and Alex rose expectantly.

In walked T'ai with a sleepy-eyed Willie in hand, followed by Khumud and Prasad.

Willie, barefoot and in his nightshirt, flung himself down the hall and into May's outstretched arms. "Aunt May, I've had the most incredible adventure. These Chinamen wearing red headbands came into my room, trussed me up like a Christmas goose, and carried me off."

May crushed him to her. "Are you all right, Willie? The men didn't hurt you, did they?"

"Oh, no," he said. "They were pleasant chaps, actually, and gave me tea and almond cookies." He suppressed a yawn as he looked around. "Where's my Mama?"

"Sleeping," May told him.

Willie stared at Alex. "Are you Aunt May's gentleman friend?" he demanded, trying to keep his head up.

Alex came forward and extended his hand. "My name is Alexander Wolders."

Willie shook it gravely, while rubbing his eyes with his free hand.

"I think someone is ready for bed," May said, extending her hand to him. "You can tell me about your adventure tomorrow, Willie."

"Oh, all right." And he let her lead him upstairs.

After putting Willie to bed, May went back downstairs, where she found T'ai and Alex talking in the hall.

T'ai regarded her with his unblinking stare as she came down the stairs, then he bowed. "I beg your forgiveness for putting you in danger, Missie May-Ling, but, since I had insured our safety by taking the boy, I did not think you were in danger."

"You were taking a risk," Alex said sternly.

"Once again, my apologies. I wanted her to see for herself the taipan's treachery. Also, what is the word of a Chinese in a court of law? You know as well as I that, in Shanghai, Chinese who work for the English are exempt from Chinese law. But if an Englishwoman saw with her own eyes . . ." He shrugged.

"You told him about Nelson?" May asked Alex, who just nodded.

T'ai's eyes narrowed further. "He died with more honor than my father."

May sighed. "Friends of yours were holding Willie?"

He immediately inferred that Alex knew nothing about the Sons of the Celestial Phoenix, for he said, "Yes. After we left for the godown, one of them was left to watch the house. When he saw the taipan leave, he took the child. We suspected Wright would try to move his stolen goods tonight, and I thought it best to have an element to bargain with. His love for his son is well-known."

"His Achilles' heel," May said softly.

"Saving his son's life is probably one of the few noble acts Nelson ever performed," Alex said.

"No," May replied, "he was a good man once."

T'ai looked from May to Alex. "Where is the other snake?"

"He has gone," May said, knowing he referred to Win-Lin.

"The fox has eluded us once again," Alex said.

T'ai's face hardened. "Then my father has only been half avenged. I had hoped to return to Paoting, but I can see there is still much work to be done before the dog is caged. Much work." A slow smile spread across his mouth. "But he will not elude me forever. There will come a day . . ." And his voice trailed off.

"I wish you good joss in your quest," May said.

T'ai bowed. "Again, my thanks."

"And our thanks to you," Alex said.

Then T'ai bowed, turned, and walked out of the house.

May looked up at Alex. "Do you think he will find Win-Lin?"

"Perhaps someday. But I'm not concerned about Win-Lin right now." And the warmth in his eyes made her catch her breath.

"Well, Dutchman," she said quietly, "what's to become of us?"

He took both her hands in his and held them against his heart. "In the midst of all this excitement, I received a telegram from England yesterday. Uncle Clarence has died, and Dudleigh Hall belongs to me now. Since you're so enamoured of England, I thought we could take possession and become lord and lady of the manor. You could wear your green dress and stand in the foyer to receive guests, and I could tell them all how my Chinese demon saved my life."

May stared at him in disbelief. "But . . . but China is your home, Alex. You would give it up for me?"

He dropped her hands and walked over to the door to stare out into the darkness. "Don't you realize that there's nothing I wouldn't do for you? I admit, when I first met you, I thought of you as another conquest, like Java, or Dinah. But that day in the pagoda, you saved my life when any other woman would have had a fit of hysterics. You intrigued me. I found you constantly on my mind, haunting me—and I wanted you." He turned, a look of appeal on his face. "If we never made love again, I would still want you. I realized we were two of a kind, and I'd be a fool to ever let you go. But even then, I was too proud and thick-headed to admit that I loved you. I've always been a loner, as you know, half-afraid to surrender myself completely to any woman."

He became a blur through her sudden tears. "Well, you had just better put Deadly Hall up for sale, because I've no intention of going back to England. I've a mind to oust Tobias as the next taipan of Benton and Black, don't you know, now that Nelson's gone."

"This is no time to lie to me, May Monckton."

"I'm not lying," she retorted, going to him and encircling his waist with her arms. "I've changed since coming back to China, Alex. I've belonged here all along, like Mother, only I've been too stubborn to realize it until recently. And," she added, "you'd never be happy in England, no matter what you say."

"Are you sure you want me? You know what kind of man I am."

She nodded. "An adventurer . . . thoroughly disreputable. But I don't want to spend the rest of my life without you."

"What about your ghosts, May? Your husband . . . Robin."

She grasped his hands, found them to be ice-cold, and rubbed the warmth back into them. "That's all in the past, Alex. I realize now that I married Nigel without really loving him because he represented everything my life in China lacked—sanity, rationality. He offered me what I mistakenly thought I wanted in exchange for my being a perfect wife for his perfect life. And Robin . . ." She took a deep breath. "I loved him, but we never existed beyond stolen afternoons in his rooms, because we couldn't risk being seen together in public." She looked deep into his eyes. "I need to feel that every upcoming day of my life is going to be an adventure and different, somehow. I never want to be able to anticipate it. And only one man can give me that." May smiled. "I suppose we'll just have to die young together having an adventure."

He threw back his head and laughed, a great joyous sound. "And I've never loved a woman more, as God is my judge."

"And what of Java?" she asked softly.

"I sent her away. When I first returned to Shanghai, I knew that somehow I would win you, but I had to make a trip to Macao to dissolve one liaison."

"That left only Dinah."

"No," he corrected her, taking her chin in his fingers so he could look at her. "There was nothing there to dissolve. When I first met her at your mother's house, I was blinded by her beauty, but she soon revealed herself as grasping and opportunistic. Dinah's chief concern is Dinah, and I only let her accompany me to Shanghai to obtain information from her, and to see if there was any connection between her and Win-Lin. The opium was my undoing, and I'll regret that til the day I die."

"I don't want Dinah ever to come between us," May said. Without warning, her face crumpled in panic. "Alex, I must ask you . . . are you sure you want a woman who can't give you a son?"

"Oh, May," he murmured, "how many times do I have to tell you, it doesn't matter?"

Then he kissed her, fiercely, possessively.

When they finally parted, she whispered, "Will you play your violin for me?"

"If you are an obedient wife."

"In that case, I suggest you sell it."

He grinned his rogue's grin. "I can see that I'm wedding a demon after all."

And he slipped his arm around her waist, and they strolled together into the moonlight and then across the lawn to the fish pool.

Alex knelt down on one knee, plucked a lotus from the water's edge, and tucked it behind May's ear. Then they walked back to the villa, to wait for the sun to rise.